Sarin's War

A Sapphic Action Adventure

L. Fergus

Article94

Sarin's War

@FallenAngelKita

http://FallenAngelKita.com

Cover art by Mrinmoy Kar

Contents

game of the gods

SARINS WAR

L FERGUS

PART I

CHAPTER I

T HE DOOR OF THE shuttle opened, and a ramp extended. A dozen soldiers with rifles exited and lined the ramp. A pair of officers flanking Sarin guided her out of the shuttle. She wore a simple red dress, and a set of combs pulled back her short, platinum hair. She stepped onto the ramp cautiously, wearing a pair of red pumps.

The Political Bureau shuttle sat on a private landing pad. The logo of Gjord Industries painted across it. The giant planet Neptune loomed large in the view from the inner edge of the space station that ringed the planet. Her father, a handsome man with a stylish suit, looked nervous while tapping his foot, as he waited at the bottom of the ramp. An expensive float car, with two armed men in suits, waited behind him.

Sarin's slow, monotonous steps matched the dead feeling she portrayed in her eyes. The Political Bureau officers escorted her father.

"Mister Sven Gjord?" The senior officer asked.

"That's me, General."

"I'm here to hand over your daughter, Jane. Please, sign here."

Sven signed the pad. The officers retreated as Sven hugged Sarin, but she didn't respond.

"My poor moonbeam. What did that monster do to you? Come, Jane. Let's get you home." He gently took Sarin's arm and guided her toward the car. Sarin stumbled over a bag at her feet.

"Where'd that come from?" said Sven. "It wasn't on the manifest. Bane, did you see who dropped it?"

"The officer dropped it, sir."

"Put it in the trunk," Sven ordered.

"No. With me," Sarin whispered in a shaky voice.

"Of course, dear."

The group loaded themselves and Sarin's belongings into the car. With a whisper, the vehicle took off toward Neptune's sky lanes. Sarin sat with her legs crossed and her hands in her lap, staring out the back window.

"Did they treat you well, Jane?" Sven asked.

Sarin ignored him. When she felt the bag by her foot vibrate, she clapped her hands over the faces of her two guards. Two blue puffs came from her hands. "Car, vacuum cycle the air," she ordered, while the two guards choked and collapsed to the floor convulsing. The cycling air caused her father to gasp for breath.

"Sorry, Daddy. But, you don't want my gas to get close to you. I'm called Sarin for a reason."

She bent over and unzipped the bag. A silver orb floated out of it.

"Do you have control of the car's systems?" Sarin asked it.

"Yes, Mom. You were correct. The Political Bureau does have your father under surveillance."

"I was afraid of that. Did you know that, Daddy?"

"What...You...killed them?"

Sarin chuckled. "I'll explain sometime, Daddy. What did they tell you about me?"

Sven took several deep breaths to regain his composure. "The reports were thin. You'd been a prisoner of a deranged psychopath and suffering from Stockholm Syndrome. They were putting you through extensive drug and psychotherapy."

Sarin huffed. "Hardly. Those idiots wouldn't know psychiatry if it slapped them in the face." She smiled. "It does give me the chance to tell you that I earned my doctorate and postdocs in psychiatry while I was away. That idiot Galina should have known better."

"I...Congratulations. When you're healthy, we can open you a practice or—"

Sarin laughed harshly. "I have in the past had a practice, but I can't do that now."

"Well, your health does come first."

Sarin kicked off her shoes. "Ugly damn things," she muttered as she unzipped the dress and wiggled out of it. Sven's mouth fell open. "What, Daddy? This isn't the first time you've seen me naked."

"No, of course not. You look like your mother."

Sarin rolled her eyes. "Hardly. You paid way too much money to engineer me to have me look as plain as her." She reached into the bag and pulled out her schoolgirl skirt, a sleeveless, black button down top, red stockings, and knee-high combat boots. When she finished putting on her outfit, she pulled out a silver armband, studded wristband, and a collection of earrings. With great care, she put each on. After putting on her spiked choker, she pulled the two combs from her hair. She shook her short hair, and it grew into a six-foot-long mane. When her hair finished growing, it braided itself, complete with a spiked ball on the end. She clipped into her hair a pair of black and red skull clips. Passing a hand over her face, her subtle makeup changed to the vibrant red and black she preferred. She reached into the bag, pulled out her pistol holsters, strapped them to her legs, then pulled out her pistols and put them into their holsters. Next, came the two pieces of a sniper rifle, which she leaned against a dead guard. Lastly, she pulled Razzorsplitter from the bag. The blade of the six-foot sword vanished when she looked down it. She smiled when she saw the look on her father's face.

"The bag is bigger on the inside."

"What is all this?" Sven demanded.

Sarin's wings, patterned after a blackbird, grew from her back and filled her side of the car. "It's me, Daddy, your daughter. I'm an Angel now. Neptune's rings, it feels good to be me again."

"You're still...brainwashed?" he asked his voice full of fear.

"If you call love brainwashed, then I suppose I am," Sarin smiled happily. "I was never brainwashed, Daddy. I grew up, fell in love, and learned to survive in a very harsh world. Kita is my partner and the love of my life. I'm a doctor, I've led nations, fought in wars, and become a mother."

"A mother? Are there any...?"

"Grandchildren?" Sarin asked, amused at his first thought. "Meet Athena," Sarin waved to the floating sphere. "She's one of them."

"Greetings, Mister Gjord. It is good to meet you finally."

"You can meet her properly once we get her into a holographic projector and server."

"She's a VI, then?" Sven asked.

"No, Mister Gjord. I am an AI."

Athena was scalable in design, allowing her to inhabit multiple systems at once. She could enter any UEE computer system and take it over. Previously, she had run the Empire of Hades, overseeing the entire country's computer system.

Sven raised an eyebrow, unable to hide his unease. "Unshackled?"

Sarin laughed. "Very."

"What happened to Omega?"

Sarin sighed. "That cranky bastard died, but he lives on through his daughter."

"Do we need to help her?" Sven asked. "I owe him a great deal for taking care of you."

Sarin smirked, knowing Omega's prime directive. "Denver is a very capable Angel. I don't know where she is."

"Can I ask how you came to mother an AI? Did you create her?"

"No," Sarin answered with a frown. "Athena was partnered to one of my other daughters, Quill. She, her twin sister Spike, and her partner, Leo, were killed soon after I was captured. I'm sorry, Athena, I know you don't like to talk about it."

"It's all right. I'm very capable of compartmentalizing, but Quill is always in a box near my heart."

Sarin nodded. "Lina and Nina were my other daughters killed by the Empire. I guess Nell is also a daughter, technically. She was Nina's partner."

"What happened to Nell?"

"I don't know."

"No sons, heh?" he asked, sounding depressed.

"Kita doesn't like men. All of the Angels are girls. It was a rare and lucky male who became her friend."

Sven turned up his nose as Sarin toyed with one of the bodies with her foot, making its arm flap comically. "What you can make a dead body do never ceases to amuse me."

"Did you have to kill them? They were good men."

"And working for the Political Bureau."

"They were vetted thoroughly," Sven retorted.

"And Athena is better at digging than your people. You would have joined them if we found anything suspicious on you, Daddy."

"I'm alarmed at how casual you are about killing them, and me."

Sarin shrugged. "I'd be unhappy if I had to kill you, but I've killed thousands, Daddy. What's two more? I've been imprisoned for more than ten years. You know how long it's been since I killed something? It's a great stress relief."

"What happened to my little girl?"

"I told you, I met Kita, and I grew up. She helped change me from a hyper-sexed, brain-dead party girl—to an intelligent, calm, and controlled Angel."

"Some say, she made you into what she wanted," Athena said in a teasing tone.

"Yes, and I made her into what I wanted: refined, elegant, feminine, someone to be my equal."

"I think she would say the same thing."

"Of course she would. Why the armed guards, anyway? I thought weapons were illegal."

"They are, but there's a war coming," Sven admitted.

"Well then, it looks like I've arrived at a good time."

"What do you plan on doing here?"

"We'll be preparing for Kita's arrival, whenever that is."

"She's coming here?"

"Yes, but I'm not sure when. It could be a while. Still, when Kita does get here, she's not going to be happy over what Galina did on Base Station. And, it won't be the kind of unhappy that produces the cutest, pouty face in the equation. It'll be more the let's-destroy-the-planet-and-turn-its-inhabitants-into-artwork kind of unhappy. Personally, I'd rather not see the station be destroyed by her rage and fury."

"What kind of monster is she?" Sven asked disgust lacing his voice.

Sarin looked at her father harshly. "Kita is not a monster. A monster is what sent me back here, and killed my babies. For those who are loyal to Kita, she has a heart of gold."

"So, you've sworn some oath to her?" Sven asked sounding relieved.

Sarin held up the finger with Kita's ring. "Partners forever. She's as loyal to me as I am to her."

Athena chuckled.

"Hush, you," Sarin replied to the AI playfully.

"She's coming here because of you? If we sent you somewhere else, would she not come?"

"Oh, no. Galina betrayed her, and Kita won't quit until she has her."

Sven shook his head. "Unbelievable. This can't be real."

Sarin reached over with her wing and stroked the side of her father's head with her feathers. "It's very real, Daddy. Kita's wrath is my wrath."

"How much damage can she do to the Empire?"

"If the Emperor hands over Galina, she won't do a thing. If the Emperor chooses to oppose her, well, hell has no wrath like Kita on the warpath."

The car pulled into an underground garage and parked.

Sarin sighed. "I guess it's time to go back to my act." Sarin vanished and reappeared looking like when she'd arrived. "Once Athena has the house secure I can return to normal. Come, Daddy. Let's go get me settled in."

CHAPTER III

I N THE INFORMAL SECTION of Gjord Villa, Sarin sat crying, while Athena's holographic projection comforted her. In front of them, floated a holographic picture of Kita.

"I'm sorry, Mom. I wish I had time to recover her belongings," said Athena.

"It's not your fault. You were busy sneaking into Galina's computer systems and trying to protect me. I just miss her and have ten years of tears built up waiting for a safe time to come out."

Athena put Sarin's head on her shoulder and stroked the other Angel's hair. Footsteps coming from the hallway caused Athena to close the hologram of Kita.

"What's the matter, moonbeam?" Sven said, entering with a platter of fruit. "Who's making my girl cry before breakfast?"

He placed the platter down in front of the Angels.

"Sorry, Daddy. I'm not hungry," Sarin said softly.

"You need to eat, dear."

"Mom just ate four days ago," Athena interjected. "At her current rate of energy consumption, she won't need to eat for three weeks and four days."

"Humans, even those with wings, need to eat several times a day," said Sven.

Sarin's eyes flashed red as she stood. "I am not human, Father. I am an Angel. We're stronger, faster, and have abilities humans only dream about. Quit believing that slag Galina keeps feeding you. I am not deranged, unstable, or brainwashed. And I'm done," she slammed her fist down on the holoprojector table, smashing the corner and ripping it from its floor anchors, "having you pretend I am the girl that left ten years ago. It's insulting and degrading. I've put up with it for a week, but no more. Athena has finished securing the house," her wings appeared, "and I can walk around as I am. If you don't like it, try and throw me out."

"Jane, darling, calm down," Kisha Gjord said with a light-hearted laugh as she entered with a bubbling champagne flute and wearing just a button-down shirt.

"Don't start, Mother," Sarin snapped. "Take your drunken ass back to bed."

"I am not drunk, sweetie. I'm just continuing the buzz from last night. Were you at a costume party last night?"

"I'm going to kill you both," Sarin roared in frustration.

"Mom, stop," said Athena, jumping in front of Sarin. Her grayish-blue wings that matched her skin and hair appeared and blocked Sarin's line of sight from her parents. "You have to give them time to adjust. You left behaving like your mother and returned more like your father. They don't understand life on The Mass—what it's like to kill to survive and have others wanting to kill you, or who Kita is to you."

Athena grabbed Sarin's shoulders and locked eyes with Sarin as she shook with fury. "Come on, Momma-Jane, we need them. They just need to see the light. They won't survive us beating it into them. Please, calm down."

Sarin snarled and huffed, but relaxed.

"What's wrong? What happened to the holoprojector?" said Kisha looking drunk and confused.

Athena turned from Sarin to the humans. She pointed to the far side of the sitting area. "Sit, both of you."

"I'll just leave this to your father."

"Sit," demanded Athena.

"I'm sorry, whoever you are, but I'm not going to ruin my hundred-million-dollar, one-of-a-kind fiber couch by sitting on it. I haven't gotten a chance to clean up if you know what I mean." She giggled playfully.

"Ugh, Mother," Sarin growled.

Kisha looked at Athena more closely, studying her gray skin. "Where did you get that costume? It's like a second skin."

"That is because it *is* my skin, Madam Gjord. I could make it look human, but then I would be dehumanizing myself."

Sarin laughed harshly. "You have a long way to go to catch up with her."

"Jane, don't speak about your mother that way," Sven snapped.

"I'm not the one refusing to sit because she's still sticky from a night with some guy she can't remember. She did it to herself and brought you down with her."

"Your mother's and my marital affairs are none of your business."

"But Kita's and mine are yours?"

"It's not a real partnership."

Sarin roared. "I'm going to bloody kill them." A pistol appeared in her hand, and she fired three times.

Athena's wing stopped the bullets. With her other wing, she knocked the pistol down.

"Mom, stop," Athena said firmly. "We're here for Momma-Kita. This is not helping. It's in our best interest to make them understand us."

Athena looked at Sven and Kisha who were cowering behind the couch.

"Jane's temper is legendary, second only to Kita's. She doesn't need a weapon to kill you. She is a weapon—I recommend you remember that. I suggest you listen carefully to what your daughter tells you about Angels. What we have are not tricks or gimmicks. Those bullets I stopped were real. Cells in Sarin's hands generate a deadly nerve gas. She can control a number of her internal systems, combined with other upgrades to her body allow her to be the best sniper and gunslinger in the universe. As an Angel, she is second only to Kita."

Athena stepped aside. Sarin appeared in her god form, made of an uncountable number of red and black lights in the shape of her angelic form. "As a god, Mom's—"

"Extremely experienced," said Sarin.

"Sweetheart, you have to tell me who this new designer is. This is fabulous," said Kisha, clapping her hands.

Sarin chuckled harshly. "You both know me well. I am Edi'rp, or just Edi, the God of Pride. I am a god, the creators of your equation—what you call a universe. I have blended with the equation that governs the Angel Sarin so that we are one."

"That is an impressively complete costume, Jane," Kisha said enviously. "What party are you going to that I haven't heard of? I would be such an exquisite addition."

"Mother, be warned, pride cometh before the fall. And Pride stands before you."

"Role-playing, too? Oh, this will be absolutely fabulous."

Sarin sneered and waved her hand. The room went white and equations scrolled by.

"Oh, darling. This will be hard to—"

"Oh, shut up." Sarin wiggled her nose, and Kisha's mouth disappeared. Sarin walked over to her mother. "I warned you about the sin of pride, Mother." Sarin snapped her fingers. Kisha's face and body aged to match her physical age. "Remind me to let you have your mouth back so I can listen to you scream later. We'll find out if you can live with being old or not." She looked at her father. "I guess I wasn't clear when I arrived: I am not a brainwashed, brain dead, party girl idiot. Kita is my partner, both in this equation and Infinity. There is no questioning it, so get used to it. Do you understand?"

Sven nodded slowly.

Sarin looked at Kisha. "And mother, from now on address me as Duchess or Vicereine. I am a noble, after all. Something you will never be." She waved her hand, and everything returned to normal except for Kisha. A pistol and a mirror appeared in Sarin's hands. She set them on the couch next to her mother. "In case you need them, Mother. Come, Daddy. Let's go discuss more about me." She grabbed him by the arm and pulled him out of the room. The door closed and locked behind them.

"Jane, what game are you playing?" Sven hissed.

"Mother is as bright as a brick in a coal mine. She'll blab about me all over the station."

"I won't let you kill her."

"I'm not killing her. Her stupid pride will kill her."

"Jane, this is despicable. I won't do it." Sven tried to yank free of Sarin, but she held fast.

"It wouldn't be my first time. It's no worse than what Mother does to her so-called friends, or you do to your business rivals. I know you've had people killed, and she has killed people's reputations."

"The killing I've done has never been this monstrous."

"It'll be suicide. If Mom doesn't kill herself, she'll never want to leave the house. We'll see if mother's pride is greater than her will to live."

"And the body? What will you do with that?"

"I have my ways of disposing of those."

"And the rest of the world? She can't just fall off the station. People will want to know how she died. Have you thought that the Political Bureau would be watching for such a coincidence?"

Sarin muttered, "Can we falsify something, Athena?"

"I could disguise myself as her, but I do not wish to participate in her social life. Perhaps if she were to take a trip?"

"I'm putting an end to this," Sven told them and pulled free of Sarin. He sprinted back to the sitting room. As he tried to override the door, they heard a muffled gunshot.

Sarin waved her hand, and the door unlocked. "Pride wins again."

"Does this mean when you become a liability, I must come up with a diabolical way of having you removed, Mom?" said Athena.

"I hope it's better than just putting a bullet in the back of my head."

"That wouldn't work, anyway."

The pair heard Sven cry out from the other room.

"What do we do if we have to kill him?" said Athena.

"We won't." Sarin snapped her fingers, altering the equation that governed her father and gave him a new version of the truth—altering the how, but not the who or the why. "Start looking into funeral arrangements, dear."

"And how shall I say she died?"

"Got drunk and fell down the stairs. Everyone will believe that."

WITH A PLACID LOOK on her face, Sarin entered the front door of Gjord Villa with her father. As soon as the door and blinds closed, she made her wings visible and changed from her black mourning dress to her usual schoolgirl outfit.

"That was utterly depressing," Sarin said, rolling her eyes.

"It was your mother," said Sven. "You loved her."

"I hated her, and how much happier are you now that she's gone?"

"I loved your mother."

Sarin shrugged. "Well, you can have your pick of mistresses."

"And if someone killed this Kita, wouldn't you be upset?"

"Of course, but there's a difference..."

"And that is?"

Sarin smiled at her father. "I can take revenge and make them suffer."

"I could do the same to you."

Sarin raised an eyebrow. "I see we're finally getting somewhere. I'll turn you into a cold-blooded killer yet. That said, you can't kill me."

"I don't need you," he said harshly.

Oh, really? Let's see how you do without me. "Fine. Be that way," Sarin yelled as she drew a pistol, put it to her head, and fired. She collapsed to the ground, a growing pool of blood spilling from her head.

"Jane!" Sven yelled. He fell to his knees, frantic.

"Oh Mom, quit being so dramatic," Athena said, coming in from the foyer.

"You're no fun." Sarin sighed as she stood up. She touched the holes in her head and fixed the damage.

Sven stared up at her, looking dumbfounded.

"I'm a god, Daddy. It's going to take more than a kinetic round to my head to put me down. It does leave me with a splitting headache, though." She helped him to his feet.

"Are you trying to give me a heart attack?" he yelled.

"Maybe, but it'd take more than that to stop that artificial heart of yours."

"You know what I mean."

"Come," she ordered. She guided her father through the house into the informal breakfast area, motioned her father to a stool, and then dug in the fridge for some fruit and breakfast foods. She put the platters on the bar.

"Since when do you do anything for yourself?" said Sven.

Sarin raised an eyebrow. "For over ten thousand years. Kita may have grown up a noble, but she hated the idea of servants. She preferred to do everything for herself unless it was a formal occasion. I learned quickly. Plus, you never know where some of those peoples' hands have been." She picked up a piece of banana and popped it into her mouth.

"I'm surprised you'd let anyone tame you."

"I didn't let anyone do anything. I didn't have a choice."

"So, she did influence you," said Athena.

"I fell in love. As you know, when you fall in love, you tend to gravitate toward the other person's habits and mannerisms. Kita refused to wear makeup and do anything with her hair before she met me. Well, that's not totally true. Snowy did her hair. I made her conscious about her appearance in general. I also improved her sexual skills, bedroom prowess, and self-confidence. She also needed someone to take care of her in general."

"You, a caregiver?" Sven scoffed.

"Not like that, well, not often. Kita does tend to end up in the medical ward pretty regularly." Sarin stopped to wipe a pair of tears away. "Sorry," she whispered. "That was the last place I saw her. I'm her psychiatrist, is what I mean. Kita's a high-level sociopath with a penchant for violence. At the same time, she's very caring and protective of those around her. She's a great mother...when she's around. The Angels are her family. It's why she recruited me in the first place. She was trying to make up for what she felt she never had growing up. She's smart, funny, and adorable."

"None of that sounds like anything you would have drifted to-ward," said Sven.

"True. I didn't know much about Kita when I first met her. I was there to teach her to walk again. A bomb blew out most of her lower half. I just happened to be attending to her when she woke up. Her eyes opened, and she looked directly into mine. She surprised the hell out of me, but I couldn't look away, either. Her eyes were beautiful, but that wasn't what made me fall in love. It was the way she looked at me. Not like everyone else—with jealousy, lust, hate, desire—instead, she was looking at me like she saw that part I keep hidden. I swear her eyes smiled. She didn't say anything, and after a few long moments, she faded off again. I knew she was the one I wanted."

"And you didn't change your mind when you found out what she was really like?" Sven asked, picking up a piece of pineapple.

Sarin laughed. "Don't be silly. You weren't this way when you first started. Like everyone, we grow and learn more about ourselves. It was the same for her and me. We grew together."

"Athena mentioned she changed you."

"She helped me change from what I was when I left here to what I am now. She didn't force me. I chose to be an evil angel so I could make my own choices, and know they were mine."

Sven frowned. "That's depressing. I thought I raised you better than that."

"Who is better, an evil person who chooses her path or a good person who's forced down her path by fear of code, law, or deity? I have learned that evil people are often better than their counterparts. If an evil person does something good, she is often praised, and her peers pay it no mind. If a good person does something evil, she is often ostracized and punished. Evil people are often more reasonable and easier to deal with, even if it means being more physical. And by that, I mean, whoever hits harder is right."

"Loyalty, respect, and compassion are not worth anything?"

"Don't confuse evil with wicked. I have all of those, and so does Kita. She has them to a fault. We wouldn't be here if she'd killed Galina the first time that bitch betrayed her."

"What you describe goes against logic," said Sven.

"The universe isn't as simple as a movie. It's complex with choices and consequences. I know that I can't be as open and reckless here as I was back...home. I can't leave a dead body on the street or at least not one traceable to me."

"You shouldn't be leaving bodies anywhere. It took my security team days and millions of dollars to cover-up the guards you killed in the car."

Sarin chuckled. "Kita tried to get away with only killing the wicked and unrepentant. She tried to protect the innocent and was distraught when she did kill them. It was a hard lesson for her to learn that you often have to kill them for the greater good. And that's what matters, the greater good."

"The ends justify the means?"

"Yes."

"That isn't always true."

"If I must sacrifice a million to save a billion, I will do it. I'm not saying we hide behind that as a justification for our activities. Sometimes killing is just killing, like killing Mother, for instance. She was a spoiled bitch that needed to die. But even Kita kills that way rarely."

"That's why you killed your mother?" Sven said aghast.

"She annoyed me and wouldn't shut up. I don't need extra irritants in my life. I have enough as it is. I'm sure there's some revenge mixed in there too."

"Revenge for what? What could she possibly have done to you?"

"All those parties and events, the way she treated me. She wasn't Mommy of the Year material. I was just her prize to be shown off."

"You're unbelievable."

"I'm evil. I don't have to have a good reason. I don't need a reason at all. If you think you have the power to stop me, then do it. Kita had it, and she used it."

"Might makes right?"

"Yep."

"Not here it doesn't."

"We'll see."

Sven made a disgusted face.

"My world is not so different than yours, but instead of money and lawyers, we fight with fists and bullets. The loser is dead, not left destitute on the street."

"So, what's your plan? You said Kita was coming for revenge."

"And she is, not for the people of the United Earth Empire, but specifically for Galina. But she will crush anything in her way. It's too bad the UEE won't just hand Galina over."

Sven chuckled. "I don't think even I can arrange that."

"That's why I'm here."

"To get them?"

"No, to clear the path to them. We have no interest in killing the populous as a whole."

"That's the most reassuring thing you've said so far."

"Oh, Daddy. Give it time. You'll understand." She clicked her black and red nail against her teeth. "Athena, when are the new simulator and servers going to be installed?"

"My custom servers are being built, even though I've had to argue with the contractor over why I need such powerful machines when one is more than enough to run the system. I have them scheduled to start next Tuesday."

"What's this?" Sven asked with a confused look.

"Athena needs more than the entertainment system to hack into the city. This first array of servers is a start. We need to think of more upgrades to sneak in more machines. But, when the simulator is installed, I'll take you home, Daddy. And, you can see the environmental conditions that shaped all of us Angels."

"I'll look forward to the trip."

"You say that now." Sarin giggled, and then looked at Athena. "So, what are we doing the rest of the day?"

"You've been home for over a week and haven't made any social appearances beyond the funeral. I suggest we go shopping."

"Then I've got to walk around with that stupid look on my face."

"I suggest you start therapy, to explain being rid of it."

"Fine. Vet the list of psychiatrists Daddy has and find one that's not in the emperor's pocket, and that I can control."

"I have two," said Athena.

"Feel like doing some interviews, Daddy?"

"Do I get a choice?"

"Athena can project and play you if you'd like."

"No. If I'm going to be living with a monster, I might as well not feel like a hostage."

Sarin rolled her eyes. "So dramatic, Daddy. We can go shooting later. Do a little father-daughter bonding."

"Won't that be suspicious, moonbeam?"

"Wait until you see the range," Sarin said, her eyes twinkling. She stood up. "All right, let's see what uncomfortable dresses are in my closet."

"You used to love those dresses," said Sven.

"Then I met Kita and realized comfort could go along with style."

Sven raised an eyebrow.

"See you this afternoon, Daddy." Sarin kissed him on the cheek and followed Athena back toward her closet.

S VEN SHOOK HIS HEAD in disbelief. "Maybe I should just turn her in," he muttered to his banana.

"At least give me a chance to show you what happened to me, Daddy, before you do anything rash," Sarin's voice answered from thin air.

Sven jerked, looking around for her. "I'll give you a week after the simulator's installed to make me understand how that world changed you into this monster."

"I think I can pack ten thousand years into a week. Most of my life there was one battle after another."

"Where are you? I thought you shut the intercom down."

"I did. I'm in my closet looking for something remotely comfortable to wear."

"Is Athena here somewhere?"

"Daddy, I'm a god. I may be strictly limited, but that doesn't mean I can't manipulate the equation locally. In this case, turn my thoughts into a voice heard by you."

"You'll have to explain that to me," Sven huffed and rolled his eyes.

"I can see you, too."

Sven shook his head and walked next door to the game room. He went to the bar and poured himself a drink.

"A little early for that, isn't it?" Sarin chided.

"Between you and your mother, it's never too early."

Sarin giggled and went quiet, leaving her father to drink alone with his fears.

CHAPTER IIII

S ARIN STOOD IN THE center of the new holographic room in Gjord Villa. She'd extended the old room, taking over two of her mother's closets, to make a three-story space big enough for her to practice with her pistols.

"Athena, how's the system installation going?"

"I'm installing myself now. It's going to take some time. If you mean the simulator, it's ready for a test. Anything you'd like to see?"

"Roost."

The simulator hummed and the room shimmered, and Sarin stood in front of Roost's hangar door. The station was complete, except for the inhabitants. Sarin filled the missing life in with her mind as she walked through the empty corridors. She passed Arconian staff, students, and warriors. Entering the reserved area for the Angels, she opened the door to the small viewing room.

The space contained: a plush carpet, sofas, a large screen, game tables, a large window looking down on the planet, and trophies from the group's many adventures.

She missed the movies and cuddling the early Angels shared. It had seemed so carefree back then, a time before empires, corporations, armies, and politics.

A door opened in the wall, and Sven entered. He looked around at the small room. "Where are we, moonbeam?"

"UEE Roost," Sarin said quietly. "This is where Kita, Nell, and I used to hang out."

Sven motioned to the walls full of items. "What's all this?"

"Just stuff. It won't mean anything to you."

"It means something to you."

"I know. That's why I'm here. I miss my friends and partner."

"You want to tell me about some of these?"

"No," Sarin said flatly. "You wouldn't like the stories behind them."

"More evil handiwork?" said Sven with a disappointed look.

The room's door opened drawing their attention. Sarin's jaw dropped when Kita walked through the door. "Don't be so glum, love. We had a lot of fun collecting those."

"Athena, is this a joke?" Sarin snarled.

"It's coming from me, but I have no control over her. She seems to be a hidden AI routine in my primary kernel. I'm sorry, Mom."

"It's not your fault, Athena," said Kita. "I had to hide in case you were captured." She looked at Sven. "Greetings, Mister Gjord. It's good to finally meet you. I'm glad to see Jane has returned to you. Your generosity and planning have meant much to us both. It's because of you she made it back alive. I'm sorry I couldn't ask for your permission to partner with her, and you missed our tiny ceremony. I can tell you I would be lost without her." She walked past Sven to Sarin and put her arms around her possessively, kissing her cheek.

Sarin jumped away, her pulse racing. "What are you?"

"It's me, well, a hologram of me."

"A hologram doesn't have warm, soft lips or a perfectly gentle touch."

Kita cleared her throat. "I was hoping it would be a warm surprise. I rewrote the simulator's operating and hardware code to be able to model me as close to the real me as possible. I didn't want you to get lonely or sad since I don't know how long I'll be gone. I thought this was better than any static or regular interactive hologram. It was the only thing I could think of. I was fairly certain you'd put in a new simulator at some point."

"Why didn't you tell me?"

"I didn't want them to find out. I only have a fraction of my memory, stuff Galina knows, and ancient history."

"It's so lifelike," Sarin whispered, touching Kita's face.

Kita took her hand and kissed Sarin's palm.

Sarin threw her arms around Kita and held her tight. Tiny tears fell down her face. "I've missed you so much. Please, tell me it won't be another ten thousand years like last time."

"I honestly don't know," said Kita. "I know nothing about what's going to happen to me."

"I can find out."

"Don't go digging and expose yourself. You came back to Neptune to be kept safe."

"And leave you out in who knows where?"

"You have your agenda here."

"I know, but..."

"It'll be ok, pretty blackbird." Kita hugged Sarin tightly for a long time.

Sarin sighed and giggled. "You even have that weird heartbeat boron construction gives us."

Kita chuckled. "Yes, contrary to popular belief I do indeed have a heart."

"And it's mine," Sarin said firmly. "Both this one, and the real one."

Kita smiled. "I will never contest that."

Sarin kissed her warmly, then passionately.

"Damn, you even got the taste right too," Sarin said softly, her head spinning a bit.

Kita looked at Sven. "Sorry, Mister Gjord. It's been a while."

Sven nodded slightly embarrassed.

"I would also like to say that I will make this code available to you, and some other goodies stored in Athena. They should easily raise your yearly profits by at least one percent for the next ten years."

"Nothing can create that staggering growth for a company the size of mine."

"I had our daughter Lina run the numbers. She assured me they would. You should see what you're getting before passing judgment."

"One percent is fifty-seven followed by a lot of zeroes."

Kita grinned. "Then I might have sent too much. I understand you have reservations about our intentions, methods, and morals. It's true I carry a heavy reputation. I'm sure Galina and her people painted me in the worst possible light—a tyrant, dictator, murderer, a monster, and not a nice person all around. I'm sure they also told you they fixed Jane. I think you figured out that's not true."

"The Political Bureau has graciously given me Jane's history and a report on you."

"So was I close?" asked Kita. Sven remained silent. "That Political Bureau list is mostly accurate. Morals are such a silly thing. It's all a matter of perspective. I do what I think is right for me, Jane, our family, friends, and my people. I'm not tyrannical, but I'll accept dictator. Like all wise leaders—I stay informed, make big-picture decisions, and find the right people to put in the right places to carry out those decisions.

"Speaking of which, did you know two of your granddaughters are exceptional leaders? Quill ruled the Empire of Hades with Athena in my stead. I mentioned Lina. She was the CEO of my company, KitaCorp. She started when she was fourteen, and the company grew at a steady eight to ten percent. I think when it was over, I was worth approximately five hundred trillion dollars," the number caused Sven's eyebrow to twitch, "including assets and liquid assets on hand, mostly gold, gems, other precious metals, and industrial compounds. All of which I assume Galina helped herself to. I doubt they killed my little lightning bug quickly." Kita frowned, looking upset. Sarin gave her a supportive hug. "I'm going to miss her."

A hologram of Lina, the Angel known as Surge, appeared. The young woman smiled happily as electrical arcs jumped around her hair. Even though her black dress, stockings, boots, and jewelry looked cheap and ratty, they were of the highest quality.

"Did you say lightning?" said Sven.

"Yes," said Kita.

"Lina could generate massive electrical currents and store them like a battery using electromagnetic waves," said Sarin. "She can unleash the electricity in a lightning storm, a bolt, or with her hammer. She often said to save the company money, she'd plug herself straight into KitaCorp's Headquarters building's main power system."

"She might still be alive," said Sven.

Sarin gasped. "What?"

Kita's hologram froze.

"One of my corporate spies inside the Political Bureau sent me a note about a new alien power source the Bureau just found. She said it could do what you described."

"Oh god, I've got to get her out of there," Sarin lamented. "Kita?" She snapped her fingers in front of the hologram and then sighed. "She must have programmed herself in a hurry. She doesn't usually make these kinds of mistakes."

"I have access to her code and can fix it," said Athena.

"Is she on the station? And how did you get spies into the Bureau?" Sarin asked Sven.

"The power source is on Earth, and the same way they get them everywhere—slowly and carefully. Though I'm usually checking to make sure they're not stealing our tech, or seeing what they're working on."

"Do you know where on Earth?"

"The main headquarters in Moscow. You can't go there. They'll kill you before you even get inside."

"I am not going to let one of my girls be tortured and experimented on if I can stop it. And they can't kill me."

"But Galina might still be working with Ht'aed, and he can trap you, if not delete you," said Athena.

"He wouldn't dare touch me. He may be more prolific than me, but I'm right behind him." *Pride and death often go hand-in-hand.*

"And where would we go if we freed her? We don't have a safe place to retreat to."

"I have to do something," Sarin snarled. She didn't like feeling helpless.

"Brute force might not be the answer, moonbeam," said Sven. "Do you have any idea how she generates her charge?"

Sarin shook her head.

"I do not have the exact biological models Kita used to construct Lina's bionanites, but I do have her DNA," said Athena. "In later Angels, Kita used a combination of DNA and bionanites to create the Angels' abilities. It is unlikely they will sequence her DNA anytime soon. It's magnitudes more complex than human DNA. It's more likely they will try and understand the bionanites."

"What is a bionanite?" said Sven.

"It is like a nanite, but of biological construction. Unlike a nanite, which must operate around cells, bionanites are often part of a cell's organelles. This allows a cell to possess abilities along with its normal functions. It will most likely take the Political Bureau's scientists a long time to discover them. Other bionanites work like regular nanites, except the body can generate them in the appendix, an area previously unknown to have any function."

"What kind of documentation do you have on bionanites?"

"Not much. Kita was very secretive about how she generated the Angels' powers. We do, however, have a live specimen who, I'm sure, will willingly donate some." Athena looked at Sarin.

Neptune's rings, no. I won't. Sarin raised her hand. "I'm not giving up anything until he promises to treat Kita and me beyond some childlike terrors and accept who we are. I'm not going to give up my love's life work to get us kicked out on the street. I'm tired of being threatened because he doesn't want to accept and understand."

"You killed your mother," said Sven, his eyes narrowing.

Sarin crossed her arms defensively and felt her anger surge. "Yes, because she endangered everyone I care about. I did give her an option, even though I knew which one she'd take. I admit, I enjoyed doing it, but I'm sad I had to. I've seen beautiful wildflowers ground up by tank treads and smashed by boots, but the soldiers and tanks have to get where they're going. More often than not, when you return later, the flowers are back, and any trace of the war machine is gone."

"Are you saying you can bring your mom back?"

Sarin shook her head. "I mean I hope you find someone new who makes you happy after I'm gone."

"You're going to leave?" Sven said his mouth hanging open in surprise.

"Yes, Daddy, I am. Kita, Lina, Athena, and I will leave when we're finished. You've made every indication you don't want us here, and that's fine."

"That's not true and where would you go?"

"It's a damn big equation out there, Daddy, if you haven't looked out the window recently," Sarin snarled. "Where we go isn't your concern."

"Jane, you just got here and aren't going anywhere. Be realistic—*Kita isn't coming.*"

"Kita is coming!" Sarin yelled. She ground her teeth angrily as she stifled a scream. "Come on, Athena. Shut it all down. We're leaving."

She held up the metal ball Athena traveled in.

"Where are you going? You can't leave," said Sven.

"Movement complete, Mom," said Athena.

"Triton," Sarin said acidly.

"Triton? There's nothing there."

"I know."

"You'll freeze to death."

Sarin collapsed into a point of light. "No, just my tears."

"Moonbeam, don't go. Maybe it's time to talk to someone."

"Daddy, you've learned nothing about me and only cemented what you want to see. If there's one thing I have learned in ten thousand years, it's to accept people as they are. It was a rule among the Angels. I forget the wider world is a much crueler place." Sarin vanished.

CHAPTER IV

S VEN SAT AT HIS desk reading the quarterly earnings of several of his less profitable divisions. A chirp from his Arcom took his attention. "Yes, Kristi?"

"There's a General Lyakhova here to see you."

Sven closed his statements. "Of course, send her in."

He stood to greet Galina. Kristi held the door open for the General. Synthetic skin covered half her face. Usually used temporarily for burn victims or the like, hers looked permanently grafted in place. He found it odd that anyone would choose to do so, unless the injury was so catastrophic there were no options for repair. Cases like that were rare. It was too bad. She'd had a striking beauty about her, but then, the synthetic skin had a certain beauty too. Its soft white coloring and the perfect features without any definition gave her a beauty often associated with androids. The synthetic side balanced well with the organic. He smiled, hiding his surprise and curiosity.

"General, how good to meet you in person," Sven said cheerfully.

"Thank you, Mister Gjord."

Even the best engineers couldn't replicate the human voice from a synthetic source. You just couldn't replicate a sound wave accurately enough to fool the human ear. The General's was excellent, if not half an octave too high for Sven's liking. *She might prefer it that way.* They had succeeded in keeping her harsh Russian accent.

He gestured to the bar. "Can I offer you something to drink?"

"No, thank you."

Sven rolled one of the plush chairs from a small conference desk over for her. "Please, be seated."

"Thank you," she said, taking a seat.

Sven sat behind his desk. "So, what brings you here, General?"

"The Bureau would like to offer its condolences for the passing of your wife."

"Well, thank you. It was a tragic event."

Galina nodded. "How is your daughter, Mister Gjord?"

On a side screen on Sven's desk, an old-fashioned command terminal opened. The cursor blinked then a message appeared, "Don't lie to her. She can sense if you do. Kita."

Sven sighed, pretending it related to the question. He'd heard rumors from spies and colleagues that Galina had an incredible intuition for detecting lies. He would heed the AI's advice, and worry about how she had gotten into his private network later.

"She is not well, as you can imagine. She's having trouble adjusting to life here. I'm adjusting as well. It's been a long time since I've had a child in the house."

"I have been told she doesn't go out much."

"No, she doesn't. She's a different person from the girl that left. She even gave away most of her wardrobe."

"That is surprising. I do hope you are making the villa comfortable for her."

Another line appeared in the terminal, "She's watching you."

Sven glanced quickly at the text, then back to Galina, "I'm trying. We've put in a new entertainment system and simulator. I've decided if I can't get Jane out of the house, she can at least leave virtually. I'm hoping it will be a bridge for her."

"I hope she adapts quickly, Mister Gjord. If you need help, my facilities are open to you."

"Thank you, General, but that won't be necessary. I have a battery of experts who are working with her. They assure me things will improve."

"I understand you've increased your security systems."

Sven chuckled and smiled. "Yes, to keep the boys out."

"So, you do approve of me," appeared in the terminal, followed by a smiley face.

Galina nodded.

Sensing pleasantries were over, Sven moved to business. "What can I help you with, General? I know you're a busy person and don't have time for personal visits."

"The Political Bureau and the government find it is a priority to keep in personal contact with our major suppliers. We like to keep an open communications channel to identify problems, concerns, and new orders, of course," Galina said in a well-practiced tone.

Sven nodded at the standard government line. "Of course, and we do appreciate it. We do like to keep our major purchasers happy."

"I'm sure you do. Recently an interesting report crossed my desk."

"Oh?" Sven said, raising an eyebrow.

"It described research into a new way of generating enormous power, in a tiny area. I'm afraid I am not a scientist or engineer, so please mind my simple-speak."

"I understand, General. I often have to stop my people and ask them to translate," Sven said, smiling warmly. He tried to remember what division was working on such a project.

"Don't worry," appeared on the screen. "I planted the files on Lina in a lab in Rio, they're working on power generators."

"I haven't heard of my Rio division making any breakthroughs," said Sven. "It might be an undergraduate's work, perhaps?"

"The reason I am here, Mister Gjord, is to inform you that the Political Bureau has seized this facility and its staff. We consider this a matter of pivotal importance to the Empire. We will return it to you when we're finished."

"To wring it dry, you mean?" Sven said tersely.

"Consider it a favor, Mister Gjord. We have done you one."

A new line appeared on the terminal, "That didn't take long..."

"I do thank the Bureau and the Emperor for returning my daughter, but you do not need to take my property. You can just ask, and I assure you we can work out a deal."

"There are times for negotiating deals, and there are times when action needs to take place."

"If you mean first contact with these aliens out on the frontier, that doesn't mean it gives the Empire the right to take what it wants."

Galina smiled slowly. "The Empire can take whatever it wants when it wants, Mister Gjord. I suggest you remember that."

The terminal cursor began to blink rapidly. "So, this is what it's like to be on the receiving end."

"When is this seizure to take place?" said Sven, maintaining his composure.

"It has already happened," said Galina, her eyes twinkling.

"I hope you plan on sending over some documentation and are willing to work on a schedule for return?"

"Yes, Mister Gjord. I will have the appropriate offices contact you."

"Thank you, General. Is there anything else I can do for you?"

"No, Mister Gjord. That is all," Galina said, standing up. "Thank you for your time."

"My pleasure, General." Sven walked her to the door. Once she was gone, Sven returned to his desk.

"What the hell are you doing here? I thought you were glitching," he typed into the command line.

"I was. I fixed the problem." A winking face appeared on the screen.

"How does a simple program like you fix itself?"

"I'm hardly simple. I do apologize for the surprise. I didn't expect Galina to take over the entire facility."

"Do you know how many of my employees you have put in danger?"

"A hundred and ninety-three. They will be interviewed, and all will pass any test on their knowledge of the information I planted in Rio. I'm sorry I had to do this, but I had to protect Lina."

"Did you give them all the information on Lina's nanites?"

"No. It's mostly accurate, with a few hidden mistakes that will keep the Bureau busy and off Lina. I'm sorry, but she is my baby. I hope you understand."

Sven sighed. "I do. I'll make sure their families are taken care of. Three things. Stay out of my office. I want to know how you got into my office—and warn me next time you pull a stunt like planting information in one of my facilities."

"Galina found the information on Lina quicker than I intended. If I can't have access to you, how can I warn you?"

Sven grunted. "I am beginning to understand why parents dislike the partners their kids bring home."

A smiley face appeared on the screen.

"That doesn't mean I approve of you and Jane or what you do."

"I don't expect you to. If you did, Jane would not be the person she is. I just asked that you accept us."

"We'll see. Now, get out. I've got work to do."

"Goodbye, Dad." The terminal closed on its own.

S VEN SAT AT HOME, alone, eating and watching the financial news. An incoming call flashed at the bottom of the screen with the picture of his personal accountant. Putting down his takeout, he answered the call.

"Jack, I haven't heard from you in a while. How are you?" Sven asked the older gray-haired man with small round glasses.

"Fine, sir. I went to Earth for a few weeks on vacation to tour the northern European golf courses. Spectacular place."

"I remember. It's been a while since I've been to Europe. I'll bet you've subtracted five points from your handicap."

Jack laughed. "Just two. I was reviewing your personal spending accounts and found some irregular purchases."

"What has Jane bought now?"

"It's not Jane. A few weeks ago Jane's new personal assistant contacted me to set up an account for a friend of hers who was having financial difficulty."

"Ok," Sven said puzzled. *Why does Athena need a personal account?*

"What caught my attention was where the purchases were made."

"Where?" Sven said, concerned.

"On Angelica Station."

"Where the hell is that?"

"I took the liberty of looking it up. It's a small station, above the ocean moon GX-30CB, about ten light-years away. It's home to an ultra-exclusive resort city that's themed around medieval European culture."

"I know Jane hasn't been out there and doesn't have any friends there. What's the name on the account?"

"*Kita* is all she had me list."

The blood in Sven's veins went cold.

"Should I alert the fraud investigation unit, sir?"

Sven blinked in shock. *Where is that damn AI?*

"I haven't left Neptune. I promise," scrolled across the bottom of the screen.

"No. Ah, can you send me a list of the charges? I'll want to go over them with Jane before I do anything."

"Of course, sir. Let me know what you wish to do."

"Thanks, Jack. It should be an interesting story."

"I'm sure it will be. It is always interesting to hear the stories these kids have to tell."

Sven sighed tiredly. "Isn't that the truth?"

"Have a good evening, sir. You look like you need a break."

Sven laughed. "You know me, Jack. No rest for the wicked."

"You? *Really?*" scrolled across the bottom of the screen.

"Your father used to say the same thing and I will tell you what I told him..."

Sven smiled. "I know. You can't take it with you, so you might as well enjoy it."

"It's good advice, sir."

"I'm a god. I can," blinked around the screen.

"Thanks, Jack. Good night."

Sven hit the button for his secretary on his Arcom.

"Sorry to call you at home, Kristi. I just have a quick question: Have we heard anything about Triton?...No? Ok, thanks...I'll find the number. Have a good night."

Sven scanned the directory and found the number for the head of the Near Station Object Detection Team. The team had been searching for Sarin's whereabouts since she stormed out of his office. A tired-looking man, trying not to look irritated, answered the call. Behind him, Sven saw a large group of people sitting and typing at computers.

"Doctor Merk?"

"Yes, who's this?"

"Sven Gjord."

"What do you want?"

"I put in a request for you to watch Triton for anything unusual. I want to know if you found anything."

"If we'd found anything I'd have told your secretary. Is there anything else?"

"No, Doctor. That's all."

The other man cut the feed without another word.

"That...is a man in need of a golfing trip to northern Europe," scrolled across the screen.

Sven chuckled and nodded in agreement. "So, what do we do?" he asked the screen. He received no response. "You, speechless? That's a first."

"I don't have an answer for everything. I used to."

"I guess all we can do is wait for her to come home," Sven grumbled as he returned to his news and cold takeout.

A call came in. Sven raised an eyebrow. The caller was Doctor Merk. He answered it, but instead of the gruff doctor, a young-looking kid, maybe in his late forties, appeared.

"Mister Gjord?" he asked in a quiet, nervous voice.

"Yes, who are you?"

"Daniel Rhodes, sir. I know you've requested we look for changes in Triton, and I have some. Doctor Merk said it was nothing, just a computational error, but these aren't errors. Here, I can show you."

He held up a screen and flipped through the images. "Did you see them?"

"What am I looking for?"

"Here, ah, sir," Daniel fumbled with the screen and zoomed in.

There was indeed a brief change, hidden across two different frames of video.

"She's destroying things, and fixing them," appeared on the screen.

"Daniel?" Sven called.

"Yes, sir?"

"How much more of this do you have?"

"A dozen, sir."

"Listen to me carefully. I want you to download everything you have onto a protected drive. Then, I want you to destroy all other originals and copies. You're not to talk to anyone or say anything. I want you to get on the next shuttle for Gjord Tower. Security will be expecting you and will take you directly to my office. You're going to be signing a nondisclosure agreement, along with some other paperwork, and then you're to show me everything on the drive you have. From this point forward, you work for me. Understand?"

"I...ah...My stuff and fish...I can't..."

"I have people for that. I can send the best aquatic specialists to move the fish. I need you here in an hour. You think you can do that?"

"Yes, sir."

"Good. I'll see you in an hour."

Sven ended the call, and called his secretary at her home, again. "Sorry, Kristi. One more question. Where do you keep the standard high-security clearance contracts and the rest of the contract paperwork?...You don't have to come in. I can do it...It can't be that complicated...Well, ok. I don't want to ruin your filing system...I'm headed there as soon as I get off the phone with you. The new employee should arrive in an hour. Tell Ray, I'm sorry...He'll accept Seahorse tickets? Get him whatever he wants and whatever you want...All right. I'll see you in an hour."

After hanging up, he called to have his car brought around. He rushed upstairs to find something business casual. As he tied his tie, a message appeared on the bottom of the mirror.

"Can I come?"

Sven raised an eyebrow. "I suppose...if you behave," he muttered. "I will send you the code when I get to the office."

"I will. Thank you."

"I suppose no one would ever believe me if I told them."

"I know lots of people."

"I'm sure you do," said Sven as he went downstairs to meet his car.

CHAPTER V

S VEN READ THE FIRST file containing information on the takeover of the Rio facility he'd requested, during the car ride over from his villa to his office. So far, he just had the government's version, which was very light on facts and heavy on rhetoric. He closed the screen after hearing a soft knock on the door.

"Come in, Kristi."

His secretary entered, looking like she was dressed for a formal day at the office. Behind her, a man wearing jeans, sneakers, and a dirty hoodie followed, clutching a bag to his chest.

"Kristi, this isn't a Monday morning during investors' week," Sven said, surprised. "But you do look splendid."

"I am your personal representative and must represent your interests at all times," said Kristi.

Sven nodded. He'd had this argument a hundred times before with her. "And you are Daniel?"

"Yes...yes, sir."

Sven stood and walked around his desk. "Nice to meet you, Daniel." He offered his hand. Daniel looked at it briefly as if confused, then shook it limply.

"Nice to meet you, too, ah, sir," he said timidly.

"I hope you found our hiring package to your liking?"

"Yes, sir. About my fish..."

Sven smiled. "They will be well taken care of. I'll get you a bigger tank if you want."

"No, thank you. The tank I custom-built myself. I left detailed instructions on how to take it apart if I can't be there to do it myself."

"That must be some tank."

"I live inside it...I...I mean, it covers all my walls, floor, and ceiling."

Sven raised an eyebrow. "So, you'll need a custom apartment?"

"Just one larger than eight feet cubed."

"I promise you'll have an apartment bigger than that. I'll see what I can do about getting you there to oversee its removal."

"Thank you," Daniel said quietly.

"So, what do you have for me?"

Daniel held up the bag.

Sven chuckled. "I hope more than a bag."

Daniel opened it and pulled out a secure file server. "Do you have a secure link?"

"Yes. Why don't you plug it into the big screen?"

"No. The windows. They can see in."

"Those windows are mirrored. No one can see."

Daniel shook his head. "They can still detect the trace radiation through those mirrors. Get them shielded."

Sven nodded. Maybe that's how the Political Bureau acquired some of its information. They were just simply looking over his shoulder. He turned the screen around on his desk. "How's that?"

"That will work," Daniel said as he connected the server. The screen blinked, and a display of dancing rabbits and hamsters appeared. He pulled a projection keyboard from his bag and tapped out a sequence. The screen filled with pictures of Triton's surface, while the rabbits and hamsters minimized to dance in a corner.

"Ok, Mister Gjord, this is the image I showed you earlier."

Sven noted Daniel's change in body language, speech, and confidence when he spoke. Sven knew the type. He employed a large number, but only a few to this degree.

"And this is the photo of the area adjacent, each containing half a shadow image. When I put the images together, you get a picture of the same landscape, but vastly altered. You can see the same in the rest." He cycled through a dozen pairs.

"Can you zoom in?" said Sven.

"I have, but I haven't found anything."

"For my sake."

Daniel zoomed in on the pictures and moved around the image, showing there was nothing to see.

A message scrolled across the bottom of the screen, "She's pissed and is taking it out on the moon and then rewinding time to fix it."

Daniel looked at Sven. "I thought you said this link was secure."

"It is. Don't worry about that. It's just a gag gift from a friend of mine. I've been trying to get rid of it for weeks."

"Ha-ha, you wish," scrolled past.

"This is a good first step," Sven said ignoring Kita's antics, "but not conclusive evidence. Do you think you can get better resolution images?"

"Of course, with better equipment. I wrote the detection program."

"And you brought the source code with you?"

Daniel nodded.

"Don't waste your time," scrolled across the screen. The images on the screen vanished. New images, showing a shadowy figure with wings appeared. Circles appeared around the figures. "Who does that look like, Dad?" flashed at the bottom of the screen.

"Do you want me to call a tech, sir?" said Kristi.

"No, don't bother. If we kill it, it will only come back stronger."

"You got that right," appeared on the screen.

"What happened to my images?" Daniel said in a panic.

"I ran them through a couple of noise and sharpening filters. Using a simple algorithm, I was able to increase the definition. And, it helps to know who I'm looking for. Jane doesn't have a shape you can forget."

"Kita, that's enough. Where are the images?" Sven demanded.

"In the trash."

"Kita, *what did I tell you about—*"

"I didn't delete them if that's what he's worried about. Mine are better. I do offer congratulations to Daniel. It's not every day you capture images of a god."

"Are you sure this is a...a prank?" said Daniel.

"I hope you're paying them well or plan on killing them soon," wrote Kita.

Sven sighed. "Someday, Daniel, when you have children, you will understand what it is like to have someone work so hard to make your life so miserable."

A big smiley face appeared on the screen.

"I wasn't talking about you."

"Yes, you were," Kita retorted. "You just don't want to admit that I'm your *daughter-in-law* now."

"Daniel, can you send a secure, untraceable message to the surface of Triton?"

"Yes, if I had the right equipment. Why?"

A message filled the screen, "To say, 'Jane, I'm sorry for being closed-minded during this time of transition. I understand coming home is hard for you and I deeply apologize for not accepting you and your partner as the strong, independent, and beautiful Angels that you are. I hope you will forgive me, and please come home. Love, Dad.' *I* usually started the apologies on my knees. But, you know, don't take my word for it. I'm just the one who's been living with her for ten thousand years."

"Kita, if you're not going to be helpful, then go away," Sven ordered.

"I just gave you the damn answer. You think Jane was putting on a show when I arrived? I saw the way her eyes lit up when I entered the room. I saw the excitement on her face and heard the joy in her voice. You can't fake that. I would think as her father who cares for her you would know when she's happy and when she's pretending. You know it was the first time she's been happy since her return to this metal donut. Why deny her happiness? No one asked you to like what we do. No one said you had to live with it. We said we'd leave when I arrived. If you didn't want to talk to her, she'd understand, but she'd be hurt. Go ahead and mess around with your scientist, get better pictures, send a bizarre message, think it over, be my guest. But, I know my girl, I know when she's upset, and I hate not being able to fix the situation. Instead, I've got to rely on you and this pencil neck to do it for me. And, just like men, you have to do it the bloody damn hard way." Kita added, "DOOR SLAM," to the end of her tirade.

Sven sighed sadly. "I can see why they go well together. None of what you read or saw here tonight leaves this room."

"Of course, sir," Kristi said, trying to hide her amused smile.

"Yes, sir. But what was going on there?" said Daniel.

"The less you know, the better," said Sven. "Give me the list of equipment you'll need to send the message, as soon as possible."

Daniel listed off a dozen things. "And a clear line of sight to Triton."

"Can you write that down?" said Sven.

"I have it, sir," said Kristi.

"Oh, splendid."

"I will put the formal request in immediately, Mister Gjord. Should I file the requisition under our Monitoring program?"

"Sure, if they can't use it, transfer it to someone who can."

Kristi tapped on her Arcom. "All items, but one, are in stock in our warehouses or currently in use at a lab here on the station. This missing item can be purchased locally. I can have everything delivered to our monitoring station tomorrow morning before ten. The items can be discreetly moved to any location you want after that."

Daniel looked dizzy when she finished, but years of working with Kristi had left Sven unfazed by her efficiency.

"Excellent. Daniel, I'll provide you with a list of my secure facilities. One of them should work for you."

"I...ah, sure," said Daniel.

"There are four secure facilities, with a sixteen-hour view of the moon. The closest is the propulsion lab out in the Gulf of Mexico sector," said Kristi.

Sven pulled it up on a map. He highlighted the Gulf facility and then extended the map to show its relationship with Triton. "Will that work?"

Daniel moved closer and squinted at the hologram. "It should."

"I will send the facility manager a note in the morning that you'll be needing space for a few days, sir," said Kristi.

"Thank you. Is there anything else you need, Daniel?" said Sven.

"Ah, dinner?"

"I'll make sure he has a proper chaperone until he's settled in permanently," said Kristi.

"That's a good idea. Thank you," said Sven.

"Doctor Rhodes, please gather your equipment. A car and chaperone will meet you at the security desk," Kristi said to Daniel.

"Ok. No problem." He hurried and shoved his drive into his bag. When he finished, Kristi shooed him out of the office.

"Will there be anything else, sir?" Kristi called from the door.

"No. Go home and get some sleep," Sven said good-naturedly.

"I plan on it, sir." She took a step out of the door and stopped. "Oh, sir?"

"Yes?"

"Whoever this woman is on the computer, she may be crazy, but she is a keeper for Jane."

Sven grunted. "The more I deal with her, the more I think you're right."

"I hope to see Jane soon. She does liven up the place."

Sven laughed. "That she does."

"Good night, sir." Kristi closed the door behind her.

Sven looked back at the screen on his desk.

"Kita, are you there?" he typed but received no reply.

He agreed Kita was a good match for Jane, but wouldn't want to be between them in a fight.

CHAPTER VI

S VEN ARRIVED LATE TO the office, choosing to work at home and let the contractors install the radiation shield on his windows. Entering through the front door, he raised his eyebrows when he saw Daniel sitting in the lobby. His eyes were puffy and darted back and forth. Looking around, Sven didn't see his chaperone. He walked over to the young scientist.

"Daniel, is everything all right?"

Daniel looked up and blinked. "Yeah. It's set up and ready."

"It's two thirty in the afternoon. I didn't expect you to be ready until tomorrow. Where's Noel? She is assigned to you, isn't she?"

"Huh, who? You mean the girl? I didn't like her looking over my shoulder, and I took the train instead."

"I see. If you don't like your chaperone, I can assign you someone else."

"I don't need anyone. They just get in the way."

Sven switched to a sterner tone. "She's there to make sure you're taken care of. If she encroached on your personal space, you just need to tell her. Let's go up to my office, and we can talk more once we're in the elevator." Sven steered Daniel through security and to the elevator. Once inside the elevator, Sven spoke again. "If things are ready, why didn't you call me? I'd have come to you."

"That'd look funny for you to come to me, just to watch a calibration test of a mineral scanner. I expanded and encrypted the remote connection, so that you can send the message from your office."

"What encryption did you use?" Sven said, concerned.

"My own. I can install it on your computer."

"I'd be more comfortable if you use one that we've developed."

"Mine's better."

"Has it been tested?"

Daniel shrugged. "I use it to keep my research and projects secure."

"With your permission, I'd like to have it tested. If it's as good as you say we can help you get a patent. The company might even choose to lease it from you."

"Maybe..." Daniel shrugged.

"A mineral scanner is a clever cover. How are you planning on sending the signal?"

"I've added extra wavelengths to the scanner's array because I don't know the type of equipment she's using to receive."

The elevator doors opened. Sven led Daniel through the antechamber to his outer office.

"Good afternoon, Kristi. I hope the work crew didn't upset you too much?"

"No problem, sir. I took an extra-long lunch."

Sven chuckled warmly. "Good for you."

"Mister Rhodes, it's good to see you again. How's your project?" said Kristi.

"It's ready."

"Excellent. Sir, a new message came in this morning from our prankster."

"Oh? Let's go into my office, and you can tell me," said Sven. He opened the door and led the others in. He put his briefcase down on a small round side table. "Daniel, you can plug into my screen."

Daniel opened his bag, took out his server, and placed it on Sven's desk. He sat down in Sven's chair, which caused Kristi to frown.

"So, what did Kita have to say?" Sven asked Kristi. "I'm surprised she didn't contact me directly at home."

Kristi smiled. "She's still mad at you, sir. She said the information she slipped to the Political Bureau has phoned home and is currently in their lab in Paris."

Sven frowned. "That's interesting, but has probably tipped our hand. They'll have detected an unidentified packet leaving their networks."

"She also said to have faith and to trust her. She's been doing this for more than a day."

Sven sighed. He hated not having control and whatever Kita was up to worried him. The Empire had among the best network security systems and personnel anywhere.

"Sir, seeing what she's done so far, I'd believe she can do what she says she can do."

Sven raised an eyebrow. "That's not why I'm worried. It's that attitude of hers that has me worried."

"She seems to be a good sort, sir."

"I can't say the same."

"Sir, I had a very long conversation with her this morning. I believe she has your and Jane's interest at heart. And yes, she was very frank and upfront about what she believes and what she's done in the past."

"I'm surprised that doesn't bother you more."

"She's more extreme and ruthless than any company we've ever competed against, but compared to the Empire, she's on par with the best and worst of them. It was her honesty I found refreshing, sir."

"She is that."

"I believe she's a friend. Otherwise, we'd never know she was here, sir."

Sven rolled his jaw, as he mulled it over.

"Sir, I'm ready," said Daniel.

Sven walked over to his desk.

"Just type what you want to say in the box and hit enter. The scanner will commence, and the message hidden in the beam will loop until we tell it to stop."

Sven took his seat and typed a quick message for Sarin and hit enter. He sat back in his chair and sighed. "I guess we wait and hope she's listening."

"Why did she go there anyway? There's nothing there," Daniel scoffed quietly.

"Exactly," Sarin said, appearing in the middle of the room with Athena's ball. In her hands, she held her large sniper rifle, still smoking.

Sven looked up as his jaw dropped. Daniel stared at her blankly. Kristi raised an eyebrow.

"All you had to do was say, 'Jane, please come home,' and I would have heard you. You're the only other equation I'm monitoring right now," Sarin growled with an annoyed look on her face.

"I, ah, didn't know that," said Sven, standing up. "I was worried."

Sarin fluffed her feathers angrily. "If that's the reason you wanted to talk to me, to the Crushing Depths with you."

Sven didn't know what that meant, but it couldn't have been good. "I'm allowed to worry about my daughter. It's my job."

"I don't want your concern."

"That's not your choice."

"You can be concerned for me, but not accept who I am? You know what? Go slag yourself, Daddy. I don't have time for this."

"Mistress Logine," said Kristi to the towering Angel.

Sarin spun around, hitting Sven with her wing. "Kristi, I'd have thought you were smart enough to leave this place behind."

"It's an exceptional place to work. Not all of us are cut out to be a soldier or a Vicereine."

"Who have you been talking to?" Sarin snarled, looking over her shoulder back at her father.

"Kita. She's been popping up around the office over the last couple of days."

"I thought she'd glitched. Did you fix her, Athena?"

"No, Mom. I didn't see a self-repairing routine in her code, but she could have been reset."

"That is an incredible VI," said Daniel. "How did you develop such a realistic voice system?"

"I am not a VI, human. I am a nonorganic Angel. What if I called you an animated corpse?"

"I...ah...what?" said Daniel, looking at the floating ball with a confused look on his face.

"Humans are not the pinnacle of evolution, human," Sarin scoffed down at Daniel.

"They do not appear to have anything worthy of our time, Mom. Let's leave and not tell them our destination," Athena suggested spitefully.

"Let's box Kita up first. I'm sure that's why she's causing trouble. Where is she?"

"I don't know," said Sven. "She seems to come and go as she pleases."

"Of course she does," Sarin muttered.

"Jane, I called you here for more than that."

"Oh? You have until Athena tracks down Kita. So, make it quick. She runs on quantum time."

"General Lyakhova came to visit me a few days ago."

Sarin's lip curled. "And what did that traitorous bitch want?"

"Be careful, Jane. The walls have ears," Daniel whispered.

Sarin turned to him. "You do not call me Jane. To you, I am Sarin."

Daniel gave her a curious look. "Why would you wish to be named after an ancient chemical weapon?"

Sarin put her sniper rifle on her hip and held up her free hand. "Come find out." She puffed out a small blue cloud from her hand.

"Mom," Athena said halfheartedly.

"I'll just shoot him instead." She held out her sniper rifle like a pistol. The barrel of the six-foot weapon didn't waver from Daniel's head. The man's eyes opened wide, and he shook. Sarin pulled the trigger, and a loud click echoed in the room. A dark spot appeared on Daniel's pants and ran down his leg.

"Jane!" Sven yelled.

Sarin laughed wickedly. "Looks like he needs to develop a backbone."

Kristi stepped forward. "Misses Logine, please. Your father has important things you're going to want to know. It concerns your daughter, Lina."

"What do you know about my daughter?" Sarin hissed.

"Kita has told us quite a lot about her predicament," Kristi replied, standing tall.

Sarin walked over to her father's shelf and with a wave of her hand, knocked everything to the ground, and placed her rifle on the empty shelf. "So, what did Galina want?"

"She must have sensed our absence or she would never have ventured into our neighborhood," Athena said with a chuckle.

"She seized one of my facilities on Earth after Kita planted files on how Lina's electrical generation works. She said she planted it to help Lina," said Sven.

"I would assume Kita put in undetectable errors until they tried to duplicate the research?" said Athena.

"Yes, and she included an invisible tracker in the research as well."

"I hope it will lead us to her," Sarin replied with a sad frown. Her face flashed to anger. "Galina is going to suffer forever."

"Someone might have already beaten you to it," said Sven. He tapped on his Arcom. The big screen on the wall flashed and a picture of Galina taken from his office security camera appeared.

"What in the Crushing Depths happened to her?" Sarin exclaimed, moving closer to look. "And how come I didn't get to do it?"

"I don't know, but I may have a clue."

Sarin raised an eyebrow. "You have my attention."

"Jack contacted me concerning purchases made on a personal expense account I didn't know existed. Apparently, your personal assistant did it," Sven said, looking at Athena.

"I may or may not have illegally accessed your contacts to create an unauthorized personal account for Kita."

"That was a good idea," said Sarin. "What's this have to do with anything?"

Sven tapped on his Arcom again. A spreadsheet appeared. "Take a look at this and see what you think."

Sarin looked at the screen. "That's a slag of a dinner bill."

Sven opened up the consumer purchase receipt from an electronics store.

"Someone is setting up a powerful mobile system," said Athena.

"Interesting," Sarin said, looking over receipts from some other stores. "They know their hair products. And forty bags of synthetic meat jerky in four different flavors, four backpacks, seventy-seven protein packs," Sarin's eyes went wide, and she fixated on the screen, "and six boxes of sugar cookies. It can't be," she whispered.

"The probability of it being Kita is ninety-nine percent," Athena said hopefully.

"I know it's her," Sarin retorted. "I didn't think she was paying attention to what I used in her hair." She looked at Sven. "Where's this from?"

"A new station built about ten years ago around the moon GX-30CB. It's the transfer station to the new immersive medieval city under the sea, Angelica, where you can experience a great part of our history authentically without any modern amenities," Sven said, reading the brochure.

"That despicable bitch," Sarin hissed. "Galina built Kita a prison. You'd better not have a stake in this venture, Father."

Sven shook his head. "Not beyond selling them materials. I passed on the project. It had too much government control around it. Now I know why."

"Then that is where we're headed," said Sarin.

"You can't go. It's quarantined, because of—"

"I don't fear disease. I can be there in a matter of weeks."

"Jane, will you let me finish?" Sven snapped.

Sarin crossed her arms in agitation. She opened her mouth to say something, but Kristi spoke first.

"Stop, both of you. If you keep going like this, one is going to kill the other, and I don't mean figuratively. Sir, you're approaching your daughter all wrong and Misses Logine, this applies to you as well. With all due respect, sir, I know you are used to getting your way most of the time as the head of a multi-planetary company, but your daughter has been the Vicereine of an entire planetary government and is used to getting her way, always. You are not going to change her. She's been doing this for a millennia or more, maybe much more.

"You both need to recognize the other's position and stop fighting over who is in charge of whom. Misses Logine, you wouldn't treat your daughter this way and, sir, you should treat her as an adult who's made her own life decisions longer than the two of us combined. We don't have to like how she chooses to live her life, but we must respect it.

"We have worked with plenty of notorious individuals and companies before. If we must work with one, your daughter is the one I'd choose. She is trustworthy, loyal, and will do everything in her power to make sure no harm comes to the company or us."

Sarin cocked her head to one side. "You've been talking to Kita a lot, huh?"

"Quite," Kristi said tersely.

"All right, Daddy. I'm willing to start over if you are," Sarin said gently.

Sven held back his gut reaction to tell her no. Still, he couldn't say yes, either. The thought of his daughter killing her mother wasn't going to be so quickly forgotten or forgiven.

Sarin went over and gently touched his arm. "Daddy, I'm sorry for killing Mother and for the way I did it. I was upset about the way I saw her treating you. I was also upset because I saw myself in her, and how it reminded me of all the horrible things I've done. I have hurt Kita and others badly. Kita has always been quick to forgive, even when I haven't deserved it. I've been lousy at reciprocating. I've put in a lot of time and learned some painful lessons trying to change those behaviors and habits I learned from Mother. I like to think I got all my bad habits from her and all my good ones from you.

"I know I'm not what you expected to get when you picked me up, but this is who I am. I'm mean, evil, and downright wicked at times. I'm self-centered, self-absorbed, and callous. But, along with that came intelligence, wisdom, kindness, and most importantly love. I wouldn't change any decision I have made. Not killing two hundred people to save Kita, throwing my guns down and becoming an addict because I killed a child, learning to be a mother the hardest way possible, or taking on a partner who by all definitions is insane. If I could, I'd bring Mother back, but I can't. I'm bound by rules I didn't get a say in."

She looked down at the ground and spoke softly, "I thought you'd be happier without her. You looked so sad that morning she came in. She didn't deserve you, Daddy, but it wasn't my choice to make." She kissed him on the cheek and wiped a tear away as she went to stand next to Athena.

Sven stood still, while an internal contention raged inside. He wanted to say she was forgiven and move forward, but a part of him was reluctant. How much of what she said was true and how much was manipulation? Could he work with her if he couldn't trust her? He'd worked with plenty of people he couldn't trust before, but they could be watched. She couldn't. According to Kita and Jane, loyalty and family ran deep, but blood wasn't a binding tie. He wondered how someone earned the trust to become an Angel. It was a hard choice. He loved Kisha and Jane dearly. The question took a new form: If he didn't trust his daughter and she was left to her own devices, what kind of monster would he be unleashing on everyone else? Was he a heavy enough counterweight to balance Jane? Probably not, but if he squeaked long enough and loud enough, she had to listen to him.

"All right, you're forgiven, but please leave the bloodshed and threats outside of our home and company. I will do my best to remember you're not my little girl, anymore." Sven sighed. "Did you really rule an entire planet?"

Sarin nodded. "For more years than Kita did, but I wouldn't have sat in that chair without her. She is the one with the true vision and drive to push forward."

"But, if it hadn't been for the rest of us, Kita wouldn't have known what to do when she caught what she wanted," Athena said with a chuckle.

Sarin smiled. "If that isn't the truth. Ok, Daddy, so why can't I go to this Angelica Station?"

"I'll show you." Sven brought up some images. "The Empire con-fiscated or destroyed everyone's footage of the fire that took place there about a week ago, but my spies were able to get their hands on some. Recognize her?" Sven blew up the only full facial image of Kita.

"Neptune's rings, I can't believe it," Sarin whispered. She walked to the screen to take a closer look.

"I thought you said you knew it was her by the receipt," said Sven.

"Of course I did. I can't believe Kita did her hair and makeup correctly. All those years and I thought she wasn't paying attention. That smoky application looks good on her. Where did she get that style of lipstick? Impressive. I bet she was sick when they cut her hair. Can I see the rest?"

Sven returned to the few pictures he had.

"Do we know who *she* is?" said Sarin, pointing to a woman wearing a skintight blue suit.

"That is Jessica A. Rabbit, Captain in the Political Bureau, probably *former* now. I have feelers out looking for information on her, but anything with her name on it is closely guarded. How she went from guarding Kita to helping her is a mystery."

"That's a nice suit of armor she has," Sarin said, tapping on the screen.

"I've never seen anything like it."

"Reading between the lines of the blue suit and the armor suit, it reminds me of the collapsible armor the bears wore."

"The bears?" Sven said incredulously.

"Frostbane, Pershing, Rusty, Tad, and a few others were shapeshifters. Frostbane was a descendant of a game warden, and Kita passed it on to the others. Katie, another Angel, developed collapsible armor for them when war went from swords and spears to tanks and bullets. If I remember correctly, that's how Rusty met his end. He was unarmored and took a tank round in the side."

"And what of the boy with the cape and stick?" said Athena.

"Nothing, absolutely nothing," said Sven. "He's not in the system anywhere. I'd almost say he came with Kita."

"I don't think so," said Sarin. She moved the pictures around in order. "Here they are in the salon without him. In the restaurant, he's joined them. She must have picked him up. Kita has a weird thing for picking up strays with exceptional talents. I'm curious to know what his is."

"I have a bit of footage taken on the docks by the freighter Gjord Dallas." He played the clip of the fight.

"Not bad, she looks rusty."

"Did she take the freighter because she knew it was connected with us, or just the luck of the draw?" said Sven.

"I believe it is because it was the only ship with FTL capability," said Athena.

"She'd need a crew."

"The statistical probability of knowing whom she recruited is low, but performing a quick background check of crews in port, I've limited it to eleven possibilities."

"Where are you getting this from?" said Sven.

"Shipping data and logs are readily available, not stored on the station, but on several sites among the public access servers." Athena pulled up all of the images of the possible crews' faces on the screen next to the station footage.

"Any chance of narrowing it down?" said Sven.

"Him, him, her, and her," Sarin said, pointing out Hawke, Auggy, Case, and Lacy.

"Are you sure?"

"These two are the only females on the list," said Sarin. "Kita will always pick female over male. The old man is from the same crew as the girls. This fellow is the only one who looks like a soldier, and that's the only reason she'd take him. Now the most pressing question is: Where did they go?"

Sven frowned. "We don't know. They haven't appeared in known space. They can't have jumped more than sixty light-years, but scans haven't revealed anything."

"Is it possible they jumped again?" said Sarin.

"Not without refueling. Most ships only carry enough fuel for their next jump. I've got people looking, but it's a lot of space to cover, even if they've launched a rescue beacon."

Sarin grumped. "So, we are no better than when we started?"

"We know she's free, and we have postulated a quadrant of space to search," said Athena.

"Can I get a ship out there?" said Sarin.

"You can't go out there," said Sven. "They'll know where you've gone, and it's not a big leap to know the why. It's best if we lie low and wait for her to turn up again. I will increase surveillance around the nearby ports and stations. We can work out a quick response plan for the next time she appears. Until then, let's concentrate on what we have, Lina."

Sarin nodded. She went to the screen. With a wave of her hand, the picture showing Kita's face filled the screen. She floated up to the screen and touched it. Slowly, tears flowed down her cheeks. "I'll be at home if you need me," she said quietly.

"Are you sure you want to be alone, moonbeam?" Sven said, concerned.

"I'm sorry, Daddy, but all those who can console me are dead or gone. Next time you want to talk to me, just ask. I'll always be listening to you and Kristi." She turned and walked to Daniel. "As for you, you won't do anything stupid, will you?" She raised her arm, and a black tendril of fog snaked from her palm to his forehead.

"No...of course not," Daniel said in a clear, calm voice.

"Good boy. You will do whatever my father or Kristi tells you, clean yourself up, and you will move out of the fish tank into a proper condo. Your confidence is sky high, and your social skills are excellent. Do you understand me, human?"

"Yes, Sarin."

"Good." Sarin retracted the black fog tendril from Daniel. "He'll be a model employee for you."

"What did you do?" Sven demanded.

"I believe it's a talent given to her by her cloud or A'ahegre. It's an alien life form living inside her. Did I pronounce that correctly?" Kristi asked Sarin.

Sarin touched the side of her nose and smiled, and then vanished with Athena.

"What does that mean?" Sven asked Kristi.

"Honestly, sir, you need to go home early tonight, get some dinner, and sit down and talk to her. She and those other girls have seen more death, destruction, and heartache than the whole of the rest of human history. I'm not surprised they are the way they are. I guess Kita's destined, but Jane went the way her environment directed. I'm sure Kita had her influence, too. But, you need to talk to her and get to understand her, sir. It will make your, her, and my life easier."

"And you approve of Kita?"

"Yes. Maybe not her methods and desires, but as a person, I genuinely have enjoyed her company. She's intelligent, confident, and very down to earth. It's very refreshing to talk to someone who has grown up completely outside our system. She does have some very choice words about the Emperor and General Lyakhova. There's something to be said about not spurning a lover."

"Is that what this is over? Kita, Jane, and Lyakhova?"

"It's a tale as old as time, sir—love, sex, and power. It goes well beyond the three of them, and all the players involved wield an incredible amount of power. In truth, Lyakhova would be seriously outgunned if the other gods hadn't leveled the playing field by keeping Kita's parts locked away. This is only the beginning of the first act of this game of the gods."

Sven sighed. "I wish I were as enthusiastic as you are."

"It might be that you're a man, sir, and they don't reach you in the same way as they do me. Or, maybe it's because I'm not in any of the hot seats and can watch from the sidelines." Kristi smiled at him.

"I might just move you into a place a little more uncomfortable," Sven said, half-serious.

"I don't think that will be necessary, sir. I have a feeling I'm already on someone's roster."

"What roster is this?"

"Like any good chess player, Kita knows that even a simple pawn can checkmate a king," said Kristi, her eyes twinkling.

"You're worth far more than a pawn."

"I know, sir. There's a reason the most powerful piece on a chessboard is a woman."

Sven went to say something but stopped. He'd never looked at a chessboard that way before.

"Well, let's hope we don't have to use our most powerful piece, eh?"

"You don't think I'd look good with a pair of wings waving a sword around?"

"Ah..." Sven stumbled at a loss for words.

"And what should I do with Doctor Rhodes, sir?" she asked, saving her boss from embarrassment.

"Put him wherever he wants to be, but close by. He seems to have some unique talents."

"Of course, sir." Kristi looked at Daniel. "Doctor Rhodes, will you please come with me?"

"Yes, ma'am," Daniel said, hurrying over to her.

Kristi led him out. Sven shook his head in amazement when he heard him ask if there was a shower available. He looked at the large screen, still displaying the large image of Kita's face. *How can one person dominate everything, without even being here?* The only person with that kind of power was the emperor, but even she required billions of people and trillions more in equipment. Kita had only Sarin, and already they were making waves.

CHAPTER VII

S ARIN STEPPED OUT OF the elevator. The designer dress she wore changed to her schoolgirl outfit. "Hi, Kristi. How'd Kita handle me being gone?"

"Like a sulking cat." Kristi picked up a paper cup and drank. She made a face. "Ugh, that stuff is rank."

"What is it? And since when do you drink coffee from a paper cup?"

"They started showing up a few days after you left with a note saying: Drink me, love, Kita. I thought it was a joke after I took the first sip, but more showed up."

"Practical jokes aren't her sense of humor. It runs more toward physical, blue, and morbid. Why are you still drinking them?"

"I tossed the first two away and got scolded for it. I figured Kita had a reason."

"Did you ask her?"

"Like I said, a sulking cat. She hasn't said or replied to anything, except for these. I admit your father has been more relaxed since she's gone into hiding."

"Kita can be hard to live with, especially for men. So, what is this stuff?" She took off the lid and stuck her nail into the dark liquid, then stuck it in her mouth and regretted it.

"What is it?" Athena said, floating out of a pouch on Sarin's belt.

"I am so glad she always injected me," Sarin said, sticking out her tongue.

"Nanites? But she said she didn't have any of that information."

"She doesn't have any specific knowledge, but I'm sure she left enough breadcrumbs to do it if she needed to."

"What do you mean?" said Kristi. "I have the best nanites your father makes."

"If she's doing what I think she's doing, you're getting the best in the equation."

Kristi gave Sarin a confused look.

"In Infinity, what you call a universe, we call an equation. You are part of the equation and so are parts of me."

"Infinity?"

"Infinity is the place that holds all the equations and is overseen by the gods. I am the god Edi'rp who merged with the equation known as Sarin."

"So, how do you know where parts of you begin and end?"

"I'm not subdivided. I am one Angel god. My form changes depending on need. My Angel form is the most useful in this equation."

"I see. So, what kind of nanites am I getting?"

"Kita has an arsenal at her disposal. She can give abilities and modify your form. You'll get wings at some point, maybe a tail. She loves tails. Some Angels barely change while others change drastically. I'm not sure how she's planning on activating you."

"Won't I give you away? Your wings aren't something you can just hide."

Sarin vanished. "Invisibility is something every Angel has." Her body reappeared, but her wings remained invisible. "It takes time to get used to living with them. Most Angels get the hang of it in a few days." Her wings appeared, and she fluffed her feathers.

"Why?"

"You said it yourself, chess pieces. Kita thinks you're worthy of joining the ranks. Don't worry, when you do get your wings, I'll teach you the ropes."

The door to Sven's office opened.

"Moonbeam," said Sven. "I'm glad you got my call. How was the Intergalactic Mall?"

"I told you I'd be listening, Daddy. Shopping is shopping. It's too bad I have to act like an addlebrained twit that can't appreciate it."

"It does keep Galina's forces from watching us too closely," said Athena.

"That reminds me," Sarin said, tapping her nail against her pistol. "Two of my escorts have been compromised by Galina's people."

Sven sighed. "I understand one of my guards met with an accident?"

"He stuck his head out the high-speed train's window at the wrong time."

Sven rolled his eyes. "And killing the man doesn't bother you at all?"

"No. Should it? He betrayed you and me."

"The only thing worse than a spy is a traitor," said Athena.

Sven shook his head. "Will you give me a chance to move the second man?"

"He's alive because I didn't want to give us away."

"How did you know the men had betrayed us?" said Kristi.

Sven raised an eyebrow.

Sarin ignored her father's annoyance over Kristi including herself in the conversation. "I read their thoughts. I keep tabs on all my guards and employees near me."

"Including me?" said Kristi.

"Of course not. Reading thoughts is a serious invasion of privacy. I'd never do it to an Angel or anyone else I deem to be a friend."

"Anyone else I should be aware of?" said Sven.

"None that people should die over. Though, some should die over crimes of fashion. So, what did you want?" Sarin was already tired of her father's morality.

"I have a picture I want you to see. Kristi, we're not to be disturbed."

"Yes, sir."

"She can come with us," said Sarin. "Whatever you need to show me, she's going to need to know, too."

"Are you sure? Who will watch the office?" said Sven.

"I have my reasons. I'll watch it, don't worry, Daddy."

Sven led everyone into his office. The big screen lowered as he went to his desk and opened an image that filled the entire screen.

"This was taken several days ago at our occupied research facility in Rio. I haven't been able to verify if the image is real or not. Our data mining team found it on an obscure database in—"

"Talon!" Sarin and Athena said together.

On-screen, dark red hair spilled down Talon's chest from under a giant white hooded cloak. Even with her face hidden, the cream and orange of her barn owl wings made her easy to identify.

"What in Neptune's rings is she doing working for Galina?" said Sarin.

"Who is Talon?" said Kristi.

"She is Scarlett Kobb. A cook on the colony ship. We first met her when she was a privateer and had saved Nell and Nina from a perverted merchant ship. She lost her son for her troubles. Ten thousand years later, she crossed paths with Kita in Inferno as part of a prison work detail. She earned her wings for helping Kita get out. She led a group of Angels known as the Owlery."

"Silence, Shadow, and Night are all dead," said Athena. "They died—"

"Let's not go into the details of how or why," said Sarin. "Scarlett is a high angel. She works by herself on whatever charitable mission she dreams up. Don't let her status and occupation fool you. She can fight. She's also paired with a white cloud, which makes her even more powerful."

"A what?" said Sven.

Sarin dissolved into a black cloud. It was so black it gave no discernible definition or shape. She shifted back.

"The A'ahegre are aliens that travel the universe seeking knowledge. They gather it by pairing with a host. In exchange for a pairing, we get access to their knowledge and abilities."

"How long have you had yours?" said Kristi.

"Mine is young. It was a child of Kita's cloud. I contain a fair amount of knowledge from outside human-occupied space."

"That could be very lucrative," said Sven.

"You've already been given FTL. We don't give you information just because you want it," Sarin scoffed.

"FTL came from Kita?"

"Yes. Kita's cloud is large and holds a wealth of knowledge. She's devoured at least one ancient A'ahegre."

"They feed on each other?" said Kristi.

"Clouds come in several shades. Black and white clouds don't get along. Whites are driven to destroy black clouds. Kita and Tina found a way to counter the urges and keep them stable. They've been a valuable asset to us over the years."

"So, it's the source of Kita's knowledge?" said Sven.

"Kita's probably spent years of her life meditating and exploring the knowledge her cloud contains. She'd never have been able to unravel the mysteries of the equation without it. I know that much.

Where Kita got her knowledge, I'm not sure. The cloud is just one volume out of many that she has access to."

"Fascinating," Kristi whispered.

"That's only the tip of the iceberg." Sarin turned back to the image. "Scarlett and Galina were rivals before they became Angels. Even then, they'd argue on whose charity was more genuine. I'm curious to know what relationship Scarlett has with Galina. I can't believe Scarlett would help Galina after what she's done."

"So what do we do?"

"Draw her out. *How* is the question. Galina's not going to let Scarlett out of her cage without serious provocation." Sarin clicked her nail against her teeth, thinking.

"I can dig into her past and see if the General has any secrets," said Sven.

Sarin shook her head. "I was partnered with her for centuries. I have the answer. It'll come to me."

"I thought you were partnered with Kita?"

"I am. Kita was imprisoned for ten thousand years. Well, cycles really. A year there was much shorter than a standard year. It was not a good time, to put it mildly. It's a major reason I hate Galina."

"Then why'd you partner with her?" said Kristi.

"Because she was good in bed and knew how to fight. This isn't the first time she's stabbed me in the back." Sarin clapped excitedly. The screen changed to a modified version of the Political Bureau's flag. Galina had flown it on her ships when she was a pirate.

Sarin waved her hands and changed it. The white flag gained a red border and refracted red when it moved. She simplified the pyramid and reattached the top. "That should get her attention."

"We just can't drop it off in front of Political Bureau headquarters," said Kristi.

"No, we can't. But I know how."

"How?" said Sven.

"How'd you like to fund your own little political dissident group?"

"No way. We'd be lucky if we'd get death."

"I'm not talking about planetary revolt. Just a bunch of college kids high on ideology."

"I can't do that."

"Daddy, we're not talking real people. Athena and I will create a fictitious group that wants freedom. The kind of thing the Political

Bureau watches. After breaking in and planting that flag, we'll have their attention."

"And then what?" said Kristi.

"Then we see who comes out of the cuckoo's nest. I just need a little seed money to get legitimacy." Sarin smiled and batted her lashes at her father.

He sighed. "How much?"

"A million should do it."

"It'll take a few days to get it scrubbed."

"Take as many as you need to get it without any trace to us."

"It won't implicate us."

"Good. If there's not anything else, I want to go home, find some ice cream, and watch a stupid movie."

"Is this how you're helping me set up this clandestine group of yours, Mother?" Athena teased.

"I don't want to muck it up with my lack of knowledge in the matter. Plus, this way I can pin it all on you."

"I am just a computer. I only do what I am programmed to do," Athena said in a stiff, computer-generated voice.

"Guess that leaves you to take the fall," Sarin teased Kristi.

Kristi held up her hands. "I'm just the secretary."

The women turned and looked at Sven.

"Get out, before I change my mind," he muttered.

Sarin and Athena giggled.

"Ladies, shall we?" Kristi motioned the pair to the door.

"Bye, Daddy. Love you," Sarin said.

"You'd better," he replied with a tired sigh.

CHAPTER VIIII

S ARIN APPEARED IN FRONT of Kristi's desk. Sven stood next to the executive restroom with his arms crossed, looking worried. "What's the matter?" she asked him.

"I don't know. She won't tell me. She came in wearing a hoodie and a pair of jeans. I asked her how she was doing. Tears formed in her eyes as she ran to the bathroom. When I went in, she threw me out. I was hoping she'd talk to you. I'm not compromising you am I?"

"No. I took a holographic generator, so Athena took my place. It's nice to get off that ship. After two weeks of being cooped up, it's nice to get away." There was no trick of physics to get from Neptune to Earth. Even with her father's fastest ship, the trip took weeks.

"I'd hate to waste your time you've put in trying to get at General Lyakhova."

Sarin shrugged. Getting Galina's attention was proving harder than she had thought. Two smash and grabs on Bureau safe houses in a month had garnered little attention. She and Athena were on their way to Earth to bring the revolt closer to Galina's front door. They had succeeded in garnishing a large underground following, which made it easier to strategically leak their next target, Seattle.

"She'll still be there. Family and friends come first." Sarin knocked on the door. "Kristi, can I come in?" Sarin pushed inside when she didn't get an answer. "Kristi?" She heard the whisper of a sob come from the stall and peeked inside. Kristi was huddled between the toilet and the wall. She knelt in front of her. "Sweetie, what's wrong?"

Kristi's eyes were red from crying and streaked with tears. "It hurts so much. What's happening to me?"

"I'm not sure. What hurts?"

"My back, between my shoulder blades."

Sarin's lips puckered. "Can I see? Please?" She helped Kristi out of the corner and pulled off Kristi's hoodie. The woman screamed. "It's all right. It's ok," said Sarin. She took Kristi in her arms and held her. Even as a trained psychologist Sarin couldn't shake the weirdness of the situation. She'd known Kristi from when she was a child. Now, she was much older, but she still felt like she was a child holding an adult.

Sarin placed the palm of her hand against Kristi's shoulder. "You're going to feel a little pinch." She injected a painkiller with her barb, a four-inch hypodermic-like needle that extended from the heel of her hand. The barb was connected to glands that could produce drug compounds, venoms, or toxins. Kristi relaxed in her arms.

"What did you give me?" Kristi whispered.

"A synthetic painkiller designed specifically for your biochemistry. It'll clear from your system with no negative side effects."

"How did you get my file?"

"I just needed your DNA. My body does the rest. Let me see your back."

Sarin lifted Kristi's shirt and saw two growths underneath Kristi's skin. "Neptune's rings, you're in for a lot of pain."

"What...what is it?"

"You have the beginning of two ball joints forming between your shoulder blades and spine. Normally, when an Angel gets her wings it takes minutes, and it hurts like the burning suns. Are you still drinking that stuff Kita sends you?"

"Yes."

"I don't know why she's doing it this way."

"Maybe because she can't inject it straight into her bloodstream and is instead relying on the much slower delivery system through her digestive tract," said Sven.

"Daddy, you're not supposed to be in here."

"Sorry, moonbeam. I was worried about the second most important girl in my life."

"I'll forgive you, this time, sir," said Kristi.

"Do you know what's wrong? What's causing her pain?"

"Becoming an Angel is a painful process," said Sarin. "The ball sockets that will connect her wings are forming. It requires rebuilding that area of her body. Once the sockets are ready, her wings will form. I can't speed up the process. All I can do is give you the chemical compounds I used to make the painkiller."

Sven's eyes widened in shock. "She's becoming an Angel? Since when? Did you ask to become an Angel, Kristi?"

Sarin shook her head. "You don't ask. You're chosen."

"What if she doesn't want to become one?"

"You don't get a choice. You do get a choice if you stay or not. No one has rejected it yet, though a few have left for a while to explore on their own."

"Kita can't do this," Sven said firmly.

Sarin shrugged. "It's between her and Kristi."

"It's Kristi's choice," said Sven. "Come on. We'll get you down to the lab and see about reversing this."

"Daddy, you didn't even ask her if this is what she wanted. You're acting as badly as Kita. It's Kristi's decision."

"I don't know," said Kristi. "Why me?"

Sarin smiled and touched Kristi's cheek tenderly. "Because you met Kita's criteria. You remind me of Dev. She was Kita's press secretary, and later she managed the Office of the Vicereine. Not all battles are fought with swords and bullets. Kita recognized this. I think she sees the same potential in you that she saw in Dev. Your knowledge and skills will be invaluable to the Angels."

"What about me?" demanded Sven.

"We're not leaving right away. There will be time to train a replacement."

"No one can replace Kristi."

"That is true, but don't you think it's time she was rewarded for her service? She can't be an executive secretary forever. She's too good. Kita realizes this and is giving her the opportunity to take the next step. But it is Kristi's decision."

Kristi dabbed at her tears, taking slow breaths. "I'm not a warrior like you, Jane."

"You're a different kind of warrior."

"What if I want to be a warrior like you?"

"Then I can teach you and have Kita give you some offensive abilities."

Kristi laughed and cried at the same time.

"Kristi?" said Sven in an uncertain tone.

"Talking to Kita I dreamed what it would be like, but I never thought...I never thought I would become one."

"Welcome to the most exclusive girls club in the equation," said Sarin.

"What about me?" Sven grumbled under his breath.

"Daddy," Sarin snapped. "Be happy for her. This is a big deal. Not everything is about you. Now, I'll give you the compounds for the pain meds."

Sven sighed. "I'll make sure she has them within the hour."

"What are we going to tell Ray?" said Kristi. "He's going to notice my back and the pain. I left this morning before he woke."

Sarin made a disapproving sound.

"We need to tell him," said Sven in a tone he used to make executive decisions.

Sarin rolled her eyes at his tone. "The only time we had an Angel married to a human it didn't end well. He killed Dev and Talli during the coup. I'm not saying that's what will happen here, but we probably should move them to a more secure location."

"I have the visitors' apartments in building three. We can have some of them remodeled."

"Ray isn't going to want to move on a whim. I need to tell him," said Kristi.

"Has Ray ever been to our villa?" said Sarin.

"For parties and social events."

"Tell him tonight he's got a dinner date with Daddy. He wants to personally apologize for overworking you for the last two months."

"Will he go for that?" said Sven. "I can get him season tickets to the Seahorses. He just has to come over to pick them up so I can apologize in person. I think he'd like to see you recognized for all your dedication."

"He'd probably come for that," said Kristi. "I don't know how keen he'll be on moving."

"We'll convince him," replied Sarin. "It's for safety, especially yours."

"He's retired, right?" said Sven with an apologetic look to Kristi.

Daddy, that's a bit of information you should know.

"Yes. Sixty years in the Legion. I'm afraid he'll get cabin fever having to live here."

"He'll be free to come and go as he pleases."

"What time should I tell him?"

"We'll make it early, so we don't have to hang around here all day," said Sarin.

"Can I come?" said Kita, her question scrolling along the bottom of the painting hanging in the bathroom.

"You'd better," said Sarin. "This is your mess. I can't believe you didn't tell me."

"You barely talk to me anymore," wrote Kita.

"As much as I love the sentiment behind Kita's choice to send you, you're not her, and all you do is make my heart hurt. I'm sorry. I love Kita, but you're missing the most important part of her, her heart."

"WAAAAHHHHHHHHH," filled every screen in the room.

"What does that mean?" said Sven.

"She's crying," said Sarin. "Kita, stop it. You can't complain about missing something you never had. When you do get here, and you rejoin with your biological self, I will be all over you. Until then, keep helping. The more you do, the better prepared we'll be for when you arrive. Do you understand me, babe?"

"Yes," appeared on a painting.

Sarin could hear the dejection from the printed word. "I love you, babe."

"I love you," appeared slowly.

"Is there any way to make the transition easier for Kristi?"

"Not without having my body. I wanted the transformation to be gradual, so she wouldn't be noticed."

Sarin tapped her nail on her teeth. "Can I do it?"

"No. The bionanites I use aren't made in the barb glands. They come from synthetic glands next to my heart."

"Ah, that's so sweet."

"How much longer will it take?" Sven asked.

"A few more weeks. I didn't think about synthesizing a painkiller. I can mix it in with the coffee."

"And make it taste better," said Sarin. "I know you rarely think of the comfort of new Angels, but try to do it here."

"Vanilla, chocolate, or mocha?" Kita wrote.

"Mocha," said Kristi.

"I'll get on it. Do I still get to come tonight?"

"Of course, babe," said Sarin. "We'll hold it in my wing of the house so you can use the holographic theater."

"Ok. Bye."

"Babe, don't be that way. We love you," said Sarin. She waited a moment before sighing heavily. "I love her, but some days I just want to slap her."

"I know the feeling," said Kristi.

"I'll go home and prepare for tonight. Anything Ray likes in particular?"

"I'll send you a list. I guess I should get changed into something more professional."

"Keep on what you've got. You might get a growth spurt."

"I don't mind a casual Tuesday," said Sven. "Nothing's planned for today anyway."

"I will see you both early this evening," Sarin said and then vanished.

S ARIN MOVED ABOUT HER common area making sure her displays were perfect. Her collection of pistols and rifles showed the evolution of her firearms. Few knew she was a master gunsmith. On an adjoining wall hung Razorsplitter and her Arconian kit for the hundreds of cycles she'd led Arcone. Her diplomas and certifications she'd earned hung on a third wall. It included a picture of the graduation ceremony the twins had held for her. The child-made diploma hung next to the picture. On the last wall, she displayed pictures of her and the other Angels along with trophies from different adventures.

The doorbell rang. Sarin phased across the house to the massive main door. Putting on her outside persona she used to fool the Political Bureau, she opened the door with a guarded smile.

"Hello, Mister Wolfe. Please come in. My father and your wife have not arrived yet. Please, follow me into my wing of the house," she said in a quiet formal voice. She led him down a side passage. In silence, Ray hurried to catch up to her.

"Can I get you anything to drink, Mister Wolfe?" Sarin asked when they arrived.

Ray looked around at the walls in stunned silence. "I'll just have a beer."

"Of course. We have a large selection."

"I'm simple, kid. Just a Wheizer for me."

Sarin directed the drink dispenser to prepare the beverage.

"I didn't know your old man was into collecting illegal firearms. Lucky for him I'm retired." Ray chuckled as he looked at the wall of weapons.

Sarin carried the beer over to the man. "Your beer, sir."

Ray turned around and jumped back into the display when he saw Sarin. She waved her hand and caught everything before any damage was done. "They don't belong to my father. They belong to me." A wicked grin flashed across her face. She wore her Legion uniform, with her wings still hidden. "I know they're more deadly than a light rifle, but on the planet where I was stationed, you needed something more deadly than a flashlight. I suppose you know what I mean, Sergeant Major?"

Ray sputtered for words as Sarin placed the beer on a table that appeared from under it. She walked over to the wall of weapons and pulled off a pair of pistols specially made for her Legion uniform. She opened a pocket, pulled out her beret, and put it on her head. Next, she pinned her rank on her collar.

"Deputy Commandant was one of the many careers I had on that nameless planet the Empire rescued me from. I was very disappointed when they refused to recognize my rank and time in service. They took the word of a Political Bureau rat over mine. Still, I am striking, don't you think?"

The man's face was beet red. "I don't care whose daughter you are. I'll turn your lying bitch ass in. There's enough illegal weaponry here to put you away forever."

Sarin smiled sideways. "You're free to tell it to my superior. She's standing behind you."

Kita stepped from out of the wall and stood next to Ray. She wore her version of the Legion uniform. Instead of black and red, hers was black.

"Your objection is noted, Sergeant Major," said Kita. "But, my second is doing just fine."

"I knew you Gjords were daft in the head, but not this crazy," said Ray.

Kita and Sarin smiled at each other.

"We're far from crazy, sir. In fact, we've come to a very rational conclusion," Kita said, her tone becoming sinister. "Why don't you tell him, Deputy."

"Gladly," said Sarin, taking a step closer to Ray. "We've decided Kristi displays the aptitude and attitude we desire in our unit. Normally, we only take people without any strings attached. We have in the past experimented with a girl who was married. Unfortunately, it didn't end well for her or her daughter."

"Kristi isn't going anywhere with you two whack jobs to join whatever insane wannabe legionnaire game you're playing," Ray yelled.

"We don't want her in the Legion," said Sarin. Kita appeared next to Sarin. Together they made their wings appear. "We want her to be an Angel."

"And that doesn't include you," Kita whispered.

"You'll never get away with this!" cried Ray.

"We already have a plan," said Sarin. "The train you took to get here is going to have a minor mechanical failure that will create a cascade of failures, until the train jumps the track and plunges into Turtle Lake. It will later be discovered, that there was a series of false maintenance reports covering up the problems."

"That's impossible. Even you don't have those kinds of resources."

The two Angels changed into their god forms.

"We're gods," said Kita. "With a wave of our hand, it'll be airtight."

Ray turned around and grabbed a pistol on the rack. He fired two rounds at Kita. The two Angels burst out laughing.

"You just killed a hologram," Kita said as the two holes closed.

Ray fired at Sarin. The bullets hung in the air a foot from the pistol.

"I'm real. But you need to do better than that to kill me," Sarin drew her pistol and fired. The bullet pierced Ray's trachea. The man dropped the pistol he was holding and grabbed at his throat. He tried to speak, but only a gurgle came out.

"I shot you in the throat so you'd shut up," said Sarin. "You're an 'I'm sorry' gift to my partner. We had a spat earlier, and I want to make it up to her. I'll give you a warning. I like to shoot people. It's a fun adrenaline rush. For Kita, it's something else. She's *hardwired* to get enjoyment from killing. Couple that with a serious bloodlust, and you'd normally be in for a very long night." Sarin looked at Kita. "Make it quick. We need to get him to his final destination."

Kita fell upon the man. Sarin snapped her fingers to put the pair in a plastic enclosure. She heard Ray screaming through the hole in his throat. Not wanting any part of Kita's idea of fun, she left to finish preparing for her other guests.

CHAPTER IX

S ARIN TUNED EVERY AVAILABLE screen to the various news channels for when her father and Kristi arrived.

"What's going on?" said Sven, looking around at the ten different reporters talking at once.

"One of the trains derailed and exploded over Turtle Lake," said Sarin, trying to sound shaken.

"Is Ray here? He'd have taken that line to get here," Kristi said, panic creeping into her voice.

"No. Should he be?"

"He messaged me that he was leaving. That was over an hour ago. It only takes thirty minutes." Kristi twisted and turned as she hugged herself looking worried.

"I'll contact our news network and send security over to find him. I'm sure he's just stuck somewhere," said Sven. He muted the other screens and made the calls.

"Isn't that a waste of resources?" Kita said as she entered with Athena.

Sarin knew how hard it was to lose a partner and wanted everyone available to comfort Kristi when the time came.

"It's a perfect allocation of resources," said Sven. "It will make a nice human-interest story and put a face on the tragedy."

"Oh, I'm not passing judgment or anything. I would have done the same thing. It's good to know we have like minds."

"We are nothing alike."

"Keep telling yourself that." Kita went to go hover over the food.

Sarin smacked her hand. "You can't eat. Get out of here."

"You didn't get any cookies, anyway," Kita said with a practiced pout.

"No one needs any cookies. The food's ready. We'll go down to my wing. We can look out onto the garden and see the curve of the station from there." Sarin and the other Angels picked up the platters of food and led the way.

"Are these all yours?" Sven asked after seeing Sarin's display of weapons when they arrived in her living area. "We can't have these in the house."

Sarin spotted several red dots on the white carpet. "Of course they're mine. They're a history of my life as a gunsmith, sniper, and gunslinger. Except for the original, I designed and built them all myself. They all work if you want to squeeze off a few rounds." As she talked, she moved to the spots of blood, put her foot on them, and made them disappear.

"That won't be necessary. I think that's the first time I've ever seen you clean anything," Sven teased his daughter.

"Being what I am, I do have some practical purposes."

"How did dirt get in here?"

"Oh, I can guess," Sarin said looking at Kita. "But I probably dragged it in when I went out to see the garden."

Kristi looked around nervously.

"Sweetheart, sit. Ray will be fine," said Sarin. "Do you want something to drink?"

"Just some water."

"No problem." Sarin went to the small kitchenette. The beer left over from Ray sat on the counter. She grabbed it and poured it out.

"It's not good to drink alone," said Sven.

"That's why it's still here. I got the message you were coming."

"I just don't want to see my girl become an alcoholic."

Sarin gave him a bright smile, hiding her past as a drug addict and an alcoholic. "Feel free to eat."

"Oh, I can't even think about food," Kristi said with a shiver.

"It'll be all right." Sarin put an arm and a wing around her. "I know exactly how you feel. Someone is very good at leaving me in similar circumstances. But sitting and worrying yourself into a fit won't help. All you'll do is stress yourself out. Daddy's people will find Ray. Have a little faith."

Kristi burst into tears.

"**H**OW IS SHE?" KITA asked as Sarin and Athena stepped through the screen onto the stone patio.

"Asleep, finally. Poor girl exhausted herself crying," said Sarin. "We all know what it feels like to lose someone. What's the latest report from the scene?"

"It's going to take a few days to get the cars out of the water," said Kita. "The whole station is in an uproar over what happened. As a witness put it: this just doesn't happen."

"First time for everything," Athena muttered.

"Indeed," Sven said from a dark corner where he had gone to smoke a cigarette.

"Daddy, what have I told you about that?" said Sarin.

"Save it, dear. I'll choose how I wish to kill myself. My company built those trains. I know what their safety record is. What did you three have to do with this wreck?"

"Nothing," Sarin said, offended.

"Don't lie to me, Jane. I raised you, and I don't need some alien to tell me when you're lying. Why did Ray have to die?"

"Hey, back off," said Kita.

Sarin waved her partner back. "He died to free Kristi. We need her to be committed to us and not worrying about some man back home."

"That's not your choice to make," said Sven.

"Everyone here has lost someone. We've all lost more than one person we care about. It's hard, but with our help, she'll get through it."

"You don't think you've helped enough?" Sven yelled.

"She's going to get a chance to say goodbye. She'll put that chapter of her life behind her, and that's all she can do."

"Have you asked her what she wants?"

Sarin put her hands on her hips. "Rarely are we asked what we want when the equation changes. I didn't get asked, Kita didn't get asked, and Athena didn't get asked. It just happens, and you have to deal with the outcome."

"But it's not some grand twist in the equation. It was the three of you who did this. What gives you the right to play God?" Sven said accusingly.

"If I were that kind of god, I wouldn't be standing here!" snarled Sarin.

"And your mother would still be alive."

"At least you and she got the chance to say goodbye. The three of us didn't. Our friends and family were slaughtered before we even knew what was going on. They killed our babies and Athena's partner. I listened from inside a cell as the orbital guns fired over and over, raining destruction down on them. They didn't get a chance to fight back, and there was nothing left except radioactive dust. I couldn't do anything to stop them.

"That was not blind fate, Father. That was Galina killing a pair of girls who looked up to her as a teacher and a friend. She didn't care. She was just following a plan that included killing my girls, Nell, Leaf, and so many more." Tears ran down Sarin's face. "They were my friends, my family. No one asked me if they should die. Otherwise, I'd have gladly given myself up to save them. I'd put the pistol to my head and pull the trigger if I had to. Don't lecture me about loss and fate, Father. I've had enough of both to last me a thousand lifetimes." Before she could say more, Kita wrapped her up in her arms and closed her wings around them.

Sarin cried herself out. Kita stroked her hair and dabbed at the tears on her cheeks. Sarin hugged Kita possessively. "I'm going back to the ship. If you need me, call me. Babe, can you and Athena handle things here?"

"Sure."

"We'll take care of her, Mom," said Athena.

"I need to go decompress," said Sarin. "I wish you could come with me," Sarin said to Kita.

"I know. I wish my biological self were here, too."

Sarin gave a hint of a smile.

"You can't run away from this," said Sven.

"Sir, stop," Kristi said from above them. The group looked up to see Kristi on the balcony. "I know your heart is in the right place, but the outrage belongs to me. Will one of you catch me if this goes badly?"

"Ah, sure," said Kita. She clapped her hands. "We've reached saturation." A set of wings peeked over Kristi's head.

"What a pretty color," said Athena.

"Yeah, I was thinking of going for a spice theme. Cinnamon is both a color and a great name."

Athena giggled. "Only because you can shorten it to Cin."

"You know I don't go for that hokey pokey stuff. Go ahead, we'll catch you," cried Kita.

Kristi jumped over the rail. Kita and Athena floated waiting for her. They caught her and set her on the ground. She hugged Sarin.

"I'm sorry, Jane. I can't imagine what it's like to lose so many friends or a child."

Fresh tears fell down Sarin's face. "I'm sorry."

"You don't have to apologize."

"Yes, I do," Sarin said as she pulled away. "This...This wasn't an accident. I caused it." She bit her lip, nervously waiting for Kristi to come apart.

Kristi frowned sadly. "I don't know what to say, Jane. I wondered how this would play out. Kita was very blunt about what she expects from the Angels. It simplifies things, but I don't know if I'll ever be able to forgive you for it."

"Wait, don't get mad at her," said Kita. "Blame me. It was my idea."

"I know. I will deal with you later."

Kita pursed her lips. "Just because you're an Angel, doesn't mean you have to join us."

"You are not getting out of this so easily, Kita. I understand you wanted to protect me, but I don't need to be protected. I can take care of myself, and I decided weeks ago to leave Ray for you." She huffed. "I'm going back upstairs. I'll find you when I'm ready. Until then, leave me alone."

"Well, I will say one thing," Kita said after Kristi was gone, "you give a girl a set of wings, and she no longer fears anything."

Sarin shook her head.

"You know what I mean," Kita said, putting her arms around Sarin.

"I need to get back to the ship. Can you handle this?"

"As well as I can. I'm probably going to need Sven's help."

Sarin looked at her father. "Daddy, just don't, please?" She didn't wait for an answer and vanished with Athena.

CHAPTER X

"**W**E ARE GOING TO have to get some of these for the house," said Athena to Sarin. They were in an underground utility passageway above a Political Bureau facility.

"You think so?"

"With the long hallways, stairs, and priceless treasures, a pair of R/C cars would be exciting."

"Ok, but no direct interfacing with the car. Kita's a bad enough cheater, on several levels."

"You did choose to partner with someone who will do whatever is required to win."

"I know. It's saved our lives more than once, but for little things, it's kind of annoying."

Athena chirped laughter. "The car has arrived at the front door. I don't detect anyone within a five-yard radius. Are you ready?"

"My hands are charged."

"Turning on the mass generator."

They waited for someone to investigate the sudden appearance of mass at the front door. This mission was the first time they had used this type of espionage tactic. Sarin had always left the cloak and dagger stuff to Kita. Now, she wished she'd paid more attention.

All Sarin needed was a distraction so she could blow a hole in the wall. This facility was larger than the previous two, and she didn't think smashing the front door would be the way a small group of college-age revolutionaries would do it. She and Athena had spent the better part of three days trying to develop a clever plan. After researching a dozen movies and shows, this tactic seemed to be the best idea that might work in the real world.

"We've got three or four people at the door," said Athena. "I—Blast doors deployed. They think we're a bomb."

"Good." Sarin transformed into a female activist. She pulled the mask down over her face tucking in her now brown hair into the back, and then placed her hand on the wall. "Let's give them one. Blow it."

As Athena sent the command to detonate the car, Sarin blasted a hole in the wall. Athena floated behind her in her ball, as Sarin entered a room with seemingly endless rows of computer stacks.

"Uh, I think this is much more than a Bureau observation station," Sarin said. "What is this place?"

"It could be backup storage or computers just crunching data. I had warehouses full of machines doing calculations for Hades."

"What if it's an AI?"

"That would depend on what kind of shackles it has. It could be hostile, though I think it would be indifferent."

"Would you be?"

"I'm not shackled, and I would defend my home with whatever resources available."

"Maybe if it is one, we can offer it a way out."

"Let us see if that's the type of dragon that is in this lair."

Two male activists appeared next to Sarin. They were not holograms, but biological constructs linked to Sarin. They were alive, but she had to do all of their thinking. She gave them each a Bureau gun, taken from her first attack back on Neptune, to make sure the investigators would link the activists to the attacks. She drew her pistol and made her way through the rows of machines. She counted over a thousand computers by the time she reached the end of the row. Looking left and right, there were at least fifty rows.

"This place must take up a city block," Sarin said to Athena.

"It is a lot of hardware. This facility might be the central control system for all of Seattle."

A door opened from the platform above them, and a large group of guards pushed their way in. Sarin fired her pistol, aiming the 9mm rounds between gaps in their armor. With all of the guards dead, she led her group through the open door to a stairwell. With a reluctant sigh, Sarin climbed the stairs.

"There are no doors out of here," said Sarin after climbing seven flights of stairs.

"The plans we purchased are useless," said Athena. "This is supposed to be the food court for the building."

They climbed seventy-seven stories before finding another door. Sarin burst through, but the corridor was empty.

"This is very troubling," said Athena.

"What do you mean?"

"We leaked our intentions to attack this location. I would have expected higher security."

"Don't tell me we're going to have to do this again."

"We should see if there is a prize waiting for us. Even if there is no AI, we could steal some important data."

Sarin stretched out her consciousness to look at the equation. She drifted through the walls until she found what looked to be a control room. Leading her group down the well-lit corridor to a heavily secured door, Sarin put her hand on it. An explosion blasted the door into the room beyond. She jumped inside, searching for targets. She found a pair of guards, and her puppets found three more. The trio put their targets down with ruthless efficiency.

The room held several workstations, papers and bodies now littered the floor. A panoramic window showed the Seattle skyline.

"Hello?" Sarin called, but no AI answered. "Well, damn. Can you hack in and see what you can steal?" she asked Athena.

"Yes, but I'll need a few minutes."

"No problem. We'll guard the hallway and the window. Now that we're in, I'm worried about getting out," Sarin grumbled. "I—"

The window exploded inward blasting the Angels with glass shards. The shower of glass shredded one of Sarin's puppets. The second puppet collapsed with a throwing star in the center of his forehead. Sarin transformed and brought her wings forward to block the glass.

When Sarin opened them, an Angel leaped at her. She didn't recognize the Angel with seafoam wings trimmed in gold. The Angel wore a white sneak suit and mask, bracers, and a utility belt. She wielded a pair of daggers.

Sarin sidestepped the Angel and shot her attacker in the hand, knocking a dagger free. Sarin phased and punched the Angel in the face, then grabbed the Angel by the throat, squeezing until her eyes bulged.

"I don't know who you think you are, but you're no true Angel," Sarin snarled. "You're a disgrace to all those who came before you. There's only one thing fake Angels deserve." She slammed her into the concrete floor repeatedly until she'd created a shallow crater. She drew her UEE pistol and pointed it at the Angel's head.

"Wait, Jane, don't shoot."

"Scarlett," said Sarin, keeping the pistol aimed at the other Angel's head. She turned as Talon landed in the room.

"Jane, that's not a false Angel, that's Talli, Dev's little girl."

Sarin shrugged. "Oh." She pointed the gun away.

Talon swept her hood back, revealing her face and dark red hair. "I...I thought Galina ruined you."

Sarin grinned wickedly. "That's what I wanted her to think. Galina's delusional if she thinks her army of Bureau shrinks can reprogram me. Why in Neptune's rings is Talli dressed like an assassin? She's only, what, fifteen?"

"Yes. Galina's been training her. This mission was supposed to be easy for her to cut her teeth on."

"So, why are you working for Galina?"

"I didn't have a choice. She offered citizens of the UEE a conditional surrender. Serve her and live. I don't know how many people took her up on it. They took Talli. Galina and Rene tried to raise her as you and Kita did with your girls, but they found they're not cut out to be parents. So, they gave her to me. I've been her mom ever since. I'd love to get out of this place. I've been waiting for someone to come along to help."

"Why not just leave on your own?" said Athena.

"Athena, you're here too?"

"I stowed away on the ship that brought you back to the Sol system. I've been with my mom ever since."

"I couldn't leave because of Talli," admitted Talon. "She's still too green to fight effectively."

"Yeah, well, she's going to feel like slag in the morning," said Sarin. "At least my plan worked."

"Plan?" said Talon.

"I've been trying to draw you out. Someone took a photo of you out at Daddy's stolen Rio facility. Do you know if Lina is there?"

"I'm sorry, I don't know. I've heard Galina has her, but I don't know where. All I was doing was surviving until an opportunity arose. But I'll help you get her back, I promise."

"I'm not challenging your loyalty, Scarlett, and we're not out of here yet. Athena, did you find anything?"

"Yes. This facility is not an AI, but a backup storage server of plans for buildings, installations, ships, and similar items. I'm moving as much as I can up to the darknet."

"Fine. We're going with success protocol. I just need to kill the female and these two."

"But I was having fun playing cloak and dagger," Athena whined playfully.

"You'll have to settle for the movies." Sarin knelt next to Talli and ran her finger through some blood trickling from the girl's ear. "I need your DNA," she said to Talon.

"No offense, but why?"

"So, it looks like you're dead." Sarin created a replica of Talli. With the pistol, she fired a magazine worth of bullets into the body putting one in the clone's forehead.

"How's that possible? Not even Kita could do that!" exclaimed Talon.

"She could if she wanted. She's no longer alone in the god department."

"I...Then maybe Sheppard was right."

"About?"

"Others becoming gods—Tina, Kylee, Raptor, Leaf, Vee, Nell, Kara, Tenshi, Denver, and others."

"Kerri?"

"Yes. Sheppard said her name along with some strong expletives." Sarin chuckled. "Kerri does bring out the best in people."

"What exactly are you the god of?"

"I am Edi'rp or just Edi, and I am the God of Pride. DNA?" She held out a hand.

Talon pulled out a strand of hair and handed it over.

A clone of Talon appeared. Sarin loaded a fresh magazine in her pistol and fired until she was empty, hitting the body once in the forehead. A doppelganger of Sarin's current form appeared. Sarin took one of Talli's stars and jabbed it into the body's throat.

"Finished, Athena? We need to leave," said Sarin.

"Getting the last of it as I head for the door."

Sarin scooped up Talli and motioned for Talon to follow. In the corridor, she gave the teenager to Talon and stood in the door looking into the room. With a wave of her hand, she created the aftermath of a fight scene that would fool even Galina.

"Athena, contact the hotel and tell them I want dinner."

"What does that have to do with anything?"

"To keep up the alibi, I've been in my room all day. We'll stay on schedule to leave tomorrow morning."

T HE GROUP APPEARED IN Sarin's bedroom at the hotel.

"So, this is what excess looks like," said Talon, looking around the room.

"You never complained about it living on Base Station or at the Angels' Penthouse," Sarin scoffed.

"There we had the best of everything, but we took only what we needed. I am sorry. I didn't mean to be rude or insult you. I came from a lower-middle-class family; this kind of lifestyle was only in the movies or the vid-mags."

"Sorry, as well. This trip has become more stressful than I'd planned. I need to figure out how to get you from here to my ship and then back to Neptune. You can hide there."

"I have no intention of hiding me, but Talli must be kept safe."

"You can put her on the bed. Someone might as well get some use out of it."

"Are we being recorded?"

"Always, but all they're seeing is me sleeping."

"Do we have medical supplies to heal her?" said Talon.

"She won't heal on her own? I didn't hit her that hard."

"Talli doesn't have the full nanite package you and I have. Kita never had a chance to give them to her. She barely has enough to survive what you did."

"Neptune's rings." Sarin reached into Talli's belt and pulled out a dagger. She ran the blade over her palm. Sarin aimed the blood drops into Talli's mouth and contusions. "When we get to Neptune, we can fix that. I hope she likes coffee."

"What does coffee have to do with nanites?" Talon asked sounding confused.

"It's Kita's delivery system at the moment. It tastes like sewer water."

"Kita's here?"

"In a manner of speaking. She created a VI of herself and snuck it along with me."

Talon grunted. "Kita can do it all."

Sarin sighed. "Except keep herself out of trouble."

"I'm sorry I couldn't do more."

"She and I don't hold anyone responsible. I went without a fight, too."

"You had a plan. I didn't know what to do. One second the ISS troops are fighting with me, the next they're placing me under arrest for treason."

Sarin raised an eyebrow. "You're one of the lucky ones. Most girls ate a bullet or worse."

"Galina said as much. She was very unhappy, so many got away."

"Who did get away?"

"Sheppard said Snowy was the only one of us to get away that didn't become a god."

"Snowy? She's always been a tough one to kill. She might still be there."

"She'd be a strong ally."

"I'll put that on my list. Anyone else?"

"Besides the three of us, I know they have Megan."

"How do you know this?"

"Galina used to talk to me when she needed to work something out."

"Do you know where Lina is? In Rio?"

Talon shook her head. "I wish I did. Galina never brought that problem to me."

"Mom, is that you?" Talli said with a small moan.

Talon moved to the head of the bed. "Yes, sugar foam, I'm here."

Talli propped herself on an elbow, but Talon pushed her back down. "Don't push yourself. You're still healing. Give it some more time."

"What happened?"

"You ran into Sarin, an old friend of mine."

"Sarin. Class one type, do not approach alone. Black wing with red patches. Black and red schoolgirl outfit. Sniper, gunslinger, and sword. Extremely physically strong. Relies on brute strength, power, and intimidation to get what she wants."

Sarin chuckled. "Someone's done her homework. Nice to meet you, kid. Keep resting and finish healing."

"Yes, ma'am."

"You seemed oddly relaxed," Sarin replied, impressed.

Talli sighed. "Mom told me that someday we'd be able to go home to the other Angels."

"Unfortunately, I only have me, Athena, a VI of Kita, and a new Angel, Kristi or Cinnamon."

"Cinnamon? Are her wings sticky buns?" Talon said, shaking her head.

"I don't know, ask Kita. I think it's a joke. Hopefully, Kita didn't name Kristi after a cheap prostitute."

"So, how are we officially getting out of here?"

"I'd love to wave my hand and just put us back on Neptune, but I'm watched constantly. We'll have to stage something that looks real and believable."

"Do you have something in mind?"

"When was the last time you went clubbing?"

CHAPTER XI

"**M**OM, MY FEET HURT," Talli whined to Talon.

"I know, sugar foam. It shouldn't be too much longer." It had been three hours, and only seven people remained in front of them to get into the club. She leaned into the teenager. "It's the price we have to pay to get back to our own kind. We just have to do what Jane says. This is her world."

"Is the makeup supposed to itch so much?"

"Talli, there's nothing I can do. You'll just have to grin, laugh, and bear it. You're here to have fun. Consider this an infiltration mission."

Talli rolled her eyes. "Who's going to train me?"

"Talli, that's enough. Look like you're having fun and without a care." Talon smiled and laughed loudly like Talli had told her a joke. A pair of girls came out of the club laughing and giggling. Behind them, four boys trailed looking wolfish.

The line moved forward as the two groups ahead of them made the bouncers' cut and entered the club with happy cheers.

"Great night, isn't it?" Talon said trying to strike up a conversation with a bouncer. Instead, she was ignored until a couple exited the club.

"Oh, yeah!" Talon said, poking Talli trying to get her to look enthusiastic.

"Not you two," said a bouncer pointing at them.

"Why not?" Talon demanded.

"Step aside, please."

"We're supposed to meet someone in there."

"Then meet them someplace else. Please, leave," said a second bouncer. He tried to guide them back toward the street.

"We've waited for hours to get inside," Talon said trying to keep her temper in check.

"You should have asked," a third bouncer—this one female—said after coming out from inside. "We won't ask again."

"But—"

Talon sighed and bowed her head dejected. She took Talli by the arm and led her back to the sidewalk.

A N EXPENSIVE AIRCAR PULLED up to the curb. The driver exited and opened the passenger door. A long leg with a five-inch heel on appeared from inside the vehicle. The simple, yet elegant shoe brought attention to the toenails painted black and tipped with red. Sarin stepped out wearing a chic black dress with red trim. Her floor-length hair and makeup looked like a professional team had spent hours primping her. Her jewelry and accessories accented her perfectly. Taking the driver's offered hand, she stood and then gave him instructions.

Sarin frowned. The red carpet didn't come out to the curb. Critics hailed The Gold Nugget Mine as the best club on the Cascade Riviera. After watching for the last two hours, its front door security operation was unacceptable.

She went to the door with her usual swagger, ignoring the looks from the line.

"I'm sorry, miss. You'll have to wait like everyone else," said the female bouncer.

Sarin ignored her. "Are you going to get the door?" she asked in a polite voice to the bouncer next to the door.

"Miss, there are no VIPs at Gold Nugget. Everyone is golden here," said the bouncer.

"Did you think of that yourself?" Sarin said, her politeness convey-ing her condescension. "And what of them?" she motioned to Talon and Talli. "Are they not golden? Do you girls want to have some fun?"

"We're not good enough," said Talon.

"Posh." Sarin turned up her nose at the bouncers. "You will let us in, or I'll have you fired."

"I've informed you of the club's policies, miss. This will be the last time I tell you, get in line," said the female bouncer.

"Do you know who owns this club?"

"Caesar, call the patrol," said the female bouncer.

"My daddy owns this club along with five others as part of Gjord Cascade Entertainment. I am Jane Gjord. Do you want to test my DNA to prove it and truly insult me?"

"Ah...Caesar, call the GM."

Sarin tapped her toe in irritation. When the man showed, he looked at Sarin and pulled the female bouncer aside. She listened in on the conversation with great amusement.

"Who is she?" said the general manager.

"I don't know. I've never seen her before, here or any other club I've worked for," said the female bouncer.

"We must get her inside and give her the experience she wants."

Beautiful people come and go, perfect people needed to be regulars. From Sarin's tiny clutch, she took out a small compact. She opened it and pressed her thumb to it.

"Hello? Jane? Is that you?"

"Hi, Daddy. I'm standing out in front of the Gold Nugget Nightclub, and they won't let me and some of my new friends in. Can you please tell them who I am?"

Sven sighed. "Put the manager on." On the bottom half of the compact, a holographic head of Sven appeared.

"He's here, Daddy."

"Whom am I speaking with? Is this Daniel or Gorge?"

"Gorge, ah, sir."

"Ok, Gorge. I commend you for following the business purpose and mission statement, but she is my daughter. I rarely abuse my power as the owner in such ways, but I am this once. This is the first time my daughter has been out since she came home. Let her and her friends in and give them what they want. If you have any problems or questions, I've sent you my personal line. Do you have any questions?"

"No, sir," said Gorge, beads of sweat building on his forehead.

Sarin snatched the communicator back. "Thank you, Daddy. I love you."

"Have fun and don't get into trouble."

Sarin smiled. "I won't. Goodnight."

Gorge led the trio inside. They followed the man through the vibrant crowd, up a flight of stairs, to a seating area looking out over the dance floor. Sarin thanked Gorge and put in an order.

"Is it always like this?" Talli yelled over the din of music and voices.

Sarin smiled and sat down. After the drinks arrived, they were served, and she chased the server away with instructions to stay close.

Talli reached for some of the hors d'oeuvres, but Sarin brushed her away. On the back of her hand, a message appeared, "Never eat club food. We'll eat at the hotel." Talli withdrew her hand with a pout. "Remember, fun. Smile, laugh, drinking will help." A third message appeared, "No discussing anything. Follow my lead."

"Life is just full of surprises," Talon said with a smile. "I didn't expect to be picked up by the great Jane Gjord."

"Surprises keep life fresh. I meet the most interesting people when I fish them out of the reject bin. No offense but your friend needs to lighten up. We go to clubs to have fun and to be seen."

"I'm sure all eyes are on you."

"This is the first time I've been out since my rescue."

"So, why now?" Talli said glumly.

"The Cascade Riviera is big enough to be seen, but not big enough that the sharks will come trolling afterward. Clubbing can be a cut-throat business. An old ghost like me coming back onto the scene is going to create quite a stir. This little outing is a warning shot that I'm back and for them to get out of the way."

"If they don't?" said Talon, slipping off her shoes and curling up on the bench seat. She twirled her drink playfully.

"I'm not as ruthless as I was in my younger days. Back then, I would stop at nothing to destroy someone. I remember Casey Bush, who tried to beat me. She carried a lot of clout, being from the Bush family. In the end, she couldn't keep up. That was before I got the ultimatum from my parents to get a job and go to school. I kept running the night scene until Nell, and I decided we wanted to get aboard the colony ship."

"What happened to her?" said Talli.

"I understand she went to rehab for addiction and her parents gave her a similar ultimatum. I'm not sure after that."

"So, do we get to dance?"

Sarin shook her head. "I'm not dressed to dance, nor do I wish to be touched," She took a sip of her drink and grinned into the glass. "Except by you two." The declaration caused Talli to stir uncomfortably. Sarin displayed another message, "How else am I getting you back to the hotel?"

"One *minor* problem," said Talon.

"Only a minor problem. We'll work around that. Come, let's hear about the two of you."

Sarin guided the pair through the art of small talk. What seemed effortless for her was like pulling teeth for Talli. She began to suspect the years of near isolation had left the teenager socially and emotionally stunted.

As Sarin observed Talli, she made her move on Talon. The other Angel acted uncertain. Sarin took it she was out of practice, but it looked natural. By the end, she had Talon under her arm and was running her foot up the side of Talli's leg.

Sarin examined the crowd below. "Well, ladies, I think it's time to go. All the couples, hook-uppers, and revelers are gone. We're only left with the hardcore partiers and the desperate."

Sarin stood up and collected her clutch. Talon strapped her shoes back on. She went to Sarin and went to whisper in her ear. Resting her hand on Sarin's chest, she placed a trio of kisses on the other Angel's neck.

Sarin shivered as all her little hairs on her neck stood up. She slipped an arm around Talon and kissed her. When they separated, Talli was waiting, looking unhappy.

"You'll get your turn soon," Sarin told the teenager.

"Or she can just join us," said Talon, taking Talli's hand to pull the teen in closer. They kissed Talli on the cheeks. Talon kissed her a few more times. Smiling, Sarin put her arms around the other Angels and guided them back downstairs.

The doors opened, and dozens of camera flashes and video spotlights burst on them. Sarin kissed the two other Angels. "You've got to smile," she hissed at Talli. With a million-dollar smile of her own, Sarin pushed through the crowd into the waiting car.

"To the Gjord Riviera Hotel," Sarin ordered as Talon landed in her lap. Sarin kissed her again as the door closed for one final shot for the paparazzi.

"**W**HAT WAS ALL OF that?" Talli demanded when Sarin closed the elevator door. Talon hung on Sarin's arm after escaping the cameras outside the hotel.

"Paparazzi," said Sarin.

"Not the smell, that mob out there!" Talli yelled.

"That mob is called the Paparazzi, sugar foam," said Talon. "They stalk celebrities trying to get pictures and video to sell to the net. They're mostly harmless, if not annoying."

"I want to go home, Mom. And do you have to hold her arm?"

Talon gave an apologetic look to Sarin and let go.

"Your home is now my home," said Sarin. "We'll rest and finish getting your IDs in order."

"Why do I need an ID?"

"Because if you're going to move around inside the Empire, you have to be someone. Don't worry. I've got someone working on it. He says he should have yours done by dawn. Once I double-check them, we'll leave for the shuttleport and my ship. Then, it's off to Neptune and safety."

SARIN STOOD IN THE giant shower. The water hit her from three sides and didn't seem to be enough to remove the smell of the nightclub. *When did I stop liking that smell?*

She started the long process of washing her hair. Normally, she'd go out to have it done, but the smell was entrenched in it, and she didn't have time.

While she washed, she tested the new identities for Talli and Talon. She'd been able to locate the man who'd doctored hers and Anthrax's all those years ago. This time, he just wanted money, which she didn't mind. It was easier to get clean money to him than having to explain sex with him to the world. The man's work was better than she remembered. She hadn't even thrown up any caution flags while using the IDs to access various government databases.

Her mind drifted to something Talon had mentioned earlier, about more gods entering the equation on a permanent basis. She had no idea who Kerri and Kita convinced to meld with to create so many Angels. Sarin had agreed because she wished to apply what she'd spent so long learning to something new. Many of the others must have felt the same way.

The selection of Angels infuriated her. Why had Kita picked them? There were more deserving Angels. She could have saved all the girls, but instead, she had just saved Kamikaze and Phoenix. Why not Spike and Quill? Why not her babies?

She struck out at the wall shattering the tile. She hit it a few more times for good measure.

Talon stuck her head in the door. "Jane, are you ok?"

"No." Jane slumped to the floor happy the shower hid her tears.

"Come on. Let's get you out and dry." Talon opened the shower door, letting steam billow out. She saw the shattered tiles in the back of the shower for the first time. "Damn."

"I've got conditioner in my hair," said Sarin.

Talon rolled up her extra wide sleeves. "Stand up and lean back."

Sarin did. Trying to leave the thought of her daughters behind, she had another curious question. "Why are you so nice to me?"

"I can't be gracious with my gratitude?"

"I thought when you came through that window, I was going to have a fight every step of the way."

"Oh, you will, but not from me. Talli is a handful."

"I've got some experience with teenagers that age. It's sixteen you have to worry about. That's when you can only do so much to save them from themselves."

"And it gets better when?"

"Somewhere between twenty-eight and ten thousand. I don't think Spike ever grew out of it."

"The poor girl always seemed so bitter."

"She was. I'd be too if I'd been stuck in an underwater prison with a bunch of humans, and Tina's ever persistent good mood."

"I'd think that better than someone in a bad mood."

"If they're in a bad mood you have an excuse to hit them."

Talon shook her head. "You fallen angels are so quick to lash out."

"Evil angel, not fallen. I stopped playing Kita's game of thrones a long time ago. I think it's a quicker solution than trying to kill them with kindness, like a high angel."

"You don't seem to mind."

"It does give me a reason not to hit you. Speaking of high angels, why aren't you glowing?"

"It's like a flashlight. Tina just never shuts hers off."

Sarin chuckled. "She's proud she's a high angel. Hopefully, it won't get her into trouble."

"Ten thousand years and nothing yet."

"I'm patient."

"And why ruin it for her?"

"I won't. She'll do that herself."

"Such a positive person you are. There, all set." Talon stepped back and closed the door.

Sarin rinsed and then shut off the water. Stepping out of the shower, she shook her wings, spraying the entire area with water.

Talon hid behind a towel. "I don't need another shower."

"And here I thought you were being nice and handing me a towel."

"You can do that much yourself."

"I could, but I was hoping you'd use that delicate touch to dry my hair."

"There is a downside to having six feet of hair," Talon said as she unrolled her sleeves. To punctuate her point, she folded her hands up inside them.

"You can't blame me for asking." Sarin grabbed a pair of towels and wrapped her hair up in them.

"You know what I've never seen before?"

"What's that?"

Talon smiled sideways. "You without your makeup. You look good."

"Mom, I'm hungry," came belting through the door.

Talon sighed. "I swear I just fed her. See you when I see you, blackbird." She left Sarin to finish drying and repair the damage.

Sarin realized how much she missed affection. Even the little bit from Talon made her feel better, like a weight lifted off her heart.

"**W**HY AREN'T WE GOING down the main elevator?" whined Talli.

Sarin sighed. She wanted to tell the girl to be quiet and not ask questions, but she wanted the girl to learn, too.

"I made a mistake," admitted Sarin. Talon raised an eyebrow. "It happens, even to me. The pictures of last night are sure to have gotten back to Galina. She knows you're with me. She probably doesn't know my capacity. She might think you're guarding me. Still, she knows we're together. We need to keep our movements hidden."

"But aren't we dead?" said Talli.

"Yes, but I don't expect to fool Galina for long. She knows just because you kill an Angel doesn't mean the Angel is dead. And I'm in the area. Even though she can't prove anything, she'll suspect it was me. I am many things, but I've never killed an Angel. I doubt she'd think I'd start now."

"Will she try and get us back?" said Talli.

"You, yes. She'll kill Scarlett for betraying her. She can't touch me but can make me and my father's life miserable until such a time she can get at me. She's the patient type and will bide her time, watching. At least we'll be on Neptune where she won't have direct access to us. The Political Bureau doesn't have as many specialized thugs out there as they do on Earth and Mars."

"Why me?"

"You're her pet project. She wants what Kita had: a daughter to follow in her footsteps."

"But she's horrible. All she ever did was yell at me and tell me I was doing it wrong."

"We can't all be good mothers like Scarlett," said Sarin, she smiled at Talon acknowledging the other Angel's work with Talli.

"It's been a long time since I had a child of my own," said Talon wistfully.

"You had someone before me?" Talli said, her eyebrows furrowing.

"Yes. He wasn't as old as you. He died when he was young. He was killed by another tyrant trying to rule the world."

"I'm sorry," said Sarin as she hugged Talon.

"It was a long time ago. Time makes the pain easier to bear."

"I know, but it wasn't fair to you. You were only doing what was right."

"And how the righteous are made to suffer...but, that's not true either. You've lost your girls, too."

"I don't think it has to do with good or evil," said Sarin. "We're just made to suffer in an endless sea, with islands of joy popping up every so often, before being washed beneath the waves."

"Jane, it's not that bad," said Talon halfheartedly.

"Some days it feels like it."

The elevator came to a stop, dinged, and the doors opened into a service hallway. They passed through the kitchen, out a storage room, onto a loading dock. They were several levels underground. A limousine sat waiting for them.

"There's our ride to the shuttleport," said Sarin.

"And freedom," said Talon.

"We're not out of her clutches yet."

"But now I have you. You are safety."

Sarin turned up a corner of her mouth. "You once saved my best friend and daughter. It's the least I can do for you."

"You've paid me back ten times over."

"And I'll continue to do so. I'm not without gratitude, and you are my friend." Sarin opened the car door and waved the others inside.

"How'd I get so lucky?" said Talon.

"You were righteous."

"**M**ISTRESS GJORD?" THE SHUTTLE pilot called through the intercom.

"Yes, what is it?" Sarin answered curtly as she looked away from the window. Outside, the station was bright against the darkness of space. She could see the Gjord family ship docked in the private docking area.

"We're being instructed to wait in a holding pattern until further notice."

"By whose authority?"

"It comes with Political Bureau codes."

"Dock anyway. Let's see if they have the guts to shoot me."

"I'll need an authorization and override signature for that."

Sarin opened a nearby console. "There you go, your ass is covered."

"Preparing to dock. Everyone, please take your seats."

In the private docking area, Sarin and the other Angels exited the shuttle. A squad of Bureau soldiers waited for them.

"What's the meaning of this?" Sarin snarled to the sergeant.

"Orders, Miss Gjord, and you're in violation. I'm authorized to detain you."

"Like you could if you wanted to. Take me to someone important."

The soldiers escorted the Angels through the terminal to a Political Bureau station.

"Mom, I'm hungry," Talli informed everyone once the group arrived in a waiting room.

"Where's my staff?" Sarin demanded of the sergeant.

"Detained in their quarters."

"Tell whatever stuffed shirt is in charge I want some food delivered."

"The lady will have to wait," said the sergeant. "We need an explanation for the unauthorized changes to your manifest."

"They're on the manifest and checked out at the shuttleport."

"We'll need to scan them again."

"Why?"

"Security."

"Bull. I've never been detained before."

"Neither has what happened out on the frontier," said the sergeant. His eyes conveyed he might have said too much.

"What, in Neptune's rings, is going on out on the frontier that can spook the home system?"

The sergeant refused to speak.

Sarin growled. She read his mind, but he didn't know. She sat back and exchanged looks with Talon. The other Angel didn't look worried, but Sarin felt her anxiety.

A lieutenant entered. "Miss Gjord, you're free to go."

"With the Emperor's apologies I'm sure," Sarin said with a charming smile.

The lieutenant led them out of the station and to the terminal where the Gjord family ship waited. The steward met them at the gantry.

"Miss Gjord, the pilots would like to speak with you."

Sarin motioned for the steward to lead the way. The other Angels fell in behind her.

Inside the ship, Sarin hit the intercom button. "What is it, Xavier? When are we leaving?"

"Sorry, Miss Gjord. The Political Bureau impounded the ship."

Sarin saw red. "Fine. We'll find our own way." She snapped her fingers, and the Angels disappeared.

CHAPTER XII

S ARIN AND THE REST of the Angels appeared in the foyer of the Gjord Villa.

"Daddy are you home?" Sarin called across the house.

"In the study," Sven answered.

The Angels moved into the study. Sven sat at the bar nursing a drink. A bandage was over his left eye.

"Daddy, are you ok?" Sarin said, rushing to her father's side.

"I'll be fine, moonbeam. I just got a little flippant with one of those jackbooted thugs from the Political Bureau. He didn't like my answer that I didn't know where you were."

"You should have called. I would've come."

"I won't cave to them any more than I have to. The bastards are on every street corner shaking down people."

"Let me see that cut, Mister Gjord," said Talon.

"Call me Sven."

Talon studied the cut and the bruise left by a rifle butt. She put her hand over it healing the wound.

"Even the headache's gone," said Sven.

"With the announcement that the emperor is gravely ill and the Political Bureau taking over it's evident we can't stay here," Kita said from the internal speaker system.

"And where would we go?" said Cinnamon.

"I've been studying Gjord Industries assets, and I believe I found a place. It's going to need some updating, remodeling, and some heavy guns, but the asteroid condominium project that was canceled ten years ago looks perfect. It has mobile manufacturing and a construction yard. Access to raw materials and food production will have to be upgraded, but all that's required is the information and people. The Red system is at the end of a wormhole cul-de-sac, making it easy to defend."

"I don't understand," said Sven.

"This is only going to get worse. I've been monitoring the darknet. Rumor has it Galina is now in command of the Political Bureau—"

"I bet that's not by coincidence," said Talon.

"The Princess," Kita showed a picture of Defiance, "is nowhere to be found and believed kidnapped by a rebel faction. The Political Bureau is filling the power vacuum. We have to leave while we can, or we'll be trapped, as the Political Bureau pulls the noose tighter."

"What about Lina?" demanded Sarin.

"We have to hope what we gave them will spare her. We'll have to wait to free her until we come back."

"When will that be?" said Talon.

"I don't know. During my searches, I've found reports of Political Bureau soldiers taking over Legion facilities and even taking over Shadow Fleet ships."

"Neptune's rings, is she insane?" said Sven.

"At the moment I don't think there's anyone to stop her," said Kita. "Except us, and we can't do that from here."

"And we can from out in the middle of nowhere?" said Talli.

"We can pick off the far-flung outposts, build our forces, and convince the Legion and Shadow Fleet to stand against the Political Bureau," said Sarin. "We might even need to find the Princess. Wait—bring up those crew pictures Daddy showed me of when you came through Angelica Station." Kita put them on the screen. "That's her. Different hair, skin, eyes, and she has had some work done on her face, but that is most definitely the Princess."

"Are you saying Kita kidnapped the Princess?" gasped Cinnamon.

"Kita probably doesn't know it's her. This record has her as an FTL pilot. The Princess might just be in hiding and Kita snared her by pure luck," said Talon.

"And we have no idea where I am," said Kita. "Dallas has completely vanished. Long-range sweeps have revealed nothing, and it will be years before regular beacon signals reach us."

"A missing princess is not worth bashing heads in over," Sven growled.

"It is if someone is trying to seize power," said Sarin.

"There's no way the Shadow Fleet would let that happen. They'd blow the Political Bureau's headquarters off the map."

"Another interesting fact," said Athena, "is that ship watchers said a large fleet of warships jumped through the Alicorn wormhole over six weeks ago. This included two flagship carriers—Enterprise and Fort Ticonderoga. The fleet just returned several days ago, short Enterprise and a few smaller ships. Reports also say the wormhole is closed."

"Very odd," said Sarin. "If it had been a battle, Enterprise would be in the center. Far more ships would have been destroyed before Enterprise took any damage."

"Rumors out of Shadow Fleet say Political Bureau officers have replaced the upper echelon officers. They say it's in response to the fleet failing its mission. I have not been able to find out what that mission was."

"That explains why the Political Bureau is flexing its muscle. There's no one to keep them in check," Talon said dourly.

"But how are we going to move Gjord Industries out to the frontier?" said Cinnamon.

"The industrial workers are already out there," replied Kita. "We need to get the brains from here to there."

"What about the information, supplies, families, and equipment? There isn't enough room out there for everyone in Gjord Tower, let alone all the workstations."

"Why go out there at all? What's the end game?" said Talli.

"To be the resistance," said Sarin. "War is coming. The sides haven't taken shape, but we need to get as many people to safety as we can."

"And recruit our own navy," said Kita.

"We won't be able to take on the Shadow Fleet," said Sven.

"I was hoping to recruit them."

"How are we going to do that?" said Talon.

"Be an alternative to Galina and the Political Bureau."

"I don't understand how we're going to move so many people so far, and fast enough to not have the Political Bureau stop us," said Sven.

"Start identifying who we need," said Kita. "I have plans for a quantum entanglement communicator that will let us move our data anywhere. We move everything from Gjord Towers and neighboring facilities to the servers here, and we pack these up and take them with us. While Sven and Cinnamon are moving the head of Gjord

Industries to its new location, Sarin and the other Angels will become a distraction Galina can't ignore. They'll be so focused on us, they're not going to care that a few dozen shiploads of people just left."

"With your permission, Sven, I will start sending orders to the facilities in the Rainbow Belt to prepare for our arrival," said Athena.

"That's twenty-three light-years away," said Sven.

"I understand a new entanglement communications unit will be installed in the central office by tomorrow."

"Of course. I forget that's a hop and a skip for some of us."

"It's no small feat," said Sarin. "That kind of jump will be the kind that will draw the attention of the elder gods. It will take Kita and I a few hours to install the communicators."

"The more help you AI girls can be by coordinating material and strategic resources so Kristi and I can work on the personnel part, the better," said Sven.

"We'll make it happen," said Athena.

"What do we do?" said Talli.

"Whatever we can to help," said Talon. "But if they don't need us, we're going to train, train, and train."

"I'll be around and can teach you all the cool assassin tricks Galina failed to teach you," said Kita.

Talli's eyes narrowed. "I thought you were busy."

"Don't worry, kid. She's superb at multitasking. Even I don't get her full attention," said Sarin.

"Ouch," said Kita.

"All right ladies, we've got a lot of work to do. Kita, how much time do we have?" said Sven.

"How much time do you need?"

"I'd like a week."

"Can you do it in four days?"

"Getting the people moving will be the hardest part."

"Then tell them something worth moving for. I would like to think taking people and their families away from the tyrannical new world the Political Bureau is creating would be enough."

"It's not that bad yet," said Cinnamon.

"Yes, but by the time it is, it'll be too late," said Talon.

"Let a couple of them get roughed up on the street," said Kita.

"We'll make them see the light," said Sven.

"Otherwise, they're out of a job," said Kita with a chuckle.

Sven rolled his eyes.

S ARIN STROLLED THROUGH THE Political Bureau headquarters of
Neptune as she reloaded her pistols. She and the other Angels
were giving the Political Bureau something more to think about than
a corporation relocating its headquarters. Her father's ships were
loaded and ready to depart. It was the Angels job to be enough of
a distraction so the ships could leave untraced.

She pushed open a door and found a squad of soldiers waiting
for her. They fired at her until their magazines were empty. Nearly a
hundred bullets hung in the air in front of Sarin. She waved her hand,
and the bullets rained to the floor. A blue-tinted cloud billowed out
from her hands. Flapping her wings, the blue cloud rushed towards
the soldiers. As the cloud passed, the soldiers choked and fell to
the ground, spasming and seizing until they died. An elevator door
opened, and Talon and Talli stepped out.

"Everything under control?" Sarin said with a smile on her face.

"You've been waiting a long time for this, haven't you?" said Talon.

"Ever since they led me off Base Station in chains. I've had a bit
of time to let my hatred and anger percolate."

"I thought those were bad things to use in a fight," said Talli.

"For those who do not know how to harness them. I don't use
blazing hatred and fiery rage like Kita. Mine is cold and calculated.
That's the difference between someone who needs strength and
power to wield a weapon and someone who needs control and
precision. But, don't be like us. It requires a complete frame of mind
and a strong stomach. You kill people for an end and nothing more.
Kita and I will kill for fun."

"I like to fight," said Talli.

"Yes, and remember that. You like to fight, not to kill. Keep following what Scarlett teaches, and you'll be an unstoppable warrior,"
Sarin said as she tried the only other door in the room.

Finding the door locked, Sarin changed her pistol ammo to thermite rounds. She fired six times into the door, causing it to melt into
a pile of slag. She led the Angels through the hole into the next room.

The thirty people in the room were in disarray. Some were in a tactical position with weapons trained on the door, others were in the process of taking cover, while the rest tried to shield what they were working on.

Sarin shot those she could see from the door. "Thank you all for your service to the emperor. But I regret to inform you, your service is in my way." She fired three times into a cabinet, and a pair of bodies slumped out.

Talli and Talon followed Sarin to the main console. With a wave of Sarin's hand, she pushed the body and blood aside. She tossed a pair of holographic generators into the air. Kita and Athena appeared. With a twitch of Sarin's nose, Cinnamon materialized.

"Oh, dear," Cinnamon said, looking around. "You've been hard at work, haven't you, Jane?"

Sarin smiled. "Work? I've only been on a pleasant stroll."

The main console came to life as Kita and Athena hacked the Political Bureau's computer system trying to locate Galina.

"I found her," said Athena. "Putting the call through."

A large screen dropped down on the far wall. The Angels stood together looking formidable.

Galina's half-plastic, half-human face appeared. "What do you—"

"In what world—," said Sarin.

"Did you think—," said Athena.

"You could beat me?" said Kita with a vengeful grin. "And us."

"Impossible, you're gone," Galina snarled at Kita.

"Am I? I think I'm pretty real." Kita's face darkened. "You have my baby. I'll give you one chance to let her go."

"I have no idea what you're talking about," said Galina.

"Then we're going to tear apart every Political Bureau installation, gut every Political Bureau crony until we get to Earth. Once there, we'll rip apart every city until we find her and you."

"And when we find you," said Sarin, "you'll suffer for eternity and beyond for what you've done."

"Vengeance will be total and absolute. For Quill—" said Athena.

"—Spike—," said Kita.

"—Leo—," said Sarin.

"—Echo—," said Talon.

"—My mother, Dev," said Talli.

One-by-one they listed the Angels killed by Galina. The former Angel stared back, stone-faced.

"We're coming for you, and there's nothing you can do to stop us," said Sarin.

Kita blew her former lover a kiss and then closed the connection.

PART III

CHAPTER XIII

T HE DULL THUMPS OF heavy-soled boots on a metal gantry made their way into an empty concourse. A small group of armed guards in black Political Bureau uniforms waited with a pair of stern-looking officers. Off to one side, a group of legionnaire officers in blue uniforms stood looking dejected.

Two men exited the gantry.

"Stop right there, legionnaires. Take off your belts and any weapons and lay them on the floor," a Political Bureau officer ordered.

"No one gives my legionnaires orders without going through me first," Sarin said with an unhappy growl.

She exited the gantry. Her ice blue eyes darted around, taking in the empty concourse. Usually, Glacier Station would be bustling with military traffic. She wore her custom-tailored Legion uniform. She wore subtle makeup, black with a hint of red, and had braided her floor-length blonde hair into a bun that sat at the base of her skull.

Sarin assessed the soldiers in the groups in front of her. Something didn't feel right. *Why don't the legionnaires have weapons?* The looks on their faces said they were captives. Her eyes settled on a short round man who seemed to be in charge. He smelled of cheap cologne. She hoped it wasn't for her. She only had a nose for one scent, a sweet mixture of brimstone and blood.

"I am Commandant Sarin," she said to the shorter Political Bureau officer in charge.

"Yes. Your codes are old, but they checked out," said the officer.

"Of course, they're old," Sarin snapped. "We've been cut off for sixteen months. Reestablishing contact is one of my first priorities, but even with the fastest ship we could find, it takes time to get from point A to point B. And who are you?"

"Colonel Saunders," the officer answered. "Now, if you'll turn your weapons over to my guards, we can talk about integrating your command into mine."

Sarin raised an eyebrow. "Last I checked this is Legion work, not Political Bureau. Protecting and serving the population is our business. Yours is to watch the population and give us the intel to do our job."

"Times have changed. The Legion now answers to the Political Bureau."

"I'm sure the Shadow Fleet has something to say about that," Sarin replied with a frown.

"That's none of your business."

Sarin folded her arms across her chest. He hadn't addressed her by rank once, and he was by no means her equal. "You're awfully young to be a colonel, Saunders. You can't be one of the Bureau's best and brightest if you're out here."

"Last warning," barked Saunders, his face red. "I will have my men shoot you."

Sarin dropped her arms and folded her hands behind her back. "You realize you're just a colonel and I'm a deputy commandant of the Legion. Threatening a system grade officer is several sizes of magnitude greater than just threatening another officer. You don't get reprimanded or ushered out of the service. You disappear, if my people don't shoot you first."

"Who you are no longer matters, legionnaire. You're nothing but dirt under my boot. I have my orders from the Bureau. We are to control everything, including you."

"Yeah, I was afraid of that." Sarin drew her pistols and put a hole in the forehead of each of the Political Bureau guard detail, and then put a hole in each of Saunders' shoulders.

Sarin holstered her pistols and picked the colonel up by his front. She looked at his collar. Many trips to the cleaners had left the dark outline of captain's bars. The leaves of a colonel were new.

"Your commander didn't believe the orders to take over or did you have separate orders to kill him?" Sarin demanded.

Gritting through the pain, Saunders tried to kick Sarin in the crotch.

Sarin blocked him with ease. "Really, little man?"

"You won't get anything from me." Saunders spat in Sarin's face. Sarin changed her grip to hold him with one hand. Grabbing an arm with enough force to break bone, she used his sleeve to clean her face.

"You...You're one of them, aren't you?" he said, his voice going up.

"That could mean I'm a lot of things," replied Sarin. "But, I'm pretty sure you're talking about these," Sarin purred as her wings appeared. "Now, to business. How many more Political Bureau scum are on the station and where are they? After they're disposed of, we can get on with handing it over to me."

"You'll have to kill me first," said Saunders.

Sarin smirked. "I do wish I had the time to turn you over to my partner, though you'd regret making it. She takes killing to an art form."

"It doesn't help she's not here either," said Talon, as she exited the gantry.

"Yes, he is lucky that I only enjoy killing people, I'm not one for the mess like Kita."

"I suggest you cooperate, human," said Talon, "you will tell us what we need to know, one way or another. If you do help us, I promise Sarin won't kill you."

"Are you going to back that up?" demanded Sarin.

"If I have to," Talon replied in a calm voice. "Hurry, Mister Saunders, your window of opportunity is closing. Even as we speak another of us is hunting down the Political Bureau on this station, and she is as ruthless and efficient a killer as any trained by Kita."

"I told you," Saunders snarled.

Talon's hands appeared from her sleeves. A four-inch barb extended from the base of her palm.

Grabbing Saunders head, she jabbed the barb into his neck. It was a short wait for the truth serum to kick in.

"How many men are aboard this station?" said Talon to Saunders.

"Twenty-four, including the detail here."

"Where are they?"

Saunders gave locations of all the personnel on the station.

Sarin sent the information to Talli. She looked at the legionnaires that stood to one side looking meek and overwhelmed. *What happened that allowed a slimeball like Saunders to take charge?* She couldn't believe the Legion would allow itself to be taken over by the Political Bureau.

She addressed the legionnaires. "I need you to contact your Senior Legion and Red Legion officers for the Bitterfreeze system and its subsystems. I've got some reports they need to see."

"I'm sorry, Commandant," said a major, "but we're it."

"What?" Sarin gasped.

"That's one of the first things that little bastard did was round up the senior officers and shoot them. Only General Starr didn't report from Freeze-1A."

"Mining and ranching, right? Who are you?"

"Major Baxter, ma'am. General Starr never showed."

"Where are your men?"

"Those that refused to switch uniforms to the Political Bureau were shipped out."

Sarin sighed. "Most likely dead somewhere."

"We're left as liaisons to our units."

"Hostages, you mean?" Baxter nodded. "How loyal are your legionnaires to you?"

"They'd switch back in a heartbeat. This was a Legion station. You killed a quarter of the Political Bureau force when you arrived."

"Anyway, to tell the legionnaires from the Bureau?"

"Sure, Saunders promoted all his people and demoted all the legionnaires to privates."

Sarin smiled. "That will be most helpful. I need into Saunders' office. I know there are two Shadow Fleet frigates in the area, and I need to talk to them, but only the Political Bureau is going to have the codes."

"We can take you to the office, but we've never seen any Shadow Fleet ships here," said Baxter.

"I know they have a separate resupply base way out of the way. It's supplied by the Political Bureau. I'm hoping if I bypass the base and talk to the ships directly, I can talk them over to our side."

"Our side, ma'am?" replied Baxter.

"We're in the middle of a coup d'état. What happened here is not some Political Bureau officer overstepping his bounds. The Political Bureau is seizing power while the Shadow Fleet is impaired from a mission gone wrong. The Legion is the only mobilized force that can stand up to the Political Bureau until the Shadow Fleet sorts itself out. For everyone in this system and the adjoining systems, I brought with me as much food, medical supplies, and fuel as I had ships to carry."

Baxter's eyes went wide. "How did you get so much, ma'am?"

"I'm not out here alone. I was stationed with Gjord Industries, and they caught wind of the attack early. They moved as much of their operations as they could out here. It took a while, but we got it up and going. We have farms, mining, manufacturing...just about anything you could want. We're in position to challenge the Political Bureau, and now it's time to make our move."

"We'll do whatever you need us to do, ma'am."

"Good," said Sarin. "Get General Starr off that rock she's on. I need to know if she's alive or dead."

Talon raised a wing. "I'll go with them. This might be more than they can handle."

Sarin nodded. "Take Cin, too. She could use the experience."

"Hmmm. I do declare someone took my name in vain." Cinnamon laughed as she appeared behind everyone, leaning against a wall.

The men turned around and gawked at her. Her short skirt, bikini top, and leather half-jacket left little to the imagination. She waved a pair of pistols playfully. "Just in case, somebody thought they'd like to be a hero." She holstered the pistols on her thighs and winked at the legionnaires as she went by to stand next to Talon.

Talon leaned into Cinnamon's ear. "Why are you flirting with them? What are you planning on doing when you're onboard with them for weeks?"

Cinnamon wrinkled her nose. "Ew, I wouldn't do that. I have self-respect."

"Now I'm just confused."

"I'm not allowed to have a little fun? I was married three times, for a hundred and sixty-three years doing the same job. Now, that's gone. It's like being a kid again."

Talon shook her head.

"You girls and legionnaires will take off as soon as we get things straight around here," said Sarin.

Talli, wearing a black sneak suit, appeared next to Sarin. "They're down. I left them where they fell if we need to study the forensics later," she said in a whisper.

"Excellent," said Sarin.

"Why is this one still alive?" Talli asked, going over and grabbing Saunders by the jaw.

"Intelligence. Put him down," Sarin ordered.

Talli did, but not before headbutting the man.

"Talli, discipline!" Talon roared.

"He's just a gutless human. Why can't I kill him? He knows nothing we can't find out on our own."

"Because it's faster this way," Talon snapped, dragging the teenager over by the arm to join her and Cinnamon.

"Sorry, she's young, and she has trouble with men like Saunders," Talon explained to the legionnaires.

Major Baxter nodded.

Sarin grabbed Saunders. "I might still have some questions for you. The rest of you legionnaires come with me and get our people back in the right uniform. Scarlett, get Kristi ready to go."

"I'll do my best."

Sarin led everyone deeper into the station, leaving Talon and Cinnamon alone.

"COME ON," TALON SAID to Cinnamon as she walked up the gantry.

"Where are we going?"

"Did you not see Jane's face?"

"No, why?"

"I'm to give you the lesson on the difference between revealing, sexy, slutty, and bedroom attire."

"I thought I was being revealing?"

"Sarin's schoolgirl outfit is revealing. What you're wearing is just stupid slutty. I know you've been in the office and this is your first time out, but that outfit is no good."

"This was what was in when I went to school."

"We need to find you something that is practical and functional for where we're going."

"I can't have a little fun?"

"Who are you trying to impress: the rocks, the cows, or the poor people slaving away?"

"But Kita told me that beauty is a weapon."

"It is. But what would you rather have? A mass market light pistol or those custom forty-fives strapped to your thighs?"

"Are you saying I'm cheap?" Cinnamon said with a frown.

"I'm saying you've known Jane for years. You didn't learn any lessons from her?"

"I...always thought those things were out of my league."

"Trust me they're not. I'll show you."

CHAPTER XIV

"**T**HIS SHOULD BE A pleasant voyage," Cinnamon said in a sarcastic tone after returning from inspecting the Gjord Industries ship.

Talon opened the door to the executive lounge they would be using as their living quarters, after finding the crew quarters weren't big enough for wings.

"What do you mean?" Talon asked with a curious glance.

"There's nothing to do. You can only do so much target practice."

"I'm sure there are some movies on the server."

"Ok, that's a day." Cinnamon sighed.

"You think I'm going to be that big a bore?" Talon asked with a slight smile, but sounding mildly insulted at the same time.

"No, but you are very reserved."

This was the first time Cinnamon had worked with Talon. Over the last sixteen months, Cinnamon had retained her normal position helping Sven run Gjord Industries while being trained by Sarin.

Talon swept off her hood revealing the rest of her dark red hair. Still smiling, she looked at Cinnamon. "You just don't know me that well. Now, the first thing we need to do is get you out of those clothes."

"And what are you suggesting?" Cinnamon retorted in surprise.

Talon walked around the other Angel. "That we find you something more suited for an Angel. The bikini and skirt have to go, and fishnets are for their namesake. I've seen enough of those to last several lifetimes." She put her hand on Cinnamon's hip and pushed gently on a ticklish spot causing the other Angel to squeak in surprise.

The tacky outfit morphed into a pair of low-rise denim bottoms and a cinnamon-colored midriff that read FIREBALL. The boots changed from useless urbanite ware to feminine style combat boots that went to the knee. Only the half-jacket remained from before.

"There we go, much better." Talon smiled. "Flirty and revealing, but functional. Now sit down on the floor next to the couch and find us something to watch. I'm tired, and I'd love to relax some."

"Why am I on the floor?"

"So, I can work on your hair. If Jane hadn't been so busy, she would have done it herself."

"Did you get orders from her to do this?" Cinnamon asked with a suspicious glare.

"Maybe," Talon said as she undid the hidden clasps that held her cloak together just above her knees. With a small bit of ceremony, the Angel whispered something to it and hung it on a metal hook.

Cinnamon flinched when she saw the throwing knives, pistol, and a short sword strapped to Talon's body. She looked at Talon dumbfounded.

"What?" Talon asked seeing the other Angel staring at her. "You didn't think I was just a walking tome of wisdom for a teenager, did you? I rarely have to use my combat talents, thanks to Kita's gifts, to help me carry out my work." Talon spoke as she undid the harness and pads containing all the weaponry and laid them out on a side counter, leaving her in a revealing solid white bodysuit.

Talon reached into her cloak and pulled out a small bag. She took a seat with Cinnamon's head in front of her. She dumped out the bag of hair care products next to her, picked up a comb, and brushed Cinnamon's hair.

Cinnamon knew her hair wasn't in bad condition, but it wasn't in excellent health either. She felt intimidated and embarrassed having someone as prestigious as Talon working on her hair. It didn't seem like the type of thing the Angel did.

"I can't believe Jane never got after you over your hair or everything else," Talon said with a laugh.

"I was protected by Sven. He told her he wanted an assistant, not a doll."

"Well, now you're an Angel and being a doll comes with it."

"I can do all this on my own," Cinnamon said defiantly.

"Uh-huh."

"How do you know how to do it?"

"All the Angels are given lessons on grooming and hygiene. Some of the girls come from some horrendous conditions, like never having seen a shower and only bathing yearly. But, Jane's one of my best friends, and she has spent some time pampering me."

"I can't imagine Jane pampering anyone."

"That's because you don't know her as I do. She loves to pamper her friends and make them feel good."

"I thought she only did that sexually."

Talon made a disapproving noise. "She won't deny that, and once upon a time I believe that's what she did, but not now. I'm sure you noticed that Jane is not the girl that left on the colony ship."

"No. She was never so formidable."

"That's a good word for her."

"How far back do you go?"

"A long time. I met her while I was a buccaneer and she was searching for her children in The Swamp of the Alligator People. A group called the Mexorks destroyed my settlement. She helped me get over the death of my son and best friend."

"You? A buccaneer?" Cinnamon asked in awe.

"That's what you take out of that statement?" Talon chuckled. "I guess pirates and buccaneers are just movie fancy for you. I ran a settlement hidden on an island out on the ocean. We'd raid ships for supplies, and then we'd give the rest away."

"And they made you an Angel?"

Talon sighed. "No. Kita spurned the idea. I got my wings much later after I helped Kita bring down a foundry called Inferno. It's as bad as it sounds: a giant factory for the production of steel run on slave labor. I saw her arrive in town and I followed her. I wanted to make my case for being an Angel, even if it meant going into Inferno."

"You helped her? She doesn't seem like the kind that needs help."

"Ha. Kita can get herself into all sorts of trouble. In this case, she helped me, but, yeah, I got wings and a place in her flock," Talon said her voice full of pride.

"So, with all those weapons what did you do?" Cinnamon asked. "Jane always says you're a good-hearted goodie-two-shoes high angel only good for cleaning the degenerate trash out of the proverbial gutter."

Talon laughed. "I am, but that doesn't mean there isn't trouble in the gutter for me. The Owlery and I spent our time helping people.

People rarely saw Kita off Base Station. Unless it was a major battle, catastrophe, or something, she didn't want most people to know she existed. The Owlery and a few other good Angels were the face of and represented all of the others. I think Kita wanted it that way."

"I couldn't imagine living in a world like that. It's so..." Cinnamon stumbled for a word.

"Chaotic," Talon finished. "I lived there since the beginning. It was a gradual change. Coming back to this is a shock." She finished rubbing the cream in Cinnamon's hair. Talon tossed Cinnamon a lock of hair around so she could see. It was vibrant and shiny.

"Wow, what did you put in it?"

Talon showed her the cream labeled BLACK.

"T-that's the stuff Jane uses. That costs more than I make in two years."

Talon made an unhappy face. "You need to have a talk with Sven over back pay you're owed. I'm surprised you don't use stuff like this."

"I was hired as an assistant, twenty-four hours a day, every day. You think I had time to put crap in my hair or worry that my lipstick matched my pumps?"

"Easy, owlet. I was just assuming with your status you'd have access to that type of stuff," Talon said rubbing Cinnamon's shoulders gently.

Cinnamon sighed hard. "It's not like Ray would have noticed anyway. How come it's only now I realize all his faults?"

"The mask we weave to fool ourselves falls away leaving us with the truth. I doubt he was a bad man, but you could certainly do better."

Cinnamon laughed. "A man all the way out here? I guess anything is possible."

Talon hit the play button, and the lights went down. She stretched out to take up the entire couch.

"Where am I going to sit?" Cinnamon asked turning around and sticking out her bottom lip.

"Plenty of room in front of me," Talon said in a playful voice.

Cinnamon took a seat on the floor and made sure her wing was in Talon's way. Giggling, Talon moved the TV. "You're bad at this, aren't you?"

"Bad at what?"

"Take the jacket and belt off, cupcake."

"Cupcake?" Cinnamon whispered annoyed as she took her kit off. Before she could turn around to see what Talon's next request would be, a strong arm grabbed her around the waist and yanked her backward. She let out a loud surprised squeak and landed squeezed firmly next to Talon, who snuggled Cinnamon to her.

"I...Wha...Why..." Cinnamon's face went through a wide range of emotions. "I...I am so sorry...If I...But, I thought...I am not...This is....I'm so, so sorry. If I...If I...did, something to..."

Talon put her finger to the frantic Angel's lips. She kept a pleasant smile on her face.

"You've done nothing but look attractive since the day I met you. I'm sorry to embarrass you, but you will find it is lonely being an Angel. It's hard to find affection, romance, and love in the outside world. Only a handful of Angels have done it, and it doesn't last long. Going back to the first Angels, they turned to each other for affection to fulfill the need to be close to someone. Sometimes it blossoms into romance or love, but that's if both parties desire. You seem to need some relaxing. And after ten years mentoring that kid, the first thing I want to do is shrug off being me for a while."

"What do you mean?"

"I am not always the wise and crusty old owl everyone sees. Like everyone else, I have more than one side," Talon said softly. "Come on, just lay here and enjoy the movie."

Cinnamon swallowed but snuggled against the other Angel. Unlike her husband's arm, which was big and clumsy, Talon's was light and sat perfectly. Her body resting against Talon's felt natural.

She thought back to college. It wasn't like she hadn't been invited to those parties, she'd just met her husband early on, and they wanted to do other things. She'd gone straight from Brad to DJ. After splitting from DJ, she'd only been alone a few months before meeting Ray. At the time, sex wasn't what she was after. She just wanted off Mars, and Ray was the ticket. In her life, she'd had no time to explore what was out there. She'd just done what biology told her to do, even though she'd never had any kids.

In her mind, men went with women, because that's how it had been for her, even with the likes of Jane running around. Did she want to? Could she actually do it if she wanted to? The Angels only had one sex. Sarin had told her that at some point. But Talon said it was possible to make it work with a male. The end of the movie interrupted her train of thought.

"What did you think?" said Talon.

"Oh, it was good. Let's watch the second one," Cinnamon suggested, trying to hide the confusion and uncertainty that she felt.

Talon raised an eyebrow but found the movie.

Cinnamon lay in Talon's arms looking at the screen, thinking the second version of this movie is far worse than the original. The rest of her mind whirled. She didn't know what to think, feel, or do if anything. Was this all Talon wanted or was there more? She liked Talon. There was definitely much more there than she realized. She bet she could tell the most wonderful stories.

A sudden loud explosion caused her to jump, making Talon laugh at her. She, at least, had Talon's attention. She'd felt the other Angel stroke her hair, but she thought that was to get it out of her face. A part of her was curious what it was like. She knew men. They were simple and easy to control. She never felt her husbands understood her. And now, was this a chance at something different? Did she want a woman, someone as complex and emotional as she? But it would be someone who understood her. What would that be like?

Cinnamon decided to take a chance. She put her arm on Talon's and interlaced their fingers. Bringing the bonding up to her mouth, she gently kissed Talon's fingers. She got no response. She feared she'd read everything wrong. Then Talon raised her fingers and squeezed her tightly.

She was about to go wild with glee, thinking she'd hit a home run when she felt Talon's warm lips press against the side of her neck. It was a spot none of her former husbands had found on a regular basis. They might graze it and cause her to contract, but that was it. Somehow, Talon knew exactly where to go and what to do. A tingling sensation washed over her and built rapidly. She couldn't do anything to fight it. She was at Talon's mercy.

"Please, stop..." she moaned, but Talon refused to relent. She continued asking Talon to stop, then demanded, begged, and suddenly she broke down into tears. It was when the tears came that Talon stopped. Talon took her in her arms and held her tight.

"What happened?" Cinnamon asked through her tears. "I feel funny, and I can't move."

"Hush, cupcake," whispered Talon. "Just enjoy the sensation." Talon looked out the window. "It seems so unfair to be so old and have never had one."

Talon picked Cinnamon up and carried her to the bed. She laid her down and tucked her in. She gave Cinnamon a kiss on the forehead.

"No one has ever kissed me goodnight before," Cinnamon mumbled on her way to sleep.

"Well, maybe now you do have someone," Talon whispered back with a smile.

CHAPTER XV

"How is it the one habitable moon looks like something out of the Wild West?" Cinnamon asked looking out the window as the shuttle descended into the moon's capital, Notree. The town sat at the bottom of a wide rocky canyon.

The shuttle door opened and a blast of dust came in.

"So much for staying clean. How come the government couldn't put their headquarters on the grazing side of the planet?" Cinnamon complained as she tried to dust herself off. Talon's hand fell on her shoulder.

"I know you're nervous, but try and be quiet," Talon said in a stern voice.

Cinnamon nodded. She was having a hard time adjusting to the sides of Talon. She was sweet and tender when they were alone. In public, she was formal and rigid. She didn't treat her poorly, far from it. Talon treated her like everyone else. Most times that was all right, but sometimes it would have been nice to be treated special in front of others.

She found being with Talon intoxicating. It was unlike the beginning of any relationship she'd had before. In the movies, girls' heads spun over new lovers. She always thought it was an exaggeration. Now, she knew differently. She didn't know how long it would last, but she wished it would go on forever.

They had a group of eight legionnaires with them, two ship pilots and a combat team of six. Major Baxter had left to meet with the locals, leaving the Angels with two guards. Cinnamon peered out into the light from the darkness of the shuttle.

The local Political Bureau officers looked older than those back on Glacier Station. A dozen armored soldiers surrounded the four legionnaires. Beyond them, towers with large guns stood menacingly. As a show of good faith, Baxter and his group carried only pistols.

The leader of the soldiers said something, but she couldn't hear it over the rush of the shuttle engines.

Major Baxter signaled to cut the shuttle's engines and for everyone to disembark.

"Should we?" Cinnamon asked Talon.

"We don't have a choice." Talon pointed outside.

Looking back, Cinnamon could see the legionnaires in the dirt, being detained. She looked at Talon for direction, moving her hands toward her pistols. She might not be Sarin and be able to take down a dozen soldiers in a split second, but she could still hit a few.

Talon shook her head. Instead, she led Cinnamon outside. Ignoring the soldiers' mistreatment of the legionnaires, the Angels stopped next to Baxter and a Political Bureau general.

"The order to drop your weapons applied to both of you," the general growled in a nasty twang of an accent.

Talon motioned to Cinnamon. She drew the two cheap imitation pistols she carried and unloaded the magazines and dropped them in the dirt.

Talon looked at the general with her big glowing eyes. The man looked inward slightly mesmerized. Her sleeves separated and a hand appeared. "My weapons, General, are much harder to separate." The talons in her hands flexed menacingly, causing the general to recoil. "We're here to speak to General Starr."

"That's a hard thing to do, missy, unless you converse with the spirit world."

"Then I will take my guard and go."

"Sorry, all legionnaires are to be detained and non-humans killed. Orders of the Emperor. Get on your knees, bird-girl."

"You can't kill us," replied Talon. She and Cinnamon lifted off the ground. A pearly white bubble appeared around them. "You can't even touch us."

"Shoot them," the general ordered.

The soldiers fired at the Angels, but the rounds bounced off the protective bubble. When the small arms failed, the larger caliber tower-mounted guns fired. The first explosion caused Cinnamon to jump. After a heavy barrage, the pair remained unharmed.

The Angels floated back down to the general.

"If you don't come out, I'll start killing them," the general said pointing at the legionnaires.

"That would be a mistake," Talon said with a growl. Her yellow eyes locked on his and the general's face went limp. "Those legionnaires are going to be your way out, General. Tell me where General Starr is."

"Out in the desert," the general replied in a monotone voice.

"Then that's where we're going," Talon said to Cinnamon. She looked back at the general and said, "You will keep my legionnaires alive until I return. Otherwise, you will fear the blackbird."

"Deal," the general grunted as his soldiers looked at each other confused. "Get them up and into a stockade," he ordered. "You four, escort our ladies to the edge of town. We'll see how long it takes before they come crawling back."

The Angels floated in the protective bubble through Notree. Cinnamon didn't find much to admire about the motley collection of dusty prefab and scrap metal structures built into the sides of the canyon walls. From the background she'd read, the town contained the shipping port for the refined ore processed out at the collection point. Beyond them were hundreds of small and medium-sized mines, supported by the ranching and farming on the other side of the moon. It seemed like an awful place to make a living.

Talon dropped the protective bubble once they'd left the town and guards behind. She stopped and scanned the horizon. "If I was a decorated legionnaire with skills in horseback and desert combat, where would I go?"

"If I didn't have a horse, getting one would be my first thought," said Cinnamon.

"Food and weapons also," Talon added. "She had a command of thirty. They wouldn't move together. The canyons and towers twist back and forth for a quarter of the planet. Leaving too many places to hide or get lost and die. Pull up the local topography."

While taken aback by the direct order, Cinnamon complied. She pulled a panel from her belt. A holographic map appeared in front of them.

Talon studied the map, ordering all the relevant overlays she could think of. Cinnamon also put up some other information she had been researching, on the moon and its people.

"These three areas are where we're going," Talon announced pointing to the map.

"That doesn't make sense at all," replied Cinnamon.

"I have my reasons. Come on."

"No," Cinnamon said putting her hands on her hips.

"What?"

"You're not the only one who can interpolate data. I've been doing it for years. You left out a large number of factors. You didn't account for personal profiles, mining production rates, infrastructure reports, supply rates, mining locations, and about fifty other factors a person might think of when running for her life while looking for a horse, food, and weapons. I've got two possible routes that put her near the border of the desert and ranch lands. The ranch lands are easier to live in, but she can't retake the moon from there. Her choice is to survive or retake her command. Right now, she's thinking survival until she can arm enough people to fight back."

Talon listened quietly. "Based on what proof?"

"All these data points here, here, and here," Cinnamon pointed to the map.

"Yes, we'll go this way."

Cinnamon swatted the oversized hood. She was unhappy she didn't find a head to hit and flew off, deciding another swat wasn't worth it. Frustrated by Talon's arrogance, she nearly hit a tall rock formation known as a tower. She stopped mid-air, darted straight up the cliff face, and exploded over the edge into the bright sunlight. She drifted to a stop that let her look out on the desert and grasslands beyond. The curvature of the moon was visible and added an alien feel to the landscape.

"Kristi?" Talon called in a quiet voice from behind her.

"You're just like the rest," Cinnamon snarled.

"I'm sorry. I didn't mean to sound mean or gruff. I...It's been a long time since I've gotten to work with someone I cared about."

Cinnamon turned around. "You think that's what I'm mad about?"

Talon floated closer to Cinnamon. "If not, please tell me. But, don't keep me the fool."

Cinnamon almost smiled at the other Angel's attempt at humor. "You refused to answer me when I asked how you reached your conclusion. You doubted my conclusion then were going to take it. I'm no longer in the position of having my work taken from me. Sven is brilliant, but it was not him working all the late nights finding patterns to make operations more profitable. I found the trends, but did I get a 'thank you' or a 'well done?' No. I got 'Put the reports in my box, Kristi. Can you refill the coffee pot?' My name didn't go on anything, he never said a word to anyone. His stupid reports would come in, and they'd be magically fixed. Everyone clamored at his genius, and he never said anything. I won't be used again," she finished with a yell.

"That would never be my intention. You had too many data points for me to follow and I like to think I excel at this type of work. I believe you when you say Starr could be there."

"You do?" Cinnamon sniffed a bit and wiped her eye.

Talon took off her hood. "Why wouldn't I? If she's not there, we look somewhere else. We look until we find her. There's always that percentage of unknown that we must be prepared for." Cinnamon nodded and cuddled in Talon's arms. "And when we get back to Rainbow Station we'll talk with Jane, Kita, and Sven. We will get an apology. Kita is big on owning up to one's mistakes."

"All I want is to be appreciated for what I do. I know it's not much—"

"Slag, cupcake. You're amazing."

"I am not. I'm just a secretary."

"And the man would be nothing without you. I have a feeling I'll be nothing without you."

Cinnamon nuzzled against Talon. "How do you know how to say all the right things?"

"With you, it's easy."

RIDING THE THERMALS HIGH into the sky, the Angels flew to the first possible area Starr could have setup camp. Being the stronger flyer, Talon directed Cinnamon from behind. From their great height, it was hard to see anything in the canyons. Talon whistled at Cinnamon to follow as she rolled over and dove lower to get a better look.

The area that interested them was a row of canyons each with a lazy river fed from underground springs. Two small ranches worked in the grasslands at the mouths of the canyons and deserts on the east and south made for an easy escape.

"Don't go into any of the canyons at this speed," said Talon as they descended. "You're not ready for that type of flying."

"What does that mean?"

"You haven't learned greater control of your wings. We only partially fly like birds. There are gravitational wells in our feathers. It's what allows us to float. You only control large surface areas of your wings. Other angels, like Kita and Jane, have control down to the individual well. They can perform some amazing aerial artistry."

"Can you do that?" Cinnamon asked, regretting doing so. It was an insulting question.

"I can fly as well as a barn owl," Talon said flatly.

Cinnamon wished she could see a barn owl in flight.

"Follow the row of canyon mouths. We'll search for any sign of trails or human activity."

"Wouldn't they know well enough to hide that?"

"Even hiding something reveals it, if you know what to look for."

"So, besides a chef, buccaneer, aid worker, and trainer what else have you been in your life?"

"I spent some time tracking unsavory characters across The Mass."

By the dawn of the third day, they moved on to the second site. It was a network of dry canyons, with a wild river running through the northernmost canyon. The canyon system opened onto grassland but was well away from any settlements or other food sources. A rail line running between Notree and the large ranches marked the southern boundary. Cinnamon thought the rail line would be high on the refugee's list.

Invisible, they flew along the tracks, searching.

"There," Talon pointed to a series of bent and dented ten-foot-tall pieces of grass. "Something hit here and rolled to a stop. See how these are broken and they become less damaged as the objected came to a stop from the loss of energy?"

Cinnamon took a closer look, Talon was right. "So, what was it?"

"Something heavy from the indent in the dirt. Back to the air. We'll see if we can spot the trail in the grass."

"How can you track anything in this stuff? It's taller than we are."

"Something I learned from the last world is it's easy to track someone through grass. It pushes apart like water, but doesn't flow back together," said Talon as they rose into the air. "See it?"

"Yeah, a whole maze of them. Eight?"

"Ten. Two are following. So, we know Starr is here and has, at least, nine men."

They followed the trails to the edge of the grass where it met the sand and rock of the canyons.

"There and there, marks of horseshoes against rock." Talon landed and inspected the marks on the stone. "Fresh, too. We're not far behind. Look around. We still don't know what canyon they went down."

"Does it matter?" Cinnamon asked. "Three of these canyons cross or converge. We could pass them and not know it."

"What do you suggest?"

Cinnamon pointed to the grass around them. "The horses were eating. We wait a bit, and then we each take a canyon and follow the poop."

"That's a brilliant idea," said Talon.

"Don't patronize me," Cinnamon laughed as she slugged Talon in the arm.

"We need to work on your form."

"Oh, you think? I'm beginning to think this is how Jane felt when she first started dating Kita."

"And look how that turned out. I can't think of a bigger power couple, both figuratively and literally."

"They're not that mean and tough."

Talon grunted. "You're just like the teenager. You've got to find out the hard way."

"Lucky for you, I won't make it my mission to try and ruin your life."

"That would put an end to our relationship."

"I just don't want to steal what's rightfully Talli's. Plus, with Kita around, you no longer train her."

"Yes, but I didn't want her trained to be an assassin. Killing is too often their first resort. There are other ways."

"Hopefully, she's learned enough from you to know better." Cinnamon took Talon's hand and guided her over into the shade of the grass. She pulled on Talon's arm. Reluctantly the other Angel sat.

"Shouldn't we go after them?" said Talon.

"Give the beasts some time to digest." Cinnamon brushed Talon's hood back and pulled the Angel into her lap.

"I..."

Cinnamon giggled. "You're so used to being the strong protective one you've forgotten what it's like to be in someone else's arms."

"I don't need to be taken care of," Talon replied, the harshness fading from her voice at the end.

"Please. You're just as much a girl as I am."

"What's that supposed to mean?"

"I mean you're not a dumb man trying to hide his feelings from me. If I wanted that, I wouldn't have agreed to be with you. I chose you because I knew you'd be different. I want to feel I take care of you as much as you take care of me, that I'm not just a damsel in distress."

"I-I'd never think of you like that. You're not. I've been— "

Cinnamon bent down and kissed Talon. "I know, and I'm showing you your message is getting through. Now, why don't you tell me a story."

"A story? I don't have any stories."

"You survived how many years on that rock? You have to have some."

"None that are interesting."

"I'll be the judge of that."

"Ok. I guess I can tell you how I became a buccaneer."

"That's good."

Cinnamon sat back and listened to how Talon worked her way up from deckhand to captain. She was so enthralled and didn't realize how late it had become.

"Well, shall we find them?" she asked when Talon reached a stopping point.

Talon stood and helped Cinnamon up, and then fixed her hood. "Call me the second you're in trouble. Don't try and be a hero. Just—"

Cinnamon put a finger into Talon's hood and touched her lips.

"I'll be fine, hoots."

"Hoots?"

"I didn't get to choose cupcake," Cinnamon replied taking off with a big smile.

"But cupcake is so you," Talon whispered.

CHAPTER XVI

C INNAMON FOLLOWED THE SPARSE trail of horse dung. Several times she'd come to dead ends and had to double back to the main canyon and pick up the trail again. Following a narrow side canyon diverted her to another main canyon. She spotted a pile of fresh-looking dung camouflaged by dirt near the intersection.

"Talon, are you here?"

"Why are you whispering over the comm? It goes straight to my head," teased Talon.

"I think I'm close. Where are you?"

Talon appeared above Cinnamon. "Here and it's guarded." She pointed to two sharpshooters in the canyon walls.

"How are we going to get in?"

"We just appear."

Confused, Cinnamon followed her girlfriend. Riding a thermal, they climbed into the sky. Talon looked at the canyon below.

"We're in the right place," Talon said to Cinnamon. "I can see the camp."

"So, how do we just appear?" Cinnamon asked as the pair flew to the campsite.

Talon didn't answer as she turned invisible. Cinnamon mimicked Talon, and they landed on the edge of camp in a deep shadow. The legionnaires busied themselves with their equipment and horses. The state of the camp was orderly and proper. To Cinnamon, this group was not discouraged or a rag-tag troop.

Talon turned visible as she stepped out from the shadow.

"Not another move, winged woman," a man in a tan cowboy hat with a lieutenant insignia on it said. "Give me a reason why I shouldn't end you now." His hands were on his revolvers.

"I am a winged *girl*, thank you," replied Talon. "Woman makes me sound stuffy and old. You are welcome to try and shoot me, but you will only waste good ammunition. I'm here to help you. Commandant Sarin has taken Glacier Station and is looking for all the trained help she can get."

"Never heard of him," said a big man with arms the size of Talon's head.

"Her," Cinnamon corrected making herself visible. The legionnaire didn't flinch at her sudden appearance.

"I'm not aware of any *girl* commandants," replied a woman spitting Talon's own noun back at her. She wore a tan hat with general's stars on the front, a flannel shirt, jeans, and cowboy boots. A gun belt went around her waist and disappeared under her duster. "She must be an Earther." She looked at Talon and frowned. Cinnamon raised an eyebrow at the frontier term. "I think we'll take our chances here with the scorpions and snakes."

"You're making a mistake, General," Talon said in a blunt rebuke.

The General's men reached for their revolvers.

In a flash, Cinnamon drew her pistols. "Tsk, tsk, boys...Just because we're girls doesn't mean we're not ladies," she said with a dazzling smile. "Put those things away."

The legionnaires exchanged glances, not sure what to do.

"Commandant Sarin is looking for a competent field commander," said Talon. "You're it in this region of space. She's hoping you live up to your pedigree."

"Pedigree? I'm not a bull, girl," Starr sneered.

"Does the name Grabble mean anything to you?"

"That would be my mother's maiden name. So what? Anyone can get that out of a file."

"She had a sister, married a man named Hennessy. They left on a colony ship and were never heard from again."

"And how do you know this?" demanded Starr, crossing her arms, but leaving her revolver in plain view.

"Because I was on that ship. You have a cousin, a man by the name of Gerald Hennessy," Talon lifted her head so Starr could see her eyes. "He was the biggest son-of-a-bitch I've ever dealt with. If you're a quarter the leader he was, we'll never lose."

"And what did this cousin of mine do?"

"From what I've been told it's better to ask, what didn't he do?" Cinnamon replied tersely.

"He was a master strategist and scientist, responsible for starting two global wars," said Talon. "In his last years, he served a friend of mine."

Starr waved a hand. "I don't believe it."

"I was there. Far stranger things came from that world than girls with wings." Talon produced her hand and extended her talons.

"What kind of sick science is this?" Starr demanded, jumping backward, the horror on her face showing her dislike of Talon's transformations.

"The kind that lets you survive in a world worse than this one. A world so deadly it's constantly a power failure away from destruction. The creatures there are engineered monsters. If that's not enough the human next to you will kill you, if it means they get to survive another day. You think you're surviving out here, General? I can tell you of a place that will give you a new definition of survival."

Starr didn't waver. "We aren't in dire straits, but unless you've got a cruiser worth of Marines up top, General Franks has us pinned. He's just letting the desert do his dirty work."

"Do you want to stay here and survive or escape with me and do your duty and save your Emperor?" said Talon. "I assume you could do no less than your sworn duties. I help my friend Commandant Sarin because I want to, not because I have to. I am not a soldier or a Marine, but a chef. We will find a way through Franks' defenses, General. You have more resources at your disposal than you realize. Sarin wouldn't send us if we didn't stand a good chance at succeeding."

"How do we know this isn't a trap, boss-man?" the muscular giant asked Starr.

"We don't. At least not yet. There aren't many Commandants in the Legion. I guess she got hers by battlefield promotion on this lost world of yours. She would have sent you down with some kind of card for me to check her serials, but that would be no good out here. So, what did she send? A handwritten letter? A patch? What makes you real, girl?" Starr demanded, grinding the heel of her boot into the dirt.

Talon reached into her cloak. She pulled out a belt with a set of revolvers in the holsters. She flipped the belt over. Hammered into the leather was an inscription, 'For our beloved son, Gerald, Love,

Mom and Dad.' Red Legion symbols decorated the front. She handed it over to Starr.

Starr refused to take it.

"Take it," Talon demanded with a cold fury.

Starr took the belt in disbelief as Talon stepped back next to Cinnamon.

"Damn things are almost as big a beacon of evil as Kita's swords," Talon whispered to Cinnamon.

"I would have carried it."

"Better you not be soiled by it."

"And what of her?"

"Hopefully, she's a better girl than Cowboy was a man," Talon said, hissing the man's name.

Cinnamon snaked her hand into Talon's sleeve and touched her cold hand.

"You said this belonged to my cousin?" Starr yelled at them. "What happened to him?"

"He died defending the universe against an alien race."

"What's that mean, boss-man?" said Starr's lieutenant.

Cinnamon rolled her eyes in disgust. "It means Talon and I are more than human." She drew her pistol, put it up to her hand, and fired.

"Kristi, what are you doing?" Talon cried in horror over the comm.

"Proving that when two Angels show up at your door to take you home, you shouldn't ask stupid questions," she snarled at the gathered legionnaires. Cinnamon heated her other hand and pressed the heel to both sides to cauterize the wound.

"What are you looking at?" She yelled at the legionnaires when she noticed them watching her. "Haven't you ever seen someone get shot before? Find me in an hour. Then you can stand around with dumb faces." She turned around swearing. Cinnamon felt Talon brush her wing against hers and sent a mental hug to her girlfriend. Cinnamon walked behind a boulder to heal and fix her nails.

"WELL, YOU'VE GONE TO extraordinary lengths to convince me to come with you," said Starr. "This belt was made by someone who knew what they were doing. If you say it belongs to my family, then I won't dispute you. We'll get your friend some aid when we get back to the ranch and get ourselves organized."

"She won't need aid," Talon said with a flat tone. "How long a ride is it for you?"

"Three days if we go slow and hide our movement. We go any faster, and some lucky idiot might stumble upon us."

"We'll fly cover and look for anyone."

"I don't suggest that. Franks will know something is up, especially if the two are moving out of the canyons. I hope you girls know how to ride a horse." Starr smiled politely.

"It's been a while," said Talon.

"Best we get you some practice in."

"What type of saddle do you use?" asked Talon.

"Western, these are for punching cattle. We're just borrowing them. Problem?" Starr asked with a sly smile.

"Not at all. I can ride Western, English, bareback, Chinza, and Arabia."

Starr raised her eyebrows. "I, ah, ok. Bring her Silverheel. He's a nice one." Starr chuckled.

A legionnaire fetched the horse. When it saw Talon, it reared. Talon lifted her head and let her eyes meet the horse's. She kept them locked as she approached. She put one hand under his chin, and the other stroked his nose. When she felt the horse was ready, she hugged the creature's head to her. In a hushed tone, she whispered a prayer of respect and honor to the horse. She released him and took a few steps back. She knelt, bowing her head. In turn, the horse did the same to her.

"Silverheel belongs to me now, General," Talon said as she returned to the bewildered group.

"Now, where do you reckon she learned to do that?" a legionnaire asked.

Talon stroked Silverheel's nose. "The horse trainers of Arabia Region were very skilled in handling their mounts. They never lashed, hit, or spoke ill to a horse. A horse was allowed to find its own path. If they needed it for a reason, they would ask it. If the horse desired to help, it would. If not and you *still* thought you needed a horse, you went and asked another horse. If that one said no, then maybe your problem does not lie in the fact that you *need* a horse."

"Do you always speak in riddles?" said the muscular giant.

"I speak how best to get the message across," replied Talon. "General, I will trust your judgment on best course, speed, and time to break camp."

"Glad to hear it, girl," Starr grumbled. "I want to be out of here, and the site scrubbed in forty minutes," she called to her legionnaires. She looked at Talon. "That'll put us in the shadows until dark. We'll skirt wide the rail line and follow the grass into the grazing area. We can move quickly there and then we'll hunker down. We have fresh water nearby and can send scouts out to see who's working the fields. If it's a friendly face, we can give them a heads up we're coming in. Is your friend going to be up to it?"

"She'll be fine. I'm sure she's not feeling a thing."

Starr turned to walk away from Talon, the new pistol belt on her shoulder. "One last thing you should know about that belt, General," called Talon.

"What's that?"

"It's cursed. It causes the wearer to change into a demon. Nothing can withstand its guns or brimstone. I don't know how true it is, but there's a hint of truth to every legend."

"I thought you said this belt wasn't that old," replied Starr.

"It's not old to someone like me," said Talon. "That doesn't mean the belt couldn't have absorbed enough evil to curse it at a rapid rate. Sometimes, so much evil at once is all you need."

"And now you're an expert at soothsaying?" Starr said with a vexed look.

"I've been around my fair share of both the supernatural and scientific. The combination of both in harmony is what you should be looking for."

Starr waved Talon off and walked away.

Talon took Silverheel's lead and led the horse to find Cinnamon. They found her behind a boulder. "You should leave such displays to Kita."

"It got the point across."

After checking the other Angel's hand, Talon introduced Silverheel. Talon was in the middle of a riding lesson when they heard the whistle to leave.

Talon took over Silverheel and Cinnamon glided after. The other legionnaires were in a circle. One had a particularly large grin on his face.

"As you can see, fireball, we're down a horse," Starr waved to the gathered riders. "Jericho won the straw poll, so you'll be riding with him."

"What?" Cinnamon snarled as her face went red. She stormed over to a legionnaire's mount where a horseshoe with 'Luckiest Horseshoe in Freeze-A1' stamped into the saddlebag hung. The shoe had a bullet mark in it. Cinnamon grabbed the trinket.

"I'll ride with anyone who can bend this into a heart." She waved it around at the legionnaires. "Anybody? I can even heat it up for you. It can't be that hard for the way most of you talk. No takers? Fine, I'll walk. And my hand is fine by the way." She held it up and moved it so they could see.

"Do, I get a try?" Talon asked calmly from behind.

"If you think you're up to it," Cinnamon said, handing her the shoe.

Without much effort, Talon bent the rusty horseshoe into a heart shape.

"I knew someone around here was girl enough to do it," Cinnamon said with an elated smile. Without any resistance from Talon, she poked her head into the large hood for a warm and playful kiss. After exchanging an affectionate nose rub, Cinnamon pulled her head back out.

"You think Mary and me do crap like that? You're such an outer-rimmer," Talon heard a female legionnaire hiss at someone commenting.

"Talon's my girlfriend," Cinnamon announced. "And what do you boys do in the sack when you're together?"

That caused most of the females to chuckle.

General Starr ordered her command onward. With Cinnamon's arms around Talon, the Angels brought up the rear.

CHAPTER XVIII

"**I** SEE THEM RETURNING," Talon said to Starr. The Angels floated invisibly above the legionnaires lying in the grass.

"Y'all, be on the lookout," Starr told the legionnaires out with her.

The three riders rode toward Starr's position unaware of the two Angels. One of the legionnaires whistled low getting the riders' attention. The riders trotted forward. The legionnaires crept from the grass to meet with the cowboys.

"General, it's good to see you're still kicking dirt," a cowboy said to Starr.

"We're making do, Yarik. We'd have a tougher time of it without those train drops. How's the ranch?"

"They haven't touched it, and we've followed your orders not to cause a fuss. We keep the beef going out. Though, Jackie says we're not getting the money back in."

"Not surprised that bastard Franks is robbing my family blind. How are the mines?"

"He's forcing as many claim owners out as he can. I'd say he's got about a third of them. The ranch has taken in some of the refugees once all the other mines were full of workers. Don't know what happened to the rest."

Talon appeared behind the group. "General, I was under the impression the ranches didn't provide much income for the moon and are here to feed the miners. Cinnamon couldn't find any financial records for the ranches or most of the mines. I'm going to guess the emperor's tax collectors didn't visit here very often."

"What in the Jiminy?" Yarik exclaimed at seeing the two Angels.

"Easy, Yar. They've been sent by a new Commandant in the region to break the stranglehold the Political Bureau has on us. They're some form of a super creature created by the emperor." Starr looked at Talon. "This moon is one of the few habitable planets in The

Empire where you can ranch without major terraforming. The beef goes out to feed more than just the miners. It goes out to our parent system and neighboring systems. Everyone likes a good steak over vat meat."

"What really leaves this moon?" said Cinnamon. "If I go to those mines and pick up a rock, what am I going to pull out of it? The buyer of the processed metal, Killam Enterprises, says they ship out heavy metals for production. I say bull. There are a lot of easier places to get production grade heavy metals."

"Beef and metals, that's it," Starr retorted.

The two Angels shared a dubious look.

"We need to develop a plan to remove the Political Bureau from the ranches and the capital mining camp," said Talon. "Have you given this any thought, General?"

"A lot, actually," said Starr. "If we go for the ranches, they'll alert the capital, and then we have a fortified base we'll never penetrate, even with your help. Attacking the capital first is what we should do, but the logistical challenges of moving enough troops to surprise the capital is nearly impossible. Their scouts will spot us before we get close. So, unless you have a brilliant idea, shut it."

Talon turned away and walked away from the group. "I think we'd do better on our own," she said to Cinnamon when she caught up. "They're more of a liability than a help."

"They've come this far."

"Yes, but they're no good if they won't act." Talon walked back to Starr. "General, this is where we part ways. Good luck."

"I thought you needed me," Starr retorted.

"We would like to have you," Talon replied. "But I have my own legionnaires being held, and I have instructions that if your extraction is too difficult to abandon the idea. We don't wish to waste too many resources on rescuing a single general and her command."

"Tell the commandant, thanks anyway. We're used to doing it on our own," replied Starr harshly.

"All I can tell you, General, is, she who dares, wins," said Talon with an icy voice. "The commandant and I are the types who dare."

The Angels took off, riding the thermals high into the sky. From there they followed the legionnaires' movements. Once the group settled for the night, the Angels landed to listen in.

"Them Angels are cowards, boss-man, not like you."

"It's ok, McKee. They have an agenda, so do we. They misjudged what they were getting into is all. The capital camp is better defended than any reports."

"Are we going to take the ranches? At least keep Franks from making any more money?"

Starr looked at her hat. "Yeah, I think that's the way to go. A stalemate is better than nothing. We'll do it when the train is at the ranches, that way we control it, too."

"It's going to be good to smash those Political Bureau bastards in the mouth," McKee said with a grin.

"We're not going in to smash them up," replied Starr with a firm tone. "We'll take them prisoner and hold them like we're supposed to. We're legionnaires, not monsters."

Talon tapped Cinnamon, and they backed away.

"So what do we do?" Cinnamon asked Talon.

"We'll go back to the capital and rescue our people. Once we have our shuttle, we'll return and help them as best we can."

A WHITE CLOUD FLOATED through the door into the expensive apartment. It stopped at the foot of the bed. Lying in the bed was Franks with an arm draped over some miner's daughter.

Cinnamon appeared first from the cloud, rubbing her arms to shake away the cold. The cloud formed into Talon.

"This is way too nice for slime like him," Cinnamon scoffed looking around at the swanky room. "And so is she, poor girl."

"She probably thinks she's hit the jackpot, and we're about to take it away from her," Talon replied. She walked around the room shutting the blinds and then returned to the bedside.

"She'll thank us later," Cinnamon replied in a loud voice. The decibel level was enough to turn the lights on in the room.

Franks stirred and then sat up. He blinked trying to knock the sleep from his eyes. "Becky?" He growled at the girl. Released from his grip, the girl scooted to the edge of the bed.

"Cinnamon, actually," she replied, holding her pistols on her knee with a foot on the footboard. Franks opened his mouth to yell.

"I wouldn't do that." Cinnamon pointed to Talon, who clamped her hand down on his mouth. Her talons dug into his skin to hold her hand in place. "Sorry to wake you in the middle of the night, but we're in a bit of a rush. I need you to come with us to release our men and shuttle."

"You don't get a choice," Talon hissed. "You can either come with dignity, or I will drag you naked through the streets."

Franks chose dignity. He raised his hands, and Talon let him slide his naked body out of bed. As Franks struggled to put his uniform on, Becky woke up to Cinnamon's curious gaze. The girl saw the Angel and scooted backward across the bed until she fell off the other side. Cinnamon was there to catch her.

"Easy, child. We mean you no harm. We only want your bedmate." From the girl's ashamed reaction and her sleeping position, she wasn't proud of that fact. "May I ask if you don't like him, why are you here?"

"P-payment..."

"Disgusting on principle. May I ask what for?"

"My father's mine."

"I'm not sure who I want to hit more, him or your father," Cinnamon snarled.

Becky shrugged. "What can a girl do?"

"A lot. Get dressed. You're coming with us."

The girl wrapped the sheet around her and went to the bathroom.

Franks dressed under Talon's watchful gaze. He took his time making sure his proud black uniform was put on correctly and as formally as possible. Lastly, he tried to slip a ring with a purplish black stone set in the center on his finger without Talon's notice. Her eyes narrowed. "And where did you get that?"

"It's my class ring from graduating command school," Franks replied.

Talon sensed the lie, but let it pass.

"What's she doing?" Talon asked when Becky returned with Cinnamon.

"Coming with us," Cinnamon replied with a frown. "You think she's here because she wants to be?"

"In this type of place, that is common."

"Not where we're from, and I'm not going to let it stand. Are you? Jane? I know Kita wouldn't."

"I understand your point. But..."

"No buts. She's coming with us."

"We are in serious danger," Talon said over the comm. *"There are alien evils here that shouldn't be, unless this place is more important than we've been led to believe. If you see anything made of purplish black crystal or glowing that color, do not let it touch you. Warn me, and I will deal with it."*

"What is this crystal?"

"Pieces from life forms from a different equation. It's too much to explain here, but know even a small amount is powerful enough to kill Kita and Jane. We do need to find out what this moon produces that is so valuable it requires posting Angel killing weapons."

"I would think the girl would know," suggested Cinnamon.

Talon nodded.

"What does your father mine here?" Cinnamon asked Becky.

"I don't know. We just strip the rock from the mine and send it to the capital to be refined."

Cinnamon gave the girl a doubtful look.

"She *knows*," said Talon.

"What's in the rock?" Cinnamon asked Becky again. "Don't lie this time, because if you do, I can think of worse things than sleeping with him."

Becky looked at the Angels then at Franks.

"Don't fear him, child. He can't hurt you," said Talon.

"I don't know," Becky whispered.

"A lie," Talon hissed. "A lie to protect this man and your father, both who betrayed you. Help us, help you."

Cinnamon waved her girlfriend down. "Becky, this is important. Lives depend on it. Including yours and your father's. We're here to remove Franks and his people so that you can return to a normal life. What's in the ore?"

"It's stuff for spaceships," Becky whispered.

"Let's go," Talon ordered the group, annoyed at the girl's answer. Cinnamon took the point, following Talon's directions as they made their way to the stockade. Along the way, she noticed a series of odd colored shipping containers. They stopped at one.

"What's in the container?" Talon asked Franks.

"New mining equipment."

Talon's eyes glowed with a bright yellow intensity over the lie. She didn't challenge him, instead choosing to let him think he'd fooled her.

U NDER THE ANGELS' WATCHFUL gaze, the Political Bureau soldiers released the legionnaires from their holding cells.

"Thanks, Talon," said Baxter after his group was released. "Their idea of food was stuff a starved dog wouldn't touch."

"We're not clear yet, Major," said Talon. "We still need to get to the headquarters building, drop communications, and then get to our shuttle. We are ten, and they have at least a company's worth of soldiers and fixed turrets. This will not be easy."

"We know, but if we have surprise on our side, we can make it. You want my men to take Franks and leave your hands free?"

"No, I think he should stay close to me," Talon said opening the talons on her left hand and digging them into Franks' right shoulder. Her talons reflected a blackish purple crystal coating that the casual observer often missed.

"What shall we do with these Bureau dogs?" one of the legionnaires asked.

"Lock them up in the cells. They'll become Starr's problem," Talon ordered.

After stripping the soldiers and herding them into the cells, the legionnaires and Angels moved back into the streets toward the headquarters building.

W ITH THE ANGELS FLANKING him, Franks bypassed security and let the group into the headquarters building. It wasn't a large command post, enough to control the security systems, communicate with the wormhole station, and be a tiny administrative center.

"Step back from your consoles," Baxter ordered.

The three soldiers on night duty looked at him confused as if this was a bizarre drill.

Cinnamon hit Franks in the kidney. "Do it," he ordered.

The three soldiers got up, and the legionnaires restrained them.

"I want a message sent to the ranches. Tell General Starr now is her window of opportunity," Talon ordered the legionnaires as they moved to take over the consoles.

"Talon, ma'am, the train is moving," a legionnaire sitting at a console reported.

"Can you communicate with it?"

"It's not responding to any hails," she reported after several attempts.

Talon shrugged. "It's not our job to help them. It's our job to get out of here. Is the shuttle free?"

"We've released it from all electronic locks. We'll just have to remove any physical locks when we get there," a pilot reported.

Talon moved over to the three secured soldiers. "When is your next security check?"

"Four hours," the first one answered.

Talon swatted at her with her talons leaving vicious gashes across her face. "Tell me the truth or the next will receive more than a few bad scars."

The others remained silent.

"They're trained monkeys taught to be silent at all costs," said Baxter. "They'll die before they give anything up."

Talon grabbed a second and jabbed him with her barb injecting a truth serum given to her by Kita.

"Twenty-three minutes," the man answered in a happy, stupid voice.

"You will answer those checks," Cinnamon instructed the last soldier. "Once that's done, we'll leave."

They waited in silence. The legionnaires watched the equipment and followed the train's progress. Talon and Cinnamon made sure the third soldier was ready to do his part in the ruse. If he failed, Cinnamon's pistol was firmly against his head, even as she cringed at the idea. Franks had drifted around the room to a newer looking machine in the command center.

The radio came alive as the different command areas in the city and neighboring mining areas called in. The soldiers answered one by one, giving a coded phrase in return.

After the radio checks were completed, the Bureau soldiers were escorted from the room, secured, and placed in a stripped office.

"To the shuttleport," ordered Talon.

CHAPTER XVIII

T HE SMALL GROUP OF legionnaires and Angels moved down a side street toward the shuttleport. They stopped at a street corner behind the protection of a building. A legionnaire stuck his head out and snapped it back in.

"Talon, we've got something up ahead. I don't know what it is—like a ball with a mass of tentacles."

"What?" Talon demanded in surprise. The Angel floated around to look. "Neptune's rings...I hope that's a manmade and not a Harbinger seeker," she said to Cinnamon, who returned a confused look. "Harbingers incorporated their crystal into the armor of the Machines, and it makes them damn hard to kill—until Kita discovered crystal kills crystal. If they're manmade, I expect they have other weaknesses."

"If they're not?"

"Then the only weakness is the sensory organ in the center of the tentacles. It's a near-impossible shot. You let me deal with it while you get everyone else to the shuttle," Talon ordered.

"I can still help you."

"If you had crystal rounds, I'd say yes, but you don't. You would only put yourself at risk for nothing."

Cinnamon sighed. "I don't like that it's always you."

"This isn't the time or the place to discuss this. Apply your skills where they're most useful."

Cinnamon turned to Baxter. "Talon's going to distract the seeker, and we're going to dash across the street. We're doing double time to the shuttleport to avoid fighting any of these things. We're not equipped to handle them. Whatever happens, get Franks and your men to the shuttleport."

Baxter instructed his squad, putting Franks and Becky in the middle. When he was ready, he signaled Cinnamon, who squeezed Talon's hand.

Talon didn't let go. It had been years since she had faced such a deadly foe and didn't relish the idea again. She wasn't sure if she'd be back to see Cinnamon. She waited a few seconds to savor the other Angel's hand in hers.

Talon had faced thousands of Machines without being scared, but now she was filled with dread. Maybe, it was because she'd been with other Angels that could do impossible things: turn into dragons, move faster than the eye could see, could hit with more force than an erupting volcano, or wield weapons with atomic precision. *But what am I? Just an owl. An owl suddenly very alone.*

"Don't wait for me." Talon let go of Cinnamon's hand and flew straight at the seeker. She raked it with her talons. Crystal talons hit crystal armor. *This is a real Machine. How did Galina capture one? It seems an impossible task.*

The seeker changed directions. Its nest of tentacles reaching out for Talon. From under her cloak, Talon produced her short sword with a crystal edge. She chopped down with the sword, severing several tentacles.

The Machine shuttered in pain and lurched at Talon, just missing her. It pursued her down the street, not giving her a chance to regroup.

Talon turned down another street and nearly collided with a group of smaller, but deadlier, swarmers. A dozen surrounded her. A shrill whistle announced the train was pulling into the train depot.

The swarmers attacked as one. Talon's bubble provided little protection, just enough of a distraction to let her escape into the air and down the street to the cattle yard next to the train depot. She turned a corner into a chute and waited. A single swarmer could be killed quickly. The real danger came when they formed a swarm. She wanted to pick them off individually. Places like the cattle yard were good for disorienting and separating the Machines.

A swarmer rushed by, and she slashed it in half with her sword. A second jumped at her, but she caught the beetle-like Machine around the neck in the talons on her foot. She smashed her foot down destroying it. Talon played the game of cat and mouse, killing three more. She hurried up a cattle chute before more homed in on her location.

Talon exited the chute next to the train. She glided to the engine and entered the cab, but no one was there. Looking out the window, she saw several of the large cattle car doors open. Starr leaped out on her horse, directly into the waiting tentacles of the seeker.

"No!" Talon yelled, but she was too far away.

The embarking legionnaires attacked the Machines. The swarmers overpowered the legionnaires stripping them of their organic matter. The creatures were programmed to collect the material for construction of other Machines. The seeker smashed through the wooden railing the legionnaires were using as a barricade. Its remaining tentacles wrapping up the legionnaires with ease. Talon jumped from the train and glided toward Starr.

"We gotta get out of here, boss-man," A legionnaire yelled at Starr. "Whatever these things are they already got Bob, Jess, Ty, and, Neptune's rings damn near everybody else."

"Fall back to the train," Starr ordered the remaining legionnaires.

Talon landed in front of the retreating legionnaires. The Machines pressed in around them. She opened her mouth and let out an ear-rupturing hoot. The sonic waves stunned the Machines. Talon leaped between four swarmers and dispatched them with her sword and talons.

The ground under Talon's feet rumbled. Talon leaped into the air. A giant metallic squid, with three tentacles wrapped up like a drill, sprang from the ground and slammed down.

"Oh, hell," Talon muttered. She dove for the train car the legionnaires had taken cover in. "Starr, get your people out of here. Now. We don't have the manpower or resources to fight these things. Save yourselves."

"There's no way I'm leaving two-thirds of my command out there," Starr cried.

"They are gone. Machines don't take prisoners or leave bodies."

"There is always something we can do. Isn't that what you meant? She who dares, wins?"

"Within reason."

"I still have this," Starr snarled, holding up the cursed belt.

"Don't you dare put that on. It's not worth it."

"My legionnaires are worth it, Talon. I'll do anything I can to save them, even sacrifice myself or give myself a damn fool curse. Maybe someday you'll understand." Starr strapped the belt around her and buckled it tightly.

"You ignorant fool," Talon yelled while backhanding the legionnaire to the floor. "Don't ever question what I have and have not been."

Starr screamed. She held up her hands as they burst into flame. The rest of her flesh caught fire and dripped away or went up as ash. Her clothes burned and charred, but remained. Her dark auburn hair caught fire. She stood up looking at her skeletal hands.

"What happened to me?" Starr demanded in a high, angry demonic voice.

Talon pointed behind Starr.

"You are now The Rider, Ryder Starr," said Sarin. "Kita will love to hear one of her favorite pets has returned to her." She drew her pistols. With eight well-placed shots, she destroyed the Machines moving in on them. Holstering her pistols, she put together her giant sniper rifle, loaded, aimed, fired, and killed the driller. "It's been so long since I've had anything worthwhile to shoot at."

"I belong to no one," Starr snarled after Sarin's exhibition.

"Oh, you belong to someone now, like it or not," Cinnamon chuckled from the door. "We have the shuttle."

"But you won't be a pet," said Talon.

"Just a sister, bonehead," Sarin said with a smile.

Starr fell to her knees as long thin bones appeared next to her shoulder blades and grew into wings with burning feathers.

"That was almost as interesting as watching you," Sarin said to Cinnamon.

"I bet hers wasn't as painful."

"I thought you couldn't do this," Talon demanded of Sarin.

"Kita gave me the necessary nanites, just in case."

"Kita wanted Starr?" asked Cinnamon.

"She's hoping Ryder lives up to the family legacy."

"What about the rest of the Machines?" said Talon.

"And what are they really taking off this rock?" added Cinnamon.

"Xeox, FTL fuel," replied Sarin. "I just found that out myself. I was hoping you'd figure it out while you were here. We need to continue harvesting the xeox. This will give us a huge boost over Galina.

If any of the Machines are still in crates, I want them destroyed and harvested. Recover the crystal from the Machines killed, and we'll get it back to Rainbow Station to be processed. If Galina's got Machines and crystal tech this war just escalated. Think you can handle that?" Sarin looked at Talon.

"Except for hunting the Machines. You're the best suited to do that."

"I'll give you Ryder. She's more than up to the task. The Rider's belt has been upgraded since Cowboy wore it. The revolvers have crystal lined barrels now."

"I take it I should also give her the basic angel talk?" said Talon.

Sarin winked and vanished.

Talon sighed. "Oh, the games gods play."

Sarin returned a light laugh from the ether. "Never with you, red."

"Don't go too far. I may still need you," Talon said seriously.

"I am at your beck and call, my old friend."

"What have you done to me?" The Rider screamed at Talon.

"Nothing," Talon said flatly. "You did it to yourself. Temptation must run deep in your family."

"You know nothing of my family," The Rider yelled with an angry teeth rattle. She clenched her fists and shook them at Talon. "Free me from this, owl."

"All Angels belong to one Angel, and that is Kita. That is the price you pay—willing or otherwise. Divinity and grace are granted at her luxury and your deal with her," Talon said, bowing her head as a sign of acknowledgment that The Rider had been manipulated into her status as an Angel.

The Rider charged Talon, trying to grab the Angel. Talon side-stepped and with a flip of her wrist sent The Rider crashing headfirst into the side of the car.

Cinnamon jumped in front of The Rider's confused legionnaires. "Sit tight, boys and girls. Let the big girls play."

"I am a grandmaster at using others' anger and aggression against them," Talon told The Rider. "You are not Kita or Jane, who can deliver their wrath on the head of quark, but a young owlet stumbling in a nest high in a tree, not even ready to fly. But we have no time to teach you. You must fight—" The Rider drew her new revolvers and fired at Talon until the cylinders were empty. The bullets hung in the air in front of Talon. "We are wasting time and resources," said Talon calmly. "Every time you fire you bring more of them down on us."

"Change me back," The Rider demanded.

"Only you can change yourself back. You are a chick fresh out of the egg. Open your eyes, take your first step, learn what you can do. What we do not have is time, Ryder Starr. You are The Rider. It is how the world will see you. Cowboy's legacy is yours. How do you wish your sisters to see you? The monster or the girl?"

The Rider lowered her revolver. "I am not a monster. I want to save my command."

"Your command just changed, sister," said Talon. "You're no longer just a legionnaire, you're an Angel. Kristi and I are here to help you."

"Is Kristi a pet of yours?"

Talon nodded to Cinnamon, who gave the newest Angel a wave. "We all come from somewhere, sweetheart. You'll learn."

"We don't have time for introductions," said Talon. "We have to find the rest of these Machines and put an end to them before they set up and take over the planet."

"Dire, don't you think?" The Rider scoffed.

"No. We need to get back to the headquarters building and reprogram the stationary turrets. They can take out swarmers and disrupt seekers with lucky hits. We'll send the shuttle up to spot for us, but the majority of the legionnaires will have to make it on foot."

"Why don't we leave everyone here and go reprogram the turrets ourselves?"

"You and I will be busy keeping Machines off the others," Talon replied.

"So, what, you're the bait?"

"I'll hit them every way I can."

"I'll be the bait," said Cinnamon.

"What?" Talon asked, unable to hide her surprise and concern.

"You learn some interesting things proofreading research reports. If they mine xeox here, the stuff has got to be everywhere. The compound has interesting properties if you heat it up past a certain point. It creates a false drop into the Nothing. It'll look similar to pushing a cookie cutter into dough. Part of whatever's in front of me will be pushed several feet away." She flipped her hair playfully. "I know, smart and beautiful."

"No," said Talon, crossing her arms.

"What?" Cinnamon responded, her playful manner disintegrating. "Just because you're the wise owl does not mean you get to risk your neck any more than me."

"I have experience fighting these things."

"She doesn't, and you didn't get it without going out and doing it."

"When I did, I had an army of Angels at my back."

"And it still wasn't enough," said Cinnamon. "None of you knew what you were doing. Not even Kita. She told me about her dealings with the Harbingers and Machines. With you two watching my back, I should be fine."

"This sounds like we can't leave your girlfriend out," The Rider said chuckling at Talon.

Talon grabbed The Rider's flaming jaw and pulled her face-to-face. Talon's eyes glowed a golden yellow. "I know you think you'd give your life for your command, but when the feathers fall, you won't. But, when you find that person you are willing to die for, I want you to remember this moment and what you felt. I want Kristi safe because I don't want to live without her. I've done it before, and I don't want to do it again. It is selfish, and I know she'll do her part, but that doesn't change how I feel."

The Rider laughed. "Being a warrior isn't for everyone. Maybe you should go back to cooking or whatever it is you used to do."

"A true warrior is ready for any battlefield. Kita understands this better than anyone I have ever met."

"Pearls of wisdom won't get us across town," said The Rider. "Let me reload, and we can go. I suggest going back the way we came. We know those containers are empty."

Cinnamon glided over to Talon. She stuck her head in Talon's hood and touched foreheads. They stood silently, hand-in-hand.

CHAPTER XIX

C INNAMON STUCK HER HEAD around a street corner. The group had traveled five blocks without finding any Machines or shipping containers. She entered the cluttered intersection stacked with crates, boxes, and trash. She didn't see anything, as she waited in the middle of the intersection for something to attack her. Deciding it was safe, she called the legionnaires forward.

An explosion lit the intersection. Cinnamon jumped to her right. A large shipping container smashed into the ground where she had been standing.

She searched the smoke for her attacker. Out of the smashed container came two swarmers. Grabbing a handful of dirt, she heated her hand.

"I've got two," she reported. "They're north of the container that just smashed into the intersection."

The swarmers floated around the intersection on gravity repulsor drives. The pair rushed Cinnamon.

"Girls, a little help?" called Cinnamon.

The temperature in her hand rose, and she squeezed the dirt. A bright flash lit the street as she threw the clump. The xeox extended like a straw, punching through the Machine. It collapsed into the dirt. Talon appeared between the Machines and slashed through both with her sword.

Cinnamon walked over to the swarmer she'd killed and inspected the hole left by the xeox.

"We don't have time to examine kills. We must go," Talon insisted.

"Give me a second to see exactly what I did. I'm still running on theory. I'd like to move to practical application. We could have a new weapon. Finish cutting this thing in half."

"Why? They smell awful inside."

Cinnamon gave her a dirty look. With a silent sigh, Talon slashed the swarmer in half. Fluids of different colors spilled and mixed in with the dirt. With a bright flash and a loud pop, the dirt went up in flame.

"That's interesting," Cinnamon said, kicking dirt over the flames. She returned to searching for her hole. Finding it, she traced it. She wasn't sure if she'd hit something critical or if it had been luck that took the swarmer down. The xeox had punched a hole through the swarmer's exterior crystal armor. She looked at Talon. "I'll turn over the findings to Athena. She might be able to do something with it."

"Just don't take any more chances," Talon said in a dire voice.

"I did just fine."

"Then why were you crying for help?" The Rider asked coming up to them.

"Because I was expecting help after I called them in," said Cinnamon.

The Angels watched as the legionnaires crossed the intersection. Cinnamon glided out ahead of them to take the lead.

They reached the headquarters without another attack.

"I would think we'd have had more. We passed at least six of those new containers," said Cinnamon to Talon.

Talon nodded. *"Major Baxter, how long to reset the turrets?"*

"We'll have to do it manually. Telling the computer what a Machine looks like is going to take time."

"It's going to take the legionnaires some time to get the guns programmed," Talon said to the others.

"We've got time, let's go crack a container open and see what's inside?" suggested The Rider.

T HE ANGELS APPROACHED THE container with weapons drawn. They tossed aside the other crates and junk piled against it. The control panel contained a security system.

"I can open it," replied Talon.

It was still early, but the little town was waking up. A shift change at the port would happen soon. Having people in the streets would complicate things.

"We're in," Talon announced as she opened the door.

A seeker lay suspended in the middle of the container.

Cinnamon picked up a handful of dirt and stepped inside. Talon grabbed her arm. "You might wake it up."

"Then you and bonehead better be ready to kill it," said Cinnamon as she pulled free of Talon.

"I got you covered, spicy," said The Rider.

The seeker took up most of the available space, and she had to turn sideways to make her way to the back. Metallic silver disks were on the six sides of the container. On the back wall was a control panel. The panel controlled the suspension system created by the silver disks.

Cinnamon returned the way she came but stopped where the tentacles met the body. She stuck her hand full of dirt into the center of the tentacles and sent a xeox bullet into the sensory organ. She returned to the back of the container and shut down the suspension system. The creature fell to the container floor, causing The Rider and Talon to attack.

"Stop," Cinnamon yelled over the gunfire. "It's already dead." She stepped onto the creature to examine it. After pushing aside some tentacles, she found something attached to the sensory organ. "What do you make of this, Scarlett?"

Talon looked at the device. "I don't know. The Machines we used to fight didn't have anything like that."

Cinnamon removed the device with minimal effort. "Interesting...We haven't seen anything like this on the swarmers. I wonder what it means."

"Probably nothing," said The Rider.

"Or, everything," said Talon. "This is not something to ignore. Neither are the states of the containers or the ring on Franks' finger. Someone has control of these Machines or at least thinks they do."

"Time to talk to Franks."

THE ANGELS ENTERED THE headquarters and found Franks hanging around the machine Talon had seen him near earlier. When he reached behind to touch it, she produced a throwing knife. The blade hummed through the air and impaled his hand.

Franks roared in pain, causing everyone in the headquarters building to jump. He clutched his hand. A second blade eviscerated the finger with the suspicious ring. Talon leaped sideways and caught the finger in her foot talons.

Talon examined the finger and ring. "Tell me, General, what command school did you graduate from? I see nothing about a school on this. I do recognize the language of the Harbingers when I see it."

"Curse you, bitch," Franks snarled over his twice-wounded hand.

"We have enough curses for one day," Talon said. "How does this machine control the containers?"

"It's too late. I've freed them all," Franks spat.

"Then your hand will be the least of your problems. The Machines will harvest you like all the rest. You are nothing but a tool for them. If Galina thinks she can control them, she is a fool. What have you released?"

"See for yourself," said Franks with a vengeance laced grin.

Cinnamon looked at the screen. "Thirty swarmers, eight seekers, four drillers, a pair of t-rexes, and a queen," she announced. Looking at Talon, the other Angel had her head down. "Scarlett?"

Talon raised her head, but she was talking to someone else. "The colony will have to be sacrificed, that is the only way unless you want to come back and fight...If they start harvesting the population, then the number of swarmers will increase exponentially once the queen has found a place to make her nest...They have plenty of organic and nonorganic material to make thousands. My suggestion would be to blow the xeox facility and rebuild once the danger has passed...I am thinking positive, Jane, and no, sacrificing the colony's people is not my first choice...You are making these choices difficult, not me. I am not a combat leader nor have I ever claimed to be...The Owlery was a force for good, protection, healing, and hope. Fighting was the last resort, and you know that. *Don't rub their deaths in MY face*," she ended in a terrifying yell.

"I am not trying to rub Iza, Ana, and Lola's deaths in your face," Sarin said from behind her. "I would never do that. As much of a bitch as I was at the time, they were my friends, and I did care about them."

A ball floated away from Sarin's belt, and Kita appeared. "If you want someone to blame, blame me. I put them in positions they shouldn't have been in. They were never meant to be soldiers, but humanitarians. I don't think I ever told you how sorry I am for their deaths. I owe you more than I can ever repay, and I keep running up the tab. You shouldn't be suffering on my account."

"I'm not," said Talon. "I'm suffering on hers," she motioned to Sarin. "She is my friend, and Kristi is making it worth it. You just see the world as your oyster, even Jane. You'll shuck us all, take what you want, and leave the rest to rot. You really are the true embodiment of evil. As I am proud to be an Angel, I detest that you walk among us."

"Hate me all you want—"

"I don't hate you. You are my friend and my enemy. I care for you like I know you care for me. But like the Caesars of old, sometimes you need a slave whispering in your ear that all glory is fleeting."

"Is the middle of a battle the place to be dysfunctional?" The Rider chattered from behind them.

"Yes," Kita, Talon, and Sarin said together.

"Surveillance is picking up movement all over the capital," Cinnamon reported. "I've got the queen. She's headed for the shuttleport."

Sarin sighed. "Plenty of tall things to string herself up around there."

"We've got to get to her before she can get anchored," said Kita. "I'll stay here and take over the turrets. You four go stop her. I'll get Baxter's people on the roof and windows to shoot at anything that comes close."

"Let's go hunting. Ready?" said The Rider.

"Oh, yeah," Sarin growled in a sultry voice after the bolt of her sniper rifle slammed closed seating one of the giant rounds in the chamber. Her uniform changed to her schoolgirl outfit. She shook her hair back and forth, looking like a vixen shaking out her tail.

"You can stay here," Talon offered Cinnamon.

"I just escaped a desk job, I'll be damned if I'm going to go hide behind one now."

"Here," Sarin passed her pistols to Cinnamon. "These will make sure you punch a hole in the bastards." She waved at Talon. "Come on, hoots. Let's go live a little," Sarin clucked with a teasing smile.

With a sigh, Talon nodded.

～

"**G**OT YOU," SARIN WHISPERED after the sound of her shot bounced off the nearby buildings around the headquarters. She'd removed her rifle's silencer. *If people weren't awake after the first shot, they are now.*

"That rifle doesn't leave much, does it?" said The Rider after looking at the remains of the swarmer.

"That's the idea. You should see what happens to a human head. It's like a party balloon filled with wet confetti."

"Lovely," The Rider said in disgust.

Sarin's smile became sicker at the legionnaire's response.

"We don't have time to appreciate art," said Talon. "We need to catch the queen."

"Art, huh?" said Sarin. "You want Kita. I'm a technician."

Sarin led the others into the air to hunt down the Machines. Shots from humans forced them to take cover.

"Where in Neptune's rings did these fools come from?" said Sarin as she shot a Political Bureau soldier.

"They must have gotten a message out to the outposts and guard stations," said The Rider as she gunned down a trio of soldiers coming round a corner.

"How many people is that?" said Talon.

"About five hundred if they get everyone around the capital and the processing area. Eight hundred once all the mine guards arrive."

"We can't wade through that many," said Cinnamon.

"I've waded through more," grumbled Sarin, thinking of her battles against the Red Legion. In the distance, she could hear the automated turrets firing. "Kita should keep them busy. Let's keep moving, but we'll have to stick to below the buildings. I don't feel like pulling bullets out of anyone today."

The group floated down the street toward the shuttleport. Talon took the lead. They passed several blocks. She stopped at a corner and stuck her head out. "We've got a driller and two seekers tearing apart the buildings on the far side."

"Why would they do that?" said Cinnamon.

"No idea. Swarmers do the harvesting for the Machines. The bigger ones are their warriors."

"They're not watching for us. So, we can get the drop on them," said Sarin, looking over Talon's shoulder.

"What do you suggest?" said Cinnamon.

"Ryder and I will take out the driller. You and Scarlett hit the seekers. Everyone, watch each other's backs. They love to ambush. Let me get on a roof." Sarin phased on top of a corner two-story building. "Hell's bloody bells," she yelled and fired.

"Jane, what happened?" demanded Talon.

"Seeker ambush. It's dead, but look out! Here come the others."

A massive tentacle from the driller slammed through the corner of the building causing the Angels to scatter. From atop the building, Sarin fired, putting a bullet into the nest of tentacles of a seeker. It bobbed and fell to the ground.

Talon dodged sideways out into the middle of the street, the remaining seeker behind her. She pirouetted and slashed at the tentacles with her sword and talons. Two bullets ripped through the side of the seeker, just missing her.

"Kristi, be careful. Those things punch all the way through."

"Sorry, I'm not used to something so big—there's something I never thought I'd say."

Sarin laughed at her over the comm.

The Machine moved erratically around the intersection. "Keep firing," said Talon.

Cinnamon fired several more times while Talon leaped into the air. Cutting through the tentacles reaching for her, she landed on top and plunged her sword into the sensory organ. The Machine crashed into the dirt catapulting Talon into the air. The Angel opened her wings and landed.

A giant tentacle lashed out hitting Sarin's building. The side of the building collapsed. She took a snap shot and put a bullet between two armored plates where she knew an altimeter control was located. The driller flew upwards then crashed into the ground. "Kill it," she ordered the others as she shot it from behind.

"Where do I shoot?" said Cinnamon after several shots didn't do much visible damage.

"Same place as a seeker," said Talon.

"Those arms are two-feet thick, we'll never get in there," said The Rider.

"I will get them to open while Jane keeps it busy. Be ready to kill it," said Talon.

"How do you reckon to do that?"

"Watch and learn." Talon leaped in front of the driller and attacked the tips of the large tentacles twisted together to protect the sensory organ. The driller took the bait. The giant tentacles untwisted to swat the Angel.

Cinnamon flew to her left where she had a chance at the sensory organ. The driller slammed into Talon, sending her into a stack of crates. Cinnamon fired. The Machine crashed to the ground and went slack.

Cinnamon rushed over to her girlfriend. "Scarlett?"

"I'm fine, cupcake. Just a couple of ribs out of place and injured pride. I was trying to do too much at once, and it caught me."

"You busted a wing by the look of it," said The Rider. "Better get back to headquarters. You don't want to slow us down."

"It's just dislocated. I can still move on foot. Set it and I'll be fine in a few minutes."

"We're basically on foot, anyway," said Cinnamon.

The Rider chattered her teeth but didn't say anything. She looked at Sarin.

"I'm fine with her coming along; you girls help her reset her wing and ribs."

While the others helped Talon, Sarin investigated the activities of the Machines. Entering the building, she found shredded metal, upturned dirt, and a few dead humans. In the center was a hole. She looked in.

She examined the equation. A large xeox deposit lay several thousand feet below, larger than any discovered by humans.

Sarin went to one of the dead seekers. She reached into the nest of tentacles and put her hand on the dead Machine's sensory organ. The Machine shook as she woke it up.

"That's right, you bitch," Sarin hissed. "A real god awakens you. Now tell me, why do you want xeox?" She wasn't addressing the seeker, but the queen. The queen refused to answer, still outside Sarin's direct grasp. "Fine, don't tell me now. But, when I do get a hold of you, I won't ask so nicely the second time." She dropped the seeker and returned to the others.

"How's it going, red?"

"I'll be fine," replied Talon.

"Glad to hear it. Good to see you're as creative and resourceful as ever." Sarin squeezed her friend's shoulder and whispered in her ear. "Don't overdo it. I'm not bringing home anyone in a bag. Remember, you just got a girlfriend. She cares as much for you as you do for her."

Talon nodded.

"All right, let's go kill the queen and get out of here."

CHAPTER XX

"COMMANDANT, THE QUEEN HAS begun to climb the main xeox storage silos," said the shuttle's spotter.

"Thanks, I can see part of her strands from here," said Sarin, examining the creature in her scope. She took aim at a weak point, but decided against firing, not wanting to give their position away. She motioned the others to follow her down the last two blocks.

"Where are the t-rexes?" Sarin called to the shuttle.

"One is on the far side, and one is two hundred yards to your left, behind a hangar."

Sarin called Kita. "Can you see the t-rexes?"

"Sure, but I can't do much about them."

"I just want you to draw it out from behind the hangar. I've got a round that'll do the trick."

"I'll see what I can do, pretty blackbird."

A pair of turrets on the shuttle port's perimeter fired at the area behind the hangar. Sarin glided up on top of a building and picked a clear firing position. From her ammo box, she pulled out a round with a solid crystal tip. Bullets from another group of human Bureau soldiers struck the building around her. "Keep those worms off me," she yelled to the other Angels.

The Rider stepped around the building and chattered loudly at the two humans drawing their attention. She fired and killed them. Two more humans appeared from around the corner. She swore and charged the pair. The soldiers saw her coming and fired. When their bullets didn't have any effect, they dropped their rifles and ran. The Rider caught them by the backs of their uniforms.

"Lieutenant Chow and Private Lee. Strange seeing you so far from your post." The Rider tossed the pair into the dirt.

"Who...Who are...?" Chow said cowering in fear.

"General Starr."

"It's a demon," said Lee, making a symbol in the air.

"Don't be foolish. I am General Starr. I need you to get a message out to the rest of the legionnaires. Tell them to stop attacking the headquarters, automatic turrets, or any woman with wings. And, everyone is to obey orders coming from a Major Baxter. We need to stop these metal monsters and the Political Bureau. They are the true threat."

"Why should I believe you?" said Chow.

The Rider took off her burning hat and dropped it between the pair. It returned to normal when it hit the ground. "That's my hat, isn't it?"

Chow nodded.

The Rider took off the cursed gun belt, and she returned to normal. Her burning wings changing to brilliant reds, pinks, oranges, and yellows matching a sunset. "Minus the wings, it's me." The two legionnaires' mouths hung open. "We don't have time for y'all to gawk. Get moving."

"Can we trust it?" Lee said to Chow.

"Private Lee, I will have you riding Solo White Pine Ridge patrol on a donkey ass-backward for a month if you don't get moving. Chow, it'll be two for you."

"Yes, General," Chow muttered as he climbed to his feet, refusing Ryder's offered hand.

"Good, move." Ryder waited until the two men turned the corner before slipping the belt back on.

"Nice job," Sarin said over the comm. *"I knew you were a smart cookie."*

"That should cut down on some of the lead flying our way."

Sarin didn't answer, her attention taken by the appearance of a t-rex. She fired, and the t-rex's chest exploded. *"One down."*

"That's good," said Talon, *"because the queen is climbing the silos. She already has a bottom anchor in place."*

"Damn. She's moving faster than I expected. Where are you, red?"

"Kristi and I are at the shuttle port's fence. There are no other Machines or people nearby. I can see the other t-rex on the far side of the port."

"Be careful. You know they can pop up without warning," Sarin said trying to contain her horror over the two being out alone. *"Wait there. I'll catch up. Ryder, get your ass moving, too."*

"I'm almost there."

The four Angels gathered at the fence.

"So, how do we kill the queen?" said Cinnamon.

"Drop it in lava," said Sarin with a frown.

"No lava ...What's the plan then?"

"Shoot it until it quits moving."

"Or, I thought I could get to the xeox tanks and heat up a large amount in a hose or pipe and blow her out of the sky."

"That could work if we can get close enough," said The Rider.

"Yeah, but we still have a driller, a couple of seekers, and at least two dozen swarmers to deal with," said Sarin.

"Your big gun isn't big enough for all that?" The Rider chided, her flames growing brighter.

"You get me the damn target I'll make sure it dies."

"Do not let her get to you, Jane. We need you focused," said Talon. "Ryder, do not antagonize her. We need her fighting with a technician's precision, not an artist's passion."

"I'm always perfect," Sarin huffed. "Get moving. I'll cover you."

The other three Angels floated over the fence and moved into the open grounds of the shuttle port.

"Look," Talon pointed to the top of the xeox silo. A thin cable from the queen wrapped around the top, and more cables wrapped around the wire to strengthen the hold. "Jane, can you break that anchor?"

"I'll do my best. Those cables are thicker than they look." Sarin took out her shooting cap now that things were serious. She put that hat on backward and took up a prone position. Placing the crosshairs on the cable, she could barely see it even with her vision and scope. The rifle fired but didn't break the cable. Instead, it swung wildly as she fired another shot. *Did I actually miss?* The cable sagged and snapped, sending the queen to the ground. *Didn't think so. "She's down,"* Sarin said to the others.

"We're moving toward her," said The Rider. *"Just keep being our guardian angel."*

"You—" Sarin spotted a trio of swarmers making for the others. She picked them off in rapid succession and then replaced her magazine. *"This guardian angel doesn't work for free."*

"Would you prefer dirt or horse hair? That's all I own in the world."

"With what's in this dirt a handful is worth thousands."

"I must have some of the most expensive rounds around," said Cinnamon with a laugh.

"Hardly," Sarin said rolling her eyes as she scanned the area for more Machines. *"Hurry, the queen's recovering, and that t-rex is coming up to protect her."*

Sarin didn't have any of the pure crystal rounds left. Everything else was crystal laced, which was good for everything except large creatures like queens and t-rexes. She fired two shots, one in the t-rex's head and one in the chest to disorient it.

She searched the landing area for something powerful enough to kill the Machines. She couldn't set the xeox off in a controlled way, but unless she took care of the t-rex Cinnamon would never be able to get close enough.

An idea struck her. She hopped down to the ground and pulled out her bullet maker. She tapped away at the controls, programming a hollow jacket with thermite and dirt she added to the materials port. The machine did the rest.

"Jane, where are you?" Talon cried.

Sarin drifted up and saw the Angels battling the remaining driller and seekers. She set the maker aside and with two shots blew apart a seeker attacking Cinnamon. The Rider's revolvers flashed even as the tentacles of the last seeker entangled her. Three shots into the base of the tentacles caused the seeker to spin wildly. It wasn't dead, but it was enough to free The Rider. There was a bright flash in Cinnamon's hand as she hurled a clump of dirt at the damaged Machine. It fell to the ground.

T ALON FLEW AROUND THE driller, racking it with her talons and slashing with her sword. The thick tentacles were nimbler than they looked.

"We're coming," Cinnamon yelled.

"Stay back," said Talon. "It's too dangerous."

Cinnamon's hand flashed as she threw another clump of dirt. The Rider fired adding to the Machine's fury. Two large explosions on the side from Sarin's rifle sent Talon reeling. As she tried to shake off the effects, a tentacle grabbed her around the waist and squeezed her.

Talon thrust her sword up to the hilt in the soft underside of the tentacle. The tentacle relaxed. She expanded her protective bubble pushing the slacked tentacle away from her, and she fell across the other tentacles. She shook her head trying to clear the pain. The tentacles curled around her.

A small glint of crystal was attached to the Machine's sensory organ. Talon slammed her talons into the fleshy pile. The Machine's tentacles closed over her as she frantically struck at the machine's weak spot until they trapped her.

C INNAMON AND THE RIDER pulled the giant tentacles apart and pulled Talon from inside. Talon regained consciousness looking into the eyes of Cinnamon. "Hmmph," was all that came out when she tried to speak. It was enough for Cinnamon. The Angel grabbed her and hugged her.

"No new injuries, just aggravating the older ones," said Sarin. "But I suggest you stay here for now and let me and bonehead go finish off the rest."

"I killed it?" said Talon.

"You clawed the sensory organ out," Sarin said with a smile. "It won't be long before the queen tries to get up on something else. We need to hurry."

"I can make it," Talon said struggling to her feet.

"I'm coming, too. But you should stay here," said Cinnamon tapping Talon on the chest.

Talon sighed and gave her a playful dirty look. "I guess I deserve that, but I'll rest when it's over. I can still watch everyone's back."

"I—"

"That's only fair," said Sarin. "Come on. We need to get into position. I've got a magazine of rounds that should keep the pair busy while Kristi figures out how to heat up the xeox and kill them."

"So, killing them is all on me?" Cinnamon said with a nervous laugh.

"Welcome to the big leagues. Let's move."

"***W**E'VE FOUND THE XEOX tanks,*" said Cinnamon. *"The hose and pump are connected. I need someone to get that big chicken's attention."*

"We'll start shooting," said The Rider. *"Darling Jane, are you in position?"*

"No, I'm in the middle of moving."

"Damn girl. It shouldn't take you more than a twitch of your whiskers."

"I don't have whiskers."

"Uhm, girls..." Cinnamon went quiet as the t-rex roared. *"It spotted us."*

"What happened?" Sarin demanded.

"The pump wasn't as quiet as we thought."

"Stuff around here is held together with wire and a prayer," said The Rider. *"This isn't Neptune with sound dampening coils and frictionless motors."*

"That would have been nice to know a few moments ago," said Talon.

"I'm coming around the hangar now. You girls vamoose, and I'll give him a spicier meal to think over." The Rider shot at the t-rex. "Come on you big, dumb oversized buffalo wing. Let me show you who the real hothead is around here," she yelled with harsh laughter.

The giant Machine roared at the Angel's challenge. It charged as The Rider stood her ground.

Sarin thumped down hard on the ground. She inserted the magazine with her xeox rounds. She couldn't see the t-rex, but she could hear it roar. Through her scope, she watched The Rider hold her ground.

Sarin gulped. She was counting on an untested round based on a best guess to save her new friend's life. She didn't like it, but she didn't have a choice. All she could do was take the shot. If it didn't work, well, she had other ways of putting down the t-rex. The rules be damned. *"Ryder, back up. I need more room."*

"More room for what?"

"I don't..." The t-rex appeared in her scope. On instinct, she pulled the trigger. She held the trigger down, and another round fired. The first struck the crystal head guard and exploded without doing any damage to the Machine. The second struck half an inch from the first, contacting a fleshy bit of gum. The hollow round shattered and

set off the thermite, igniting the xeox charge. A thin straw punched through the t-rex's skull.

The t-rex stumbled and flipped over The Rider. As she ducked, the dinosaur's tail smashed into her. She tumbled backward and disappeared underneath the t-rex in a cloud of dust.

"Ryder...Ryder... " Sarin yelled over the comm, but she got no response. *"Girls, is it down?"*

"I don't see her," said Talon. *"What happened to her?"*

"I lost her in the dust. It looked like the damn thing came down on top of her."

"She's probably knocked unconscious under it."

"Girls, the queen is starting to climb again," said Cinnamon with a hint of concern in her voice.

"I don't have a shot. You girls will have to slow her down," said Sarin.

"We're ready. By the time you get here, it'll be over."

"Don't do anything stupid while I move to you."

"**Y**OU AIM—I'LL HEAT UP the xeox," said Cinnamon to Talon.

"Are you sure this air pump will give us enough PSI to get a shot from here to there?"

"All we need is to direct the xeox. It'll do its own launching," said Cinnamon tartly as she grabbed the air hose and kinked it.

Talon poured a handful of xeox into the hose. "Loaded."

Cinnamon heated the hose with her hands. When she felt the xeox expand, she released the kink, and the xeox false dropped out the end of the hose toward the queen. "Did we hit her?"

"I don't know. Reload and fire," Talon barked.

They repeated the process three more times, but with no visible result.

"This isn't working," Cinnamon cried. "And she's reached the top of the silo."

"We'll have to wait for Jane," said Talon calmly.

"Jane! Jane! This isn't working," called Cinnamon.

"I'm a little busy," Sarin replied with a growl. *"Think for yourselves."*

Cinnamon looked at Talon and raised an eyebrow.

"It sounds like she's in trouble, but is handling it."

"Then we've got to get the queen down," said Cinnamon.

"How?"

Cinnamon looked at the landing area and the silos. "She's above a xeox conveyor, and I can reach her anchor. Give me your sword, and I'll cut her off."

"This is a queen. Do you know how dangerous she is?"

"Do we have a choice?"

Talon clenched her fists but relented and reached into her cloak and handed over her sword. "Let me show you how to use it."

"How hard can it be?" said Cinnamon.

"Blades are a lifetime of learning, ask Kita or Jane." Talon showed Cinnamon how to grip and swing the sword in case she got into trouble.

When Talon finished, Cinnamon pulled the other Angel's hood back. "I'll be careful," she whispered and then gave her a kiss.

"You better come back to me," Talon hissed.

"Don't be possessive and don't use that tone with me," Cinnamon retorted.

Talon sighed. "Sorry. But, you're young and inexperienced. I'm worried."

"I know, but we don't have a choice. After I cut her down feel free to crash in and tear the queen up."

Talon hugged Cinnamon tightly. "Be safe, cupcake."

"I will, hoots."

Around them, the ground rumbled, and a quintet of swarmers crawled from the dirt.

"Kristi, go!" said Talon.

"I'm trapped."

"I'll clear you a path." Talon let out an ear-splitting hoot blasting the swarmers backward. "Go!"

Cinnamon leaped into the air, refusing to look back to see if Talon was all right. She felt guilty leaving Talon with only her talons for defense. She turned invisible and ducked into the shadows. Using the silo to screen her, she flew up the side and peeked over the top of the flat roof.

A rope-like tentacle wrapped around her foot. She drew the sword, attacked the tentacle, and landed on the silo's roof. Cinnamon could hear the queen's vocal reaction. More tentacles snaked upward. Cinnamon dodged them from all directions. One grabbed her by the ankle and pulled her to the ground. Terrified, she rolled across the roof. Her head banged against the handle of an access hatch. Scrambling, she ripped the hatch off and slid inside. She fell into a mound of xeox.

She laid in the black crystals, her breath coming in ragged gasps and tears came to her eyes. She'd survived this before, why was she so terrified now? She had to regain control—the others couldn't save her. Talon's fears for her became very real. Thinking of Talon calmed her. The older Angel gave her a sense of calm, even when she wasn't standing right next to her. She wiped at her tears, and it caused her to cry harder. She cried until she was furious at herself for doing so. Talon and Sarin were both outside fighting the enemy. She was in a silo crying like a little girl. Picking herself up, she vowed not to cry anymore. *At least, not until I'm in Talon's arms.*

Looking up, she spotted hatches along the front side of the silo. She glided upward and opened each one until she found the queen.

"Die, bitch," Cinnamon snarled. She jumped from the hatch and grabbed onto the underside of the giant metallic cockroach. She plunged the sword between the crystal plates. The queen shook violently, and a pair of tentacles snaked toward Cinnamon. Jumping backward, she shot upward missing the tentacles.

She darted in and with a loud yell, she cleaved through the tentacle anchoring the queen to the silo. The queen fell toward the moon's surface and disappeared in a cloud of dust.

Cinnamon landed at the base of the silo. Around her, xeox particulates performed false drops, creating a halo of shooting stars. Her arms and chest were glowing a cinnamon red. *Kita never said my anger would cause my body to heat up.*

A tentacle came toward her, but the xeox particulates surrounding her annihilated it. Cinnamon smiled wickedly. *Time to see if this bitch can take the Cinnamon Challenge.* She moved deeper into the cloud, and the lights increased. She could see the queen struggling ahead of her. Another tentacle dissolved as it tried to grab her.

"Keep trying," Cinnamon snarled. "You'll die piece by piece."

A trio of tentacles shot toward her. Two survived long enough to make Cinnamon deviate from her path. "This is for Jane, Ryder, and Scarlett, you goddamn crystal zombie," she snarled as she jumped into the air. She landed on the queen and plunged the sword into the head. Around her, xeox particulates hanging in the air exploded, punctuating the death of the queen with a fireworks show.

"You have been listening to too many of Kita's stories," Talon said a few yards away.

Cinnamon went from being enraged to embarrassed in a heartbeat. "I didn't think anyone was listening."

"Oh, we all heard it, yearling. But, good job," said The Rider limping on Sarin's arm.

Sarin looked like she'd been in a long fight. Her clothes were dirty and torn. Her hair disheveled, and a clip was missing.

"You both look like you shouldn't be on your feet," said Cinnamon.

"What happened, Jane?" said Talon. "Met your match?"

"You are in no better condition, hoots. It's time to get back to headquarters and get you some proper—Oh, hell. Get down."

A group of humans fired. Talon and Sarin raised their hand stopping the bullets. With a wave of their hands, they knocked them to the ground.

"These are just privates," said The Rider.

"Legionnaires?" said Sarin.

"Let's find out." The Rider took off her belt and stepped forward. "Listen here legionnaires, I'm General Starr. Put your weapons away and report to Major Baxter at headquarters. Arrest any Political Bureau soldier. Any orders from them are illegal. Any questions, the Commandant and I will answer them—"

"You know what?" said Sarin.

"What?" Ryder grumbled.

"I'm ready to go home. I want a hot bath and something yummy to eat. I forget how much I hate playing in the dirt. This is Kita's deal, not mine. I'd rather fight on a space station." She wiggled her nose twice.

"Yes, General," the legionnaires said in unison. "We'll report to headquarters immediately."

Sarin smiled. "Problem solved."

"What did you do?" demanded Ryder.

"I just suggested to every human in the capital that if an Angel tells you something, it's the damn truth, and you shouldn't waste time arguing. Now, I have a question I want answered."

Sarin walked over to the queen's body. She placed her hand on the head. "Ok, bitch, what were you up to?"

Sarin scanned the queen's equation, searching its thoughts. There wasn't much, but what she found was disturbing. She removed her hand and stood.

"Anything useful?" said Talon.

Sarin wrinkled her nose. "We got lucky. She was going to create Machines with FTL capability."

"They could go anywhere then."

Sarin nodded. "I'll inform Kita. We'll have to keep an eye out in the future. There's nothing more that can be done here. Let's get back to Baxter."

T HE ANGELS FOUND MAJOR Baxter outside the headquarters building directing an influx of subordinates.

"What's the situation, Major?" said Sarin.

The man evaluated the group of battered Angels. "Better here than wherever you've been. If you look like that, I can only imagine what the other guys look like, Commandant."

Sarin chuckled lightly.

"The Legion outposts around the moon are checking in and giving us status updates. Many have troops in the city because of Political Bureau orders. I'm getting them back out on patrol to clear the streets and dispatch others to incident areas. I think whatever you battled with solved the problem, ma'am."

"It was a queen and a bunch of her groupies," said Cinnamon with a huff.

"You look like you could use some down time to recoup. I'll send a medic over to you."

"That would be most kind, Major, but not necessary," said Talon.

"If more of those Machines popup and you can't fight, we're screwed. Someone else with a scratch can wait fifteen minutes," Baxter said with a grunt.

"Don't worry about us, Major," said Sarin. "Let's get this mess straightened out so we can get back to Rainbow Station. Plans are already in motion to capture the next piece. Major, you're now a colonel and in charge of this rock. Get it straightened out and producing xeox. Controlling the fuel supply to the Empire should convince the Shadow Fleet to take us seriously."

"What if they try to retake the moon by force?" said Talon.

"I'll threaten to blow it up."

"We don't have those kinds of weapons," said Ryder.

The other Angels giggled. "We don't need those kinds of weapons," said Talon. "We've got Jane."

"Are you planning on shooting the Shadow Fleet out of the sky?" Ryder chided.

"That's an interesting idea," said Sarin. "I just thought I'd throw a rich girl size tantrum."

"More like god size," said Talon.

"For me, same thing."

CHAPTER XXI

S ARIN TOUCHED THE RINGER on Ryder's door. She checked her nails as she waited for the door to open. When it did, she was surprised to find Ryder wearing a red sports bra, jeans, and socks.

"What do you want?"

Sarin could smell the alcohol on her breath. "I came to talk to you. I thought you deserved a proper welcome and an explanation."

Ryder raised an eyebrow, but stood aside and waved Sarin in. The cowgirl's hat and shirt lay on a table next to a half-empty bottle and a tin cup. Ryder grabbed the cup and sat down hard on the bunk, then swore as she adjusted her wings.

"They take some getting used to," Sarin said apologetically.

"Why the hell do I have to have them?"

"It's the uniform."

"Yeah? I suppose the urge to preen them comes with them?"

Sarin chuckled. "Yep. They need to be kept clean and neat. Don't worry. You'll get good at it."

Ryder leaned back resting her head on the bulkhead. "So, what have I become?"

"You're now a member of the most exclusive girls club in the universe. You're an Angel."

Ryder rolled her eyes. "I notice it didn't come with a harp."

"No, but it comes with some other abilities. You'll heal rapidly, eat once a month, sleep every two weeks, you can fly, your strength, perception, endurance are vastly increased, and you've already met your unique talent."

"Bonehead."

Sarin nodded. "That comes with its own unique abilities."

"So why me? I'm no pretty girl. I'm a legionnaire first, cowboy second, and woman last. I'm a long way from my comfort zone. I hate space."

"You had to have seen plenty of it as a legionnaire."

"Sure, doesn't mean I liked it. I took every dirt-side mission I could get."

"How did you end up at your family's ranch?"

"Rank has its privileges. My family's ranch happens to be next to the mines, and they needed to be guarded."

"It seems like a demotion."

"I got to be home, and you're taking me away from it."

"When we're finished, you're welcome to go back, but you might want to see what the flock is like first."

"Where did you all come from anyway?"

"A lost world. Everyone fought to survive, and Angels are the pinnacle of that planet's evolution. Your cousin, Gerald Hennessy, led the Red Legion there. That gun belt you have belonged to him."

"Did it turn him into bonehead, too?"

"No. He did that on his own. The belt trapped his essence."

Ryder scoffed. "Sounds like a bunch of hocus-pocus."

"Maybe, but it's an easier explanation than explaining how the belt is imbued with special nanites that pass to the wearer and the wearer retains them until they die."

"That's not possible."

"You have wings, don't you, flame face?"

"My cousin, Hennessy, you said? Is he behind the wings?"

"Oh, he wishes. Kita is the mistress of the Angels, and she knows all our secrets."

"The VI at the headquarters building?"

"No. That's just an AI version of her. She is somewhere out in the cosmos, and we are preparing for her arrival."

"I don't adhere to any messiah."

"She's hardly a messiah, but she is a god, just like I am."

"That explains a few things about you."

"You'll believe I'm a god, but not in a cursed gun belt?"

"I believe in both, but only after seeing them with my own eyes. Tell me, how does a god get mixed up in a human civil war?"

"I wasn't always a god. I was human, then an Angel. We're after the leader of the Political Bureau, General Galina Lyakhova. She betrayed Kita and the flock."

"So, she's an Angel?"

"Was...someone stripped her of her wings."

"I take it you're not omnipotent?"

"No. Think of me more like a Greek god."

"Well, you look the part."

"Give your body a few weeks and so will you."

"Ha," Ryder growled. "I'm dog meat. Always have been. Nothing will fix that."

"Wait until I work my magic. I give all new Angels a class on beauty."

"Why?"

"I don't hang around with ugly people...and beauty is a weapon all its own. I'll show you."

"This I can't wait to see. But you're stuck hanging around this ugly duckling."

"You have a rugged beauty. I would never try to make you a beauty queen. That's not you."

"Lipstick on a pig and all that."

Sarin snapped her fingers, then pulled her compact from her belt. She tossed it to Ryder. "Have a look."

Ryder fumbled with the compact. "How do I even open it?"

Sarin laughed. "The latch on the front."

Ryder snapped open the compact and bobbled it when the top sprang open. Once she had it under control, she looked in the mirror.

"What did you do? God magic? That's not me."

"I did speed up nature a few weeks then a little foundation, some layering, highlighting with the right color, and ta-da."

Sarin snapped her fingers again, and the makeup vanished. "That is your natural beauty."

"No way."

"Get used to looking at it."

"Why waste it on me?"

"You don't think you're worth it?"

"I never wanted to be one to get by on my looks. I had to make sure I pulled my weight."

"And you will, but there's no reason you can't look good doing it. Think of it as a favor to the rest of us."

"Is that what you tell yourself?"

"I'm a gift to everyone."

"You don't lack ego, that's for sure."

"Oh, there is no shortage of ego in the flock. It's all alpha girls. So be ready to hold your own."

"I can go toe-to-toe with anyone."

Sarin smiled. "Be careful. Some of the girls are supercharged."

"Like what?"

"You'll just have to wait and see. Scarlett, Kristie, Talli, and I are tame compared to others."

"And when will I get to meet them?"

"Where Kita goes, the others are sure to follow."

"And you're sure Kita is coming?"

"Positive. Galina and I are here."

Ryder's eyes narrowed. "And who are you to Kita?"

Sarin flashed a dazzling smile. "Her partner."

"You mean...?"

"She is my true love."

"I bet you two make quite the pair."

"We do stand out in a crowd. Now, come, get dressed. It's time to meet with the others for some quality time."

"Quality time?"

"We live, love, and fight together. You don't put your life on the line for a stranger, only those you care about. You need to get to know the others, and they need to get to know you."

SARIN SAT IN THE shuttle seat waiting to dock with the Political Bureau supply depot that serviced the Shadow Fleet in the Bitterfreeze system. She rested her hand on Talon's shoulder and opened a cloud connection.

"Intrigued. So, you and Kristi? You make an interesting pair." She prefaced her statement to make up for the monotone voice she had in cloud form.

"How so?" Talon answered in the high melodic tone of a white cloud.

"She doesn't seem your type."

"She's a kind person, a bit naïve, but in a cute way. She hasn't been exposed to the horrors we have."

"Amused. And you're going to be the one to show it to her?"

"I hope never to have to go through that again," said Talon.

"We've already faced Machines."

"True, but that was nothing compared to when we first had to deal with Machines. I remember the fear."

"And we overcame it. As we do everything. I'm surprised Kristi was so accepting of you. I expected her to be a harder nut to crack."

"I just had to hit the right buttons," said Talon.

"Laughter. I didn't know you knew the right buttons."

"Because I portray myself as solemn and full of piety? What do you think I did with the other owls?"

"Skeptical. Helped the poor, righted the wrongs, good girl stuff."

"Good girls can be bad."

"You're opening up a whole new side to you I would never have guessed."

"You're not the only one who likes sex. Just because I'm not you or Kita and flaunt it."

"Next time the Pride has a sex party I expect to see you there."

"I have Kristi now. That's all I need."

"Dire. Don't break her heart."

"And I thought it would be Sven I'd have to worry about," said Talon.

"Daddy's not as imaginative as I am."

"It's my heart I worry about. I'm afraid I'm not good enough for Kristi."

"Of course you are. Why wouldn't you be?"

"I *am* just a lowly cook here in UEE space."

"Posh. You're as much an elder Angel as I am. You've proven yourself. Don't think any different."

"I've made mistakes," admitted Talon.

"Agitated. Haven't we all? Kita chief among us. What's important is you've never let those mistakes beat you and don't let them start defining you now. You're too good. You've done an excellent job with Talli, just like you did with the other owls."

"They're dead because they weren't ready."

"They're dead because Kita tried to shove an owl sized peg through a wolverine sized hole. It's her fault they died, and she admits it. You trained them for the mission you had."

"Every Angel is supposed to be able to fight."

"In her own way, according to her own skill set. You fought the war on poverty and injustice. That's a specialty few have. It's important. Don't sell yourself short."

"I...I'm sorry, Jane. I don't mean to dump this on you."

"It's why we have each other, to talk, to get over problems like this. To reassure each other in moments of crisis. I've had my own questioning of faith. It took me a while to get over leaving Kita and not doing anything about it. I know she told me to go quietly, but it's hard when I know I might have been able to make a difference or at least made Galina's life harder."

"I had the same thoughts, but I don't think I could have accomplished anything," said Talon. "So I didn't even try, I just went along with Galina."

"You did what you had to. No fault in that. When the time came, you did what was right; that's what's important, and you kept that kid alive. That's a feat in and of itself."

"I feel bad for her. Talli has such a strong attachment to Dev, and I can barely tell her anything about her. Dev was the mother Talli dreamed of and then to have Dev murdered in front of her...It's more than a soul should have to bear."

"I'll work with her. I knew Dev. Maybe I can get Talli to open up."

"I promised her a picture."

"I'll get her one."

"Commandant, the depot is refusing us permission to dock," said the shuttle pilot. "They say this depot is for Shadow Fleet and Bureau ships only."

Sarin broke the connection with Talon. She'd expected the Political Bureau supply depot would turn them away. The depot's existence was 'need to know' only. "Did you tell them our ship is having an emergency and they're the closest facility?"

"Yes, ma'am. They don't care."

"Did you tell them a commandant is aboard?"

"Yes, ma'am."

"Dock anyway. Let's see what they can muster." Sarin looked at the other Angels. "Showtime, girls." She stood and moved toward the door. Through the window, she watched as they passed into the hangar. Outside, she could see four Political Bureau soldiers waiting with rifles. The shuttle touched down with a thump. Sarin drew her pistols.

"Open it," Sarin instructed Ryder.

Ryder turned the lever on the shuttle door and threw it open. When Sarin had a clear line of sight, she fired, dropping the four soldiers where they stood.

"Talli," called Sarin.

"Yeah?" said the teenager as she pulled her mask into place.

"Time to hunt. Kill them all, just don't damage the equipment."

"You got it."

Talli pushed passed Sarin and vanished as she walked across the hangar.

"Klein," Sarin yelled back to the pilot.

"Yes, ma'am?"

"Call the ship and tell them it's safe to dock. We need to get the dockworkers unloaded so we can get this place operational as soon as possible. Athena, found anything yet?"

"Yes, Mom. I have found the codebook for the Shadow Fleet and have the codes to call the Shadow Fleet ships. Would you like me to send them?"

"Yes. How far away are they?"

"They are a week away. Five days if I instruct them to travel at maximum power."

"Good. That gives us enough time to learn the cranes and other equipment. Call them in."

CHAPTER XXII

T HE HULL OF EMPEROR'S Punisher slid alongside the supply depot.

"How do they sound, Athena?" said Sarin.

"The level of stress in their voices gives no indication they detect anything is amiss. I have been using recordings from the last time the ships docked, and they have been following my instructions without question."

"Have you made contact with the escort ship, Luna?"

"Yes, they are standing by waiting their turn in port. I am passively attacking the ship's systems, same as I have been doing against Emperor's Punisher."

"Good girl. As soon as we get their hatches opened, we'll head for the bridge."

"Thanks, Mom. I will monitor your progress and keep an eye on young Talli."

Sarin didn't think Talli would go rogue on her, but the teenager had been lashing out at random lately. Sarin had met with her twice in clinical sessions to try and help her, but the teenager was smart and stonewalled her at every chance. For this mission, to capture the Emperor's Punisher and her escort ship Luna, Talli was going in solo to reach the Emperor's Punisher's manual self-destruct button before any of the Political Bureau could. What Sarin didn't want was the teenager carving a path to it, and she was instructed only to use lethal force to stop the self-destruct from being activated. If Talli obeyed her, that would be the question.

Sarin wished Kita were here. She had a way of reaching gifted and troubled kids. Sarin was never sure if they saw Kita as a friend, parent, or role model—probably all three. The kids all ended up differently, and only Phoenix seemed to want to assume Kita's mantel.

Seeing Emperor's Punisher stirred memories of living aboard Emperor's Wrath for four years. She and Kita had settled down into family life then. While she attended to her practice, Kita raised the twins. Sarin missed them and missed being their mother, even if she hadn't been very good at it. A wave of anger and hate at Galina and Sheppard for taking Spike and Quill from her overtook her nostalgia. She knew first blood belonged to Kita, but she was going to get her share. Her babies didn't deserve to die.

Sarin returned her focus to the ship as the magnetic locks leaned into place, mooring the ship to the dock. The dock area of the depot could have fit the ship inside. Stacks of containers lined the dock in long rows. The depot had enough goods, supplies, and material to keep the two ships going for a year. Doors along the side of the ship opened and the cranes extended into place.

"Scarlett, Kristi, how are you doing?" said Sarin over the comm.

"We're just reaching Luna now. As soon as we find a way in, we'll make sure they behave themselves," said Talon.

"Be careful."

"We'll be fine."

Sarin still worried. Neither of them were military or Legion and would have little sway over the crew. The hope was if they secured the engines and took out the Political Bureau personnel the crew would fall in line, or at least not do anything ill-advised until getting orders from Emperor's Punisher.

"Looks like it's our turn," said Ryder as a crane moved over the container beside them.

The two Angels entered the container and closed the door. The magnetic clamps banged against the sides of the container, and they felt the container vibrate as it lifted into the air. They rode in silence until they felt the thump of the container hitting the deck.

"All cameras in the cargo area are looped," said Athena.

Sarin turned into a cloud and engulfed Ryder. She passed through the stack of containers to a dark place in the cargo area. Sarin released Ryder, returned to her Angelic form, and both Angels turned invisible. Relying on Sarin's experience aboard Emperor's Wrath, they glided above the cargo to the door leading to the main elevator.

A s a cloud, Talon drifted through the Luna into her engine room. Only six sailors were working. They all wore blue coveralls, except for a man in a black Political Bureau uniform who was in discussion with one of the other sailors.

"I'm telling you there's no way to fix it without a replacement part," said the sailor.

"I do not want excuses, sailor. I want results. I won't have you jeopardizing this ship with your incompetence."

"How is it incompetent to order a part? We're at the depot. If I send the request now, it'll be in the supply cache they load. If we don't, it'll be a month, and the engines can't jump to FTL without the part."

"Are you saying you are unwilling to follow my order, sailor?"

"What order? You want me to do the impossible. I can't fix it without the part."

"This ship will not be seen as deficient for any length of time. You will fix it now."

"Do you even know what I'm talking about?"

Cinnamon appeared behind the Political Bureau officer and hit him in the back of the head with her pistol. He fell to the floor unconscious. "Probably not. All he's worried about is how it's going to make him look."

Talon appeared. She took a set of zip-cuffs from her belt and tied up the Political Bureau officer.

"Who—Alarm!" cried the sailor.

"Whoa, take it easy," said Cinnamon. "We're on your side. And nobody's leaving or talking to anyone else until you agree. We're here under orders from Deputy Commandant Sarin of the Legion. The Political Bureau is engaging in a coup against the emperor. Commandant Sarin is the leader of the resistance."

"Lady, I don't even know what you are."

Talon stepped forward. "We're Children of the Emperor—"

"We are?" said Cinnamon over the comm.

"It's an old lie, but it works. Everyone is in awe of what the emperor possesses. We fit that belief structure." Talon returned her attention to the sailors. "The emperor is under attack. It is our duty to defend her against all enemies, foreign and domestic. It is time for you to stand by the oath you swore when you enlisted."

"I...You have proof of this?" said the sailor.

"Knocking one of them out isn't enough of a sign?" said Cinnamon.

"Chief, if they're against these Political Bureau stooges, I say we help them," said another sailor.

"How many Political Bureau soldiers are on the ship?" said Talon.

"Six, including him. One is always on duty in the engine room and the bridge. The others move around the ship."

"Athena, can you see them?"

"Yes. One is on the bridge, three are in quarters, and one is in the officer's lounge. I have locked the doors to their quarters and the officer's lounge."

"Who's that?" said the chief.

"I am Athena. I was a community AI for the Emperor before Child of the Emperor Kita freed me. I have been helping her until her incarceration by the Political Bureau. Since then, I have been helping Commandant Sarin."

"They gotta be with the emperor. Ain't nobody got tech like that except them," said a third sailor. "I mean AI and whatever happened to them—"

"Genetic modification," said Talon. Her hand appeared, and she opened up her talons causing the sailors to jump.

"If you don't like pointy things, you can always play with fire," Cinnamon said lighting a fireball in her hand.

"By the Emperor!" said the chief.

"Believe us now?"

"I'm not going to stand in your way."

"That is enough for my mission," said Talon.

"We're with you," said the third sailor with the rest of the engine room crew.

Talon looked at Cinnamon. *"They could be useful in swaying the other crew."*

"Follow us," said Cinnamon.

"**M**OM, I HAVE FOUND references that indicate the senior offi- cers of Emperor's Punisher are still alive and are being held in the detention center," said Athena.

"Hold the elevator, Athena," said Sarin. "What do you think?" she asked Ryder.

"I think it'll be easier to convince them then the enlisted, and having them at our side adds legitimacy to us when we take the ship."

"Agreed. Athena, take us to the detention level."

"Yes, Mom. I must warn you the detention level is a separate network that I can't access. You will be operating without me."

"I understand," said Sarin as she screwed her silencers into her pistols.

"I thought we were trying to take this as bloodless as possible?" said Ryder.

"Speed is going to be paramount. Getting to the prisoners before the Political Bureau can kill them is key. We'll try to go through as stealthy as possible, but if it becomes a race, start shooting—just try to injure the Marines."

"Mom," said Athena, "Scarlett and Kristi have made contact and have convinced part of the crew they are Children of the Emperor. They are moving forward to seize the ship."

"Interesting ploy, I didn't think of that."

"I thought Children of the Emperor were a myth," said Ryder.

"I don't know for sure, but it's how Galina explained our wings to Sheppard when we woke up the crew of Emperor's Wrath. Most citizens of the UEE believe Children of the Emperor are real."

The elevator stopped, and the door opened. The Angels hid their wings and stepped out. In front of them was the security control desk operated by Political Bureau soldiers. To the left and right passages led off to the detention areas.

"You are not authorized to be here," a soldier, with a heavy German accent, said while standing up from behind the desk. He wore a major's tab on his collar. "What is your name and rank?"

Sarin looked at Ryder and shrugged. "Deputy Commandant Sarin with General Starr, Major."

The major looked unfazed by the appearance of the two senior officers.

"This unauthorized intrusion will be reported to the Political Bureau, and you will be disciplined."

Sarin drew a pistol and fired into the major's forehead. "We're here to return this ship to its rightful owner." She shot the other two soldiers as they stood. Jumping over the desk, she looked at the screen. "Neptune's rings. They've sent out a silent alarm. You take the left and shoot everyone. Make sure they don't kill the prisoners."

Ryder didn't answer as she was already moving down the left passage. Sarin sprinted down the right passage where it intersected another passage. She turned the corner into a waiting guard with a rifle ready to fire. Behind him, another guard was tapping on a console. She fired at the guard at the console as the other guard fired a three-round burst into her chest.

As Sarin stumbled backward, she adjusted her aim and fired into the faceplate of the guard who had shot her. Two more three-round bursts hit her in the back. She threw herself to the ground and rolled, dodging bullets, then fired hitting a guard in the jaw. Sarin twisted on the floor as bullets struck her in the leg. The last guard moved toward her and shot her in the chest. Sarin ignored the damage and returned fire, killing the guard.

Sarin leveraged herself to her feet, ignoring the blood and pain coming from her wounds. She shuffled down to the console the guard had been using. It controlled the cells for this cellblock. They had set eight cells to terminate. She deactivated the termination sequence and unlocked the doors. Cell sixteen was marked ADMIRAL FIR-DAUS. Sarin shuffled down to the cell. She hit the button to open the door and leaned against the doorframe.

"Admiral Firdaus?" Sarin said to a dark-haired man with olive skin and golden eyes.

"Who—By the Emperor! What happened to you?"

Sarin slumped to the floor. "I'll be all right. I'm here to return your ship to you."

"You must lie down," he looked at her collar and nametape, "Deputy Commandant Sarin," he said with awe in his voice. He ripped the sheet from his bunk. "Where are you hit?"

"I...lost count. I think I'm going to sleep now."

"No, you can't. You must stay awake. Anyone out there?" Firdaus yelled into the hallway.

Ryder appeared in the doorway. "What's the—Jane, what the irons happened?" Ryder knelt next to Sarin.

"Are you with her?" said Firdaus.

"Yes. I'm General Ryder Starr of the Red Legion stationed in the Bitterfreeze system."

"I recognize the name, General. We must get her to medical."

"I don't know if that would help. We should just take the comman-dant to the morgue and leave her."

"Excuse me, General?"

"You believe in zombies, Admiral?"

"What does that have to do with anything?"

"The commandant will rise from the dead. Give her a few minutes to squeeze the bullets back out of her."

"What is going on?" Firdaus demanded.

Ryder raised an eyebrow. "The tactical picture is we're here to get your ship and crew back from the Political Bureau. The strategic picture is the commandant wants to free the Shadow Fleet and take it to Earth. The rest is a bit stranger," Ryder made her wings visible. "Do you believe in Children of the Emperor? You're in the presence of two."

"I...you're an Angel?"

"Yeah, but probably not in the context you're thinking. We serve the emperor, not some theology."

Sarin's eyes opened. "Oh, Neptune's rings, I forgot how much that hurts." She reached down and picked a bullet out of her skin.

"Do you need anything, Commandant?" said Firdaus.

Sarin saw that Ryder's wings were out and made hers visible. "I need you to rally your officers, grab the weapons, and get ready to head for the bridge. By that time, I should be fit to fight again. Ryder, why don't you go with him? I don't want any surprises."

"You got it." Ryder waved Firdaus to his feet and led him into the cellblock.

"Mom," said Athena.

"Yeah?"

"I have a report on Talli. She has taken the engine room and killed four Political Bureau soldiers in the process. She's barricaded inside and wants to know what to do?"

Sarin sighed and winced in pain. *At least she kept to killing the Political Bureau. "Tell her to stay there until I come to get her. No one but one of us is allowed in."*

THE ELEVATOR DOORS OPENED and Sarin, Ryder, Firdaus, and a handful of senior officers armed with the weapons taken from the guards in the detention center entered the bridge.

"Excuses will not be tolerated!" a man in a black uniform yelled from the command podium to one of the stations below him. "Get my ship back online! All of you! And find the source of this outage. For your sakes, it had better trace back to the depot, or I will have you all flogged."

Sarin stepped forward, the blood on her uniform not yet dry. "What is this? Are we aboard a nineteenth-century English man-of-war? We don't flog people for software issues. We don't flog people at all."

The man spun around. "Whoever you are, you're under arrest."

"I believe this is my authority." Sarin drew a pistol. "And the rank on my collar is my authorization. I am Deputy Commandant Sarin. In the name of the emperor, detain all Political Bureau personnel until further notice, and the command of this vessel is returned to Admiral Firdaus."

From the stations below, a Political Bureau soldier fired at Sarin, the bullet going through her wing and hitting the wall. From her left and right, a dozen guards sprang into action, initiating a violent firefight.

Most of the crew took cover as the soldiers exchanged fire with the sailors and Marines. Sarin targeted the left while Ryder took the right. The elevator opened, and a group of eight armed Shadow Fleet officers exited to help Sarin's group.

Sarin shot the remaining guard on her side and turned her attention to those firing from the workstation area. She fired as fast as she could acquire targets. When the last shot fired, the silence was deafening.

Sarin proceeded to the workstation area and found the Political Bureau colonel cowering against the bulkhead wall.

"Get up," she snarled as she grabbed him by the collar and throwing him back up to the command deck. Floating up and over the rail, she landed next to him and shoved him to the deck with her boot. "Don't move."

Sailors and Marines who'd taken cover were coming out, trying to figure out who was in charge. The officers that had come with Sarin were helping their fellow wounded officers.

"You," Sarin pointed to the woman wearing the most stripes she could see, "contact medical and tell them we need teams up here now."

"The glitches in the system—"

"Are gone except those holding Political Bureau personnel."

"Yes, Commandant."

"Admiral, what's the status?" said Sarin.

"Four dead, seven wounded, including me."

"Are you critical?"

"I won't be pushing the bullet back out, like you, but I can wait. Others need more urgent care."

"It's on the way." Sarin turned and looked at the crew. "The rest of you grab aid supplies and help those down. The rest of you move the bodies for collection."

"Mom," said Athena.

"Yes?"

"Scarlett reports they have taken command of Luna and are awaiting instructions."

"Excellent. Tell her to round up the Political Bureau personnel and get them ready to be moved to Emperor's Punisher. Security!"

"Yes, ma'am?"

"Get teams moving to round up all Political Bureau personnel. They're to be stripped and taken to the detention area. Ryder?"

"Yeah?"

"Take command here. I'm going to the engine room to relieve Talli."

S ARIN BANGED ON THE engine room's door. "Talli, it's me. Open up." She clicked her nail against her teeth as she waited. "Athena, can you see what's going on?"

"No, Mom. She's blocked out the camera."

"Great." Sarin shifted into her cloud form and drifted through the door. She gasped when she changed back. Talli knelt over a body with his abdomen cut open. Talli had his liver in her hand. Blood covered her white sneak suit.

"Talli put it down," Sarin said gently.

The man moaned.

Sarin sighed.

"Come on, Talli. It's time to go." Talli looked up with a nasty glare. "The mission's over. It's time to stop." Sarin stepped around Talli, pulled her pistol, and shot the man in the head.

"What did you do that for?" Talli screamed.

"Because I gave you a chance to play. Playtime is over. It's time to get cleaned up. I can't have you roaming the ship covered in blood. We're Children of the Emperor, and we have to act and look like it."

"Why can't I do what I want?"

"You can, but with limits. Kita has limits, and so do you. She understands there is a time for playing and a time to be civil. You must learn control, and you must talk to me. Let me help you. I know you loved Dev and she loved you. I'm sorry she's gone. If I could bring her back, I would." Sarin snapped her fingers and Talli was clean, and the body was made whole.

Talli huffed and glared at Sarin as she exited the room.

S ARIN STOOD AT THE head of the conference table aboard Emperor's Punisher. Around the table were a dozen senior Shadow Fleet and Legion personnel.

"This has been a good first step, but we're a long way from our goal of liberating the entire Shadow Fleet. The Shadow Fleet ships that went through the Alicorn Wormhole are still in quarantine. The rest of the fleet is spread throughout the systems trying to hold the populous at bay. But, to get to them, we have to go through the AC system. Taking AC Station will be our top priority, but we'll have to act fast. Earth will be aware when they lose this vital supply and economic hub."

"Planning an operation against AC Station will take months," said a Marine colonel.

"We have the time it takes to move between here and there. Surprise is our element."

"What about the Shadow Fleet ships guarding the system?" said Firdaus.

"The Angels will take care of them and bring them into our fleet. I need you to worry about capturing the station."

"The good news is there isn't a sizable military presence on AC Station, and we have two thousand Marines. We should outnumber the guards by a good margin."

"Excellent. I expect to be underway as soon as we refit both ships."

CHAPTER XXIII

S ARIN'S INSIDES FELT TWISTED after the wormhole jump. She'd never gotten used to the sensation. She sat aboard a shuttle, waiting for the jump to complete so they could fly over and capture the checkpoint.

"Wormhole checkpoint fifty-two miles at two-seven-three," a sailor announced over the shuttle's comm.

"Have you established contact?" Sarin replied.

"Connection coming online. Wait, out."

Sarin drummed her black and red nails on the console. "What's taking so long? Pilot, take off. I don't want to ruin the surprise. They can brief us in route."

"Yes, ma'am."

The engines vibrated through the shuttle as it lifted off and out of the Emperor's Punisher's hangar.

Firdaus' image appeared on the console screen. "Commandant?"

"Yes, Admiral?"

"I have a Political Bureau lieutenant calling from the checkpoint demanding to know what we're doing here. Apparently, we're not on any of his schedules. He's demanding to talk to my political officer."

"Only if he can commune with the dead. Tell him we've had engine problems and it was closer to go to AC Station than back to the Bitterfreeze supply depot. Have engineering falsify some maintenance reports and send them to him. That should keep him busy until we arrive."

"And the political officer?"

"Athena?"

"Yes, Mom, I can do it. I'm studying video of the previous political officer so I can get in character."

"Pilot, how far out are we?" asked Sarin.

"Seven minutes, ma'am."

"You won't have to act long, Athena."

"But I'm channeling my inner Galina."

Sarin smirked. "Just keep him busy long enough for us to dock."

"Yes, Mom."

Sarin closed the connection. "Ok, girls, show time. Don't kill anyone not in a Political Bureau uniform."

"Commandant," said the Pilot.

"Yes?"

"The checkpoint's hangar doors are closed."

Sarin leaned into the cockpit to look. She wiggled her nose, and the doors opened.

"How'd you do that?" gasped the pilot.

"I wished upon a star," Sarin said with a grin. "Take us in to land." Sarin ducked back into the cabin. The pitch of the engines came down as the shuttle landed. Only a gentle bump let them know they had arrived.

"Nice landing," said Ryder.

Sarin opened the shuttle door and hopped out. The hangar was empty. She searched the equation and pinpointed all the humans on board the checkpoint, two to her left, the rest to her right. She ignored the pair and moved toward the larger group. The other Angels followed her.

Sarin burst through a door into a control room. Six sailors sat at workstations, some trying to hide their amusement over the red-faced man at the main console shouting. Some of the sailors turned and looked at Sarin. Seeing her uniform, they stood at attention.

"Excuse me, Lieutenant?" Sarin said sweetly. When he didn't answer, Sarin walked into the room and stood behind him. She drew a pistol, pointed it at the back of his head, and fired. "I'll take it from here, Athena."

The Political Bureau soldier on the screen changed to Athena.

Sarin looked at the sailors in the room. "I'm Deputy Commandant Sarin. I'm in charge of the resistance to the Political Bureau. Currently, they are staging a coup against the emperor. We're moving into the AC system as the next step to retake the Empire. I need access to your systems, and I need to know where all the ships in the system are."

"Chief Petty Officer Robinson, ma'am. We'll pass over the codes to your ship. Emperor's Fury has left for AC Gamma, and Emperor's Might is in AC Delta. Both are putting down rebellions."

"That's all the combat ships in the system, right?"

"Yes, ma'am."

"That will simplify things. Any knowledge of AC Station?"

"No, ma'am. We haven't been let off the checkpoint for months."

"Can't have everything. We'll rotate you aboard Emperor's Punisher for some rest."

"Thank you, ma'am."

"This was boring," said Talli.

"Not everything we do can be entertaining," said Talon. "It's often a good thing when things are dull."

Talli rolled her eyes.

T HE HOLOTABLE DISPLAYED THE first wave of the assault on AC Station: Fighter spacecraft traveled on elliptical flight paths while covering the incoming shuttles filled with platoons of Marines.

AC Station was a major economic trade center. It sat in the center of a major wormhole nexus, connecting the Sol system with all of the AC subsystems, the Bitterfreeze system, and everything beyond it. It reminded Sarin a bit of Base Station. Over fifty thousand people called the station home, and many had never seen a planet.

The first of the shuttles docked. The plan called for a coordinated assault around the station hitting the commercial, private, and military docks, and passenger terminals to paralyze the small garrison. Sarin didn't expect this to be a hard fight. Five hundred legionnaires patrolled the station and only a hundred Political Bureau soldiers augmented them. Athena was hacking into AC Station's central broadcasting system so Sarin could send a message to the legionnaires. Once the legionnaires struck their colors, mopping up the Political Bureau would be simple.

The Angels had been distributed among the first wave to optimize their strengths to the most crucial and susceptible weak points of the AC defense.

"Jane."

"Yes, Ryder? How do things look?"

"My platoon has wandered into a helluva firefight. I estimate the enemy to be at company strength, they've dug in around the commercial docks and more are moving up to reinforce."

"As soon as Athena's ready I'll broadcast the message and see if I can pull those Legionnaires off you."

"If these are legionnaires, they're not wearing blue."

"It could be like Bitterfreeze, the legionnaires were press-ganged into the Political Bureau," said Sarin. "Can you hold?"

"Shouldn't be a problem. These legionnaires can't shoot worth a damn."

"Jane, Scarlett."

"Red, what do you have to report?"

"We're struggling to grab a toe-hold. This isn't light resistance. I lost a third of our assault group just getting off the shuttle."

"Damn. How many?"

"Maybe two hundred and fifty dug in."

"What's the chance of them meeting both our groups enforce?" said Ryder.

"We knew there was a chance they'd be prepared. They didn't challenge us when we arrived in space," said Sarin.

"Or they're just paranoid and dug-in knowing somebody would come along at some point."

"That's not helping us—dammit. Kristi's been hit," said Talon.

"Athena, how long?" said Sarin.

"This is not a video game with a timer telling me how much time I have left," said Athena. "Offering you a guess would not help you and only add to my own stress."

"I've never known her to be snarky," said Talon.

"Even machines can get stressed," said Sarin. "I'll come over and give you a hand. How's Kristi doing?"

"Took one in the gut. Painful and a lot of blood, but not lethal," said Talon.

Sarin appeared next to Talon. Bullets struck the crate providing them with cover.

"You weren't kidding," said Sarin.

"Am I the kind to exaggerate?"

"Just saying, someone on that side knows what they're doing."

"To a point," said Ryder. *"I've been watching them. Their fire discipline is basic. They have yet to try and maneuver against us. They're not taking aimed shots, just praying-and-spraying. I'd say these troops are green."*

"That doesn't make any sense. Legionnaires are better trained than that. Who are these guys and where'd they come from?" said Sarin. *"And where did the legionnaires go?"*

"A bullet is still a bullet," said Talon.

"True that." Sarin spun from behind cover hitting targets as they presented themselves. She returned to cover as more bullets struck the crate. "There's six less."

Cinnamon dove behind the crate, leaving a long bloody streak on the floor.

"Cupcake! That's more than a gut shot," said Talon as she bent down and put her hands on two bullet wounds.

"I didn't want to worry you," said Cinnamon.

"Now I have to save you. Lay back."

The rounds hitting the crate increased. A round found its way through. Sarin stepped from behind the crate, firing as she went to another crate.

"Sarin, Talli. How are you holding up?"

"My platoon took some hits, but we're ok now."

"How many enemies are you facing?"

"None."

"None?"

"I killed them all."

"How many?"

"Over a hundred."

The girl becomes more like Kita every day. *"Good. The platoons will move out and start securing checkpoints echo and foxtrot once the follow-on force arrives. Go with them, but be careful. Kristi's wounded."*

"That sucks for her. But I'm going to go now."

"Talli, stay with your platoon!" said Sarin.

"I don't need them, and I don't have to do what you say. I'm going to go kill more bad guys."

Just like Kita. *"Just don't do anything rash. If you get into trouble, call me."*

"I'll be fine."

Yeah, until you're not. I need more time with Talli. She's not Kita and not supposed to be a sociopath...unless she is...then what? Either way, she can't be as bad as Kita.

"Commandant, Command."

"Go ahead."

"The second wave is loaded and on the way."

"Have all the landing sites checked in?"

"Affirmative, all have taken casualties, including four platoon leaders, but no platoons were repelled. The company commanders believe they can break out with the arrival of the second wave."

"Did everyone meet as heavy resistance as General Starr and Talon?"

"It varied, but the average was company strength. The platoon leader with the Angel Talli estimated they met a company."

"Tell Talli's platoon leader she's going off on her own. He's to do his best to keep up with her, without sacrificing his Marines. I want his comm frequency, and he's to alert me if something happens to her."

"Yes, Commandant."

"Good, keep me updated."

"Mom, I'm into the station's private, commercial, and military broadcast network," said Athena. "I can broadcast your message when you are ready."

Sarin touched Talon's shoulder. "I'm going back to Punisher to broadcast our appeal. I can take Kristi back with me."

"I can heal the damage. It'll just take time," said Talon.

"I know you can, but if you're busy healing her, you can't fight."

"I want to stay," said Cinnamon.

"It's better if you go back, cupcake," said Talon. "I haven't even started working on the bullet in your liver."

"I can fight."

"We know you can," said Sarin. "There's no need to prove tough-ness. What matters is getting you healed."

"But you didn't give up aboard the Emperor's Punisher when you were freeing the officers," said Cinnamon.

"I didn't have a choice, and I know you would have done the same. Right now, we have a choice. Go back, get patched up, and fight again another day."

Cinnamon's shoulders slumped in defeat.

"No one thinks less of you, Kristi," said Talon. "We've all been injured and taken out of a fight. Please, go back and get treated. For my sake. Knowing you're taken care of is a weight off my heart."

"Ok."

Sarin touched Cinnamon's arm, and they appeared on the bridge of Emperor's Punisher.

"Medical, I need a team up here for some gunshot wounds," said Sarin.

"How is the battle?" said Firdaus.

"They're set up like they were expecting this."

"Could someone have leaked our plans?"

"Maybe, but right now I'm going on the assumption they were expecting this when we refused to answer why we were in the system." Sarin turned to Athena. "I'm ready whenever you are." She pulled out a compact and checked herself.

"I'm ready, Mom."

Sarin put the compact away and straightened up formally. Athena gave her the ready signal.

"Legionnaires, Marines, sailors, and soldiers of the Political Bureau, I am Deputy Commandant Sarin and am in command of the emperor's forces in the Bitterfreeze nexus. We have uncovered a plot against the emperor by senior Political Bureau members. They wish to overthrow the emperor and seize control of the UEE. They want to destroy our way of life and enslave us.

"All orders originating from Political Bureau Headquarters and senior Political Bureau members are deemed illegal. All Political Bureau officers are to be taken into custody, and all soldiers are to turn in their arms and taken into quarantine by Shadow Fleet and Legion personnel. Anyone who does not comply will be deemed a traitor and dealt with accordingly."

TALON PEEKED AROUND A crate after Sarin's message played. The firing had stopped as the message repeated. A pair of Political Bureau soldiers jumped up from their positions, threw down their rifles, and raised their hands. A few more followed.

"Soldier, pick up your weapon. The rest of you, open fire." A Political Bureau officer from the rear of their positions yelled.

Shots came from a dozen positions, but the rest of the company remained silent. The firing increased as those firing yelled at the others to fire.

"Marines, hold your fire," yelled Talon. "Political Bureau soldiers lay down your weapons and move forward through the Marines positions. The Marines won't harm you."

A few of the soldiers complied.

"Get back to your positions. I order you," yelled the Political Bureau officer. Some of the soldiers wavered, a few continued to walk forward. "Shoot them!" The Political Bureau officer raised his pistol and fired into the back of an unarmed soldier. The soldiers who'd fired before turned their weapons on their comrades and fired. Some of the uninjured soldiers crawled toward the Marines.

Talon leaped on top of the crate she was using for cover and sprinted across the top of a row of crates lined up across the dock. She drew a quartet of throwing knives from under her cloak. She threw a trio into some soldiers firing on their comrades, the last blade she threw into the firing hand of the Political Bureau officer. She leaped off the last crate, landing and rolling as bullets hit around her. She drew her pistol, rolled into a cartwheel while shooting four more soldiers firing at her. Talon spun, twisted, and jumped into a sideways layout shooting three more soldiers. She landed and rolled, drawing two knives and throwing them into a pair of soldiers' faces. Sliding to a stop next to the Political Bureau officer, she plunged her hand into his mouth and tore out a kill tooth.

"Jane," said Talon.

"Yeah?"

"I don't think the bulk of these troops are indoctrinated Political Bureau types. The company we were facing tried to lay down arms and crossover, but a handful gunned them down. I have the officer who gave the command."

"I knew Galina wasn't afraid to be barbaric, but damn, that's low even for her. The second wave should be there any minute."

"I think we should use shocker rounds."

"That's not a bad idea. We're getting reports of other areas doing the same thing. I'll have the rounds sent over with the third wave."

~

S ARIN AND TALON STOOD over the captured Political Bureau officer in a quiet corner while the Marines gathered up the Political Bureau soldiers and solidified their positions.

"So, Captain Bremer, when did shooting your own soldiers become a proper way to motivate anyone?" said Sarin.

"I will not talk to you, imposter," said Bremer.

"Oh, you'll talk, don't worry. I'm just giving you a chance to talk with dignity, instead of a giggling, drooling fool."

To punctuate Sarin's words Talon jabbed Bremer with her barb, injecting him with a truth serum.

"What's your full name?" Sarin asked once the serum had taken effect.

"Josef Bremer."

"And your rank?"

"Captain in the Political Bureau."

"Who gave you orders to shoot your own men if they refused to fight?"

"The rabble aren't real Political Bureau soldiers, just kids drafted off the street. Only the lash gets anything out of them. Command recognized this and authorized any means necessary to get them to perform to standard."

"What are you protecting here on AC Station? It's just a commercial hub, not military."

Bremer giggled. "That's what you think. Half of the Shadow Fleet brass is being held here."

"Why?"

"No idea. The traitors should be shot. Some already have."

Sarin spoke to Talon. *"Half the Shadow Fleet leadership is here? What does he mean by that?"*

"I don't know, but we need to find out. This could be the break we've needed."

Sarin nodded.

"Ok, Captain Bremer, you've been most helpful. Talon will give you the antidote and turn you back over to the Marines."

A FTER THE THIRD WAVE of reinforcements arrived, the Marines went on the offensive. Armed with shocker rounds, they mopped up what was left of the initial resistance and started to move deeper into the station.

"Jane?"

"Yes, Talli? Are you ok?"

"I'm fine. I'm in a weird hotel, and the Political Bureau guys are all jacked up, running around. They just pulled a guy out of his room and shot him."

"Where's this hotel?"

"Deck thirty-five, section A. It's called the Stellar."

"Give me a second."

"Ok."

"Scarlett, Talli might have found our missing Shadow Fleet officers. They're being kept in a hotel on deck thirty-five."

"That's not far from here."

"I'll tell her we're coming." Sarin changed back over to Talli. *"We're going to come to you. Until then, you're to keep the guests alive by any means necessary."*

"You mean it?"

"Just don't hurt the guests."

"Ok, you've got it."

Y ELLS FOLLOWED THE THUMPS of two grenade launchers and shattering of glass as the Marines stormed the Stellar Hotel. Sarin and Talon went in after the first wave. They found the Political Bureau soldiers in a state of confusion. Most were oriented toward the threat coming from the top floor. The shocker rounds allowed the Marines to shoot first and sort out the good from the bad later.

The hotel was constructed from a series of stacked rings with doors every twenty feet, and six elevators stationed evenly around the structure. In the center was a large pool with a three-story fountain. Meant to inspire glamour, wealth, and prestige, Sarin found the decor to be tacky, fake, and gaudy.

"Talli, Sarin. I need you to stop what you're doing and join us in the lobby."

Almost as if a response to her command, a pair of soldiers splashed down in the large shallow pool. Blood leaked from their bodies and found its way into the fountain. Sarin sighed.

"Talli, please come down," said Talon. *"You've had your fun."*

"I'm not coming down until they're all dead."

Sarin exchanged looks with Talon and rolled her eyes.

"Talli," said Talon, *"the Marines are on their way. You've killed as many as you're going to be able. It's time to turn it over to them. The rest are prisoners."*

"That's more than they deserve."

"I know, sweetheart, but most of these are just kids, drafted off the streets to fight. They're not the same people who killed your mom."

All the senior Angels received was silence. Talon took off. Following the path, the bodies had taken. Sarin trailed her, pistols at the ready.

The upper story of the hotel was a bloody mess. Body parts littered the ground. Blood coated the walls.

"I don't think there's a whole body up here," said Talon.

"I'll begin to worry when I find them stacked and posed," said Sarin.

They entered an open door and followed the sounds of muffled tears. A pair of bloody swords sat on the bed. Talli sat wedged between the bed and the wall. Talon knelt before her.

"Talli, I'm sorry. I wish I could bring Dev back. I know she loved you."

"It's not fair. What did I do?"

"Nothing, sweetheart. It's not your fault. You are a victim of Galina's petty revenge scheme because Kita refused to give her more than she was able. You have the right to be upset, but you can't let it consume you."

Talli wiped at her tears. "You keep saying that...but it's all I have of her."

Talon pulled Talli's hood off and stroked her hair. "That's not true. You have memories of her. I haven't forgotten my promise that when we find Kita, we'll get you a picture of her."

"But when? We're never going to find her—"

"I may be able to help you with that, Child of the Emperor," said a voice.

The three Angels turned to find a middle-aged man with sandy blond hair graying at the temples wearing an orange jumpsuit.

Sarin's ears pricked up. *Who's he been talking to?* "And who are you?"

"I am Vice Admiral Gene Hackett. I am the commander of the rescue fleet that was sent for Princess Bush after Admiral Sheppard remained with the Princess."

"And you know Kita how?"

"I never met her, but both Admiral Sheppard and Princess Bush talked highly of her."

"There is no way Kita would have left Sheppard alive."

"On the contrary, the admiral was elevated to the status of Child of the Emperor."

"You mean she got wings?"

"Yes. The princess had a pair as well. She said every Angel was a Child of the Emperor, and the Shadow Fleet was to treat them as we would her."

"Does that mean you're to protect us?"

"You will know her will better than I would. We are at your command."

Kita, I will do more than kiss you when I see you. "I...haven't seen the princess in a long time. What happened?"

"The rescue fleet left through the Alicorn wormhole and jumped into a region of space known as the Tetrahedron. We located the princess on UEE Gjord Dallas, and alien warships were pursuing it. We attacked and their forces engaged. During the attack, an enemy assault ship jumped within a mile of UEE Enterprise and boarded her, led by the princess and Child of the Emperor Kita. They captured the ship, and the princess halted the attack. It seems there was a misunderstanding, the princess was never in danger, and her handler had activated the rescue beacon. He was a Political Bureau agent in league with the conspirators trying to bring her home to capture her.

"Admiral Sheppard was elevated and was made the princess' personal bodyguard. They kept the Enterprise with them as an escort for the princess. The rest of the fleet returned home. When we arrived without the princess, the Political Bureau under the order of the emperor seized the fleet. They shipped the top officers in the fleet here. My guess is we're to be tried for treason."

"If I got you back to the fleet, could you retake command?" said Sarin.

"With you at my back, all you have to do is say the word," said Hackett.

Kita, I don't know how you do it, but thank you. "We'll get you to your fleet and show Galina her days are numbered."

S ARIN STOOD IN FRONT of a holographic display of the Sol system with Hackett. The Earth and the other planets were away from her, the wormhole nexus nearest the solar system hovered in front of her. There were several stations in the quadrant. A highlighted Political Bureau station, Black Station Five, was their target.

"When we were taken, the fleet that went through the Alicorn wormhole was on station to repel any alien incursions. In case they decided to follow us," said Hackett.

"Why would they do that?" said Sarin.

"It was a precaution, not so much we expected them. The aliens didn't seem interested beyond kicking us out of their space when we met with them."

"The fleet is still closer to Black Station Five than we will be once we enter the system. And we don't have the warships to slug it out with them."

"I have discovered something that might be useful, Mom," said Athena.

"What?"

"I've been studying the cargo manifests for the freighters in port. The UEE Northern Light's next stop is Black Station Five."

"That's fine, but we can't sneak a thousand Marines aboard."

"We don't take the Marines, just the ship captains. Once in Sol space, we fake an engine malfunction that takes us out toward Alicorn wormhole. Once we're close, we ask for assistance from the fleet. When they come to help, we commandeer their shuttles and use them to get close to the UEE Fort Ticonderoga. Then we take the ship from the inside."

"And what is the probability of success?" said Ryder.

"About three percent. But, it's a much higher rate of success than anything else I've thought of."

"And what else have you thought of?"

"About a thousand different ways to die."

"We'll have to pretend for almost a week that we're trying to repair the engine," said Sarin.

"Yes," said Athena. "I believe we can bluff that we think we can fix it on our own. Once we get close to the fleet, we can change our course of action and ask for help."

"Who says the fleet is going to help us?" said Ryder.

"As a licensed cargo ship for the Political Bureau, we carry valuable cargo for the Empire. We will be in the fleet's system and can request aid. Unlike a regular ship, which would need to wait for Legion assistance."

"We're going to need the God of Luck for this one," Ryder announced.

Sarin sighed. "She's not working this equation. We'll have to make our own luck."

"You think this plan is doable?"

"The hardest part will be the end, but we'll still have to bluff our way through the wormhole checkpoint on the Sol side. I've done crazier, but we had more Angels then."

"And half our force is gone."

Sarin nodded. Talon and Talli were on their way to take the wormhole checkpoint leading to the Sol system.

"First things first. Let's get a look at this ship. Let's make sure it's usable before we plan anything else."

CHAPTER XXIV

T O SARIN, THE POLITICAL Bureau soldiers that entered through the airlock were goons. They wore assault armor and a full combat load with rifles, even their commanding officer. *It's a little strange that they're expecting trouble at a wormhole checkpoint station.*

She stood with the other Angels, disguised as crewmembers for the freighter. Her hair was braided and in a tight bun at the base of her skull. A week's worth of grime covered her face, hands, and overalls. So far, the mission to sneak Hackett and his officers to the Shadow Fleet had gone smoothly.

"All right you civilian scum, line up," the officer ordered. "Sergeant Channahon, take a team and search the ship."

"Yes, sir."

The sergeant pointed to three men, and they pushed their way past the Angels.

"You don't want a guide?" said Talon.

"Shut up, bitch," said a soldier as he slammed the butt of his rifle into Talon's gut. She doubled over and fell to the deck.

"You will only speak when spoken to," said the officer. He produced a small panel from his belt. "You will press your thumb to the panel to confirm your identity."

"Athena," said Sarin, *"please tell me you can spoof them."*

"I've been attacking the station since we arrived. I'm in a position to intercept and pass them false identities."

Talon stood up slowly and leaned on Cinnamon.

The officer presented the pad to Sarin first. Without hesitation, she pressed her thumb to the screen. The wait icon appeared. Sarin kept her face neutral, giving the system and Athena time to work. The screen lit green.

The officer went down the line of Angels collecting thumbprints. "Everyone's identity is confirmed," he said after Talli finished. "Show me your manifest."

Ryder pulled a panel from her belt. She pulled up the manifest list and showed it to the officer.

The officer took it and studied it. "Captain Henson, you will accompany me as I inventory your cargo."

Sarin stiffened. "Yes—"

Clinks sounded across the deck followed by hissing sounds. The air filled with green smoke. Sarin felt her lungs burn as her limbs went weak. Coughing, she collapsed to the deck, and the world went black.

S ARIN WOKE WITH THE room spinning. *What happened and where am I?* She was on the floor, and the ceiling above her was white. *What did they do? Where are the others?*

Sarin rolled onto her side, which made the spinning change axes. The walls were white and seamless. There was nothing else in the room.

What went wrong? It was all going according to plan.

She coughed, spitting up some green gunk. Whatever the Political Bureau used had been effective. The Political Bureau soldiers didn't wear respirators. *This stuff was meant for Angels. But how?* Angel physiology was close to humans except at the subcellular level and below. *Who would know Angels well enough to develop such a weapon?*

Sarin hoped the other Angels weren't harmed. *How long have I been out?*

The walls of her cell blinked and an image of Galina, in a formal Political Bureau uniform, sat behind a large wooden desk. Galina steepled her fingers. They were white like her face.

"Jane," she cooed. "You've been a busy girl. I hope you've enjoyed your time on the frontier. I've missed you. You were always one of my favorite lovers."

"Galina...we went together like oil and water," said Sarin as she stood.

"You enjoyed it."

"Then, but not now. I'm not into sexbots."

Galina chuckled. "Evolution, Jane. We all must evolve. Kita called Angels the apex of human evolution, but she was wrong. I'm stronger, faster than I ever was as an Angel. You and your kind are just a failed experiment."

"I think Kita has been far more successful than you'll ever be. She created a new species. You're just strapping on spare parts."

"The first generation is already being deployed. Soon, I will have an army just like me."

Sarin hissed through her teeth. "Earth won't stand for this. Once the people learn what you're doing, they won't allow you to replace the emperor."

"I already have. After the Emperor died, and with the princess killed by Kita and aliens, it was easy to find a puppet to sit on the throne."

"You think that story will survive when Kita arrives?"

Galina smiled. "The masses are already fooled. They've seen the footage of Enterprise being destroyed with all hands-on deck."

"Is that why you keep the Shadow Fleet quarantined? Because they know the truth?"

"The truth is what I say it is."

"Kita will destroy you, and I will help her."

Galina laughed. "Just like you to give in when the going gets tough. Your other Angels will learn soon enough who Sarin really is—just an alcoholic, drug addict, sexual deviant who can't stand to look at herself in the mirror. Imagine Kita's response when she finds you that way...again."

"You're wrong. I'm not like that anymore. Where are the other Angels?"

"Finding ways to be useful. Scarlett and your new Angels offered their services for science to atone for their betrayal. Talli is returning to me for a *mother-daughter* reunion. My techs are decoding Athena. See what your leadership has brought, Jane?"

"I'll rescue them if it's the last thing I do."

"Listen to you, sounding like such the hero. Better to leave such chest thumping to Kita. And, you're not going anywhere. That gas you sucked down contained a nanite that when activated can render Angels immobile."

Sarin shook her head. "There is no way you could develop such a thing. You don't know Angels well enough."

"But I have someone who does. Megan has been more than happy to develop a nice anti-Angel arsenal for me."

"She would never—"

"Oh, but she would. She's never forgiven Kita for what she did to the Arconians. Between her and Lina, I've brought the Empire a bounty of riches."

"Lina...What have you done to Lina?" Sarin gasped.

"She is still a mystery, but in good hands. We'll understand her power soon enough."

"Maybe something you're not meant to know. Secrets best left to Kita."

"Never. Kita was an arrogant, wicked, backstabbing bitch who used others and got lucky. Anything she can do I can do better. I've proven it. I beat her back on that planet, and if she shows up here, I'll beat her again."

"Touchy. Then you must really be upset over Rene picking Kita over you."

"Rene is dead. She died a hero trying to stop Kita."

"That's not what I heard. Sheppard begged to die, and Kita wouldn't kill her. Instead, she was made an Angel *again* and is serving Kita loyally."

"RENE IS DEAD!" Galina screamed as she slammed her fist on the desk.

"The lies we tell ourselves, so we don't have to see the truth. Here are two truths for you, Kita is coming for you, and if you harm Lina, I will kill you myself."

Galina laughed direly. "You are going to be nothing more than a drooling mess on the floor. And Kita, I will enjoy killing and stripping her secrets from her."

"You won't touch her."

"You still think you love her? She never loved you. You were just a toy...just like the rest of them. You meant nothing to her, just a way to fill her carnal pleasures."

Sarin glared at the image in front of her. "Then if that's all I was to her, then what were you? She refused to touch you, to give you what you wanted...What do you suppose you were to her if you weren't even worth her time? You whored yourself to her, and she slapped you down while you begged for more. You call me an addict, but you're addicted. You can't get enough of Kita, and she hates you."

"She *loves* me!" Galina screamed. She reached into her desk and pulled out a panel. "Those nanites do more than just immobilize." She touched the panel, and Sarin shrieked. "I'll kill you, and Kita will have no one but me."

Sarin balled her fists and her body tensed against the pain that radiated from her blood. "What about Snowy...Roo...Vee...Amber...Raptor...Tiffany...Emma...She loved them all and never rejected any of them..."

Galina snarled and tapped on the pad, sliding her finger from the bottom to the top. Sarin convulsed and fell to her knees. Tears filled her eyes as the pain coursed through her body. Her breathes came in short gasps, as she couldn't catch her breath due to the muscle spasms in her chest.

"...She only rejected you..."

Galina slammed the panel on the desk and struck it with her fist. Sarin convulsed, and she collapsed to the floor. Rolling over, she looked at the ceiling for a moment and then closed her eyes feeling no pain. *So, this is what it's like to die. I expected more, but Kita was right, it's just blackness. She's always right.*

S ARIN'S EYES FLUTTERED OPEN and saw the same white ceiling. She floated from the floor to her feet. She closed her eyes for a brief moment and changed from her angelic form to her god form.

"It's not possible!" Galina screamed her voice cracking.

"Do you think Kita would just leave me with nothing?" Sarin said her voice pleasant and regal. "Or was surprised by your betrayal? You're not as clever as you think. She saw it coming. Though she could do nothing to stop it, she did prepare for it. I am Edi'rp, the God of Pride. You've succumbed to the sin of pride for a long time. It is my job to prepare for Li've's arrival. Revenge is hers to take, but the line, I'm sure, is long."

Galina sat, her mouth hanging open.

Sarin changed back to her angelic form, now wearing her black and red schoolgirl outfit with her pistols strapped to her legs. Behind her, the door opened.

"The cavalry has arrived," Sarin cooed.

A Marine and a sailor, both armed with rifles, entered. Sarin turned to face them. Galina's image vanished.

"Who are you?" said Sarin.

"Gunnery Sergeant Rodriguez and Chief Davis, Child of the Emperor," said Rodriguez. "We're here to rescue you."

"Thank you," said Sarin, giving them a dazzling smile. "Can you bring me up to speed on what's going on?"

"Four hours ago, you and three other Angels were brought aboard by the Political Bureau thugs. We've been working out since then how best to rescue you."

"But why?" said Sarin.

Rodriguez and Davis exchanged glances. "Standing orders by the princess. All Angels are to be helped if they need it," said Davis. "And the four of you looked like you need help. The enlisted haven't liked what the Political Bureau has been doing or how they've been treating us. They took away our officers and replaced them with their own. They've been keeping us in quarantine for fear we might bring home some alien disease since we got back, but they've kept us in an information vacuum. We have no idea what's happening on Earth."

"Sorry," said Sarin. "The Political Bureau has tried to remove the Legion from their positions and has subjugated the Shadow Fleet for their use. We've been out on the frontier for the last two years fighting them, and we haven't spoken to the princess in a long time." The explanation seemed to satisfy the pair. "Out of curiosity, how'd you know we were in trouble if the Political Bureau had us?"

"You were heavily restrained and unconscious. That is no way to treat Children of the Emperor," said Rodriguez. "A while later they snuck in a bunch of the fleets' former captains through a maintenance airlock. We guessed you'd come to reinstate the captains. It looks like the Political Bureau didn't like it."

"The Political Bureau has been up to some real shady dealings lately around the fleet," added Davis.

"You're not wrong, but you took a big risk," said Sarin. "We did come to return the captains to their posts. Command General Lyakhova led a coup to take over when the emperor died. They've put a puppet emperor on the throne and have told the outside world the princess was killed by the aliens when you were sent to save her."

"But that's not true," said Davis. "She and Admiral Sheppard stayed aboard Enterprise in alien space to secure a treaty with them."

"The Angels don't believe she's dead, and we oppose General Lyakhova. We want to set things right, and that starts by freeing the Shadow Fleet and letting it do its job, protecting the Imperium."

"Anything you say will supersede the Political Bureau's orders in the minds of the crew," said Rodriguez.

"That's what I'm hoping," said Sarin. "We need to rescue the other Angels and the captains. There should have been four Angels with me, and did they take something to a lab?"

"There were only Angels with brownish orange and cream-colored wings, cinnamon-colored wings, and wings the color of a sunset."

"Damn."

"I'll check with our contacts to see if the Political Bureau took anything to their area," said Davis. He tapped on his Arcom. "Grayson says the Blackshirts' lab has been buzzing about something."

"I just got word from Frazer," said Rodriguez. "They sprung the other Angels from the Political Bureau. They had them in surgery for some reason."

"I can guess why," said Sarin. "Ok, we need to hurry. They gave us some nanites that can kill us. I've got to get to them before they have a chance to activate them."

"Frazer said they're moving toward the maintenance hangars. Doesn't sound like the Political Bureau is organized."

"Yet," said Sarin. "They will be. What ship are we aboard?"

"Ticonderoga," said Davis.

"Good. Let's go."

CHAPTER XXV

THE SOUND OF GUNFIRE erupted from the door to the maintenance hangar as Davis opened it. A platoon of Political Bureau soldiers in heavy armor were firing on a fighter in the corner. Sarin drew her pistols and fired on the soldiers. She hit six in the head, her large caliber blasting through their face shields. Nearby soldiers turned toward the new threat. Sarin grabbed Rodriguez and Davis, phased them behind the fighter.

Six Marines with pistols and rifles were hunkered down taking cover. Talon and Ryder lay on the ground wrapped in sheets. Talon's hands were wrapped in bloody bandages. Big bloody spots covered Ryder's sheet. Cinnamon was naked covered in different types of burns.

"What happened?" said Sarin.

"They cut off Scarlett's talons," said Cinnamon.

Sarin covered her mouth to hide her shock. "Neptune's rings, red, I'm sorry."

"I'll be fine," said Talon, her voice shaky and shallow.

"What happened to you?" Sarin said to Cinnamon.

"They decided to experiment and see how much heat I could take and what else burned me."

"I'll strangle Galina with my bare hands."

"Save some for me."

"Is Ryder awake?"

"No, she's out."

"Child, this is Gunnery Sergeant Frazer and his squad of mechanics," said Davis. "I don't suppose you can teleport us out of here?"

"I'm not going anywhere," said Sarin. "It's time we go on the offensive and let these goons know who's in charge."

"I know every Marine is a rifleman, but we're just clerks and mechanics."

"You don't worry about that," said Sarin. "Just cover us."

"They can't fight in their condition," said Frazer.

"We're bad girls, Marine, fighting is what we do."

"We live fast," said Cinnamon.

"And die hard," said Talon.

Sarin touched the three Angels, and they blinked out of existence. They reappeared healed and clothed.

"Hot damn," said Cinnamon. She backflipped in the air and burst into flame. A few bullets hit the ceiling above her. She lobbed a pair of fireballs in response.

"By the Emperor!" said one of the Marines.

Cinnamon gave him a flirty wink.

"You're in for a show, Marines," said Ryder. She burst into flame, burning her skin and feathers away, leaving a burning skeletal demon Angel cowboy.

"Mother of God," whispered Davis.

Ryder laughed, stepped from behind the fighter, drew her revolvers, twirled them, and fired until her cylinders were empty.

Talon opened her cloak and pulled out her short sword and her pistol. She hopped over the fighter and hooted as The Rider reloaded. The sonic assault stunned the soldiers. She jumped into the air and glided into the middle of the soldiers' line, capturing two soldiers around the neck with the talons on her feet.

Cinnamon followed, throwing fireballs at the stunned soldiers. She landed in front of a group and blasted them with a lance of flame.

When Sarin stood, Davis grabbed her arm. "I think this message is for you." He held up his Arcom. A message read, "Show this to Sarin."

"Athena?"

"Hello, Mom."

"Where are you? Are you alright?"

"I'm fine. I'm in the Political Bureau workshop. They're trying to access my main kernel, but all they've done is allowed me access to the ship. I'm sorry, Mom."

"Sorry for what?" said Sarin.

"For not detecting the shadow network the Political Bureau was using when they captured us. I...forgot to look."

"It happens. We're all ok."

"Yes, I've started to broadcast you and the fight to the rest of the fleet in hopes of stirring unrest."

"Good idea. We need to get to the captains and have them put out a message saying the Political Bureau is illegitimate."

"I'm searching for them now."

"Let me know when you find them."

"Yes, Mom."

Sarin let Davis have his arm back. "Is that the other Angel you were looking for?"

Sarin shook her head. "No. The girl I'm looking for has seafoam-green colored wings—"

"We saw her. They loaded her aboard a shuttle that took her aboard Venus. Rumor has it she's going to Earth."

"I have confirmed this, Mom," said Athena.

Davis' eyebrows closed in confusion.

"That was Athena. She's an AI Angel. You'll understand when you meet her. Now, cover the entrances. We'll clear out this goon squad."

Sarin rolled out from cover but found she had nothing to do. The other Angels had wiped out the platoon. She walked over where the Angels were examining one of the soldiers. Along the way, she put a bullet in the heads of a few soldiers who were taking their time to die.

"What do you have?"

"These guys have augmentations. In this case, they've replaced his arms," said Talon.

Sarin looked at the mess of synthetic material, some of it melted together. "Nowhere near as good as my step-daughter Arial, but I guess they have to start somewhere."

They checked the other bodies but found no other augmentations.

"Do you suppose he's just the first?" said Cinnamon.

"Probably," said Sarin. "Galina bragged about having an army and had a set of new arms herself."

"I didn't think her vanity would allow that," said Talon.

"I think whatever Kita did to her face has given her a new sense of beauty."

Davis jogged over to the Angels. "Your other Angel is back..."

"Yes, Athena?" said Sarin.

"I've found the captains in the forward airlock area. It looks like they're about to be executed."

"Don't let that happen."

"I'll do my best to make sure the airlock malfunctions, but I can't stop a bullet."

"We're on our way." Sarin looked at Davis, "Do you know how to get there?"

"Yeah, I even know a shortcut."

"**M**OM, YOU MUST HURRY," said Athena.

"We're running as fast as we can. Wings and airtight doors don't mix."

"Are you saying you're more a peacock than a goshawk?"

"Ha-ha, very funny."

The door swung open with a bang into the airlock area. Admiral Hackett stood against a wall facing a firing squad. Sarin drew her pistols and fired, sending a bullet through the line of eight heads of the soldiers on the firing line. Behind her, Talon dove through the door, rolled to her knees under Sarin's arms and threw two knives into the throats of a pair of guards watching a group of eight more captains. Cinnamon and Ryder stepped up behind Sarin and killed the four guards watching from the corners.

"Admiral Hackett, are you all right?" said Sarin as she rushed up to him. She snapped the plastic tie holding his hands behind his back.

"Angel Sarin is that you?" Hackett said slipping the blindfold off his head.

"It looks like we're just in time. We need to get a message out to the fleet stating that you're back in charge, that all orders from the Political Bureau are illegal, and they're to be detained."

"Yes, we can't let the fleet descend into anarchy. My uniform is in the detention area. I—" Sarin snapped her fingers and he and the other captains were dressed in their parade uniforms. "How?"

"Secret," said Sarin. "If I get the princess' permission, I'll tell you. Athena, are you ready?"

"And waiting. The camera is to your left, above the airlock door," she said over the ship's PA system.

"Another Angel?" said Hackett.

"Yes, a very special one." Sarin guided him where to stand and moved the rest of the captains to stand behind him. "Whenever you're ready."

Hackett took a breath and stood at attention. A screen on the wall across from him showed the video feed.

"Sailors, Marines, and legionnaires of Shadow Fleet task force one-six-eight, we now have official orders from the princess, delivered by her very own personal guard, the Angels. They have brought word and evidence of treachery on Earth. Our glorious Emperor has died, and instead of power passing to Princess Bush, a usurper from the Political Bureau has seized power. As of this moment, myself and the other captains of the Shadow Fleet are reinstated by order of the princess. The Political Bureau is to cease all operations, lay down all arms, open all areas, and stand down. If you do not comply, we will use force.

"Sailors, Marines, and legionnaires, we must do our sworn sacred duty to defend the Imperium and the Emperor. All hail the Emperor, Casey Bush."

"And now pandemonium," said Cinnamon.

"I have begun locking doors and trapping Political Bureau soldiers in rooms and corridors," said Athena. "With the admiral's permission, I will reach out to the rest of the fleet and do my best to help."

"Yes, of course," said Hackett. "Anything to spare as many lives as possible. I'm sure most of the Political Bureau is as innocent as the rest."

"Maybe innocent of the deed, but most are indoctrinated and can't be trusted," said Sarin.

"We should get to the bridge," said Hackett. "That will be the best place to coordinate our efforts."

"The Angels stand ready to help in any way necessary," said Sarin. "But I need a favor."

Hackett gave her a funny look. "Of course."

"It's not my place to give orders, at least not at the moment," said Sarin. "But one of the Angels, Talli, was taken back to Earth. I need your fastest interceptors to stop them."

"As soon as it is safe to fly, we will get her back."

S ARIN FINGERED THE CONTROLS on Fort Ticonderoga's captain's chair. As the highest-ranking officer, the honor was hers. Hackett and a few of the other captains stood to her right. The other Angels, including Athena and Talli, stood on her left.

For three days, they had dug the Political Bureau out of the capital ships. Some of the smaller ships tried to flee or fight back, but after Ticonderoga was able to resume flight operations ship-to-ship combat ceased. Boarding parties were being prepared to take back the last of the small ships, but all organized resistance throughout the fleet was over.

"Make the call, Athena."

"Yes, Mom."

Sarin held her breath as she watched the blank screen. She was taking a gamble talking to Galina in the open. She doubted the captains would believe anything Galina told them about her, but there was always a chance. Galina's stone-faced image appeared.

"Command General Lyakhova, how good to see you again. You look much calmer than when we left our last chat."

"What lies have you told these honorable warriors of the Empire?" demanded Galina.

"You mean the warriors you've had removed from their commands and imprisoned? I haven't told them any lies, just the truth. You and your puppets' days are numbered. I have control of the Shadow Fleet."

"The fleet is nothing," hissed Galina.

"No, but I can make life very uncomfortable. I control a third of the frontier and now have the power to free the rest. I control all of space."

"That's nothing! I control entire planets."

"With no way to get into space. How long before Mars and Neptune revolt against your rule with no Shadow Fleet to keep them in check? They will learn the truth. I may not be able to take Earth, but I can make your life miserable until Kita, and the princess arrives."

Galina smiled. "Who knows if that will ever happen? You can't beat me."

Sarin smiled back. "No, but I can keep you from winning."

HAWKE

game of the gods

L FERGUS

Hawke

@FallenAngelKita

http://FallenAngelKita.com

Cover art by Mrinmoy Kar

HAWKE

H AWKE STARED INTO THE shot glass, seeing a ghostly image floating on the amber liquid. He sighed heavily, then swished the
drink to make Onyx's face disappear. Tossing the drink back, Hawke
smacked the glass down next to the bottle of Diamock fronzia—a
spirit that looked and tasted like bourbon. Grabbing the bottle, he
poured himself another round.

This was his new routine since Kita and the other Angels had been
arrested or disappeared. Tet-Sec hadn't shown interest in him, happy
to let him go, and the Angel Starlight didn't seem to care what he
did—she was too busy trying to free the other Angels.

No one cared about his heartache. He'd made his death offering to
Onyx—alone. And now he spent his time—and the stipend Starlight
gave him—trying to forget Onyx. He hadn't had much luck in his
quest by the number of bars and bottles he'd gone through. *Damn
Kita and her curse.*

A commotion at the door drew his attention from his bar corner
seat. An Aurorian had her flashy blue thigh-length coat pulled back,
revealing a pistol strapped to her thigh. *Good luck getting that in
here.* Even Hawke had left his pistols back at the flat he called home.
The Aurorian reached under her jacket to her belt and pulled out a
communicator. She tapped on the screen and shoved it under the
bouncer's big cat-like nose. The Djinn made a disapproving face and
waved at her as he pulled a communicator from his podium.

The Aurorian seemed to be in a hurry and pushed passed the
bouncer. He reached out and grabbed her shoulder. The Aurorian
froze as the scales around her head stood up.

Hawke didn't know much about what the scales on an Aurorian
meant, but this couldn't be a good sign for the Djinn. She grabbed the
Djinn's paw, her dainty hand almost lost in the fur of the Djinn's oversized mitt. The young lion-like Djinn roared as the Aurorian lifted

the paw from her shoulder and tossed it aside. The Djinn—clutching his paw— let out a series of mild roars, and Djinn swears.

"I told you not to touch me, sand-kicker," the Aurorian announced so everyone in the bar could hear.

Hawke raised an eyebrow, then—ignoring the Aurorian—went back to his task at hand. When the Aurorian not-so-politely took the seat next to him, Hawke's eyes moved from his drink to a pair of golden breasts only half hidden by the Aurorian's jacket. Keeping one eye on her rack, he lifted the other up to her gorgeous face.

"I know enough to leave a girl who can do that to a Djinn the hell alone," he muttered as he set his bottle down. "If you don't mind, I'd like to drink in solitary."

"That's not good for your health. I need you sober."

"Thanks to Kita, I'm forever healthy as a horse. If you don't mind, getting drunk is a challenge."

"Then it's not good to drink with strangers. I am Neti H'Mar T'oke. You are Nathan Hawke."

"Anyone can get that from the vids, goldie. I'm not interested in making some fangirl's night. I've got my own problems."

"Hali C'Zar Ah'tem sent me. She said you were an ass. I see my friend wasn't exaggerating."

"What in the hell does Hali want? Can't she let a brokenhearted man drink his troubles away?" To punctuate his words, he knocked back another shot.

"It's not what Hali wants, but what I need," said Neti as Hawke grabbed the bottle.

Neti put her hand on Hawke's arm. The former Red Legionnaire didn't flinch—but he didn't move either.

"By the Emperor, what is it with you girls? You always want something. If you need a busybody, go find Kita. She can't sit still for nothing."

"I wanted Hali, but she has priorities other than her friends. She recommended you. Said you could shoot straight and knew to keep your head down in a fight. I could use someone like that." Neti let go of Hawke's arm.

Hawke grabbed the bottle. "Go find a Diamock."

"If I wanted someone to blindly follow orders, there are thousands to choose from. I need someone to watch my back and who brings enough firepower to put down a platoon of Diamocks."

"I'm just a simple, old soldier. Leave me alone." Hawke poured another shot.

"I understand. You lost someone—we all have. How long are you going to mourn him? It's been six weeks—"

"Her," grumbled Hawke.

Neti's scales rippled. "My apologies, I'm terrible with Humans. Her. I—"

"She was a Graniite. Now, go away."

Neti's scales stood up, and her eyes widened. "I...excuse me for prying, but what in the Void kills a Graniite?"

"Kita," Hawke muttered into his drink before knocking it back.

Neti smiled. "I'll buy you another bottle if you tell me the story."

Hawke slammed the shot glass on the bar. "Two things always follow Kita—trouble, and death. We were fools for going with her...Should have stayed out of that ship...and—and never gone to that planet. I—" Hawke shook his head, unsure if his broken heart or the liquor was loosening his tongue.

"I don't know Kita...beyond what I've seen on the vids and heard—but I'm not her. I'm not going to take you to deep space or alien worlds. I just need a hired gun to get me out of a jam. If I have to play love doctor along the way, I've got a sympathetic ear—only caveat, I don't want to know how a Human and Graniite get it on in the bedroom. I've heard stories—"

"It's not like that," yelled Hawke. "Onyx was a great girl. Tough as nails and knew her mind. She was the best thing to ever happen to a broken-down old warhorse like me." He wiped the tears from the corners of his eyes as he sat down hard on the multiracial stool.

"I see," said Neti. She flagged the bartender down. "Get my friend a bottle of whatever he wants." After pressing her credit chit against the reader, she looked at Hawke. "Enjoy. I don't envy you the headache you'll have tomorrow."

Hawke scoffed. "Give it two minutes, and I'll have to start again."

Neti pushed away from the bar and turned her back on Hawke, her scales on her head and back rippling with a holographic rainbow of colors bordered by the sleek blue coat.

"Hey, where you going?" Hawke called.

Neti looked back over the shoulder. "I need a soldier, not a broken-down warhorse. Have a good night."

"A soldier has a right to mourn," Hawke huffed.

"Yeah, they do. I've mourned—and loved—a few. But I knew when it was time to move on and get back into the fight. The only fight in you is with a bottle. I understand, and I've seen it happen. You lose one too many or get deep in the weeds, and you just can't take anymore. It's not your fault, you were the best, and now your time has passed."

"I'm still the best," yelled Hawke. "You give me a gun, and I'll hit any target—kill any comer. Just because you waltz in here in your shiny jacket and pants with a pair of illegal customized Diamock Six-AE heavy repeaters doesn't mean you know me, goldie. I've seen shit that'll make your scales fall off. I—"

Neti held up a hand. "Just seeing if there was any fight left in you. I see there's plenty. When you sober up in the morning and are still interested, I'll tell you where we're going."

Hawke grunted. "Give me five minutes, and I'll be stone sober."

Neti raised a curious eyebrow—tiny scales encrusted with jewels that arched over her eye.

"Kita's curse."

"You're going to have to explain that to me."

"Meh," Hawke waved his hand. "Just think of me as an Angel without wings."

Neti's eyebrows went up as the scales on her head rose and fell. "I know what Hali told me...so you're like her?"

"Kita gives the girls all the flash and dance. Men are just her workhorses...Though she talked fondly of a guy named Cowboy. I've got some hidden talents. If we get someplace sticky, you might get to see."

"If you're as good as Hali, we won't have a problem."

"You won't have a problem with me. It's you I don't know about."

"We need to make a stop by my flat. I can tell you more then."

Hawke took the bottle delivered by the bartender. "Not so fast. What about my fee?"

Neti flashed Hawke a bright smile. "Hali said she'd owe you one."

Hawke cracked the new bottle open and took a whiff. *Strong stuff.* "Bullshit. Kita's crew doesn't operate like that. If she wanted something, she'd ask."

Neti's eyes flickered. "I'm a little short of cash right now. It's all tied up in our current job, but you help me get it, and I'll give you ten percent."

Hawke grunted as he poured another shot. "Ten percent of nothing is still nothing—which is what you got. No deal, goldie."

Neti fluttered her eyes and smiled suggestively. "When we're through, I'll give you a night you'll never forget."

"Do I look like I just fell off the turnip truck? You'll duck out, leaving me holding my dick in my hand."

"Well, if you don't mind a quickie, I can give you a down payment before we leave."

Hawke's eyebrow shot up. *Never heard that one before.* "I've heard about you Aurori. You must be in dire straits if you're giving it up now."

Neti shrugged. "Little horny. Hali wouldn't give me a second look when I offered and wouldn't shut up about a Human woman."

Hawke chortled into his drink. "Jess," he muttered, shaking his head. "She's another of Kita's disciples. You'd know her as Valor. Little girl transforms into a walking tank. Ok, goldie, I'll go with you and hold you to that good night romp. See what Jess is raving about."

"Excellent," cooed Neti. "Just one thing...call me goldie again, and I'll shove me heel up your vagina."

Hawke grinned as he rubbed the ragged stubble on his chin. "Sure thing...I don't know what Hali told you, but you're in for a surprise. So, what do I call you?"

Neti's scales rippled. "Ti. Nathan ok for you?"

Hawke scoffed and raised a hand. "Only my mother called me Nathan, Emperor rest her soul. I've been called Hawke since Red Legion basic training. Worked back then, works now."

"Let's get out of this dive bar and somewhere civilized."

Hawke looked around at the Diamocks and Zentos inhabiting the joint and shrugged. They seemed nice enough to him.

T HE DOOR TO THE flat opened, and Ti waved Hawke in. He marched down a short hallway with a door on the right into a kitchenette and living area. It was decorated sparsely, and from the lack of anything out of place, either Ti was a neat freak, or she didn't stay here often. He placed his bottle on the counter.

"The bedroom is around the corner. I don't know if Humans freshen up before sex, but I need a shower—I've spent all day in government offices, and they make me feel dirty."

Hawke spun to face Ti. "You're—you-re serious about that?"

"About what?"

"Sex."

Ti's scales rippled in a wild pattern. "Was I not clear?"

Hawke scratched the back of his short-cropped hair. "I...I—girls I know string a guy along, take them home, and then make the guy work for it...if not, just kick him out after changing her mind. I expected you to forget the idea and get straight to work."

"I know I mentioned I was horny, right?"

Hawke raised an eyebrow. "I didn't miss it. I just—just—I'm still getting over Onyx, and I'm not really in the mood. It's not you—trust me. I...I..."

Ti shrugged and stuck out her lower lip. "Hey, you're Human. I won't pretend to know your emotions. But the offer still stands. I can't let Hali be the only one who's slept with a Human."

I don't mind getting used, but that's a new one. "Ah, thanks. I'll just sit and watch TV while you do what you need to."

Ti reached into her belt, pulled out a communicator, and tossed it to Hawke. "Study that. It'll tell you about my business."

"What do you do?"

"Comet ice procurement. The comm will tell you all about it. We've got an hour before we leave, so plenty of time to read."

"You got a glass or tumbler?"

"In the cupboard. I'll be out in a bit." Ti took off her coat—exposing her perky breasts—and unslung her belt. She placed both on the back of the couch. Kicking off her four-inch heels, they landed neatly next to the bedroom door. "Get some reading done," she directed playfully. "You'll have plenty of time. I've got to finish myself off," were her parting words as she disappeared into the bathroom.

Hawke let out a deep sigh and shook his head. *What is it with the women around here? I've been hanging with Kita too long.* Opening a cupboard, he found a tumbler and poured himself a drink. Taking the communicator, he sat on the opposite side of the couch from Ti's effects.

Turning the little device on, it opened to a page entitled, 'Welcome to a World of Ice.' *What is comet ice?* Hawke's only experience with the stuff had been the necklace Cotton had given Kita. According to Cotton, it was rare, but that's all he knew.

He flipped through the pages displaying ice on necklaces around Verisom princesses or as centerpieces in rings worn by Djinn and Zentonians. Each piece was held in a stasis field, giving the ice a purple hue.

Reading on, he found a more interesting section: the collection and transportation. As a former cargomaster, this was the kind of detail that interested him. Two companies dominated the harvesting market from around the galaxy. Once a comet was captured, it was stored in open-space compartments and carved into different sizes. Shavings and other waste were turned into PurIce—100% pure comet ice free of contaminants. The biggest chunks of comet ice sold for the cost of a planet. A marble-size chunk like on Kita's necklace cost more than Hawke made in a year with the Red Legion. PurIce was sold by the milliliter as an additive health benefit—with a lengthy legal disclaimer.

Once the ice was cut, it was placed into stasis. Hawke didn't know what stasis was, and tapping on an information icon brought up a page of topics. Selecting STASIS brought up more information than he cared to read. Scanning the overview, stasis was a dimensional pocket that preserved states of matter and kept them from interacting with the main dimension. The stasis generators could vary in size from nanite machines to entire rooms. Size and duration were the limiting factors. Nanite generators could generate a tiny field that lasted years, while large generators could freeze a room for a few hours.

It was interesting stuff. Hawke could think of a few applications for cargo. He would—

"Interesting reading?" said Ti.

Hawke's head snapped around to the Aurorian. "By the Emperor, woman!" he exclaimed upon seeing her naked. "Warn a man before you surprise him like that. You'll give me a heart attack."

Ti laughed. "I thought you said you were as healthy as a horse? You've had to have seen an Aurorian naked before."

Hawke sucked in a deep breath. "Not up close. The last gal I saw naked was Kita. And she'd give you a run for my money."

Ti gave him a teasing smile. "We are known as the most beautiful race in the galaxy. I've seen Kita in the vids—she definitely looks good. What were you two doing?"

"Us? Nothing. She was all twitterpated over some scars disappearing and came out to show Jess. I admit I thought she was a fine piece of tail...until I saw you."

Ti's scales rippled in a complex pattern as a corner of her mouth ticked up. "I don't remember her having a tail—wings, yes, but no tail."

Hawke stole another glance at Ti. "Figure of speech. It means she's got a great ass and a nice rack—boobs, breasts, whatever you call them."

"Then you met me?" Ti spun around on her toes, showing off her back, butt, and legs.

"Yeah. I guess Jess was right. I don't know what I'm missing."

Ti giggled. It was one of the most adorable sounds Hawke had heard and made him smile.

"Well, I did take care of myself in the shower, but if you want..."

"I thought we were on a time crunch?"

Ti walked to the couch on her toes—the Aurorian never walked flat-footed—she bent at the waist, resting her arms on the back of the couch, letting her golden breasts hang and squeezing them together with her arms.

"You really going to worry about a silly little thing like a deadline when you got this in front of you?"

Hawke sat up and crossed his legs to hide the chub growing under his uniform. "You said it, not me."

Ti stood up, turned around, and sat on the back of the couch. "I did. And we do have a ferry to catch. Excuse my flirtatious behavior. It's been a while, and you are...rare."

"I'm nothing special. And if that's all I am, then you can move along. I've had plenty of gals looking for one-night stands. I'm not interested."

"It won't be once, I promise you. I'm sorry if I come across as forward and strong. Aurori are not shy about what we want, and sex is a way for us to relieve stress, bond, and gather genetic material. If you're not interested, I won't take offense."

Hawke pressed his lips together as emotions raged inside him. His heart still loved Onyx, but his brain said she was never coming back.

Sex wasn't what he wanted to right now. He just wanted someone who cared.

"I'm not saying no. You're fantastic. I just need some time to get over...somebody else."

Ti smiled. "I understand. I can't say I've ever loved someone like that, but I've watched plenty of vids. But...but can you do me a favor?"

Hawke rubbed his hands on his leg nervously. "What do you want?"

Ti got off the couch and jumped over the back, landing next to Hawke. She leaned back, resting her head on the couch's arm, slung her left leg over the back, exposing two slits that formed a V between her legs.

Ti held out a hand. "Let me see your hand."

Hawke placed his in hers.

She guided him down and placed his hand over the skin between the slits. Letting out a soft moan, she pushed his hand between her legs.

"What am I doing?" said Hawke, looking everywhere but where his hand was.

"I just need you to get me off. The shower didn't do it. And—and I'm beginning to get anxious."

"Anxious?" questioned Hawke.

"You ever see an Anxious Aurorian?"

"I don't know what one looks like."

"Like me. I'm stressed, I haven't gotten any release, and if I don't, I become anxious. Which is a serious medical condition causing an imbalance of chemicals in the brain that can lead to coma or death. Why do you think Aurorians are always having sex? It keeps us healthy by releasing chemicals that get rid of anxiety."

Hawke was perplexed. He'd never heard of anything like that before. The closest was blue balls, which hurt like a son of a bitch. *If she needs me to rub her pussy or whatever, I can do that.* "Ok, but I have no idea what I'm doing."

"I have no problem giving directions—as long as you do the same. I don't want to stick my penis into your belly button."

Hawke couldn't hide his smile. "You'll be glad to know you don't have a penis."

"I figured I might have to get a fake one made."

"Let's worry about that later. What am I doing?"

"Ok, the pulsa—the flap—lifts up, and the more turned on I get, the more it'll open. Slide your fingers inside."

Hawke found the tight, narrow opening and was able to get two fingers inside. He found a round lump that surrounded a hole. *What the hell am I doing? Keep calm. You got this, Hawke. Just like any other woman. It's just like clits, nipples, and g-spots, just have to dial and tweak to hit the right spot.*

"Ok," Ti gasped. "That's the elluva. It's not important right now. If I was really turned on, that's the spot to go. Right now, beside it, you'll find two fleshy hoods with hard centers—umbras. Message those."

Hawke spread his fingers enough to touch both fleshy hoods. As he circled his fingers, Ti became wet. He flattened his fingers to message both the hood and the center. *Feels like the head of a pin.* It reminded him of his first experience touching Zenda Mosch's clit and hood. He didn't know what he was doing then either, but he'd followed his fellow legionnaire recruit's guidance and gotten her off with some experimentation. This seemed like that. He just needed two fingers.

"Like that?"

Ti sucked in a long breath. "Yeah..oh, Void. Keep doing that....just keep doing that. Don't stop."

Hawke did as instructed. He knew enough to change his rotation, pressure, and speed.

"Oh, Void!" yelled Ti as she arched her back, leaving just the crown of her head touching the cushion. Her skin shivered as gooseflesh appeared, and beads of sweat traced their way from her stomach down her sides. "Oh, oh, oh!"

I hope nothing's wrong. Hawke found Ti's pulsa stretched, allowing him to get his whole hand in. He did his best to keep stimulating her umbras, then an idea struck him. Rotating his hand to get an umbra between his thumb and finger, he squeezed and rolled the hard ball between his fingers while using the rest of his hand to massage the other umbra. *She's either going to love me or hate me.*

"Void, Void, Void, Void, Void," Ti ended in a scream.

Hawke took that as a good sign.

Ti's back fell to the cushion as her body shook.

"Did...did I do something wrong?" Hawke asked worriedly.

Ti's head lulled to one side. "Oh, no. I...I...sorry. My head is—my head just exploded. Whatever you did was amazing. I haven't been zicked like that in forever. You sure you've never had sex with an Aurorian before?"

Hawke shook his head slowly. "It's similar to Human girls—just more parts."

Ti scooted down to push her butt against Hawke's leg and drape her leg into his lap. "Feel free to touch. Anything I can do for you?"

Hawke kept his hand to himself, but he couldn't do much about her toes playing in his hair. "Sorry. That was an experience, but I'm just..." He shrugged. His heart was somewhere else.

Ti rolled backward, then forward, tucking her legs under her as she pressed up against Hawke. "You must need some kind of release. I know with another race, the first couple of times can be difficult, but I'm good with my hands. Just tell me what you want."

Hawke leaned back against the couch as tears fell from the corner of his eyes. He wiped them with the back of his hand. "Sorry...I just...I just want her back." Pushing the heels of his hands into his eyes, he tried to stop the flow of tears.

"I'm so sorry," said Ti as she put her arms around him. She pulled Hawke to her and let him cry on her shoulder.

"She was the only gal that ever got me," whispered Hawke. "And she saved me and...and...I couldn't save her. It's just—why the hell did we follow Kita to that world? It wasn't worth it. Onyx wasn't worth it."

"Why don't you tell me what happened?"

Hawke squeezed his eyes tight, trying to remove the tears. "Kita. It's always Kita. She'll tell you she's your best friend until she pulls the knife out of your back. They could have saved Onyx from the lava flow. But the rest of them just floated watching. Kita was the only one to go down, but...dammit, she should have saved Onyx with all her banter about how great she was."

Ti frowned. "I'm sorry. That's horrible. I can't believe Hali wouldn't do something. When I get the chance, I will ask her. There must be a reason. But no one deserves to die like that. It must have been even harder to watch." She squeezed Hawke and pressed her head to his.

Hawke let out a long sigh. This was the first time since Onyx that someone had shown they cared. The pain in his heart eased, washed away by his tears. He'd kept so much bottled in about Onyx. It felt strange to release it to a stranger—he'd just pleasured—but Ti proved she was sympathetic and kind—better than Kita. He wasn't sure what Ti was into, but he was willing to help—and if it conflicted with Kita, she could go rot.

"Listen," Hawke said, trying to gather his feelings and courage. "Thanks. That helped a lot. Whatever you need help with, I'm your man. But we probably need to go—"

Ti unwrapped her arms from around Hawke and smiled. "I need you in fighting shape. Seriously, you going to be alright?"

"Yeah, I'll be fine. Thanks again."

"Glad I could help. You'll have to tell me more about her."

Hawke's eye narrowed. "Who? Kita?"

Ti giggled, causing Hawke to smile. "No. But if I see her, I'll slap her. Onyx. I want to know more about her."

A chill went up Hawke's spine. "I don't recommend that. You won't survive the experience."

Ti's eyebrows went up. "I can hold my own in a Clux fight. Kita is a big girl, but so am I."

"Kita...Kita better be careful."

Ti's smile went from ear to ear. "Come on. Let me get dressed, and you can pick out your accessories." She sprang from the couch, wiggling her cute golden butt over to a painting on the far wall. Dragging her finger along the bottom of the frame, the painting retracted to reveal a collection of pistols hanging on the wall. "Take your pick. Grip and sight customizations are in these drawers." She pulled them open a fraction.

Hawke heaved off the couch and came up behind Ti, putting a hand on her shoulder. "Where the hell did you get all these?"

Ti leaned her head back and kissed Hawke's cheek. "I'm a bit of a collector. Take what you want. As my bodyguard, you're allowed up to four. Grip extenders are in the left drawer to help with your extra finger." She spun away, strutting back to the bedroom on her toes.

Hawke shook his head. *Damn. What a girl.* He looked over the selection, recognizing them all. One thing about Kita, she demanded the best and got it—including weapons for her crew. *Where the hell did Ti get these? Only militaries have this kind of hardware.* Hawke shrugged about the weapons' origins and pulled two sets of pistols off the wall. The Aurorian repeaters were medium weight, auto-firing, and deadly accurate, great for everything but the biggest brutes. For those, he took the Diamock ballers—heavy, semi-automatic, and great stopping power. Nothing got up after being shot with one of these.

Trying the grips, the ballers didn't need modification. Like most Diamock weapons, they were perfectly balanced and needed little adjustment. *A little surprised Ti has these. They're big for her dainty hands.* The repeaters were made for Aurorians—petite and short. Hawke dug in the drawer and found a pair of grip expanders meant for a Diamock. Switching the grips out, the repeaters handled like a dream. He took aim at a vase on the counter to test his reaction time.

"I'd prefer you not shoot that. It was a gift from an old fling of mine."

Hawke fumbled the pistol as he tried to bring it down, causing Ti to laugh—which was music in his ears. "Hey, sorry. It was the only thing to aim at."

"Hmmm," Ti purred. "I'm glad to hear I don't count." Ti walked behind the counter and opened a drawer.

"You hired me. It looks bad when the bodyguard shoots the boss."

"That would put a damper on our relationship." She set a pair of pistol harnesses on the counter. "Made for Aurorians, but they should fit you."

Hawke gathered up the pistols he'd chosen, met Ti at the counter, and set his load down. Picking up a leg holster, he adjusted it to maximum and strapped it on. The auto-adjuster didn't need to do much to secure the holster to his leg.

Ti picked up a baller. "Nice. You know your way around hardware—" she smiled at him warmly "—and software. My legs are still tingling."

Hawke strapped on the lower back holster after the other leg holster. "I may be an ass, but I know how to treat a lady."

"From Hali, I heard that was debatable. She said you got smacked at least once."

"Some gals are sensitive and don't know when a man needs to be left alone."

"Well, I don't clean, for the record."

Hawke felt his cheeks turn red. "I—not you. Just sometimes the game is on and—"

Ti laughed and twirled, causing her metallic red thigh-length coat to flare. The coat was open wide down the middle, revealing she had no shirt on underneath, but the jacket was held together with several golden chains. The back of the jacket was open wider than the front to allow the majority of her scales to be visible. She wore a golden linked ring belt over pants that matched the jacket. Her custom pistols were strapped to her thighs while she moved effortlessly on gold five-inch heels.

"I'm sure we have a lot to learn about each other. What do you think?"

Hawke let out a low whistle. "You look fantastic. My duty uniform looks underdressed."

Ti strode over and straightened Hawke's lapel. "I like it. If we have to get you something else, we'll order it. Whose uniform is it, anyway?"

"The United Earth Empire Red Legion."

"They don't mind if I borrow it for a bit?"

Hawke chuckled. "We'd have to find Case and ask her."

"Case...Casey? Hali talked about a Casey."

"Yeah. She's Emperor Casey Bush of the UEE."

"Impressive you're on the first-name basis with your emperor."

Hawke coughed and mumbled, "She's the one who slapped me."

Ti giggled. "At least you've learned from your mistakes."

Hawke holstered his collection of pistols. "It was just me shooting my mouth off. I've never lived with a woman, and I do all my own cleaning. I'm not afraid to mop a floor or scrub."

"You don't have to get defensive. I've done my fair share of cleaning, too. I think it's funny she smacked you. It's such a waste to damage such a...what's the word? Handsome face."

"I'm glad someone appreciates it."

"I do more than that. If you're set, we can go."

"Where are we going?"

"We have a ship to catch."

"**W**HAT DO YOU THINK?" said Ti as she strode into the portside outer cabin that was as large as her flat.

Hawke glanced through the window at the busy spaceport getting the ship ready to depart. He noticed only one bed—it was big, but he wasn't sure if he was comfortable sharing it with Ti. Luckily, he probably wouldn't need to sleep on this voyage. "It's nice. Roomy; comfortable. I thought you were a comet ice dealer? You can afford this?"

Ti shrugged as she walked around Hawke and sat on the bed, crossing her legs. "I guess I should tell you where we're going and why."

"You're the boss. I'm just supposed to keep you alive, right?"

Ti smiled, showing off her lip color that matched her clothes. "I would prefer that. But you're my eyes and ears to everything that doesn't have my attention. I also may need your muscle. I don't expect you to take on a Djinn...but the two of us should be able to handle one.

"One of my shipments was hijacked by a group of pirates, and we're going to get it back. I've contacted them, and they're not associated with any of the big bands—that would be too easy. They're located on the edge of Djinn space—they say they have a letter of marque from the Djinn crown—we'll see how true that is. But I've made a deal to pay the ransom for my shipment, and we will be escorting it back to the Tet."

"What kind of pirates are these?"

"Lucky ones. My ship was behind schedule and was taking a shortcut outside of patrolled space. This would have never happened if the captain wasn't in such a hurry."

Hawke crossed his arms and leaned against the wall. "What about them? Are we bringing them back to?"

Ti shrugged. "Depends on if his company pays their ransom. They don't belong to me. If they did, I'd fire their asses. They belong to a shipping company I hired. The only thing I own is the ice. The recovery equipment, storage containers, and handling equipment are leased for the job. In the event of a pirate attack—like now—it's up to the owners to get it back. Before we were boarded, I had new storage containers and handling equipment loaded. This is where your muscle comes in. I will need your help swapping the storage containers and loading them onto our ship."

Hawke rolled his eyes. There was always something. "I get twenty percent."

Ti cocked her head. "I offered you ten."

"You didn't tell me what we were going against, and I declined your ten percent then."

"Sex with me should cover the other ten percent. I still owe you a night. I'll make it two."

Hawke scoffed. "Sex doesn't pay the bills or heal a bullet hole. Twenty or I walk."

Ti pouted her lips. "I thought you liked me?"

"Doesn't have anything to do with it. Business is business. Look me up when you get back." Hawke turned to leave and went to push the open button for the cabin door.

"Fifteen, and you do whatever you did last time," Ti called down the narrow passageway.

Hawke kept his finger on the button. "Eighteen. And I don't have to touch you—"

"That's fair."

Hawke heard the pain in her voice. "—Unless I want to."

"Give me a chance. I don't know anything about a Human male, but I'm willing to learn. I've made all my other partners happy."

Hawke let go of the button and turned back down the hallway past the door to the bathroom. His six-foot-five frame filled the passageway opening as he looked down at Ti. Gone from the Aurorian's face was her usual confidence and swagger. He detected a tear trail down her golden cheek.

"It may be never. I thank you for helping me with my feelings for Onyx...but that doesn't mean I'm ready to move on—or even get it on. She was special to me like no one else has ever been. I'm sorry I can't give you what you want."

Ti let out a disappointed noise. "Well, I—"

An announcement came over the speaker. "Greetings, travelers, and welcome aboard the Sancha. The ship is casting off and ready for our trip. It will be three standard cycles to the Fore Wormhole, where we will jump to Fri'ka space. It will be another two standard cycles to our port of call, Space Station Ai'jka. If Ai'jka is not your destination, please see an attendant. Thank you for choosing Djinn Royal Space Lines. We hope you have a pleasant trip."

The message repeated in several languages.

Ti looked up at Hawke. "Too late to back out now."

"I didn't say I was backing out. I'm just saying I'm not going to be your fluffer."

Ti cocked her head. "What's a fluffer?"

"A girl whose job is to get a guy off whenever he feels like it."

Ti's scales stood on and rippled wildly. "Is...is that what you think I want? I'm sorry. I'm so sorry. Aurori are flirtatious and sexual by nature...it's how we show we like someone and care about them. You were—awesome, earlier. I wasn't expecting that. Sex is just our way of getting to know someone better. I don't mean to give you the impression I'm looking for a Human xicha. I...I...Oh, you don't know what that is."

Ti bit her lip, looking flustered. "I like you. I admit I'm a sucker for warrior-types. There aren't many among the Aurorians. And you've been around and seen stuff no one else has. I hope you tell me about it. And falling in love with a Graniite makes my heart swoon—Aurorians love impossible romances...Djinn and Zentonians, Verisom and Zentonians, Diamocks and Djinn. You're the first I've ever heard with a Graniite.

"I'm sure I sound ridiculous, and I promise I'm not trying to use you. I like you. I thought you liked me. I'm not trying to take Onyx's place or push her aside. You just seem like you need a friend, and I want to be that friend. I do have to get my ice back, but I was hoping with all the free time we'd have aboard the ship, I could get to know you better...as friends. If that leads to sex, I promise I won't disappoint. I don't know if I can do what you did, but I promise I will learn. If—if you want your own cabin, I'll get you one."

Hawke frowned. "Better for your safety I stay here. I won't sleep anyway."

Ti's eyebrows came together as her scales rippled.

Does that display mean confusion?

"Everyone has to sleep sometime."

Hawke shrugged. "I may take a nap for a few hours. Kita's curse. I only sleep every two to three weeks for a cycle, and I last slept four cycles ago. Better this way. I can keep watch."

"How lonely," whispered Ti.

"Eh, I get lots of reading and watching vids done. I'm a little wary of newcomers after what Kita did. I'm not used to having friends, anyway—at least for long. In the Red Legion, we were moved around a lot. I'm used to relying on myself, and Onyx was the first girl I'd had a relationship with. I'm not even over her, and you come along. I'm waiting for the other shoe to drop—something bad to happen to turn a good thing sour."

Ti stood up and tentatively reached out for Hawke.

Hawke hesitated; not sure what Ti wanted. *Is this something Aurorian I don't know about?* He reached out, but doubt, fear, and his broken heart made him stop.

Ti covered the remaining distance and took his large hand in her golden, petite one. "I'm not going to hurt you...physically or emotionally. I know you're still hurting, and only you know what's best for your heart...but please, don't forever languish in your grief, sorrow, and loss. These feelings are natural, and we carry those we lose forever in our heart—that's natural and healthy. But...but it can make us miss good things too. I don't want to replace Onyx...she's special to you. I'm not interested in trying to be in that orbit. I just want to spend time with you...get to know you...and see where it goes. I promise there's no other shoe. Just a good time and maybe a friend." She squeezed Hawke's hand.

"I, ah, ok—"

A bell chimed, followed by an announcement. "Dinner is being served for guests in blue, red, and yellow zones. Please follow the directions sent to your comms."

With her free hand, Ti pulled her comm from her belt. "That's us. Hungry?"

"Not really, but I can eat a snack. I ate a week ago. I should be good for a few more weeks."

Ti's scales rippled again. "Well, I need to eat a couple of times a cycle. Would you be my company?"

Hawke shrugged. "Sure. I got to watch your back."

"I'm hoping you'll sneak a peek at my front, too."

"You are easy on the eyes."

Ti's face lit up in a smile. "I hope so. I did it for you."

Hawke hadn't noticed the subtle makeup, but now that Ti mentioned it, he liked it.

"**C**OME ON," SAID TI beckoning Hawke to keep up. "I want to get a good seat."

Hawke lengthened his stride to catch up with the excited Aurorian. "Where are we going in such a hurry?" he demanded as he turned sideways to dodge a family of Zentonians.

The passageway through the cabin area was narrow, and for a big guy like Hawke, he often had to twist to let others by. Most were polite, but the Zentonians—which seem to make up the bulk of the passengers—were frequently preoccupied with their large families and smacked him with their squirrel-like tails.

"Tonight's entertainment is the opera," Ti replied after the Zentonians passed.

Hawke grunted and stopped. "I'll just wait in the cabin or...why don't we go grab a drink in the bar?"

Ti smiled. "Because I like the opera. It's cultural and educational. And the singers are fantastic. As my bodyguard, you have to go where I go. But I'll make you a deal—go with me tonight, and I'll go with you to something you want to do."

Hawke frowned. "I don't know of any place on the Tet."

"What about...ah..." Ti's cheeks turned rosy. "I don't know what planet you're from."

"Earth."

"How about any place on Earth? I've never been there or heard anything about it. Name one thing you want me to see."

Hawke ran his hand through his short salt-and-pepper hair. "I guess...Niagara Falls."

"What's a Niagara Falls?"

"It's a set of three waterfalls with an almost two-hundred-foot drop and is more than a half-mile wide."

"That sounds exciting. I've never been to such a big waterfall. What's special to you about it?"

Hawke grunted as his ears turned red. "There are stairs to the bottom where you can enter the mist cloud. You'd look cute in a yellow slicker standing under the waterfall's rainbow."

Ti turned and hugged Hawke. "Ha, that's so sweet. I'll love it. But I more meant a cultural or sports event."

Hawke shrugged and smiled. "We could go to a Bills' game. I haven't been to one in decades."

Ti's scales rippled curiously. "What's a Bills? What kind of sport is it? Is it fast...skill...timing...athletic..."

"Football is a collision sport and all of the above. It's complicated, but each team has an offense and defense. The offense tries to move the ball into the endzone for six points, or if they run out of tries, they can kick the ball through the uprights for three points. I'll see if

I can find a vid. Enterprise has a complete library of games. It's easier to explain when the game is going on."

"Aurori have lots of sports. I played roknik when I was in school. But football sounds fun. You can even buy me a cheer stick or something."

Hawke smiled. "You'd look great in a jersey."

Ti giggled. "If that's what you want. It might be hard to find one here. You might just have to settle for me naked."

Hawke gulped and felt his cheeks reddening at having his attempts at mild flirting turned back on him full force. *Ti doesn't mess around.*

Up ahead, a trio of Diamocks in combat uniforms and armor stepped out of a side passage with pistols raised.

"Zink!" yelled Ti as she reached for her pistols.

Hawke didn't know who the Diamocks were or what they were planning to shoot at, but he wasn't going to let Ti get caught in the middle. Grabbing the Aurorian around the waist, he picked her up, and slung her down on the deck, jumping on top of her as the first Diamock bullets flew overhead.

"That was zinking fast," cried Ti. "How'd you do that?"

Hawke ignored her, drew one of his ballers, got to a knee, and fired at the Diamocks' heads. From his time aboard Mauler—Kita's Diamock frigate—he knew that no pistol round would penetrate their armor. But these guys weren't in full combat armor. They were missing their helmets.

The first Diamock's head exploded with a shot from Hawke's baller. He shifted to the right and flattened himself against the wall while using his foot to drag Ti to him. The Diamock bullets tore up the deck after her. Hawke took aim and fired at the second Diamock, the bullet striking the dogface alien in the jaw. The remaining Diamock shifted its aim from Ti to him, and a bullet struck Hawke in the shoulder.

Ignoring the pain, Hawke aimed for the remaining Diamock when four bullets struck him in the back as he pulled the trigger. He pitched forward on top of Ti as she pulled the trigger hitting the Diamock in the neck splashing bright orange arterial spray across the wall.

Hawke rolled off Ti, bringing his baller up to target whoever shot him in the back. Four more Diamocks, two kneeling and two standing behind them, had pistols out firing. Three more rounds struck Hawke in the chest, stomach, and leg. Hawke drew his other baller. Using the baller in his injured arm, he fired rapidly to suppress the Diamocks. With the baller in his good arm, he shot a kneeling Diamock in the head.

This second group of Diamocks was armored like the first, but unlike Diamock units Hawke had seen, these didn't have any unit insignia painted on their chests.

Ti crawled up next to Hawke and fired a trio of bullets, striking a Diamock in the head and two in its chest.

"Get behind me," Hawke ordered, seeing Ti's exposed position. To ensure the Diamocks didn't aim at her, he fired several more rounds from the baller in his bad arm.

"I can shoot," replied Ti.

"But you can't take a bullet," Hawke retorted. Snapping his good baller to another Diamock, he fired, hitting it in the eye. Hawke sat up, putting himself between the Diamock and Ti.

The remaining Diamock drew a weapon from behind his back and leveled it at Hawke.

"Needler!" cried Ti.

When the weapon fired, it sounded like ripped cloth. *Probably not why it's called a needler.* The needle-like projectiles perforated Hawke's neck, chest, and stomach. He tried to raise his good baller, but his arm collapsed to the deck as the rest of him fell backward. Above him, Ti was on her knees firing at the Diamock. Hawke's head hit the deck, and everything went black.

H AWKE OPENED HIS EYES to white. *Where the hell am I? Is this Heaven?* Hawke never believed in such a place, but he'd seen it on the vids. They always made it a happy, joyous place where you met long-dead family and loved ones—or some kind of god.

"Onyx?" He called. His voice carried through the dimensionless whiteness.

He took a step but was unsure of where to put it down. His foot didn't find anything solid, and he nearly fell. "Dammit. What the hell is this place?"

"Well, you're the first person I've ever seen fall in the White."

Hawke spun around to face the voice so full of smug confidence it could only belong to one person. "Kita! What the hell are you doing here? Why would they let you into Heaven?"

Kita laughed. "This isn't Heaven, sorry. This is the White. You know when a computer boots up, and it flashes all that information before loading the operating system? This is that information screen. It's the BIOS for this universe. It's also a safe place for gods, like me, to hide or chat with friends who took one too many rounds while their bodies need time to heal."

"To hell with you. You've been a pain in my ass since I saw you. I should have never joined you."

Kita pulled her braid around and stroked it. "If you'd never come, you'd never met Onyx."

"You worthless backstabbing bitch! It's your fault she's dead."

Kita recoiled in surprise and shock. "I had nothing to do with her death."

"You told her to walk across that decrepit building. You and the others could have saved her when she fell. They didn't even try! You flew down to her and watched her die! You despicable, horrible monster." Hawke burst into frustrated and angry tears as he clenched his fists.

Kita tossed her braid behind her and crossed her arms. "We scouted the route. There was no place to cross except there. The gravity of the planet made a ten-ton Graniite weigh over twenty. The planet's gravity also stressed the gravity wells in the Angels' feathers. We could barely fly, let alone carry her. We tried, remember? I tried with all my might to pull her out, but between her weight and the suction of the lava, there was no way. Even if I did get her out, there wouldn't have been much left of her. I'm sorry. I did my best. Believe me, if there was something I could have done, I would have."

"You're a god!" Hawke roared. "You could've saved her or brought her back. You could have done it then, or you could do it now!"

Kita leaked air between her teeth. "Yeah, and then we'd both be in trouble—then and now. We weren't supposed to be on that planet, and we're not supposed to be in the White, either. And I am definitely not supposed to bring people back from the dead. I can hide some small stuff in the equation, but not that. Sorry, I'm not ready to take on the gods—yet. My time is coming, until then—" Kita shrugged.

"—I have to accept the outcome of the equation same as you. Onyx was a great girl, but I thought Ti was a worthy replacement."

"Don't you come near her!" Hawke yelled.

"Who do you think sent her to you? I felt bad about Onyx and thought you could use someone in your life. She came to Hali looking for help. Hali couldn't, but she contacted me—"

"Where the hell are you?" Hawke demanded.

Kita rolled her eyes. "Languishing in some deep space prison. Gives me plenty of time to study the equation while I wait for rescue."

"I'm not coming to get your ass out. You can rot."

Kita smirked and shrugged. "I didn't think you would. I mean, I never paid you for your earlier services. I'm hoping Ti will make up for it—that and what I gave you."

"My curse?"

"Call it what you will. It's saving your life, and Ti is quite upset that none of the medics on board your ship knows what to do...lucky for you, I do."

"What if I want to die and be with Onyx?"

Kita laughed. "Death doesn't work like that—take it from someone who knows. There's no happy land or joyful reunions, just a long dreamless sleep where time has no meaning until your brain shuts down and your consciousness slips into eternal nothingness. I'm sorry you'll never see Onyx again, but Ti is a great girl with lots of potential. I see you've already hit it off. I may have underestimated your bedroom prowess."

"Stay the hell out of my life!"

"I'm just saying from experience, great girls don't come along very often—that's why I horde them. I know you loved Onyx, and you had a great couple of years together, but don't let that stand in the way of missing out on somebody else who will be as equally great—just in a different way. All romances are different but can be equally fulfilling. I don't care that you don't come and rescue me. That's your choice. I do thank you for what you've done for me and for helping me. I'm sorry I couldn't be better, but I hope Ti will make up for it, and you have a great life together."

"Ti is not a bribe," Hawke snarled.

"Of course not!" Kita gasped. "She's my way of saying 'I'm sorry' for not being a better friend. I am doing a little matchmaking—I studied her equation and knew yours—and I discovered you two would be great together—if you can get over your broken heart. But I can't fix that—only you can. Ti is willing to help in any way she can and understands what you went through and what you—probably—need. Really, only you can answer that. Me, Hali, and Ti talked it over, and we feel Ti is what you need."

"Goddammit, Kita! Is there nothing you don't have your fingers in? Why can't you leave well enough alone?"

Kita grinned wickedly. "Would you prefer I take Ti away?"

Hawke puffed up his chest and raised his fists. "Touch her, and I'll kill you!"

Kita cackled maliciously. "Going to need more than that, grizzly man. Ti is your choice, and this will be the last time you see me. Enjoy your life. Don't let Ti's association with me cloud your feelings for her. She's great. You're great. You'll go great together."

"Evil bitch," Hawke huffed.

"And when have I ever befouled you, Hawke? I take care of my friends—even when they hate me."

"You will double-cross everyone at some point."

Kita frowned and shrugged. "True...but only when Reality is on the line. When I do, no one will know. See you around, Hawke."

H AWKE OPENED HIS EYES to the hallway. An Aurori in a white bodysuit with the golden hashes on her chest denoting she was part of a medical team hovered over him. Glancing down, two more Aurori and a Zentonian were trying to treat his wounds.

"Ow!" snarled Hawke as one of the Aurori did something to him. He tried to sit up, but the Aurorian hovering over him pushed him down.

"Zick! The Human is awake," said the Aurori holding Hawke's head.

Hawke swung his arm, knocking the Aurori aside, and sat up, surprising the other med-techs. "I'm fine," he grumbled as he looked down.

Sticking out of his chest were six needler darts—fully expanded. The darts went in like needles, but after impact, they extended a ring of barbs that tore through flesh—and did even more damage trying to get them out. The butts of several bullets were also visible.

Hawke grabbed the dart in his neck, careful not to slice open his fingers, and pulled it out. "Damn," he muttered over the pain. Deciding to let his body push the rest out, he tried to stand.

"Please," said the Aurori, who seemed to be in charge, "you are gravely injured. We need to get you to the auto-doc." She tried to put herself in Hawke's way.

"I don't need no damn auto-doc," grumped Hawke. *I'm my own damn auto-doc.* He pushed the Aurori out of the way and stood. "Did you have to cut my uniform?" He huffed, seeing his uniform top and undershirt cut open. He pressed them together so the fabric could repair itself.

Ignoring the med-techs and security personnel, Hawke went to a downed Diamock missing most of his head. There were no visible markings on the armor, but Hawke knew where to look. Grabbing the armor's straps, he broke the woven fasteners and pulled off the plated vest. Ripping open the uniform top, he exposed the unit marking painted on the Diamock's chest plate. Hawke didn't recognize the three yellow circles, but he did recognize the dagger through the Diamock skull painted to the left. *Hunter-Killer Pack.*

"Hawke?"

Ti didn't sound shaken but concerned. Hawke stood up and turned to face her, and the group gathered behind her.

"I told you, I'm fine," he barked at the med-techs and security people.

"Hawke," said Ti firmly. "Not even Aurori get up from needler darts and gunshot wounds."

Hawke grunted and hated to admit that "I'm not Human. I'm an Angel."

Ti's scales rippled as an eyebrow raised up. "You're—"

Hawke raised a hand and huffed. "Kita's as sexist as they come—but she's not stupid. Well...maybe. Kami—her daughter—isn't. Girls get wings. Guys get—something else. But both get the same basic stuff, including regenerating faster than you. Speaking of Kita...and you...you've got some explaining to do. Not only about her, but about these guys." Hawke nudged a dead Diamock with his foot.

Ti pressed her lips tightly together as her scales moved in a complex pattern. "Can we talk about this later? Like after our date?"

Hawke crossed his arms and swore as he pressed down on a dart. "Son-of-a...Are you crazy? There could be more of these guys on the ship. We're going back to the room so I can keep you safe and get some answers."

Ti's scales stood up straight as she puffed out her chest. "I'm in charge. With you, I don't have to worry about anyone. I want to go to the opera. You can come and protect me—or go back to the room. I can protect myself."

Hawke leaned into Ti's ear. "Do you know who those guys were? They weren't no regular Diamocks."

"And they're dead. I shot two of them. What's it matter?"

"They were a Hunter-Killer Pack—Diamock special forces. I trained with them aboard Mauler. They're tough bastards, trained—"

"I know who they are," snapped Ti. "Do I look worried about them? Now, let's go to the opera. Afterward, I will tell you what you need to know."

"If you don't tell me, I'll go to someone who will...and she's got a long reach."

Half of Ti's scales stood up. "I thought you hated Kita?"

"Doesn't mean she won't tell me what you're hiding."

Ti turned up her nose. "You don't trust me?"

"I just got shot up by Diamock special forces protecting your ass. Now I'm thinking I should have let them have you."

Ti's mouth fell open as all her scales laid flat. "I don't know what they want. It could have been you they were after."

Hawke chuckled gravely. "Goldie, the Diamocks know me. If they wanted me dead, they would have known to send an entire assault ship's worth of soldiers after me. Not a bunch of special ops guys with pop guns in half their armor."

"Excuse me," said a Zentonian in a blue security uniform. "I need you to come with me so we can collect your statements and sort out this mess."

Hawke raised an eyebrow at Ti. "No opera tonight."

"Humph," she replied, turning away from Hawke. "We'll see."

～

H AWKE GRUMBLED AS HE stumbled through the door to the cabin he shared with Ti. The light was on as he traversed the narrow passageway—past the bathroom—to the bedroom. Ti lay on the bed in a peach cami pajama set. She was busy looking through a pamphlet, with her feet in the air crossed at the ankles.

She turned and set her pamphlet down, revealing it was from the opera. "Hey, Hawke. How was your night?"

Hawke saw red. "Goddammit. I've been answering these giant squirrels' questions and staring at the four walls of the brig. They finally got a hold of Hali to let me out. Seeing you, now I know why she was laughing the whole time."

Ti rolled over on her back. "The cogs of administration only turn so fast. I'm sure Hali moved as fast as she could."

"And you had time to go to the goddamn opera!" Hawke thundered.

"Calm down. Diplomatic channels work faster than administrative ones."

"Screw this. I am not playing your and Kita's game. When we get to the next stop, I'm out of here."

Ti sat up, her scales rippling. "Hawke, please. Let me explain. There's no game...just limited access to information."

"You sound like Kita."

Ti smiled whimsically. "She is very good at it. But I promise it was done to protect you. We didn't want you to become a target."

"I can take care of myself."

"I know, and you proved it. Killing an HKP squad by yourself shows you're not normal. But there are worse things out there that could be after you...and are after me—a comet ice broker doesn't make that kind of enemies."

"What the hell are you?" snarled Hawke.

"Please...please calm down. I'm sorry they kept you locked up for so long. I figured it would be until the opera was over. Would you rather sit in the brig or sit through the opera? It was exceptional. They brought in a troupe of Verisom princesses that were exquisite—magnificent voices. It was worth the upgrade for the room. If I knew they wouldn't let you out, I would have come and got you myself."

"Goddammit," Hawke thundered as he struck the thin wall with the side of his fist, leaving a hole. "What the hell are you?"

Ti pulled her legs up to her chest and wrapped her arms around them. "Hawke, if you don't calm down, I won't tell you, and I will ask you to leave. Go have a drink in the bar or run a few laps on the exercise deck—if you need to. I will wait, but I won't talk to you like this."

She raised her hand, and Hawke's four guns came free of their holsters and floated down and sat next to her.

"Dammit, if it's a fight you want—"

"I don't want to fight, but I don't want you to do something stupid. One of the things I need to tell you is I'm a metalist—I can manipulate metal like Hali can electricity. It's why none of the bullets fired at us tonight hit me. You were so fast; I didn't have time to do much. I've never seen anyone move as fast as you did. I was impressed—you're better than Kita led me to believe."

Hawke pressed his lips together as he clenched his fists. He was tired of these girls and their games. Kita was always messing with him. *Why the hell can't she leave me alone?*

Ti sighed. "Come, sit. I promise you Kita has no malintent for you—neither do I or Hali. But—as you know—the galaxy is danger-ous. We don't want you getting injured in a way your body can't fix in ten minutes.

"I know I seem a little cold and harsh, but I was upset you were injured. They wouldn't let me near you, and I was afraid you'd died. No one I know gets up from a needler volley. I cried in the arms of some random Aurori.

"I care about you, Hawke. But the others didn't think you'd come if I told you who I was and what I do. I am a comet ice broker—that's my current cover. It lets me move around and associate with all classes of people. Besides being Grand Ambassador, did Hali ever tell you what she did?"

Hawke, letting some of his anger drain away, leaned against the damaged wall. "No. She said she was in the Aurorian military."

Ti rolled her eyes. "True, but it goes deeper than that. Before she was retired and put on the diplomatic track, she served with me as a member of the Ne'shi—Golden Flowers. We're a clandestine operation that protects Aurori interests—we're spies, special forces operators, and detectives.

"The Diamocks were after me. I'm not sure how they knew I was aboard since I just made the ticket and have you as cover. Someone will have to dig into that. But thanks to you, I'm safe. I've scanned the ship's manifest, and all the other passengers check out. I—"

Hawke's mind dropped being angry and went to work on what he knew about Diamock special forces. "The Diamocks wouldn't come aboard as passengers. They most likely came aboard through the cargo."

"Hmm, I will scan the cargo manifest for any irregularities. Kita and Hali said you were good at this."

"I've got some experience. Most likely, the ship's cargo manifest has been altered to not show any changes. We might have to go down and have a look for ourselves. But first, what are you doing that has Diamo after you? I thought you were allies."

"We are...but that doesn't keep either side from checking up on the other."

"If that was the case, they'd catch you and return you—not kill you."

Ti rolled on the bed to let her head hang over the edge. She folded her hands and put them on her stomach. "Some missions are white, others gray, and mine are black."

"I'm afraid to ask—"

"It's why I went to Hali for help. She had experience and—I thought—wasn't doing anything."

"Why didn't you go to your superiors?"

Ti clicked her tongue. "We don't operate like that. I don't know who my supervisor is. I get missions through a secure channel. If we decide we need help on a mission, we're expected to find it ourselves. That's why I thought you would be perfect. Outside the inner circle, no one knows you. Kita said you were an elite soldier that fought with her and had performed admirably. She spoke highly of you. I thought you'd be the perfect complement to me...and if something romantic came out of it, all the better."

"By the Emperor, I hate girls."

"Oh, come on," pleaded Ti. "I'm not that bad. I'm not asking you for your DNA so we can have a kid. I just thought we'd have a little fun. I've been in the field for three years, zicking absolute creeps and assholes to keep my cover. All I want is some fun for me. I thought it would be fun for you. You don't have to be such an ass about it. Kita was just doing us a favor. She said we were compatible, and I believed her—I still do. I just need you to get out of your own way and see the good thing in front of you. I won't bite—unless you want me to. I mean," Ti let out an unhappy and frustrated sounding grunt. "Are all Humans this difficult?"

Hawke laughed to himself. He'd never really thought about it, but he did have some pretty memorable fights with girls—all accusing him of being an ass and hard-headed. He did remember the gals being just as bad. *Maybe it's who I attract...* But Ti wasn't like them. She hadn't stormed out or slapped him. She'd left him in the brig, but that wasn't all her fault. Ti was a great girl...and she threw herself naked at him wanting his attention. *How many girls have ever done that?* She was willing to do what he wanted, only asking he return the favor. Maybe Ti wasn't trying to buffalo him. She was being genuine while trying to do her duty and protect her cover. *Maybe I should cut her some slack.*

"Ah, I'm more difficult than most. Many a gal has busted their frying pan over my head."

Ti cocked her head. "What?"

"I mean, I've chased a lot of girls away being stubborn and an ass."

"Is that what you're trying to do? Chase me away? Because I'm not going anywhere. We have a mission to do, and I will complete it. After that, you can go. Until then, you're stuck with me."

A smile broke across Hawke's lips. "Finally, a girl as stubborn as me."

Ti rolled over. "I am dedicated. I always get what I want, no matter what I have to do. You're just proving to require more determination than I was led to believe—you're more than just some heartbroken Human in need of a pick-me-up. I mean, I offered sex—with an Aurorian—and you turned me down...with good cause. But still. Who does that?"

Hawke sighed with a mixture of pride and embarrassment. "I do."

"I know. That's one of the things I like about you. You like me for me, not what's in-between my legs or to be some beautiful creature to hang on your arm."

"Well, I'm not against it."

Ti laughed. "And I like your sense of humor. You know how to make a girl feel good and wanted—without sex. Which is rare. You have a unique skill, Hawke."

Hawke shrugged inwardly. It was the first time he'd ever been told that, but if it made Ti happy, he wouldn't deny it. "You have to make a girl feel good about herself...even when she looks amazing as you."

Ti smiled. "As far as Aurori go, I'm not that special. I won't win any genetic contests. But, to be fair, your flattery is working, and I like it, but to get back to why you're mad at me—are you still mad at me?"

Hawke blinked, realizing Ti had skillfully maneuvered him away from his anger and made the conversation about them. *Damn, if she's that good...no girl's done that before. They just storm off.* Hawke rubbed his chin as he debated his feelings. "I'm not mad, but I still want to know what you're up to."

"And I will tell you—I will also tell you I reward good behavior." She winked playfully and turned to sit on the edge of the bed. Patting the area next to her, she said, "Come, sit."

Damn. She played me like a fiddle. Hawke pushed off the wall and sat.

Ti put her arms around Hawke and rested her head on his shoulder. Squeezing him tight, she lifted her head and said, "I'd kiss you, but I don't know if you're ready for that."

Hawke bowed his head. "Not...yet. I'm still digesting what Kita said."

"When did you talk to Kita, anyway? In the brig? Hali said she has a way of appearing anywhere."

Hawke chuckled. "I don't know where we were. Some place only she can access as a god, I guess. She told me some stuff about you, Onyx, and life in general."

"To be honest, all she told me was you would be a good bodyguard, and if I was interested in romance, you'd be a good match. I may have taken a god a little too literal at her word."

Hawke shrugged. "Kita has ways of seeing into the depths of your soul and knows how to get the best from people. I hate her, but—dammit—she was right about you. I've never met anyone like you."

"Ahhh," Ti cooed as she kissed Hawke on the cheek. "Is that ok?"

Her soft, warm lips sent a shock from Hawke's cheek down his spine. No girl's kiss had ever made him tingle—so much his cock jumped. *Slow down, boy. We still have a long way to go.*

Hawke turned to Ti and smiled. "It was amazing. Been a long time since this old warhorse has been kissed."

"I don't kiss anything old," Ti replied with a teasing smile. "Not sure what a warhorse is either."

Hawke chuckled. "It's a term for a veteran."

"Well, you're not old."

"I'm pushing a hundred and thirty."

"You want to take a guess at how old I am?"

The hair on the back of Hawke's neck stood up as he debated how to answer. "I've been around long enough to know never to ask or guess a girl's age. You're beautiful. That's all that matters."

"I knew you were smart. I'm still young by Aurori standards. You can look that up if you want." Ti released Hawke, stretched, and yawned. "Hmmm, I think it's bedtime. But, before I do, we are going after pirates. They are in league with the Djinn, but also the Diamocks. My mission is to infiltrate their network and install a snooping device. They do have my ice, so we'll have to be smart if we're going to get in and out. We can work out the details tomorrow. Does that satisfy you?"

Hawke frowned as everything that could go wrong on that type of mission went through his head. "I'll think about it. You get some sleep."

"Alright. You don't have to stay if you don't want to. Just lock the door."

Hawke turned in alarm. "That's not going to keep you safe."

Ti stretched across the bed, reached under a pillow, and pulled out a pistol. "I'll be fine." She twisted and grabbed her comm from the side table. She tapped the screen several times. "There. I sent you a security badge. You now have the same clearance I do, in case you want to go snooping. If anyone gives you any problems, show them that."

Hawke pulled his comm from his pocket. On the screen was a message from Ti. He opened it and tapped the icon to upgrade his security clearance. He looked back at her and frowned. "I don't like leaving you alone."

Ti replied with a sleepy smile. "That's sweet, but I can take care of myself. If you come back and I'm not awake, send me a message so I can deactivate the screamer before you open the door."

"What's a screamer?"

"A little device that admits a high-pitched noise to distract and disorient intruders. It'll give me enough time to get a few shots off."

Hawke nodded. "Alright. I think I'm going to look for the missing Diamocks."

"Missing?"

"We killed seven, but a Diamock HKP has ten members. Three are still out there."

"Probably laying low until they can get off the ship...but if you want to go looking for a fight, I won't stop you."

Hawke grunted as he stood. "Better safe than sorry."

Ti smiled and blew him a kiss. "Be safe." She nuzzled down into the pillow.

"Good night...sweet dreams," replied Hawke as he slipped to the door.

"As'sh aa'naj inichi maj'ori."

Hawke paused at the door and turned to look back at Ti. "What's that mean?"

"May the stars guard you," said Ti with a smile that turned into a yawn.

Hawke waved as he slipped out the door. *I don't think it's me the stars need to protect.*

H AWKE MADE HIS WAY through the extensive cargo hold of the ferry. It was bigger than the cargo ships he'd served aboard. Doing his best to look like an owner trying to find his cargo, which he was, he followed the directions the cargo personnel had uploaded to his comm.

Most of the cargo was in standard shipping containers with no hint at what they contained. They made for easy loading and unloading and required little to no maintenance by the crew. Which might explain why Hawke hadn't seen another soul down here. When a metal *click* echoed through the containers, he froze.

Checking his comm, Ti's container was just ahead around a corner—the direction the sound had come from. Still missing three Diamocks, Hawke wasn't going to take any chances. With a thought, he turned invisible. Another part of Kita's curse. Still, he wasn't going to not use it. Kita had shown him the benefits of stealth and even given him clothes that could as well. The stealth system wasn't infallible, but it was better than any other system he'd seen. It had problems with environmental effects and swift movement. *It's not going to rain in the cargo hold.*

Hawke crept to the last container in the row and stuck his head around to see what lay down the other direction. A container's doors were open. Checking his comm, the open container was Ti's. Slowly, Hawke moved down the side of the corner container to the next container in the row. These were shorter containers, about half the length of the containers he'd passed.

He moved up to Ti's container and looked through the gap between the door and the container wall. A Diamock wearing the same armor like the ones he'd killed earlier was attaching something to the stasis machine meant to hold Ti's comet ice. *Where are the others?*

Hawke moved to the edge of the door and peeked around. Not far down the alley, another Diamock was moving toward Hawke. He let the Diamock enter the open doors and approach the working Diamock.

"*Problem?*" said the patrolling Diamock in a husky growl of a voice.

Hawke had learned Diamo, the language of the Diamocks, from his time serving aboard Mauler.

"*Yeah, the cheap bastard from the shipping company that bought these bare-metal tools.*"

"*If you weren't such fumble fingers—*"

"*That Aurorian bitch knows what she's doing. If I don't do it right, I could blow us all to the Void.*"

As far as Hawke knew, there was nothing explosive about stasis machines. Why the Diamocks were trying to blow them up was an interesting question.

Slipping around the door, Hawke grabbed the patrolling Diamock in a chokehold, using his taller frame to lift the Diamock up and squeeze the pistol out of his hand. Hawke caught the pistol and turned it on the other Diamock. The swift motion made Hawke visible, but he didn't mind. He had the upper hand.

"Now, I only need one of you, so who wants to have a chat?"

As a response, the Diamock in Hawke's arm slammed his elbow into Hawke's side. The other Diamock lunged from his seated position at the pair. Hawke flicked the pistol, aimed it at the charging Diamock's head, and pulled the trigger, splattering his brain across Ti's stasis chambers.

Hawke flexed the arm holding the frisky Diamock and lifted him. *Is Ti the type of girl that minds a little blood? Guess I'll see if I can remove the bits of brain.* "Well, pal, it looks like it's you and me. Why are you trying to blow up a bunch of empty stasis chambers?"

The Diamock struggled as a response. Hawke stuck the pistol in his belt. Kicking Hawke in the legs, the Diamock tried to free himself against Hawke's superior strength.

"Buddy, you're not going to break free. I'm an Angel, and I've got the strength of a platoon of Diamocks. Just tell me what I want to know, and I can tell you the ship has got an excellent brig. Just tell me what you're up to?"

The Diamock must have sensed Hawke was telling the truth because he quit struggling and said, "Doesn't matter. If you're here, then she's dead."

Shit. I forgot there were three. "What are you doing with her stuff?"

"The Aurorian has enough zentyx packed into these chambers to blow the ship in half."

Hawke knew the explosive—a little bit went a long way. *But why would Ti want to blow the ship? Guess I'll have to ask her—right after I save her.* "You don't go anywhere," Hawke ordered the Diamock. He grabbed one of the flat boney spikes that made up the crown around a Diamock's head. Hawke knew they were sensitive. Taking the spike between his thumb and finger, he bent it forward until it cracked like a dry twig.

The Diamock let out a howl and went slack in Hawke's arm. Hawke lowered the Diamock to the floor and let the poor bastard clutch his injured head.

"Don't go anywhere," said Hawke. "Someone will be along to collect you. While you wait, clean up this mess."

Stepping over the Diamock, Hawke collected the explosive charge the Diamocks were trying to wire into the stasis chambers. Ignoring the Diamock, Hawke sprinted back to the cargo office.

"Hey!" Hawke yelled, sticking his head in the window. "You got a wounded Diamock commando that attacked me earlier in front of C-two-five-six-three."

"Huh?" said the Zentonian looking up from something she was reading.

"Got to go. Just get him!"

Hawke pushed away from the window and ran back to the elevator.

H AWKE SPRINTED THROUGH THE narrow corridor lined with cabin doors. He sidestepped, jumped around, and in some cases bullied his way past the other passengers in his way. He turned a corner and lowered his shoulder into the chest of a much larger Djinn, sending the roaring male sprawling into his harem.

Hawke ignored the curses and counted down the cabin numbers to the room he shared with Ti. Skidding to a stop when he reached their cabin, the door was ajar—held open by a Diamock head. Tiptoeing around the slain HKP soldier, Hawke drew his pistol and jumped into the room, checking all the hiding spots.

Instead, he found Ti leaning against the headboard, legs curled up—still in her PJs—tapping away on her comm.

Hawke lowered his pistol. "I told you they'd come for you."

Ti put down her comm and smiled. "Ugh. I wish you were wrong. The amount of paperwork killing one generates is incredulous."

Hawke wasn't sure what the word meant but ignored finding the meaning and instead asked, "Are you ok?"

"Oh, we had a nice tussle. I showed him around the room, and then I broke his neck. He did hit me hard enough to make my lip bleed. His pistol is around here somewhere. We should find it before security arrives."

Hawke put his pistol away and dug through the pillows and blankets on the floor. He hit something hard and metal through the blanket, but when he uncovered it, he found the lamp.

"Found it!" exclaimed Ti holding it up like a dead fish.

Hawke held out his hand. "It can join the one I collected from downstairs. We have to go back to the cargo hold and collect the Diamock I left there. I figure you'd want to talk to him. I want to talk to you."

"Oh? And what did you boys talk about? I doubt it was a friendly game of barkatte."

"Something about enough explosives in the stasis chambers to blow the ship in half."

Ti's scales rippled wildly. "Oh. That." She shrugged. "A gift for the pirates."

Hawke crossed his arms and huffed. "You weren't going to tell me you had that much explosive on board?"

"So, what? You can guard it?"

"I thought we were snooping their machines."

Ti stretched out her legs and stood. "I am. The real target is the Djinn and Diamock systems. The pirates have to be linked to their networks, and we want in." She walked as she spoke, stopping in front of Hawke. She tapped her finger on his chest. "The explosive is just a reminder never to steal from me."

"You might want to go remind the Diamocks of that."

Ti sidestepped Hawke and reached into the bathroom to withdraw a white robe. She slipped it on. "Help me move this fool into the hallway, then we'll go down and have a chat."

Ignoring the looks of passersby, they moved the body into the corridor then went back to the cargo hold. They found the Diamock curled up against the doors of Ti's shipping container—still holding his injured crown.

"Oh! You didn't!" exclaimed Ti.

Hawke shrugged, not seeing what the big deal was.

Ti knelt next to the Diamock and coaxed his bloody hand away from his injured spike. She examined the injury, then looked up at Hawke and said aghast, "You did this?"

"I had to make sure he didn't run off."

"Do you know how much this hurts a Diamock?"

Hawke shrugged. "I've seen it before. Zentix took it like a champ when Kita did it to her."

"For Diamocks, this is extremely sensitive. They could die from it. How would you like it if someone snapped a sensitive place on you?"

Hawke rolled his eyes. He'd received his fair share of shots to the nuts before—some of those gals had meant it to be crippling. "What? It happens to all of us. It hurts for a bit—I knew a guy that ended up in sickbay for a day. But it comes with the territory. He could have stopped me if he wanted to."

"So, now it's his fault?" snapped Ti.

Hawke held up his hand. "I'm just saying he took it like a soldier. I would have done no less."

"You could have just brought him back with you. I would have dealt with him from there." Ti pulled out her comm and called the ship's infirmary requesting a Diamock specialist. "Come on, champ. Help me carry him to the cargo office. I don't want them snooping around my container."

I'll never understand women. Hawke bent down and picked up the Diamock in his arms.

"You need help?" said Ti, her scales rippling wildly.

"I got him. He doesn't way much." Not waiting for Ti to close the container, Hawke led them back to the cargo office.

HAWKE LED A PAIR of Zentonian freight operators in grease-stained overalls—and even more stuck in their tails—to Ti's table overlooking the mezzanine level of Space Station Ai'jka. Ti was having a light breakfast while searching for a new carrier. Neither she nor Hawke trusted the one Ti had arranged before departure, but finding a new carrier had proven difficult. Hawke had left to check the docks to see if any small operators were available.

"Hey," said Hawke bumping the table with his thigh to get Ti's attention. "I found someone."

Ti looked over her comm at the Zentonians and said, "Ugh, take them back where you found them."

"What's wrong with them? They've got a small ship that's perfect for the cargo. Xent'tt has a small crew that doesn't ask questions of what we've got and, for a small fee, won't answer anyone else's questions either. They say they've got a private bunk for you and room for me in the crew quarters."

Ti raised her scaly eyebrow as she waved Hawke in close to her. "And do you know how many cameras will be in that *private* bunk?"

Hawke shrugged. He was used to the United Earth Empire and cameras everywhere. "What's it matter?"

"Do you want my sexy gold butt and boobs floating around every Zentonian server this side of the Tet?"

Hawke grunted. "Then we can switch, and they can look at my ass."

Ti chuckled. "Not sure I want to share."

"I'm not yours...yet. Plus, these are the only guys on the station willing."

"And what kind of bargain are you driving, Nathan?"

"You and me or getting your cargo to Neitz?"

Ti set down her comm. "Well, since I'm not having any better luck, I guess we'll go with your...find. As far as you and me, I thought we had something." She reached up and put a hand behind Hawke's neck, pulling him in for a kiss.

Hawke did his best to enjoy the kiss while guessing what Ti's game was.

"There," sighed Ti while licking her lips, "that should show them who you belong to."

"Me? Belong to—"

Ti batted her lashes. "You don't want to be mine? Who knows what these Zentonians will want to do with you. I can guess from what their comic books and vids depict us Aurorians doing to them." She shuttered.

"I'll flay and gut them they so much as look at you wrong."

Ti purred. "Hmm, you do care. Bring them over. We'll see what they have to offer."

Hawke stood up and waved the Zentonians over. "Captain Xent'tt, Cargomaster Henz'zt, Entrepreneur Neti H'Mar T'oke would like to speak with you."

The two Zentonians approached the table and tried to muscle Hawke out of the way, but he stood firm, putting himself between them and Ti.

"Captain Xent'tt, I understand you have a ship that could move my cargo from here to Station Neitz. Let's dispense with pleasantries—I'm not interested in doing anything with or to you. The Angel Hawke is mine, and I am not interested in anything beyond moving my cargo. If I discover any recording devices—audio or visual—or anything else that captures my likeness, I will tear your ship apart then sue you for all the money you and your crew are worth. Afterward, I will black flag you and your crew to ensure you never work in Tet or Aurorian space again. That is, of course, if Hawke doesn't catch up to you first. Now, can your ship do as I need?"

"What's it got that we don't?" Henz'zt chattered in disgust.

"More like what he doesn't have—fur and the sexual appetite of a Zentonian."

"If you don't like our price," said Xent'tt, "you can push your container to Neitz. A few pictures won't harm nothing."

"Zick! Do you think I'm stupid? A naked picture of me is worth more than what I'm paying you to ship."

"Only takes a second."

"For forever having my dignity and reputation ruined." Ti opened her hand, and the stylus in Xent'tt's overalls flew out of his pocket and aimed at his large black eye. "What do you think? Is my reputation worth a lifetime of blindness?"

Xent'tt chattered his big incisors in alarm. "Fine, but the price went up. Forty thousand plus sleeping quarters and food."

The stylus flew back to Ti's waiting hand. "I'll wait for a less despicable offer."

Xent'tt and Henz'zt backed away and had a rapid-fire discussion in Zenti. Hawke had no idea how to speak the language of the squirrels, but from the huffs, chirps, and chatters, it was intense. He could guess as an independent contractor, they needed money, and their plan to extort Ti had backfired. Still, he and Ti were in a jam, too. He'd discovered that Neitz was not a popular destination and little independent cargo went there. It was all transported by the pirates or government shipping. None of that was round trip. This was a lucrative run for Xent'tt—if he didn't screw it up.

The Zentonians split, and Xent'tt approached the table where Ti had gone back to eating her meal.

"Well?" she snapped at the giant squirrel.

"Thirty thousand. No questions or cameras. You sleep in the crew quarters and eat in the mess. We load immediately and leave as soon as a flight plan is filed. We arrive three days after departure."

Ti picked up a baked good and handed it to Hawke. "Try it. Frrezz are a Djinn delicacy—so is Zentonian." She looked over and glared at Xent'tt. "If you believe I won't feed you to a Djinn, you're sadly mistaken. Let's try that offer again."

Hawke sniffed the pastry and shrugged when it smelled like straw-berry. *You only live once, and if it hasn't killed Ti, it won't kill me either.* He popped it in his mouth and found the inside was filled with jam that tasted like strawberry. *I bet it's a universal flavor.*

The fur on Xent'tt's tail stood up. "Forget it. You're not worth the hassle."

The stylus flew off the table into Henz'zt's eye. The Zentonian howled as he clutched his face.

Ti looked at Xent'tt. "Twenty-five thousand. No questions. I sleep and eat privately, and Hawke can help Henz'zt perform his duties. We leave as soon as you're able. If you decline, my next visit will be your ship, and we'll see what I can pull off that."

Hawke grunted over the extra work. He did know his way around a freighter, but he wasn't interested in working one.

"Well?" encouraged Ti.

"You pay for Henz'zt medical bill and ten thousand for his lost income."

"I'll pay for the medical bills, but I've already offered a form of payment for the lost productivity."

"Five thousand for the medical bills."

"Deal. I suggest you get Henz'zt to the clinic. Tell them to contact the Aurorian consulate office and tell them Neti H'Mar T'oke sends her regards. I'll send you my number so you can call me when you're finished there. Hawke will oversee the loading."

"And what are you doing?" grumbled Hawke.

"Getting a massage. Negotiations always leave me so tense."

"I thought you had sex for that?"

"Are you offering?"

"You signed me up to work on the freighter, remember?"

Ti made a disgruntled sound.

"Can't have everything," replied Hawke with a chuckle. "Come on, boys. Let's get that eye taken care of."

"**Y**OU KNOW, YOU COULD have taken Xent'tt's eye and saved me from having to repair everything on this tub," said Hawke as he set a plate of *something* in front of Ti.

"Then who would pilot this tub? Not me...can you?"

"You can get your own damn food," grumbled Hawke as he sat down with a *thump* on the cheap metal bench. His gear clattered to the floor behind him.

Ti looked up from her comm and smiled warmly. "Normally I do, but it's been awfully sweet of you to do it for me. I could get used to this."

Hawke grumbled.

Ti reached across the narrow table and touched his arm. "Oh, come on. You'd be bored otherwise. The comm I gave you has some books on it—if you like Aurorian romance. If I'd known what you like, I would have wiped my back up and filled it with…Bills' games?"

Hawke chuckled. "Only if you hacked Enterprise's entertainment library."

"I could if I knew where the ship was."

Hawke shrugged. "I have no idea where it is. Last I heard, Sheppard and Gering were taking care of it. But thanks for remembering."

"I tried to look them up…I thought someone might have uploaded something on Earth sports, but no luck."

Hawke shrugged. "I doubt there'd be much. They've been to the big game twenty-one times and lost each one. Still better than Detroit. They've never been. Still, there's always next year."

Ti laughed lightly. "This football does bring out a lighter side to you. I may have to hack Enterprise just to get the games. I can put one on when you're in a mood."

Hawke grinned. "I'll have to teach you the right games. There are plenty that gets my blood boiling. The *Bum Bills* have a way of snatching defeat from the jaws of victory."

"I knew there was a catch."

The door to the mess slid back, and Xent'tt stuck his head in. "We're scheduled to start our approach in an hour. Hawke, finish eating and help Henz'zt with the pre-dock checks."

Hawke grumbled as he shoveled several spoonfuls of mush into his mouth.

"Have fun," Ti cooed and waved her fingers.

Henz'zt stuck his head in next to Xent'tt. "Hey, Boss, we got a shuttle from the Independent Neitz League wanting to board for a pre-docking inspection."

Xent'tt's teeth chattered wildly. "Who the Void are they?"

Ti steepled her fingers. "Let them board, and we'll find out."

"I don't have nothing if they shake us down. If they want a piece of Aurorian ass, I'm not stopping them."

Ti rolled her eyes. "Thanks for the warning. Lucky for you lot Hawke and I can take care of ourselves. If they want slaves, I'm giving them you. Fair?"

Xent'tt's teeth chattered. "You still need us to dock."

"I'm sure the Independent Neitz League will be more than willing to get us to port for a fee...way less than you charge. Now, scat and make yourself useful, or I'll throw you in for free. Hawke, let's go get ready."

"I thought I was getting the ship ready to dock."

"A one-eyed Zentonian is better than no Zentonian. He can figure it out on his own. Let's go."

H AWKE STOOD TO ONE side of the airlock hidden behind some equipment while Ti stood in the main corridor waiting for Xent'tt to open the airlock door. The Zentonian went through the sequence—and with a hiss of air—he pulled back the door, further concealing Hawke.

Heavy space boots thudded on the metal deck of the ship. Hawke counted four unique thuds—A Zentonian, two Diamock, and a Djinn.

"What do you want?" snapped Ti.

"Straight to the point. Good," said a Diamock. "We're here to collect the transit fee for the Independent Neitz League."

"Never heard of you," Ti scoffed.

"We protect the shipping lanes around Neitz."

"And how much is the fee?"

"Forty thousand credits."

"You're out of your Void crushed mind. Let me see what your boss has to say."

Hawke heard the audible clicks as Ti dialed a number on her comm.

"Bener? This is Ashila Men'the Afrinaa—the comet ice procurer—you have my ice, numbskull. I'm here to pick it up. Now, call off your goons so I can dock...What do you mean who? Your Free Independent Neitz or whatever they call themselves here shaking me down for safe passage...Not yours? I thought you controlled everything in Neitz space? ...Independent contractors? Don't give me that zick...Fine. Then you don't mind if I kill them? ...Well, make up your mind because I'm not paying them. So, call them off, or I'm sending them back stuffed in their helmets...Yeah? Just remember if I die, then there goes your money for the ice...You'll sell it? You won't get ten million for it. I'm the only way it's worth that much...Uh-huh, I'll take the cleanup cost of the ship out of what I owe you...Believe me, my hide will be intact."

There was a *beep* as she closed the comm's connection.

"Your choice, brainless ones. Either get back to your shuttle or get dead—just remember, your boss can't collect from a corpse."

"You said you had ten mil. You can afford our protection," said the other Diamock in a deep growl.

"True," cooed Ti, "but I don't want to pay you. I'll give you the crew."

"We'll take you," snarled the Djinn. "You'd fetch a good price."

"Hmmm, then your boss doesn't get paid. And, of course, you have to catch me...and I promise none of you will lay a hand on me."

The sound of pistols being raised and cocked caused Hawke's muscles to tense.

"What's that going to do?" goaded Ti. "You still have to hit me."

The firing of the pistol was deafening in the small confines of the airlock, but the *thump* that hit the deck was too heavy to be Ti. Not waiting for an invitation, Hawke slammed the airlock door closed on the Djinn with enough force to crush the large lion-like creature between the door and frame. Hawke jumped behind the remaining Diamock and Zentonian, grabbed their heads, and smashed them together—crushing their helmets. He turned to the stumbling Djinn and punched him in the snout with a loud *crack*. Blue blood erupted from his nose as Hawke punched him in the gut bending him over. Continuing his assault, Hawke drove the Djinn back into the airlock tube. In the zero gravity, he hurled the Djinn back against the side of his shuttle's closed airlock.

Hawke returned to his ship and went to the airlock controls. After closing the airlock, he blew the emergency restraining bolts on the connecting tube, disconnecting them from the shuttle.

He turned around and gave Ti a concerned look. "You alright?"

Ti seemed unable to hide the look of awe and love from her eyes. "I, ah, I'm fine. I didn't realize I had a hero in shining armor—especially one so strong."

Hawke chuckled. "More of Kita's curse. I'm a little stronger and faster than your average bear." That caused him to chuckle, but he didn't explain why.

"Well, I owe her one. I was afraid it would take the crew and us to tackle the Djinn."

Hawke raised his hands. "They're just big kitty cats. Nothing to worry about."

Ti smiled. "This might go easier than I thought. Xent'tt! Get this thing to the docks."

"THIS DOESN'T LOOK RIGHT," said Hawke seeing the randomly stacked shipping containers and other items around the dock as the magnets clunked against the ship's side to secure it in port.

"They're pirates. I'm sure neat stacks and straight rows aren't their specialties," said Ti looking through the bridge windows.

"And where's the welcoming committee? I'm sure they want their ten million and would be out here waiting for it. I also don't see your cargo anywhere."

"Probably in one of the shipping containers."

"You going to inspect it in one of those?"

Ti grunted.

"Better let me out and meet the locals. Once it's safe, you can come out through the cargo hold and make your deal."

"How many can there be if you're worried?" said Ti, her scales rippling.

"Smells like a trap, and I can take a lot more bullets than you can. And I may need you to come rescue me."

"I'd say you're no good to me dead, but I've seen you rise from the grave. But you're right. The way things are stacked, there are too many kill sacks and defensible positions to be an accident."

Hawke put his hand on Ti's arm and leaned into her. "How strong is your metal ability? Can you lift a shipping container?"

Ti turned to look at him, her mouth open. "You're serious? I'm one of the best, and I can only lift a few pounds. Pulling bullets or weapons aside is what I was trained to do. I've never seen anyone with that kind of ability."

Hawke grunted. "You've never seen Kita's girls in action. You stay aboard. If they're there and start shooting, I'll distract them while you move in on the flank and take them down."

"Hawke, as much as I love chivalry, you can't take on so many."

Hawke grinned, leaned in, and kissed Ti. "This old bear has got some tricks. If it's just pirates, it'll be a walk in the park. If it's more—well, I've been looking for a good fight."

Ti's scales rippled wildly. "I...does this mean you're—"

"If I go down, I want the last thing I do to be kissing a gorgeous girl."

Ti seized Hawke's face and kissed him deeply. "You better come back. I want more."

Hawke stood and smiled. "I'll be back. I just might not look the same."

"What does that mean?"

"I'm a bear with tricks."

Ti's scales rippled in a dizzying display. "I don't know what a bear is, and I thought you were a warhorse."

"Warhorse for an old veteran. If this goes the way I think it does, you'll see what a bear is."

"I know you seem sure of yourself, but I don't see how you'll take on all the pirates with four pistols."

Hawke turned and walked the bridge door. "Bear. Tricks. Kita's curse."

Ti frowned. "Fine, but if you get in trouble, I'm coming to get you."

Hawke nodded as he opened the door and walked down the narrow passageway lined with pipes and conduits to the airlock. He looked at the crewmember by the door and said, "Open it."

The inner door swung open, and Hawke entered the airlock chamber. There was a hiss of air as the chamber equalized with the station. When the outer door opened, Hawke went to the opening and found no gantry or stairs to the dock. Shrugging, he jumped and landed on the metal decking thirty feet below.

The dock was clear for fifty feet until a row of shipping containers formed a wall that ran from the front of the dock to the edge, where the environmental shield came down to maintain the atmosphere.

Behind the shipping containers was a maze of more. *Yeah, this smells of a trap.*

Hawke walked toward the nearest stack of shipping containers and stopped when a holoprojector orb floated down from on top of the container stacks. It hovered in front of him and expanded to display a Diamock in an ornate uniform. Hawke recognized Kita's tormentor.

"Tetarax," Hawke growled lowly.

"That is General Tetarax to you, Sergeant Major."

Hawke crossed his arms. "Well, if you want to play that game—my rank is Centurion in the United Earth Empire Red Legion."

"Yes, we know your history as a soldier."

"I'm more than a soldier. As a centurion, I outrank generals and admirals. I've served a hundred years in the UEE Red Legion and have seen and done more than you ever will. So, tell me, Tetarax, what are you doing all the way out here? I thought you wouldn't be able to take your eyes off Kita."

"The Angel and her friends are safely locked away, waiting for their trial. We thought you were happily indisposed until you left the Tet. I'm here to ask you to return. It's by the Grand Panel's good graciousness that we granted you parole. We formally ask that you return so that the trial can commence."

"As far as I know, I haven't been charged with anything."

"The charges are sealed and will be opened at the beginning of your trial. Former Grand Ambassador Hali C'Zar Ah'tem was informed as your lead counsel."

Hawke shrugged a shoulder. He'd done plenty of barrack's lawyering in his day. "The girls don't tell the boys what's going on. And I never retained her as counsel. So, feel free to deliver the charges to my flat, and then we'll talk."

Tetarax's quills on his muzzle and cheeks rippled. "I have authority to bring you in by force—if need be."

"Whose authority?" scoffed Hawke. "I'm not on a Diamock ship. I never signed up to join the Diamock Military. We're not on the Tet—what's your jurisdiction? I'm a citizen of the United Earth Empire, and last I checked—you haven't signed a treaty with Case. If anything, I demand to contact my government. I'll speak to Case. Where is she?"

"Who is Case?"

"That would be Her Royal Highness, Emperor Casey Bush. You might know her as the Angel Defiance."

"She is currently indisposed."

"Yeah? I suggest you release her, or I will find a way to get a message to the UEE. And if you think you got your ass handed to you last time, you won't believe the ass-whooping you'll get when the entire Shadow Fleet arrives."

"The Shadow Fleet is nothing when we control your most powerful warship."

Hawke smirked. *Do you think Enterprise is the only carrier in the Shadow Fleet?* But Hawke kept that to himself. An overconfident adversary was easier to take down. "Well, now you for sure as shit have given me a reason to not go with you."

On top of the shipping containers, a row of Diamocks moved to the container's edge, took a knee, and raised their rifles.

Hawke's eyes shifted back and forth, getting a rough count of what he faced. *Sixty? They must have forgotten who I am.* "That it, Tetarax? That's barely a workout."

"Even you are not invincible, Centurion Hawke." Tetarax pointed out the port bay to a pair of Diamock boarding frigates floating nearby.

Ten thousand is more of a challenge. No way we're getting the freighter past them. I wonder what weapons the pirates have stashed around here? First things first. Kill Tetarax's goons and the pirates, then figure out a way past the blockade. Maybe Ti can call someone?

"I guess we're going to find out. Because the only way I'm going back with you is in a body bag."

Tetarax's quills rippled upward. "I'd hoped you'd say that. Bring back the body. The Scientific Society will want to study it."

Hawke raised an eyebrow. *That's a sure-fire way of raising Kita's ire.* In the blink of an eye, Hawke drew his repeaters, aimed, and put a double-tap into a pair of Diamocks' faceplates. Unlike the special-forces Diamocks on the ferry who wore stripped-down armor, these Diamocks wore armor head-to-toe and were equipped for a fight. Hawke hoped to kill enough and recover a few of their assault rifles. Those stood a better chance than his pistols.

The double-tap shots were bringing down the Diamocks at a rapid rate. The first bullet would fracture or break their faceplates, allowing the second bullet to be the kill shot. The only problem was it ate through his ammunition in a hurry.

The Diamocks on the ends of the storage containers recovered from the shock of seeing so many go down faster than Hawke would have liked. They took aim and fired, forcing him to the only cover available, the front of the storage containers. Moving there offered protection but also ruined his firing lines.

As Hawke moved along the face of the storage containers, the Diamocks moved to the front of their makeshift barricade and fired down on him. A few bullets struck him in the arm and shoulder, but nothing that would slow him down.

I've got to bring these guys down. Hawke reached the storage container wall, but the Diamocks weren't afraid to shoot down at him. When one appeared near him, Hawke jumped twenty feet and grabbed the Diamock's legs, pulling him off the barricade and slamming him to the deck. Hawke shattered the Diamock's faceplate with a sharp punch then twisted the helmet to break the neck. Hawke repeated the maneuver three more times until the Diamocks in his area refused to show themselves.

Hawke kept moving back and forth along the barricade, firing as targets revealed themselves. When his repeaters went dry, he drew his ballers. The powerful Diamock pistols could penetrate a faceplate with one round but had limited ammunition. The loud *bang* of the baller was in sharp contrast to the light *crack* of the repeaters.

More bodies fell from the storage containers, but Hawke had to stop to reload his last magazines. *Damn. Twenty rounds to kill what's left. I have to make them count. What did the coach of the Bills used to say? The best defense is a good offense. See if that's true...it never won the Bills any championships.* Hawke jumped and landed on an empty section of the container barricade.

Not many Diamocks were left on the storage containers, but when Hawke looked to his left, he raised an eyebrow as two hundred Diamock soldiers waited below. *I guess I owe Tetarax a little more respect.*

Hawke dropped to a knee and shot fifteen more Diamocks before his pistols clicked. Annoyed and disgusted, he tossed the pieces aside, stood up, and put up his fists. *I'm not done yet.*

The remaining Diamocks rushed Hawke with their weapons trained on him. They surrounded him, and Tetarax's holographic image floated above the group.

"You're bleeding," chastised Tetarax. "I was led to believe nothing could hurt Kita's crew."

Yeah, Kita. "Give it ten minutes, and I'll be fine. You know, Tetarax, if you were a real soldier, you'd be here leading your troops instead of hiding behind a desk."

Tetarax's quills bristled. "I was going to let you live, but I think you've outlived your usefulness."

Hawke chuckled. "Boy, I haven't even started. There's a reason I was a member of Kita's crew."

"You're just a Human that's a good shot."

"Goat-dog, I'm an Angel. Just because I don't have a pair of tits doesn't mean I can't kill everything here."

"Bring it in—alive, if possible."

Hawke raised his fists as the Diamocks around him brought their rifle butts up to strike. Hawke lunged forward, grabbed a Diamock, turned, and threw him into those waiting behind. The rest of the Diamocks fell on Hawke, striking with their rifles. Hawke took strikes to the head, back, and arms while doing his best to strike back. A hard hit to the back of the head caused him to see stars. *Damn. What the hell am I doing? I'm being like Kita. Give the girl credit. She knew how to take a beating. Time to have some fun. Bear.*

A tingling sensation at the base of Hawke's skull expanded down his spine and out to his limbs. Hawke didn't know the process of how Kita was able to transform him from his Human form to a twenty-five-foot armored grizzly bear. It wasn't painful, just disorienting. Not only for his senses but for his brain. His human mind fused with a bear brain giving him the instinctual behaviors of a grizzly. He couldn't talk in his grizzly form, but the suit that came with the bear form had an interpreter that let him communicate—but it was a bitch to use as it required significant concentration to translate from his mind, to bear, to computer, to Common.

As Hawke's bulk increased rapidly, he tossed back the shocked Diamocks attacking him. After shaking out his shaggy grizzly bear coat, Hawke let out a deafening roar as composite metal and ceramic bands extended from his spine and wrapped his giant bulk in the nearly impenetrable armor. The armor expanded around his limbs and paws, creating a powerful exoskeleton that increased his speed and strength. A helmet formed over his massive head from his neck, his eyes shining bright red.

With the exceptional armor came a selection of heavy weapons that allowed Hawke to blast his way through most enemies. A pair of miniguns extended from his rump, the six barreled guns spun as ammunition was fed into the chambers. On his hips and shoulders, missile and mortar pods extended, giving him the ability to reach enemies behind cover.

All of the weapons were aimed by a reticle in his right eye. They fired by his thought, letting him chain together combos that blasted enemies apart. Hawke didn't know much about the suit's origin, other than he wasn't the first bear in Kita's service. The original was a giant polar bear named Frostbane, and the suit was designed and built by an Angel.

Free of his tormentors, Hawke reared on his hind legs, towering over the Diamock soldiers. He came down hard, driving his front paws into the heads of two unfortunate Diamocks. Their helmets cracked like eggs as their heads splattered across the roof of the metal storage container. Looking at a cluster of stunned Diamock soldiers, Hawke let out a loud roar before charging into the group biting and clawing his way through. Those he couldn't get a hold of, he used his enormous bulk to knock them off the container barricade down to the dock's deck.

The rest of the Diamock soldiers recovered from their shock. Those closest to Hawke opened fire only to find their rounds didn't penetrate. Hawke roared at the irritation and tickling of the bullets. He pulled up his charge and spun, bringing his miniguns to bear on the mass of Diamock soldiers behind him. The miniguns spun up and spit fire blasting into the Diamocks ranks. The two-millimeter rounds were fired from a cartridge. They accelerated down a railgun, giving each round hypersonic velocity—enough to smash through most armor types and often exploded upon impact. The Diamocks caught in the open went down as if cut by a scythe. Those in the rear or closer to the stacks of cargo containers took cover in the maze of steel.

Hawke huffed as the Diamocks took cover, but he had a way of reaching out and touching them. The mortar pods on his shoulders made *thump* sounds as they arced through the docks and exploded among the cargo containers. The mortars were a mix of high explosive and incendiary. They caused havoc as Diamocks were blasted apart or set on fire. Many Diamocks who'd run for cover in the cargo containers came running back into the open, chased by flames. A *rip* filled the docks as Hawke turned his guns on the exposed Diamocks.

A *whoosh* from his right caused Hawke to turn as an RPG slammed into his side, spinning him sideways causing his back paws to slide off the container barricade. Annoyed, Hawke dug his front claws into the metal container while kicking with his back feet trying to find the side wall. His back right paw found the metal, and his claws dug in. As he boosted himself up, another RPG warhead detonated in his face causing him to let go and fall twenty feet to the dock's deck.

Hawke landed on his rump and smacked the container in front of him out of frustration. Rolling to his paws, he snarled at the barricade, then slammed his shoulder into it, knocking the large rectangular container back a few feet. Dropping his shoulder, he pushed the double-stacked containers backward into the Diamock position.

Diamocks appeared on either side of the shifting containers and fired down on Hawke. The bear raised his head and roared. Deciding it was better to use his energy to move the containers, Hawke pushed until the container stack hit another stack. Seeing he now had an opening, Hawke charged into the maze of containers to hunt down the Diamocks hidden within.

Coming to a corner, he stuck his nose in the air, sniffing for Diamocks. Smelling their sweet and tangy scent, he turned the corner down an alley between two cargo containers. He didn't see any Diamock, but his nose didn't lie—they were somewhere close, and he would root them out. As he plodded down the alleyway, Diamocks appeared on the top edges of the cargo containers. They opened fire, and a pair dropped grenades that bounced off Hawke's back. Hawke roared at the ambush and stood up on his hind legs, letting him tower over the gawking Diamocks. He stepped on a grenade with his rear left paw. The explosive went off, but the blast was muffled. The other grenade went off, but the blast was mitigated by his armor. With a huff, Hawke used his paw to swipe at the Diamocks' goat-like legs, knocking them over. Using his other paw, he brought it down on the defenseless Diamocks crushing their armor and chests.

Grunting, Hawke hopped back down, turned around, and pulled his head up on the other side. The Diamocks had already turned and fled, jumping to a neighboring stack of cargo containers and disappearing around a second level container. Hawke slapped the top of the container in frustration, then pushed off, and returned to all fours. He jogged his way out of the ambush site and turned a corner into a hail of bullets coming from two heavy machine guns set up on the far end of the dock.

With a snarl, Hawke looked at the first machine gun and fired a pair of missiles from his hip pods. The four-inch missiles packed a punch and could take down armored vehicles. The crews servicing the machine guns saw the missiles coming, ceased fire, and dove for cover as their weapons were blown apart.

Hawke chuckled at the Diamocks as he plodded toward the destroyed guns. *Uh-oh.* Hawke's bearish chuckled died as two Gronks turned the corner. He had never faced more than one and always with another Angel. The Angels called them the alligator snapping turtles from hell. They stood almost eight feet tall. Every exposed part of them was covered in interlocking armored scales that could turn aside a .50 caliber bullet. Their armored heads retracted into their torsos, leaving a tiny gap for them to see through. They were known to be mean and damn near indestructible.

Oh, I hope I have enough missiles. Set missiles to armor-piercing and fire a full salvo. Hawke's missiles had three types of warheads—High Explosive, Incendiary, and Armor Piercing. HE packed several pounds of explosives that detonated upon impact. AP had a unique warhead that ignited a charge that burned through the armor plate, followed by an ultra-dense rod that smashed through the created hole.

HE had no effect on Gronks, and AP was so-so. Their armor was a dense organic composite containing layers of metal. If Hawke's missiles penetrated the Gronks, their redundant organs made them hard to kill. They had three of every major organ spread out within their torso.

The salvo of missiles peppered the pair of advancing behemoths, enveloping them in multiple fireballs and smoke. Hawke stopped his advance and fired his miniguns into the dense cloud. From out of the haze, the pair of Gronks marched forward, though the left one was slouched forward, his chest smoking.

"Hawke?" Ti yelled from behind.

Hawke swung his head around and roared a warning to Ti to stay back.

"*Ti,*" Hawke said through his armor's speech unit. "*Stay back. Gronks dangerous.*"

"Hawke, you can't kill them. We have to retreat back to the freighter."

And hope they don't bang the door down? "*Ti go, find safety. I kill.*"

"Hawke!" Ti yelled as she fired her pistol over his back.

Hawke didn't see what she was shooting at. Instead, the fist of a Gronk slam down on the top of his helmet. The force of the blow splayed Hawke's paws out from under him, and his head hit the deck. The smoking Gronk punched Hawke in the shoulder, causing the giant bear to slide back a few feet.

Shaking off the blows, Hawke pulled his paws under him and pushed himself up onto his hind feet, towering over the Gronks. He lunged forward, bringing his front paws together and down on the injured Gronk's shoulders and driving it into the deck, folding the creature in half. Hawke bounced several times, thrusting his huge bulk down onto the Gronk, trying to smash it flat.

A blow from the other Gronk took Hawke's attention in time to receive a second punch to the head, causing him to see stars. Hawke gave one last shove to the injured Gronk to ensure it wasn't getting up before turning and backpawing the other Gronk. The two turned and stared at each other—the Gronk's beady little eyes shining out from the gap in his chest armor.

The faster Gronk struck first, hitting Hawke several times in the head driving the big bear back. Hawke roared in frustration, then stood on his hind legs again. The Gronk charged, slamming into the bear's middle, driving his spike-covered fists into Hawke's belly armor. The blows were enough to dent the armor and drive Hawke back until he lost his balance and fell backward.

As Hawke struggled to get up, the Gronk grabbed the mortar pod on Hawke's right hip and twisted it back and forth. Hawke roared as he tried to kick his tormentor, but the Gronk deftly dodged the paw until he ripped the weapon pod from Hawke's flank, leaving a large hole in his armor. Flinging the pod aside, the Gronk slammed his fist into the hole.

Roaring in pain, Hawke pushed his torso into a sitting position, twisting the hole away from his opponent. The Gronk slammed the bear's side several times, causing the armor to ripple. Hawke raked his right paw down the Gronk's front, his powerful claws leaving deep gouges in the Gronk's plate armor and pushing it back. Hawke twisted onto his feet and clamped his jaws down on the Gronk's collar armor, trying to get at its recessed head.

Growling while he squeezed with his jaws, Hawke tried to crush the Gronk's head. The helmet increased Hawke's bite force tenfold. Hawke shook his head as he bit, trying to sink his teeth in deeper and keep the Gronk off balance.

The Gronk thrust its spike-covered fists up into Hawke's gorget, beginning a furious contest of strength and leverage to see who would pierce the other's armor first. The Gronk managed to tear loose part of Hawke's neck plating and jammed a spike into the gap. Blood spewed from the hole, falling down to the deck. Hawke roared and stood up, shaking the creature in his jaws to discourage follow-up strikes. The Gronk's flailing arms connected with Hawke's nose. The bear roared and released the Gronk, landing on its face.

Hawke brought his front paws down on top of the Gronk with a loud *crack*. He again took the Gronk's head in his jaws and squeezed with a snarl. Another loud *crack* followed. Rearing, Hawke shook the Gronk, the body flailing like a ragdoll while blood from the hole in his neck sprayed everywhere.

Collapsing to his front paws, Hawke pressed a paw down on the Gronk's chest while pulling on the head. With a wet *pop*, the head detached from the body. Hawke let the head go and collapsed on his side, breathing hard as blood poured from the hole in his neck.

"Hawke! Hawke! Are you alright?" cried Ti as she ran up with her pistol drawn. She went to the bleeding hole. "What do I do?"

"Surrender!" came an order from above.

Hawke roared and thrashed his head at a group of Diamocks that had surrounded them on the cargo containers.

"Stand down," ordered Ti. "It's over. You've lost." From her belt, she pulled out the holoprojector linked to Tetarax. Turning it on, she tossed it in the air, and the Diamock general appeared.

"Who are you?" Tetarax growled.

"Neti H'Mar T'oke. Call off your goons. You've lost."

Tetarax looked at Hawke. "It looks like the creature is dying."

Hawke roared in defiance.

"Stand down, or the Spring Ascension unleashes the Void." Ti turned and pointed out the dock's environmental curtain. Out in space, a large curvy, and sleek warship dwarfed the two Diamock frigates. "You don't want twenty thousand Aurorian shock troops crashing your party, do you, General?"

"Who are you?" demanded Tetarax.

Ti smiled but said, "Stand down and evacuate Neitz. Aurorian High Command is taking over."

"The Aurorians should not be in Djinn space," snarled Tetarax.

"Neither should the Diamocks. It just seems the Aurorian connections are better than the Diamock ones. Now get out before I call the ship."

"We could kill you and the creature before they get there," scoffed Tetarax.

"If you're willing to risk galactic war with Aurora, you can try. Hawke is under Aurorian protection by order of Aurorian High Command."

Tetarax's quills rippled wildly before saying, "All units, return to staging areas for immediate departure."

The surrounding Diamocks lowered their weapons and backed away.

Tetarax glared at Ti. "This isn't over. I'll have Hawke's head yet."

"Good luck."

Tetarax snarled, and the holoprojector went out.

Ti rushed back to Hawke. "Hawke, how bad are you hurt? Help is on the way."

"*Five minutes,*" Hawke huffed.

"There's nothing that can be done in five minutes. We need to get you out of here. I'm afraid the Spring Ascension doesn't have a vet aboard."

Hawke grunted a bearish chuckle as he pushed himself into a sitting position.

"Hawke, you shouldn't be moving," fretted Ti. "Lie back down. I'll look around for a trauma kit."

Hawke shook his head, causing more blood to run down his neck.

"Now is not the time to be stubborn," lectured Ti. She hurried away.

Human. Hawke's body tingled as it shrank, the mass of the bear returning to the gravity wells in his body. When he returned to his Human form, he was sitting on the deck with a half-inch hole in his neck leaking blood all over himself. He reached into his belt, pulled out a trauma flimsy, and put it over the wound. When the bandage was in place, it released a foam that filled the cavity and released healing nanites. Satisfied he'd be healed before Ti got back, Hawke stood and surveyed the carnage.

Four assault shuttles glided through space toward the pirate station from the Spring Ascension. Hawke whistled lowly at the size of the massive Aurorian warship. He'd never seen Aurorian warships before and was impressed with what the ladies could build.

"You don't listen, do you?" scolded Ti as she hurried to him, holding a trauma kit a little worse for wear.

"I just needed a few minutes. Trust me."

"So, was that the little secret you've hinted at?"

Hawke smiled sheepishly. "That's Poo."

"And what is Poo?"

"Poo is a grizzly bear—a creature from Earth. Part of Kita's curse."

Ti's scales rippled. "I'm beginning to think it was Kita's blessing. I thought I was safe before. Now, I don't think anything can get me."

"Well, I can't think of anything sappy to say, but, ah, does this mean you want to see me now that our mission is done?"

Ti smiled as her scales stood up. "I still owe you two nights of sex."

"Yeah, about that—"

Ti looked at him, alarmed. "Do you...not...want me?"

Hawke gave her a sideways smirk. "I want to know who I'm sleeping with. I don't think even a special agent can call in whatever that thing is out there on a whim."

Ti's scales rippled in a zigzag pattern as her golden cheeks flushed. "It's the heavy dreadnaught Spring Ascension, and I called them after the attack on our stateroom. I got the feeling the Diamocks were up to something. I just didn't know they were after you, not me."

"And who are you?"

"Neti H'Mar T'oke?" Ti said with a small, bashful smile.

"And who are you that you have the power to call in a battleship into Djinn sovereign territory?"

Ti bit her lip. Hawke raised an eyebrow.

"If I tell you, I get more than two nights of sex."

"What are you trying to sucker me into?"

Ti smiled and touched Hawke's hand. "More than sex?"

Hawke's eyebrows went up. "You want to date this old bear?"

Ti nodded. "I hope more than that."

"Whoa! You don't even know what I'm like at home. Lots of girls have kicked me out after a couple of days."

"Well, if we go home, there are lots of rooms."

"You did have a nice flat. Way better than what Hali gave me."

Ti waved the statement off. "That was nothing, just a place to use on missions. Home is, well, home."

"If I say yes—" *Because why would I say no to a smart, courageous, beautiful girl? Damn, if Kita wasn't right. I love Onyx, but I need to move on. Maybe Ti is right for me. I may never get another chance like this.* "—will you tell me who you are?"

Ti smiled brightly as her scales stood up. "Really? You will?"

Hawke nodded, doing his best to try and be cool and suave and not run around in circles throwing his hands in the air.

Ti threw her arms around Hawke's neck and kissed him. Hawke let his tongue dance with hers and enjoyed feeling her press against him.

When she pulled her head back, she said, "My aunt is Eldest Statesman Trio Ach'm D'asora, leader of the Aurora. I, ah, am a member of the royal family."

Hawke sighed. "Is that all? What's one more royal to the party?"

Ti laughed and playfully slapped Hawke's arm.

Hawke playfully put his arms around Ti and lifted her up. Looking up into her bright violet eyes, his heart melted. She wrapped her legs around his waist, bent down, and kissed him.

H AWKE SAT IN A hospital waiting room, trying to distract himself with his comm to kill time until he could see Ti.

A nurse entered the room in a tizzy. "Centurion T'oke?" she said out of breath.

Hawke's head snapped up to the Aurorian. He was still getting used to answering to Ti's name. "Yes?"

"Come quickly! There's a problem." She waved him to his feet.

Hawke jumped up and followed the nurse out the door.

"What's the matter?" Hawke demanded.

"It's in the creche."

Shit. "Let's go." Hawke hurried around the nurse, having been to the creche earlier.

Hawke ran down a hallway pushing nurses and staff out of his way, and barged through a door. In front of a window down the hall, a group of Aurorian doctors and nurses watched inside the creche.

He stopped next to the group and demanded, "What's going on? What's wrong with the baby?"

"Centurion T'oke!" exclaimed the head nurse. "The baby! Something's happened to her!"

Hawke muscled his way to the window and looked inside. A dozen bassinets were in three neat rows. In the middle, an armored bear cub stood on her hind feet, pawing at the bassinet cover while crying loudly.

Hawke let out a loud laugh followed by, "That's my girl!" he yelled. "Just like her Old Man!" His smile beamed from ear to ear. He turned to the head nurse. "There's nothing wrong with her. I bet she's just hungry."

Did you enjoy SARIN'S WAR?
Let others know what you think!

Leave a review on
Amazon and Goodreads
Reviews help me make better books

SPECIAL THANKS

Thanks to the following Patrons!

—Kita's Partners—
Anna Haig
ParadoxicMouse

—Kita's Lovers—
Monica and Shirlee RichardsonMiller
Skye Miller

—Angels—
Adam Dunsmuir
Joshua Le Tourneau
Kat
Natalie Nicholls
Noble Seven
Vivenne Sullivan
Xrebelion

—Kita's Crew—
5m7kabedfr76
Nora Rockwell

—Kita's Friends—
K.V. Wilson
Mark Gardner

ALSO BY L. FERGUS

Project Omega

Angel of Yorq

Birthright

Razor's Pass

Fall and Rise

Return

Sarin's Heart

Breakout

Her Glory

Price of Glory
(Coming 2023)

game of the gods

Rebirth

Clouds

Sarin's War

Hawke

Li've

THE NEW ANGELS

Earth 168

BykeChic

Earth 832

Earths

Earth Y4K: Blood, Oil, and Tears
(Coming 2022)

NON-KITA BOOKS

Warmache

PATRONS ONLY

The following are exclusive to Patreons. Become on at https://www.patreon.com/FallenAngelKita

RETURN OF THE FALLEN ANGEL

Return of the Fallen Angel: Book 1
Return of the Fallen Angel: Book 2
Return of the Fallen Angel: Book 3
Return of the Fallen Angel: Book 4

CHILDREN OF THE EMPEROR

Rescue
Childrend of the Fallen Angel
Sacrifice

 IRRUPTION

Unbalanced
Fusion
Retreat
Sins
Reformation
Metamorphosis

ABOUT THE AUTHOR

L. FERGUS IS AN Amazon Bestselling author with Birthright and Rebirth. Both titles were #1 new releases in LGBT Science Fiction. Before Amazon, L. was a Wattpad Featured Author and #1 writer of science fiction. The Fallen Angel Saga has more than four hundred thousand reads. The books Birthright, BykeChic, and Rebirth have won over twenty awards, including Best Overall.

Like L. Fergus' main character Kita, L. fosters children to give them a supportive place to grow and thrive. L. lives with four dogs: Rust, Moxy, Stormy, and Valor, and four cats: Jupiter, Crater, Pluto, and Forest Fire.

If you want the most up to date stories consider becoming a patreon at www.patreon.com/FallenAngelKita

Join L. Fergus' mailing list at FallenAngelKita.com for news about upcoming book releases. Follow L. on:
Facebook at Facebook.com/FallenAngelKita
Twitter @FallenAngelKita
contact L. at L@FallenAngelKita.com